Falling
FOR
THE
Marquess

AMERICAN
HEIRESS
TRILOGY

JULIANNE
MACLEAN

Prologue

London, 1883

LADY BERKSHIRE SIGHED CONTENTEDLY AS she handed her lover's greatcoat to him. "Come back on Thursday?"

Standing tall and sumptuous in the corridor, his golden hair spilling onto his shoulders in unfashionable disarray, the Marquess of Rawdon smiled. His devilish charm filled the corridor like a beam of sunlight, radiant and warm.

Lady Berkshire, who was still flushed from their afternoon tryst, melted like hot butter before him, for she had just experienced, firsthand, the validity behind the rumors. Yes, it was all true. The beautiful marquess had a flare for the erotic. An intensity in the bedroom. A talent for lavish, liberal lovemaking.

He was Seger Wolfe, the Marquess of Rawdon, and among the ladies who liked to whisper in the dark corners of London's late-night drawing rooms, he was England's most coveted lover.

When he did not immediately accept her invitation, she tried again. "I'll have strawberries and chocolate." Beneath the melodic intent to entice, her voice was laced with pleading.

Seger considered her invitation with great care. It was not his habit to see the same woman more than twice in a single week, and never—under any circumstances—exclusively. Most women understood the boundaries merely by instinct. They knew not to ask, and not to become possessive if they wanted him to return another day, which almost invariably, they did.

He inhaled deeply and sighed, surprised by a sudden twinge of discontent that was unusual at a time like this.

"Perhaps on Friday," he said.

Lady Berkshire's big blue eyes lit up with anticipation. "Friday, it is."

She stepped back into her bedroom and closed the door behind her with a gentle click.

Seger stood for a moment, staring down the long length of the empty corridor, questioning his response just now. Something had been missing lately from his usual enthusiasm for encounters like this, which made no sense. Lady Berkshire was a beautiful woman and an entertaining bed partner.

He continued to stand outside her door, staring at it. Then he realized something. He barely remembered what it felt like to make love to a woman because he loved her.

Her.

Seger exhaled heavily. How long had it been, and

why was he even thinking about it now?

Bloody hell, he knew how long. Right down to the day. It was just under eight years.

Thankfully, eight years of superficial encounters and casual intimacies for the sole purpose of pleasure had emptied him of almost all memories of her, and he was glad. There was no point pondering them now. She wasn't coming back. Death was rather firm in that regard.

He buttoned his coat and turned to leave, telling himself that this feeling of dissatisfaction would pass, probably as quickly as it had set in. Everything was fine, as it had been for the past eight years. Seger was content. He knew how to enjoy himself—and enjoy himself he did. He found great pleasure with women he didn't know very well, and he enjoyed the superficiality of those relationships. The women were always cheerful and smiling. Nothing was ever complicated or distressing.

To be frank, he wasn't certain he would know how to understand a woman's deeper emotions even if he wanted to.

Not that he wanted to. He did not.

Seger descended the stairs and, with firm resolve, expelled those thoughts from his mind. They did him no good.

He let himself out the front door of Lady Berkshire's London house, glanced up and down the street, then crossed to where his coach was waiting a few doors down.

He reminded himself that there was much to look forward to that evening. He had a ball to attend—a

Cakras Ball. As always, it promised to be a tantalizing feast for the senses. Exactly what he needed for a distraction. He would no doubt meet a number of interesting women there. Beautiful women. Adventurous women.

He climbed inside his coach and signaled to the driver to move on. His blood quickened as he anticipated the evening ahead.

Chapter 1

The London Season
May 1883

Dear Adele,
It is finally upon me—my first London ball.
You cannot imagine how nervous I am, for I fear
I will not fit in, that everyone will see through me
and know I am not one of them.

I hope that will not be the case, for I do long
to be a part of society here—the daily rides along
Rotten Row, the receptions, luncheons, and eve-
nings at the theater. It has been an exhausting but
glorious experience so far, though I admit most of
my acquaintances have been frustratingly superfi-
cial.

I realize, of course, that that is to be expected. I
am in England after all, and people are reserved.
I suppose my frustration comes from what occurred
with Gordon two years ago. I must be an oddity. I
crave adventure and my heart wants it, yet I know

*how dangerous it can be. I know I must strive to
move beyond that mistake if I wish to live a proper
and virtuous life. I only hope that my heart has not
become too complicated. Sometimes I find it difficult to simply smile and be pretty, which is what is
expected of me. I want something deeper than that.
Something more honest. Indeed, what a challenge
this is going to be....*

    Your loving sister,
    Clara

*A*LREADY LATE FOR HER FIRST ball in London—
quite notably the most important ball of her
life—Clara Wilson stood in the doorway of her sister's
boudoir, watching her chaperone, Mrs. Gunther, flip
through a large stack of invitations.

"I'm sure it's one of these," Mrs. Gunther said, spilling a few of them over the edge of the silver salver
onto the mahogany desk. "It has to be."

Mrs. Gunther was a staunch woman—the only person her mother trusted to act as Clara's chaperone in
London. She was a great social matriarch in America
and came from a very prestigious family, but unfortunately for Clara, Mrs. Gunther's memory was not as
sharp as it once was.

"It was at—or somewhere near—Belgrave Square. I
at least know that. I remember Sophia describing it."

Clara's tiny heels clicked over the marble floor as she
crossed the room to peer over her chaperone's shoulder. There were certain to be a number of balls "at or
somewhere near" Belgrave Square that evening.

"Is there any way I can help you remember?" Clara asked. They had to find it soon, for they were already late.

Mrs. Gunther flipped through invitation after invitation. They all looked the same—square, ivory cards with fancy titles in lavish print—and they all belonged to Clara's older sister, Sophia.

Three years prior, Sophia had become the first American heiress to marry a duke. She and her husband, James, were immensely popular among the Marlborough House set, and there was never a shortage of social engagements to attend at any given moment—which made the task of finding the correct invitation all the more difficult now.

"The Wilkshire Ball, the Devonshire, the Berkley...." Mrs. Gunther said. "No, no, no. The Allison Ball. Could that be...? Wait, Lord and Lady Griffith.... Was that it?"

Mrs. Gunther continued to guess haphazardly at the names, and Clara's hopes for the evening took a dive. Everything depended on this one night, and if Clara did not make an appearance at the ball, there might not be a second chance. For Clara—the latest American heiress to invade aristocratic London—had to pass the test. In order to be accepted and welcomed into British society as her sister had been, Clara had to glide into a London ballroom and win the approval of the Prince of Wales. Otherwise, she would end up returning to New York where her position in society was fragile, to say the least.

"Ah." Mrs. Gunther turned to face Clara and handed her the invitation. "Here it is. The Livingstons on Upper Belgrave Street. I'm certain this is it. We can go now, my dear."

Letting out a breath of relief, Clara smoothed a gloved hand over the antique lace on her French silk gown and touched the glittering diamond-and-pearl choker at her neck. She led the way out of her sister's boudoir, the precious ivory invitation safe in her hand.

A moment later, they stepped out of the brilliantly lit manor and into the dark, still night. Mantles buttoned at their bare necks, ivory fans dangling from their wrists, they walked down the stone steps to the coach.

As soon as Clara reached the curb, however, her heel imposed upon a crack and she stumbled. The invitation went sailing out of her gloved hand, and she toppled sideways into a tall, extravagantly liveried footman who caught her and righted her before she even had a chance to notice him standing there.

Clara collected herself. "My word. Thank you!"

Without a hint of a smile, the man stood like a palace guard, his face made of stone.

Clara sighed hopelessly. *The English.* Pray, the people she would meet tonight would have a little more personality. A sense of humor at least.

Clara picked up the invitation and looked at it more closely. "What's that symbol in the corner?"

Mrs. Gunther squinted at the small triangular medallion printed on the card, with the letters MWO above it. "I've no idea. I'll ask Sophia when we see her."

The footman handed them into the crested black

coach with shiny silver fittings, then hopped onto the page board as the vehicle lurched forward and turned toward Belgravia.

A short while later, they pulled up in front of a grand manor house, lit up like a sparkling jewel in the night. Clara heard music from the orchestra inside while couples moved past the large windows, twirling on the dance floor to a Strauss waltz. A mixture of excitement and apprehension sizzled through her veins, and she gathered up her silk skirt to follow Mrs. Gunther out of the coach.

They made their way up the stone path to the front door beneath a massive portico. A broad-shouldered, bald man stood at the entrance, and when Clara and Mrs. Gunther approached, he stepped in front of the door, which was closed tightly behind him.

Mrs. Gunther rolled her shoulders in that haughty way of hers, a skill she had perfected. "We are here for the ball," she said in her best matriarchal voice, with one intimidating eyebrow raised.

"Do you have an invitation?" His deep, booming voice didn't intimidate Mrs. Gunther. She kept her eyes fixed on his as she reached into her purse.

"Here." She handed it to him.

He glanced over it, then lifted his narrow gaze to assess each of them individually. Clara felt a prickling of dread, as if they were about to be turned away. Was this how her Season in London was to begin? A failure, before she even set foot in the door?

There was suspicion in his voice. "You're American?"

"Yes," Mrs. Gunther replied.

"You'll be a novelty, then." He stepped out of the way of the door and opened it. "You'll find the masks on the oak table just inside the entrance."

Mrs. Gunther eyed him incredulously. "Masks?"

Clara nudged her through the door before she could question him further about the mask theme, for Clara did not wish to appear as if they did not belong. She wanted to fit in.

Once they were inside, Mrs. Gunther said, "I did not like that man."

"Neither did I. I'll feel better when we see Sophia and James."

They found a large crystal bowl full of feathered masks just inside the door, and Clara chose a cream-colored one to bring out the auburn highlights in her dark brown hair.

A woman walked by while they were donning their masks, and Clara could have sworn she wasn't wearing a corset. Clara's lips fell open. She was about to say something to Mrs. Gunther but caught herself. Surely, she had been mistaken.

They withdrew to the cloak room to freshen up, then made their way across the crowded grand hall toward the ballroom.

As soon as Clara stepped inside, her mood lifted. She relaxed and cleared her mind of all the mistakes she feared she would make, for what a dazzling room it was. Couples swirled around the floor in bright splashes of color and glitter. The music from the orchestra seemed to come from the blue beyond, so skilled were the musicians, and all the ladies and gentlemen looked elegant and happy.

A footman approached with a tray of champagne and offered glasses to Clara and Mrs. Gunther.

Mrs. Gunther shook her head and waved a hand to decline. The man's brow furrowed, and he looked at them strangely. "Really, you must," he said in a pleasant tone, raising the tray toward them again. "Lord Livingston would be disappointed if you didn't try it."

Clara, still wanting to fit in, took a glass of the bubbly and carefully sipped, savoring its delicious taste and delighting in the way it poured heat through every limb. The footman winked at her as he left.

"Did you see that?" she said to her chaperone.

Mrs. Gunther touched her arm. "Pardon me? Oh, my dear, you don't have a dance card." She stopped a lady passing by and asked her.

Clara left the issue of the winking footman alone.

The woman, wearing a black and white feathered mask and a garnet gown trimmed in velvet, laughed. "We don't bother with names *here,*" she said, then continued on her way.

Clara suddenly felt as if she'd followed Alice down the rabbit hole.

"Perhaps it's because the Prince is coming," Mrs. Gunther surmised. "They say he is not at all as prim as his mother, and he prefers to move with the fast set."

"What if someone asks me to dance?" Clara whispered. "What about introductions?"

"No one else seems to be bothering with them." Mrs. Gunther's concerned gaze swept the room, and her voice took on that haughty tone again. "This is highly improper. Where is Sophia? I would like her to explain what we are expected to—"

At that moment, a young gentleman with gold spectacles and fair hair approached and bowed. "May I have the honor of a dance?"

Clara glanced at Mrs. Gunther who hesitated at the man's informality, then nodded, albeit reluctantly. Clara was surprised her chaperone allowed it without a proper introduction, but she supposed the woman felt as anxious and out of place as she did and didn't want these eminent lords and ladies to know it.

So, not wishing to defy her chaperone, Clara allowed the gentleman to take her champagne glass and set it on a table. She then accepted his gloved hand and walked onto the floor with him. They danced a waltz—she had yet to see any other dance performed—and when it ended, he escorted her back to Mrs. Gunther, thanked her, and went on his way.

"That was lovely," Clara said, "but this is not at all how Sophia described it. She said the necessity for social graces was as bad, if not worse than New York, and she'd had a very difficult time. That man did not even know who I was, nor I he." She leaned closer to Mrs. Gunther, and whispered, "A few of the gentlemen aren't wearing gloves. Look at that man there."

Another couple twirled by.

Mrs. Gunther raised her chin in the air. "I don't know what the world is coming to. We may be approaching the end of a century, but I hardly think society should act in such an uncivilized manner— noble or otherwise. Why, at one of *my* balls...."

Just then, a tall, imposing gentleman entered the ballroom. Clara's attention flitted away from her chaperone's social commentary and landed lightly upon the man now standing just inside the doors. He wore a black suit with tails and a white necktie and waistcoat, and his hair—golden and wavy like ripe wheat in the wind—was an unfashionable length, reaching his shoulders. He stepped into the room with his hands clasped behind his back and tossed his head in a most arrogant manner, throwing an errant lock of that golden hair away from his face.

He wore a black mask that matched his attire, and consequently Clara could only see his chin and mouth. It was a beautiful mouth, she decided as she watched him move closer and smile and nod at a passing gentleman. A mouth with full lips and perfect white teeth. There was a deep dimple centered on his chin, and his angular jaw was firm. Clara took another slow sip of the champagne.

He must have sensed her staring, for his gaze came to rest intently upon her. Briefly, they watched each other, to the point where it almost seemed improper, yet Clara could not tear her eyes away. Not that she was feeling brave or daring. To the contrary, she was dumbfounded and completely stuck, like a butterfly with its delicate feet caught in honey.

Gracious, but he is handsome. She knew it in the unexplored depths of her being, even though he wore a mask.

He wasted not a single second. He set out on a path toward Clara, his eyes never veering from hers. She sucked in a short, shaky breath, oblivious to whatever Mrs. Gunther was going on about. All Clara could do was watch that beautiful man saunter like a lion across the floor, his shoulders broad beneath his jacket, his gait slow and sure and languid.

He stopped before her, said nothing, and held out his hand.

Mrs. Gunther stopped talking. She saw the gloved hand beside her and turned to look at the man who belonged to it. He simply nodded at her, then lifted his hand another fraction to pull Clara out of her stupor and boldly indicate that he wanted to dance.

In complete silence, Mrs. Gunther stared at the gentleman. Clara could only presume that her chaperone was caught in the honey, too, for though her lips were parted, no words were coming out of her mouth.

Laying her gloved hand in his, and without an introduction, Clara allowed him to lead her onto the floor.

She picked up her train and looked into his eyes, and they glided harmoniously into the waltz. They went around the room a few times before he spoke.

"You're a fresh face at one of these things."

"I've only just arrived from America," Clara replied. She would have liked to add "my lord," or "sir," or maybe even "Your Grace," but without the introduction, she didn't know what to call him.

His lips twitched with what looked like pleasant surprise. "America, you say. How wonderful. Permit me to welcome you to our shores."

"Thank you," she replied.

This was not at all how Clara had imagined this night would begin.

"I'm visiting my sister," she told him.

He did not ask who her sister was.

They continued the dance, swirling around the room with such fluid grace, that Clara did not feel the least bit dizzy. Her partner was by far the most skilled dancer she had ever encountered. His hand held the small of her back firmly yet lightly, guiding her around the room as if she were as light as fairy dust.

When the waltz ended, they came to a graceful finish near a tall potted fern. Another waltz began—a slower one—and her partner inclined his head at her. "Shall we dance another?"

Again, she was surprised by this blatant disregard for the rules of etiquette. He should be returning her to her chaperone by now. She glanced over at Mrs. Gunther, who was trying most unsuccessfully to look at ease. Clara remembered the old adage, "when in Rome," and decided she should simply follow this Englishman's lead.

"I would be honored."

They moved into position again, and a shiver of excitement moved through Clara as his hand returned to the small of her back. He led her into the center of the ballroom, where they moved about at a more relaxed pace.

"I must say," he commented, in a deep, sultry voice, "you are an extraordinary dancer. I was fortunate to have found you before some other man. I believe I would like to keep you."

Clara laughed. "You cannot keep me."

"Ah, but I wish I could. At least until you tire of me and send me on my way."

Clara felt a hot thrill at his flattery. "Sir, you are flirting with me, quite shamelessly."

"Because I am a shameless man—at least in the wake

of your exquisite charm. You are undeniably the most intriguing creature I've encountered all evening. All year to be precise."

Clara's cheeks felt like they were on fire. "I don't know what to say in response to such overdrawn compliments. You don't even know me."

"Overdrawn? You underestimate your allure. You should allow me to prove it to you."

"Prove *what* to me?"

"That you are exquisitely charming."

Their conversation was decidedly out of her realm of experience, and though it was exhilarating in ways she had only dreamed of, it was most definitely improper. She urged herself to remember that. He was a complete stranger. Did he not realize the scandalous nature of his flattery?

And yet, she could not bring herself to change the subject. "How will you prove it?"

"How would you like me to?"

Clara wasn't sure she could speak, even if she knew how to answer such a slippery question.

"I am completely yours," he said, his expression friendly and open—a delightful change from what she had become accustomed to since arriving in England. "I am at your disposal. Your humble servant. Here for your pleasure."

She stared in shock for another few seconds, then couldn't help herself. She laughed out loud. Maybe it was nerves. "I've never met anyone quite like you."

And who was he, exactly? All she knew was that he was someone very daring and very grand. Everything about him was exciting and magnificent and lordly.

He was such a glorious change from the ordinary.

He gazed at her. "Look around you. Every man on the floor is taking notice of you here tonight and wishing he had spotted you first. They are each hoping that I will soon disappear and leave you free once again."

Clara did look around. The other gentlemen were simply dancing with their partners, not looking at her at all. "I'm afraid I don't see it."

"No? How else can I prove it to you, then? I know. Feel my heart. It's racing." He pulled her hand to his chest and held it there.

Stunned by this physical intimacy in the middle of a crowded ballroom, and flustered by the feel of the man's hard chest beneath the flat of her hand, Clara felt his heartbeat. It was not racing. He was as calm as a lake in the deep of night.

Utterly beguiled and falling into a lazy daze, Clara missed a step.

Her partner righted her and continued on without missing a beat, holding her hand out again, where it should be.

Clara's mouth felt suddenly dry. In fact, she could hardly breathe. Did this man always have this debilitating effect on women? If so, she was in for an engaging, perhaps difficult, first season there if she ever encountered him again.

They danced a little longer, and she noticed his pace was slowing, growing more leisurely. Clara found herself avoiding his gaze. He had knocked her off kilter with that last little flirtation.

The waltz ended, and the orchestra paused. The

sound of pages turning filled the silence. Clara raised a hand to her cheek and felt a bit faint in the heat of the room. Or perhaps it was this man's effect on her that was causing her to feel fuzzy-headed.

He sensed her distress with perfectly timed precision. "Would you like a cool drink? There is a punch bowl in the supper room."

"Please," she replied.

He offered his arm, and she permitted him to escort her into the next room, where a long buffet table was overflowing with tea cakes and crumpets, large bowls of colorful fruit, clotted cream and towers of frosted peaches. There were shellfish on silver platters, cheeses and meats, and cakes and candies and berries.

The gentleman led her to the punch bowl, filled a glass and handed it to her. She took three large gulps before she realized it was burning her throat. It tasted bitter with some sort of spirit.

She tried to swallow without croaking or making any facial contortions, then smiled politely at him and carefully set the cup on the table. She wasn't about to have any more of that beverage, whatever it was. She didn't want to end up smelling like a distillery.

"Better?" he asked.

"Yes, better." *Except that my throat is on fire!* She tried to clear it. "Thank you." Her response barely squeaked out of her.

"Would you like to see the Fuseli? It's in the main hall."

She swallowed again. "I'm not sure that I should be away from my—"

"You can't come to Livingston House and not see

the Fuseli."

Clara looked up at his elegant mouth, heard the sound of his seductive voice, and felt a buzzing sensation somewhere deep within herself, along with a desire to follow him wherever he led her.

"I suppose I could go and have a peek."

"'Have a peek.' What a charming American expression."

He offered his arm to her again, and she went with him to the main hall, determined to take one look at the masterpiece, then politely thank her partner and ask him to escort her back to Mrs. Gunther.

Out in the hall, other couples were whispering quietly in corners, and Clara found the whole atmosphere somewhat dreamlike. The ladies seemed to float around as if bewitched by something, and the gentlemen spoke in hushed tones. The masks gave it all a rather mysterious flavor, as if they were all supposed to keep some great collective secret.

Clara attributed her odd perceptions to the few sips of champagne she'd had, and that scalding beverage in the punch bowl.

Her handsome escort stopped before a painting that hung at the bottom of a wide, circular staircase. "Here it is."

Clara looked up. "It's *The Nightmare.*"

She sensed the man quietly studying her face. "You know your art."

"Yes, though I've only read about this one. I had no idea it would be so—"

"So what?"

"So...." Dare she say it? She looked up at the curvaceous contours of the sleeping woman's breasts beneath her gown, her arm limp and flung down to the floor. "So erotic." She continued to stare in silence at the details: the grinning devil, the luminescent horse entering the bedchamber from some other, unnatural world.

She could feel those gleaming green eyes watching her, taking in her response to the painting.

The man leaned closer. "Some say it leads to the dark recesses of the mind."

The heat of his breath in her ear caused a wave of gooseflesh to surge across her skin.

He moved silently behind her as she studied the painting, and his presence at her back was more unsettling than anything she saw in *The Nightmare,* for the man standing at his ease behind her was true flesh and blood, sumptuous and beautiful, and he was breathing hotly against the damp back of her neck.

"My word, but you are lovely," he whispered.

Unaccustomed to such open flattery, Clara grew breathless. "Thank you."

"Your perfume...strawberries."

She turned to meet his gaze and tried to imagine what he would look like without his mask. He must surely be the most handsome man in all of London. He certainly had more charm and appeal than anyone she had ever met in New York or Paris.

"Come with me, darling," he said softly.

He was smiling now, like that grinning devil in the painting. He took her hand and slowly backed up. Captivated by the playful glint in his eyes and the engaging way he looked at her, Clara followed him around the bottom of the staircase until she realized, with hazy, besotted awareness, that he was leading her away, into the dim, private shadows beneath the stairs.

Chapter 2

*W*ARNING BELLS RANG INSIDE CLARA'S head, but a more willful part of her nature—the part that wanted to experience what this man offered—somehow managed to silence them.

He backed up against the wall, pulled her toward him until her breasts were pressed firmly, thrillingly against his chest, and with a smile, he leaned close for a kiss

It was one of those life-altering moments, when all that she believed about herself would be tested. Clara should have stopped him. She should have placed her hand on his chest and pushed him back, but alas, she did not. She did nothing to stop the snowball from rolling, nor did she try to control her desires, for there in the dark, she and this gentleman were hidden from view.

He was the most exciting man she'd ever encountered. After two long years of self-inflicted emotional repression to try and fit into a strict, upper-class society, she couldn't resist the opportunity to taste freedom. She wanted to burst forth like a flash flood, breaking through a dam.

She gazed into the man's eyes and felt her proper convictions break.

His eyes were smiling when he kissed her. His tongue swept in and touched hers with the confident skill of an experienced lover, heating her blood and igniting a fire that roared like a monster in her ears. She swayed into the kiss and into his body, relying on his strong hands around her waist to keep her steady through her knees, which incidentally, in the last few seconds, had turned to warm pudding.

If she had any sense at all, she would put a stop to this immediately, but her lusty curiosity wouldn't allow her proper scruples to gain a foothold. She'd never imagined a London ball would be as exciting as this. It felt like she was dreaming. Or drowning.

"Ah." He sighed against her cheek. "That was the most enchanting kiss I've had in...I don't know how long."

He pressed his lips to hers again, closing in on her with his whole body, and she wrapped her arms around his neck.

"Come with me upstairs," he whispered in her ear.

"Upstairs?" she asked.

"Yes. It's still early, love. I doubt all the rooms would be taken yet."

"All the rooms?" What in the world did he mean?

Then all at once, panic pooled in her belly and she woke from the dream.

"If we're going to go," he added, "we should go now. The hall is getting crowded. All the corners have been taken up."

He stepped away from the wall to collect Clara, as if he fully expected her to follow, as if this little tryst were perfectly normal and acceptable.

Earlier, Clara had sensed that something wasn't quite right about this ball, but she hadn't been sure what to do about it. She'd hoped Sophia and James would arrive and make sense of it for her. Now, the need for action was imminent.

"Sir, I believe you must have me confused with someone else. I can't possibly—"

"Why ever not, love? You're *here,* aren't you? And we seem to have developed a rather intoxicating rapport."

She realized that she should have heeded her instincts sooner, for clearly, something was very wrong. "Where is *here,* exactly?"

He gazed at her for a moment, then the set of his jaw changed. His expression darkened.

"You don't know where you are?"

"I'm afraid I do not, and I would be grateful if you would enlighten me."

All the warmth and seduction from seconds ago vanished like a drop of water on a hot stove. Clara's stomach lurched.

"This is a private ball, madam. Only those with an invitation are permitted to enter."

Clara backed away from him and moved out of the shadows and into the open hall. A sick feeling crept into her belly as she watched him follow her.

"I did have an invitation," she told him.

"Was it yours? How did you get it?"

"It was my sister's."

He stopped following and closed his eyes. "Please, tell me that you're married."

Clara's brows flew up under the half mask, which suddenly felt very tight on her face. "Married!" She lowered her voice to a whisper. "No! And if I were, I would certainly *not* be here having this indecent conversation with you!"

He glanced this way and that, as if he weren't sure what to do with her. After some brief deliberation, he took her by the elbow and began to escort her back to the ballroom. "You need to leave."

"But what is this place?"

"Not the sort of place you should know anything about." He quickened his pace, and Clara had to scramble to keep up with him.

"Don't run," he said. "You'll attract attention."

"How can I help it? You're practically dragging me on my knees!"

"Don't speak to anyone else. Get out of here now, and for God's sake, don't tell anyone where you were. Do you understand?"

"What I understand is that I should never have danced with you."

He stopped and looked down at her, his eyes fierce and dark. "I must correct you on that point. You were, in fact, *very fortunate* to have danced with me. You are a tempting little flower, and another man might not have been so understanding, or so apt to let you go."

He marched her back to Mrs. Gunther, gave a polite bow, and lingered a moment, staring at Clara as if he weren't quite ready to leave. Then he directed his gaze toward Mrs. Gunther. "Good evening, madam. It is my understanding that you are in the wrong house this evening. I implore you to take your charge and leave here, immediately. Good night to you."

With that, he turned and walked off.

With trembling hands and a throbbing pulse, Clara walked into the Witherington Ball only moments after their footman informed them that the Prince of Wales was not at Livingston House. He had arrived not long ago at the house two doors down.

Clara was breathing hard, partly from her hasty escape, but mostly from the memory of following a handsome, seductive stranger into the dark shadows beneath a staircase, and feeling the shocking, sizzling lure of temptation.

She had thought she was stronger than that.

Groping for some semblance of normalcy, she glanced around the room in search of her sister, Sophia, the Duchess of Wentworth, and spotted her near the orchestra, conversing with her husband, James.

"There she is," Clara said to Mrs. Gunther, who was still unaware of what Clara had been up to when she was supposed to be sipping punch. She was now pressing Clara for answers. "Let's go and tell her that we've arrived."

Mrs. Gunther led the way around the perimeter of the room. Sophia's face lit up with a radiant smile when she noticed them. Wearing a Charles Worth gown with gold lace and jewel trimmings, topped off by a sparkling tiara—a requisite among married ladies when royalty was present—Sophia met them halfway, leaving her husband to socialize with a group of gentlemen.

"Where were you?" Sophia asked. "You were supposed to be here an hour ago."

Clara spoke breathlessly. "We went to the wrong ball."

"The wrong ball? Which one? And why do you look so pale? Are you unwell?"

Mrs. Gunther spoke haughtily to Sophia. "It was a disgrace."

Clara gazed imploringly at her sister, who knew her well enough to guess that she wished to speak privately. "Thank you so much, Mrs. Gunther. Perhaps Clara and I could have a moment alone. Would you excuse us?"

Mrs. Gunther's brow furrowed, but she nodded in agreement and snapped open her plumed fan. "I will wait by the fountain."

As soon as Mrs. Gunther left them, Sophia led Clara aside to a private corner. "What happened? You look as white as pastry dough." She reached into her jeweled purse for an embroidered handkerchief and used it to dab at Clara's forehead. "Perhaps we should find somewhere to sit down."

"I don't need to sit down. I'm fine. I just need to know where I was."

Sophia paused. "How can I possibly—"

"We had to wear half-masks, and there were no dance cards. Everyone was drinking a tart punch that kicked like a mule, and no one wished to be introduced."

Sophia covered her mouth with her gloved hand.

"Oh, dear."

"What was it?" Clara asked. "Please, tell me."

"Were you at Livingston House?"

"Yes, and what do you mean, 'Oh, dear'? Tell me, before I lose my mind."

"You went to a Cakras Ball," Sophia finally explained. "But how in the world did you get in?"

"We had an invitation."

"From where?"

"Mrs. Gunther picked it up from your desk. She couldn't remember the address of where we were supposed to meet you, so she went through your invitations and thought that Livingston House was the place."

Sophia shook her head. "Do you still have the invitation with you?"

"Yes, here." Clara pulled the tattered card out of her purse.

Sophia examined it and touched the small medallion in the corner. "Oh, Clara, I can't believe you went there. Did anyone see you?"

"Yes, but we were wearing masks."

"Did you talk to anyone?"

"Yes. And I danced—twice. No, wait. Three times, actually."

"That's all? You just danced?"

When Clara didn't answer right away, Sophia regarded her warily. "Clara, what did you do? Are you all right?"

The room seemed to be spinning. "Yes, I'm fine."

"Thank goodness."

"But I was very lucky," Clara said.

"How so? What do you mean?"

Her cheeks flushed with heat at the mere memory of what had occurred with the handsome stranger. "I danced with a man who was very charming. He took me for a glass of punch."

"That punch," Sophia said quietly, "is pure Jamaican rum, with a little juice added for color."

"I only had a few sips," Clara explained. "But then he took me to look at a painting, and we lingered there awhile. He was very handsome and—"

"Clara, what did you do?"

"Nothing!" she insisted. "Or rather…something. I went with him into the shadows under the stairs."

Sophia went pale. "Did he kiss you?"

Clara's inability to answer the question was all that needed to be said. She gazed at her sister imploringly.

"Was it awful?" Sophia asked.

"Oh no, it was nothing like that," Clara replied. "But that's what makes this so confounding." She lowered her voice to a whisper. "Even when I knew it was wrong, I *wanted* him to kiss me. How is it possible that I could have risked my reputation like that? Again? I thought I'd learned my lesson."

Sophia took Clara's hand. "Hush, now. I know how important it is to you, to be cautious and prudent. But take heart. It could have been worse. He might have believed that you wanted more than just a kiss."

"I think he did believe it. At first anyway."

"But you told him otherwise? And he accepted that?"

"He was surprised," Clara explained, "but as soon as he discovered I was an innocent debutante, he marched me straight back to Mrs. Gunther and insisted that we leave."

Sophia shook her head in disbelief. "You were very fortunate to have met that man, Clara, whoever he was. Others might not have been so understanding."

"That's exactly what he said."

They stood in silence, listening to the orchestra play a minuet. Finally, Clara's heart rate slowed.

"It was like some kind of dream world," she said. "What are these Cakras Balls?"

Sophia glanced over her shoulder to ensure that no one was listening. "The Cakras Society is a secret club that no one is supposed to speak about outside of the gatherings, so I must be discreet. They hold balls where the guests may leave the dance floor to engage in trysts in the bedrooms of the house. The MWO stands for 'married women only,' and all social rules are relaxed in favor of anonymity and liberation, but most importantly, in favor of pleasure."

Clara stared dumbfounded at her sister. "Do husbands and wives go there together?"

"Some do, but I suspect that most who attend keep their spouses in the dark."

"That's appalling. You mean to tell me that every person I saw there tonight was being unfaithful to a spouse?"

"Not all of them," Sophia replied. "As I said, some married couples go together, and many single gentlemen attend."

"But how do *you* know about it, Sophia?"

Her sister colored. "James was a member of the society before we met."

"James, your *husband*?"

Sophia nodded. "Yes, and...well... we attended a few of the balls together when we were first married."

"*You* went there? I thought *I* was the only one who ever did anything wild."

Sophia glanced over her shoulder again. "He never left my side, and I must admit, it was wicked fun. We danced as much as we pleased, drank champagne, and slipped away when we felt like it, finding some dark alcove to be alone together."

Clara grinned at her. "Sophia, I'm shocked."

Her sister gave her a mischievous little smirk. "There's nothing wrong with enjoying one's husband, and a happy marriage is a gift to everyone involved, including one's children."

Clara laughed quietly. "Leave it to you to find the charity in lovemaking."

"You can find anything you desire in lovemaking, Clara, but I should not be telling you these things. Mother would throw me to the hogs if she could hear me now. The point is, you are not yet married, and you should not have gone to that ball."

"I'm quite aware, Sophia, but it cannot be undone. You must help me get out of this as smoothly as possible. The last place I want to be is at the center of another scandal."

Sophia nodded and walked with Clara around the ballroom. "You told no one who you were? You wore your mask the entire time?"

"Yes."

"We are fortunate in the fact that one of the rules of the Cakras Society is that guests do not attend any other social functions in the same evening, to avoid being seen and recognized. We must pray that everyone will be judicious tonight."

"There's a chance they won't?"

"A chance, yes. Some people simply don't care. Either way, it wouldn't hurt to burn that dress you are wearing, and don't wear that diamond pendant again. And that comb in your hair—bury it at the bottom of one your trunks."

Clara glanced anxiously about the room. "Perhaps I should leave."

"No, you can't leave now. You still have to dance with the Prince." She began to primp the trimmings on Clara's gown. "He has an open mind when it comes to foreigners, being half German himself, and thankfully for us, he has an eye for pretty ladies. And you, my dear sister, are among the prettiest."

Sophia smiled, but Clara recognized the worry in her eyes.

"You must forget about what happened tonight," Sophia continued, "and bring some color back to your cheeks. I have already spoken to Bertie about you, and he has requested a spot on your card, so you cannot leave without insulting the Crown."

Clara nodded. "I'll do my best."

"Good. Then let us find James. It's time for your Season in London to begin. This time, we'll begin it properly. Then we'll take you straight home."

Chapter 3

Dear Adele,
I take back what I wrote before about London
gentlemen being as dull as the Knickerbockers. I
met a most fascinating man the other night. I won't
tell you how I met him, only that he was very
handsome and very exciting....
Clara

"*I*T HAS BECOME AN UNQUALIFIED stampede."

Quintina Wolfe, the Marchioness of Rawdon, tossed the *Morning Post* onto the breakfast table and reached for her gold-trimmed teacup. "Have you read this yet, Seger?" she asked her stepson, the marquess. "Another American heiress has waltzed into a London ballroom, bold as brass, and danced with the Prince of Wales, and she's made headlines because of it. I ask you, what is the world coming to?"

Seger had not read the society pages. He never read *anything* in the society pages, nor did he ever wish to, but when his stepmother spoke about it that morning, he found himself instantly diverted. He glanced up from his own copy of the paper.

"I beg your pardon? Did you mention an American?"

He had not yet managed to sweep last night's brief but consequential encounter from his mind. He could still hear the young debutante's sultry voice in that irresistible American accent, and the appealing way she'd purred and shivered when he'd whispered in her ear. He had left the ball early, for he had lost all interest in "dancing" with anyone else after she had departed, but a lot of good that had done him. Through the night, in bed, he could still smell her perfume on his hands, and he couldn't seem to forget the luster in her eyes. It was a luster he had known only once before in his life, and it bloody well kept him awake all night, tossing and turning like a flounder.

Quickly, he attributed his sleeplessness to the fact that their "encounter" had been cut short, and because of that he was frustrated. He was, after all, not accustomed to being refused. He had become an expert at spotting fruit that was ripe, and ripe fruit was generally eager to be picked and tasted. Not in many years had he bothered to approach the type of woman who would not be willing or able to take things to the finish. What in God's name had induced him to mistake a debutante for a seasoned trifler?

Perhaps it was because she resembled Daphne in certain ways—her dark hair and brown eyes, and her facial expressions. He supposed he had needed a closer look.

Quintina stabbed the paper with her long, bony finger. "It's all there in black and white. Read it for yourself. Another tart with obnoxious manners and objectionable breeding has arrived with trunks full of American dollars, hoping to become one of *us*. Pox on her. She's a trollop, like all the rest. Honestly, what can they be thinking?"

Barely listening to his stepmother's open rant about the Americans, Seger reached for the paper.

"Did you know," she said, "that she's the sister of the Duke of Wentworth's young American wife, who came from a hovel somewhere in the middle of the country where her ancestors were bootmakers and butchers. But then again..."—Quintina waved a hand— "the duke was not exactly in an enviable position in society, was he? Being so deeply in debt...."

Seger picked up the paper and found the headline: another american heiress joins stampede to acquire english title.

The article went on to describe the estimates and sources of her father's wealth, the young woman's unparalleled charm, and the details of her attire, mainly her fashionable Worth gown. "It was the color of a fresh magnolia," the writer said, "with pale blue flower sprays. She wore a diamond pendant and pearls and lilies in her thick, mahogany hair."

Seger's gut began to twist and roll as he read word after word of the excruciatingly disturbing article. The beautiful, bewitching—and idiotic—young temptress from the Cakras Ball. Her name was Clara Wilson.

What the bloody hell was wrong with the girl? Did she not know she would attract attention by dancing with the Prince of Wales, and that every man who laid eyes on her at Livingston House would be making the connection that morning, licking his chops, and planning how he was either going to ruin her entirely, or use what he knew to squeeze the largest wad possible from her rich American father?

Everyone had seen Segar dancing with her, too, and Seger was more than recognizable, even in his mask. He was one of the regulars at the Cakras Balls and had never tried to hide it. All of society knew he avoided ambitious young debutante's like he avoided the plague, for he was not interested in becoming anyone's prized acquisition.

He knew what real love was. He'd had it once, and he knew it could not be arranged, or bought, or snuffed out by a strict and sometimes cruel social code.

He would not marry to please his tenants or the royal court or his stepmother. Especially his step-mother. Such a path had been forced upon him once, and it would not be forced upon him again. It was a matter of principle now. He would not surrender to it. Besides, he preferred his life exactly the way it was.

He gazed coldly at Quintina. There were many things not yet forgotten. Or forgiven.

Seger raked a hand through his hair and pushed the still-glowing embers of resentment down into the deepest corners of his being where they belonged. They did him no good out in the open. What was done was done, and he could not change the past.

He turned his attention back to the paper and read the rest of the article about the American. No doubt, there would be conjecture about his intentions if their encounter at the Cakras Ball became known. Every-one would wonder if he would marry her. Some would expect him to, for he had compromised her reputation by disappearing with her under the stairs.

"Bloody hell." Seger crumpled the paper in his fist,

whirled around and threw it into the fire. This was precisely why he did not flirt with debutantes. He did not wish to marry until he was good and ready, and he was not ready now. He would not be forced. His marriage would be on his own terms.

Seger watched the newspaper shrink as the red flame consumed it, then he faced the table again.

His stepmother was staring at him in stunned silence, her thin-lipped mouth dangling open. After a second or two, she raised an eyebrow. "Well done, Seger. That's exactly what *I* wanted to do with that paper."

Just then, her niece, Gillian Flint, entered the breakfast room. Gillian was visiting from Wales, enjoying her first London Season under the chaperonage of her aunt. From what Seger had heard from his stepmother, the young woman had been a great success so far.

Gillian removed her spectacles, smoothed her skirt and sat down.

Quintina furiously buttered her roll. "I wish we could do the same to that American heiress, and all the others like her. Throw them into the fire. We have our own English girls to arrange into marriages and we should not have to suffer this kind of vulgar, garish invasion. They think they can *buy* their way in. It is simply shocking."

Nostrils flaring, she returned to her breakfast, and Seger turned his attention away from her. He could not eat another bite, however, for he now knew the American girl's name.

It was Clara. Clara Wilson.

Seven days later, Clara waited in the drawing room at Wentworth House for Sophia, James, and Mrs. Gunther. They were about to embark upon yet another exhausting evening of society balls and assemblies.

She gazed at herself in the enormous gilt-framed mirror above the fireplace, fiddled absentmindedly with one of her earrings, and wondered if the mysterious masked Casanova she had met a week ago would recognize her if they met again.

Thankfully, no one else had recognized her. At least she didn't think so. There had been some concern after that crass article in the paper, but when Clara went out the next evening and the evening after that, nothing untoward had occurred. It seemed the English were as discreet and reserved as they led the rest of the world to believe. Or perhaps no one wanted to stir up a scandal and make a fool of the Prince of Wales.

Clara moved away from the mirror and sat down, wondering who she might meet that night. She had become acquainted with dozens of young aristocrats over the past week, but could picture none of their faces now, though she had been able to look at them fully and without restrictions for many minutes. The only face she could conjure in her imagination possessed a pair of striking green eyes and a full mouth, a deeply dimpled chin and a strong, square jaw below a narrow black mask. Clara knew she would spend most of her evening thinking about her secret paramour, searching room after room for that thick, golden hair and striking, charismatic presence.

Sophia, James and Mrs. Gunther entered the room, and they all made their way through the doorway and into the coach.

Four long hours later, Clara entered her third ball of the evening. She was exhausted from the constant string of introductions and the challenge of making conversation with English gentlemen while remembering to curtsey to this one, not to curtsey to that one, and for pity's sake, not to become distracted and call an earl a "sir-something" or a baronet a "lord."

Later, she sat down with Mrs. Gunther, clacked open her plumed fan and watched the dancers while absent-mindedly stroking the smooth jewel in her drop earring with a finger and thumb.

Again, her thoughts drifted to the vision of that incredible man, sauntering across a ballroom toward her. It all seemed like a ridiculous fantasy now. Perhaps the champagne and the punch had rattled her senses and made it all seem more magical than it truly was.

But certainly, the man's effect on her had been real. She had not been able to extinguish the confusing, sweet longings that emerged every time she thought of him, every time she reminded herself that she did not even know his name, and that it was a very real possibility she would never see him again.

Still, Clara continued to dream of that night, imagining what might have occurred if she had gone with him to one of the private rooms as he had suggested. She envisioned a night of abandoned morality, bold and daring quests for pleasure, and the more she thought about it, the more intense and adventurous her fantasies became.

But that's all they were, she reminded herself. Fantasies. She knew nothing about the man beneath the mask, except that he had not ravished her when he'd had the chance.

And for that—despite all her daydreams that indicated otherwise—she was thankful.

She also felt justified in her private affection for this stranger, for at least she could tell herself that he possessed some integrity, and that he was a true gentleman, under the circumstances. A hero who had pulled her from the fires of scandal, just as her father had done two years ago. If that mysterious gentleman had not marched her back to Mrs. Gunther and insisted that they leave, who knew where Clara might be today? Perhaps on a steamer somewhere in the middle of the Atlantic, on her way back to America, her chances of marrying a decent man all but washed away.

On the other hand, her heroic fantasy man could have been married.

Married. She hoped he wasn't. Pity the poor wife if he was, for how could any woman survive the knowledge that a husband like him was unfaithful and uninterested in her?

Sophia approached with cheeks flushed from a dance with her husband. "It's almost time to leave, Clara. Have you danced enough?"

"Enough? Most definitely. I'm exhausted." Yet, the thought of leaving brought disappointment, for another night had passed and her dream lover had not materialized.

"Shall we go then?" Sophia asked.

Clara closed her fan, gathered up her skirts, and followed her sister out.

As they drove home in the dark carriage, Clara continued to ponder the situation. She could not continue this way, dreaming about a mysterious stranger, while opportunities with perfectly respectable gentlemen passed her by.

Later that night, not long after she'd changed into her nightgown, Clara padded down the corridor in bare feet and knocked on Sophia's door.

Sophia opened it and raised her index finger to her lips. "*Shhh.*" She held her second son, John, in her arms. Carefully, she handed the sleeping infant to his nurse, Louise, who headed for the door to take him upstairs to the nursery. Clara closed the door behind Louise.

"I'm surprised you're still awake," Sophia said.

Clara sat on the bed, not altogether certain how to explain her feelings to her sister, who already had enough on her plate with two babies barely ten months apart. All Clara knew was that she needed to do something to get over this foolish infatuation because it wasn't going away on its own.

"I'm sure you've noticed," Clara said, "that I've not been remotely interested in any of the gentlemen I've met this week, and I've met quite a few very nice men."

Sophia regarded her intently. "Is it because you're still thinking about the man you met at Livingston House?"

"Is it that obvious?"

"To me, yes. You gaze off into space most of the time, and if you're not doing that, you're surveying ballrooms, searching with your eyes."

Clara tried to explain herself. "I want to find a good husband, I truly do, but how can I, when I can't get a certain fantasy man out of my mind? None can compare to my memory of him." Clara cupped her forehead in her hand. "I know it's ridiculous, because I'm sure that everything I believe about him is exactly that—a fantasy. Let's be honest. He was present at one of these improper balls, and therefore is probably one of two things: a rake who carries on affairs with married women, or a husband who cheats on his wife. Neither of those possibilities are attractive to me. I want to marry a decent man who will be faithful to me and be a good father, and yet...."

"You can't stop thinking about him."

Clara sighed. "Something needs to be done. I need to get him out of my head."

"How can I help?"

Standing and crossing the room, Clara glanced down at the stack of cards on Sophia's desk. "I don't suppose you've received any more invitations to *a you know what*."

Sophia rose from the bed and joined Clara at her desk. "I know very well *what*, and I thought you said those balls were appalling."

"Well, they are, at least for married people who go there to be unfaithful."

Sophia slowly shook her head. "Clara. You cannot take a risk like that. What would Mrs. Gunther say?"

"Would she even have to know?"

Sophia gaped at her.

"You could be my chaperone," Clara continued. "We could go for just an hour or so."

"But I couldn't possibly go to a Cakras Ball without James," Sophia replied. "I wouldn't want to be seen there without him. People might presume we've grown bored with each other, which we have not."

"We could wear wigs and put on English accents," Clara suggested. "No one would recognize us."

"Have you lost your mind? Even if we did manage to attend without anyone knowing, what are the odds that you would see this particular man again? He might not even be there."

"Can't we at least try? I must know who he is—have a name at least. What if he's the man I'm destined to marry?"

"Then you will meet him in a respectable situation."

"How can you be sure? Maybe he only goes to the Cakras Balls."

Sophia sighed with frustration. "What about everything you just said, about him being either a rake or a philanderer?"

Clara waved a finger at her older sister. "You told me James used to go to those balls when he was younger, and now look at him. He's a perfect husband, Sophia. What if you had dismissed him because you'd discovered he attended those parties?"

Sophia was quiet for a moment. "I suppose you have me there."

"I just want both of us to keep our minds open." A thrilling ripple of anticipation shimmied up Clara's spine. "So, will you come with me?"

Her sister hesitated, then went to her desk to sort through the invitations. "The Cakras Balls don't happen regularly. Sometimes I don't receive an invitation for months on end."

She continued to flip through, then stopped and stared at Clara. Excitement fluttered in the air as she handed her a card.

"Or sometimes, they come exactly when you want them to."

Chapter 4

Dear Clara,

Please be careful. Do not forget what happened two years ago. You craved excitement and you wanted to break free of society's strictures, and you came very close to complete ruination. Remember that where young women like us are concerned, society's strictures exist for our protection....

Love,

Adele

"Jf Mother could see us now, she'd turn blue." Sophia glanced out the dark window of the carriage as Livingston House came into view, then arranged the rhinestone-and-feather mask on her face. "I don't know what James will think when I tell him where we went tonight. I hope he won't be angry."

"You can blame it on me," Clara replied. "Besides, it's not as if you're sneaking out behind his back. In fact, we would have brought him with us if he hadn't gone to Yorkshire."

"I suppose. At any rate, I'll explain everything when he returns and hope for the best. We're here. Are you sure you want to do this?"

Clara fought to suppress nervous butterflies as she, too, arranged her mask. She was about to take an enormous risk by sneaking into a Cakras Ball, but she might also see her handsome paramour again.

Anticipation rippled up her spine. "Yes, I am sure."

Sophia faced her squarely. "All right then. Here are the rules. And as your chaperone, I will allow you to dance with him, but under no circumstances should you be alone with him. This is a dangerous place, Clara, and if he's not to be trusted—"

"Don't worry, I won't do anything foolish. But I don't want to presume that he's not to be trusted. He didn't ravish me the last time."

"That was last time. What if sees you here, after you'd already been warned, and presumes you're looking for a dalliance? He might think you're fast."

The carriage stopped in front of the brightly lit mansion. "I'm not fast. I am morally upright, in perfect control of my impulses."

Sophia gave her a look. "Then what, pray tell, are we doing here?"

Clara had no choice but to surrender to her sister's shrewd observation. "I've missed you," she said.

"I've missed you, too. And despite my misgivings, I'm pleased that I can help you tonight because I understand how you feel. It was the same when I met James. I could barely get through the day, wanting him the way I did." She squeezed Clara's hand. "Who knows, maybe this man *is* your destiny. What a hopeless romantic I am."

"Or maybe I'll discover that he's the worst rogue in the world and he's here tonight cheating on his wife, after losing half his fortune playing cards, and on top of that, when he sleeps, he snores like a buffalo."

They shared an affectionate smile, then Sophia pulled on her long gloves. "With any luck, we'll find out soon enough—at least about the first two things."

The carriage door opened, and the ladies stepped out. Clara looked up at the front of the mansion where the same burly man as last time stood in front of the door.

Sophia straightened her mantle. "You're absolutely positive?"

"Yes," Clara replied. "Let's get this over with."

They picked up their skirts and walked up the steps. Sophia presented their invitation. The next thing they knew, they were inside, standing on the shiny black-and-white checkered floor in the wide hall, handing their mantles over to the masked butler while the music of flutes and violins flitted to their ears from the ballroom.

"Does Lord Livingston ever greet his guests?" Clara asked as they ascended the stairs to the drawing room.

"No, there are never any introductions. Both Lord and Lady Livingston follow the same rules as everyone else. They mingle and dance with whomever they please, but no names are ever spoken."

"You mean to say they carry on affairs under each other's noses, and they're happy with that?"

"Apparently."

Clara considered such an arrangement. If she married an Englishman who was later unfaithful, could she turn a blind eye? She had been brought up with a different ideal, as all American girls were, with a Puritan attitude toward adultery as a scarlet letter sin.

They entered the crimson-and-gold drawing room,

where elegant chintz fabrics covered the chairs and chaises, and the walls were painted scarlet with gilt crown moldings. None of the guests were sitting down. Most stood in dimly lit corners, whispering and giggling. The air was charged with the heat of secret, wicked seductions.

"I don't see him," Clara whispered. "Perhaps he's in the ballroom."

"Or in one of the private rooms already."

Clara didn't want to think about that, but she had to face the fact that it was a very real possibility.

They accepted glasses of champagne from a footman who offered it, then entered the large ballroom and watched couples waltz around the polished floor. The same orchestra was there again, and the music was stupendous.

Clara couldn't help thinking that from her vantage point, it could have been any other respectable ball—if not for the couple kissing passionately behind a potted tree fern not three feet away from where she and Sophia stood.

A mixture of shock and fascination struck her, and she couldn't seem to look away.

Sophia took hold of her arm. "Stop staring."

"Can you believe that?" Clara whispered as Sophia led her away. "I've never seen anything like it."

"I thought your mystery man kissed you."

"He did, but at least he found us some privacy."

They continued to move around the perimeter of the ballroom, watching the dancers. A gentleman caught Sophia's eye and approached. "Care to dance?"

She smiled graciously and disguised her voice with

an English accent. "Please except my apologies, but I must decline. Perhaps later."

He bowed cordially and moved on.

"I won't be dancing with anyone tonight," Sophia said, "and neither should you, except for the man we're here to see. We must remain focused."

"I completely agree."

They finished their champagne and set their empty glasses on a side table.

"Do you see him?" Sophia asked.

"No. He's not here."

"Don't lose heart. We'll stay for a little while. Maybe he's on his way at this very moment."

"Or maybe he was here earlier and left already."

Just then, a golden-haired man in a black mask strolled into the ballroom. Looking relaxed and confident, he picked up a glass of champagne and let his gaze sweep around the room. Clara's eyes narrowed.

She knew that walk...that body. *It was him.*

A thrill rushed through her like a firebrand. She stood motionless, watching him intently. He looked as handsome as she remembered. Even more so, after the week she'd spent dreaming about him. She was completely dumbstruck by the sight of him.

"Is that him?" Sophia asked. "The man who just walked in?"

Clara nodded.

"Upon my word," Sophia said. "No wonder you couldn't forget him. He's incredible."

They watched him move around the room, composed and at ease. Clad in the usual formal attire—black jacket, white waistcoat, and white necktie—he raised his glass to a man on the other side of the room, who raised his glass in return before continuing his conversation with a lady.

"Do you know his name?" Clara asked. "Have you ever seen him before?"

"Never. I only attended a handful of Cakras Balls with James, and I don't recall seeing this man, though James and I weren't here to socialize with others."

"What about during the Season last year?"

"I never saw him at any of the parties or balls I attended. I most certainly would have remembered him."

Clara took a deep breath. "What is wrong with me? My stomach is doing somersaults."

"It's called infatuation, and you're infected with it. But it's understandable, now that I've seen him for myself. Let's walk this way so you can collect yourself before you speak to him."

Speak to him. At the mere mention of it, Clara's stomach careened again. "What will I say? I can't ask him his name. That would be against the rules. How will I learn anything?"

"You'll have to be creative. Are you ready?"

Once again, Clara found herself caught in the sticky web of his unparalleled good looks and his debilitating sexual allure.

"Heaven help me, I could never be ready for a man like him."

It was the perfume that gave her away as she brushed past his elbow, in a ridiculous dark wig, no less. She smelled of strawberries again. A brief glance at her mouth confirmed it. It was indeed the American.

Seger stopped and turned to look at her from behind after she'd passed by and felt the immediate stirrings of unfulfilled arousal. Tonight, she was with a friend instead of the older woman from the week before. No, not a friend... Seger's brows drew together as he noticed the wig on the other woman as well. It was probably Miss Wilson's sister, the Duchess of Wentworth.

At that precise instant, the single heiress glanced over her shoulder. Their eyes locked and held, and recognition occurred. She stared at him for a few seconds, then faced front again.

Seger shook his head. What the devil were they doing here? It was a well-known fact that American heiresses were bombarding London in a mad dash for husbands with titles. Why would she come here to look for one and risk her reputation? Did she not realize that skirting a scandal last time had been a complete miracle? The duchess should have known better.

Or perhaps that's why the single heiress was here in the first place. To stir up a scandal and force someone's hand.

Well, it wouldn't be his hand. He had spent the past eight years learning how to guard himself against that sort of thing.

Unfortunately for her, however, it probably wouldn't force anyone else's hand either. Most of the gentlemen here were not in possession of a great deal of honor when it came to young ladies and scandals. They would simply watch from the shadows as she danced in her noose. Besides that, most of them were already married.

Just then, in his peripheral vision, Seger noticed an older man making his way toward Miss Wilson. It was not surprising. Even in that ridiculous wig, she was stunning. It was only a matter of time before every other man in the room would want to experience her delights, for she was a rare contradiction. She had the look of a professional beauty, yet with such innocence. And those lips were enough to bring any man to his knees.

The man bowed before Miss Wilson and held out his ungloved hand.

Seger tensed as he watched.

Miss Wilson politely refused the gentleman's advance. He nodded courteously and backed away. Seger exhaled a breath of relief. She was lucky that time, but how long would her luck hold?

Seger downed the rest of his champagne in a single gulp and set the glass on a table. He hadn't come there to play hero, but he supposed it couldn't be helped. He would dance with her once and do what he could to talk some sense into her. Then he could at least say he tried.

He approached the ladies and bowed slightly. "Good evening."

"Good evening," they both replied simultaneously.

He offered his hand to the heiress. "Shall we?"

Clara gazed up at her dream lover in a shock-induced stupor. She hadn't expected him to approach her after he'd been the one to march her back to Mrs.

Gunther the first time they'd met. She was surprised he hadn't turned and run in the opposite direction when he'd recognized her a moment ago.

But who was she to refuse such a gift? All that mattered was that he was there, and she was going to dance with him.

She placed her gloved hand in his. He led her onto the floor and stepped into a slow waltz. They danced for a moment or two before he finally spoke.

"Miss Wilson, isn't it?"

Smothering her surprise at his candor, she looked him in the eye. "Yes. It appears you've been reading the papers."

"I have indeed," he replied. "You're quite the sensation."

She raised her chin. "That was not my intention. The London press is very aggressive."

He inclined his head. "Yes. Which makes me wonder why you took such a risk coming back here tonight. I thought I made myself clear last time. I warned you about the dangers of a place like this for a woman like you. Did you not understand my meaning?"

"I did."

"Then why have you returned?"

Clara rummaged around her brain for an answer when she didn't want to be *giving* answers. She wanted to be the one asking the questions.

"It seems, sir, that you know all about me, yet I know nothing about you. That's hardly fair, is it?"

She barely recognized the bravado in her voice, the deep, seductive timbre. Perhaps it was something in the air. The whole room reeked of pure, unhampered sexuality.

"There are rules here," he replied. "Identities are to be kept secret."

"But you broke the rule when you revealed that you knew my name."

The corner of his mouth turned up in a sly grin. "You're not going to report me, are you?"

"Good gracious, no. Not unless you want me to."

He chuckled. "I think not. Only because it would put you in the spotlight more than me, and I don't think that's a wise place for you to be at the moment. Not among these people. They have no mercy when it comes to the violation of their rules."

Clara tilted her face upward and remembered how wonderful it felt to be kissed by those beautiful lips. "Then I should thank you again," she said sweetly, "for being my champion a second time and warning me away from danger."

"Not that it did any good the first time. All you did was leap back into the fire. Strange, you don't strike me as the type of woman who enjoys things hot and hazardous."

"No? How *do* I strike you?"

"As the type who doesn't usually take risks. You seem innocent and free of sin, which makes you stick out like a sore thumb here."

Clara pursed her lips. "I'm not sure if I've been insulted or paid a compliment."

"It was, for all intents and purposes, a compliment."

They continued to dance around the room, and Clara considered all that he had said and realized she still knew absolutely nothing about him. Sophia had told her to be creative. How the blazes was she supposed to do that?

"Obviously," she said, "you don't attend many balls other than these, or you would not find me so fresh. I'm no different from most other young ladies my age."

"I beg to differ."

Still no new information. What would it take? "Shameless compliments," she said. "Are you always so blatantly charming with the ladies?"

He didn't reply. The waltz came to an end, and her mystery man stepped back. "I had intended to talk sense into you, but all we've been doing is flirting. Stay and dance with me again."

He was certainly direct. It was quite refreshing, and Clara had no desire to refuse him. "If I am to stay for your lecture," she said, "you must tell me something about yourself first."

"Is this a negotiation?"

"I believe so."

He wet his lips. "Right, then. What would you like to know?"

She considered it for a few seconds. "If you won't tell me your name, at least tell me why I've not encountered you out in society."

"Because I prefer to avoid the Marriage Mart. Come, let's dance."

She finally stepped into his arms and let him whisk her across the floor. "Because you're already married?"

"No."

"You're not married, then? You've never been?"

He shook his head and Clara's heart rejoiced, but there was still so much more she wanted to know.

"Why won't you tell me your name?" she asked.

"Because that's not what we do here."

"I don't care. I'll probably never come to one of these things again, and I would at least like to know the name of the gentleman I danced with this evening. You're not a criminal, are you? A fugitive from justice?"

"No."

"A spy for the British government?"

He laughed. "I'm afraid not."

"Then why must you be so secretive? It's not as if I couldn't find out who you were if I asked enough people. You must be the only gentleman in London with hair that reaches your shoulders."

He said nothing for a few seconds while they continued to dance, then finally, when the waltz was nearly at an end, he said, "My given name is Seger."

The music stopped, and they stepped apart.

Clara liked the name and gazed at his face, wishing she could see what he looked like without the mask… wishing she could reach up and touch that strong chiseled jaw and those perfect, soft lips.

"Since you didn't give me a chance to lecture you," he said, "it's your turn to do something for me."

"What is that?"

"Leave. And don't come back here again."

His blunt request hurt, even though she knew he was only thinking of her safety and well-being.

Further reflection made her feel flattered that her

welfare mattered to him at all.

Clara knew she should do as he asked, but she wished it did not have to be so. There was still so much she did not know about him, and she longed to see him again. How would she survive another week of these hopeless longings?

In the end she agreed because he was right, but she wasn't happy about it. "Thank you, Seger. I enjoyed myself."

Eyes never leaving hers, he kissed the back of her hand. "As did I."

At the touch of his lips, a shiver of delight coursed through her. She began to walk away, but he stopped her. "Wait."

She turned.

"Why *did* you come back here?"

Clara stared at his green eyes and her heart began to pound. "Haven't you guessed?"

He merely stared at her, waiting for her reply.

"I came here because I've never been kissed like that, and I couldn't stop thinking about you." With that, she walked away.

Chapter 5

Dear Clara,

You must be more careful about breaking the rules, and I am not referring to your foolish desire to return to that scandalous ball. Even the smallest mistake matters. Just the other day, Mrs. Carling gave Mrs. Jenson the cut direct because Mrs. Jenson wore her diamonds in the morning. (Be sure not to do that.)

Now that I have said my piece, you must tell me all about your adventure. Was he there?

Love,
Adele

"DID YOU SEE THE DUKE of Guysborough last night?" Mrs. Gunther asked, looking up from her embroidery to peer at Sophia over the rims of her spectacles. "Did he attend the assembly?"

Sophia raised her teacup and sipped, a faint smile touching her lips. If the Duke of Guysborough had been at the Cakras Ball, she and Clara certainly hadn't known of it.

"We didn't see him," Sophia replied.

"I wonder if he'll be at the Tremont assembly this evening. He's a handsome man, don't you think? A duke, Sophia. And widowed."

Sophia inclined her head. "You think he would be a good match for Clara?"

"Naturally, don't you? Your mother would be very pleased."

"He's rather old."

"Nonsense, he can't be a day over forty-five."

"But he has children already from his first wife, who passed away not long ago. Do you think he wishes to remarry so soon?"

Mrs. Gunther poked her needle into the fabric on her lap. "I've been making inquiries, and from what I understand, he has only one son and four girls. No spare, so to speak. I should think he would be vastly inclined to marry again, and Clara is certainly a beauty."

Sophia dabbed at her mouth with the corner of her linen napkin. "I hadn't considered the duke. I don't know him well. Do you think he's handsome, and doesn't seem too mature?"

"To a woman of my age, he's barely more than a schoolboy."

Just then, Sophia's husband entered the breakfast room. "James, you're back."

He smiled at her. "Yes, I decided I missed my wife and sons far too much to spend another day away from them."

Sophia rose from the table to greet him.

They sat down and discussed the renovations at Wentworth Castle while James ate his breakfast. When he laid down his fork, Sophia stood. "Shall we go and see the boys?"

"I would like nothing more." Together, they

excused themselves from Mrs. Gunther's company and left the room.

As soon as they were alone in the corridor, James took hold of Sophia's hand, kissed it, and held it as they walked. "Perhaps next time you'll accompany me to Wentworth," he said, "and spare me the agony of sleeping alone."

Sophia's voice was flirtatious. "I didn't like sleeping alone, either. And I would have gone with you if Clara wasn't here. But she needs me, James. In that regard, there is something I must tell you, and I hope you won't be angry: I took her to a Cakras Ball last night."

James stopped and let go of her hand. "You did what? Why in the world would you do that?"

"It's a long story, but I must confess all, for I worry that the situation could become dangerous if we don't soon learn about a particular gentleman who has made quite an impression upon Clara."

"And this man was at the Cakras Ball?"

She nodded.

"That's not a good sign to begin with. But why did you take her there, Sophia? It's hardly a suitable destination for a young lady seeking a husband."

Sophia explained the whole situation—how Clara had walked into the wrong ball a week earlier by mistake, and how she had not been able to forget the man who had informed her of her error.

"We returned last night to try and discover his identity," Sophia explained.

James took hold of her hand again. "Did you?"

"Only his given name. It's Seger."

James thought for a moment. "Seger. The only Seger I know of is Seger Wolfe, the Marquess of Rawdon."

"He's a marquess?"

"If he is indeed the same man."

"Have you met him?"

"No, he doesn't sit in the House. He has no interest in politics, or perhaps he simply doesn't like to show his face. He was involved in a divorce scandal a few years ago. He was called to court as a witness to testify for a fellow peer, to prove his wife's adultery."

Sophia tried not to sound glum as she walked slowly down the corridor beside James. "So, I gather the marquess is not respectable?"

James spoke plainly. "As I said, I've never met the man, so I cannot say. But do warn Clara to be careful if she encounters him again, especially in light of what happened to her before. Is this what has you worried?"

Sophia exhaled heavily. "You don't think she'll make a mistake like that again, do you?"

"What I think is that you should try to have confidence in her. She is an intelligent young woman and from what I have seen, she is no longer naive. She has been quiet and careful these past two years, choosing to postpone her first Season. That is self-restraint at its best, especially for an adventurous girl like Clara, who attended our wedding with dreams of romance in her eyes, longing for such happiness for herself. We must trust that she will be prudent, for she has said on many occasions in her letters to you that it is her greatest wish to be sensible."

"Yes, but she is inherently passionate, and sometimes love can turn one's head."

"Like it turned yours?" He gave her a look.

"But you were a good man, James. We don't know anything about the marquess, and I fear that I might have become caught up in the excitement of her infatuation and advised her poorly. Perhaps I should have set a better example and refused to let her return to Livingston House."

"She saw him again, I presume?"

"Yes, they danced twice, and again, he asked her to leave. She was in a romantic daze the whole way home. I'm worried, James."

He nodded as they reached the door to the nursery. "You mustn't trouble yourself. We will do what we can to help Clara. I will make inquiries about the marquess. Now let us dispense with our concerns for the time being and see what our sons have accomplished today. Perhaps John has discovered his thumbs." He opened the door to the nursery, and they walked into the warmth of morning sunlight streaming in through the windows.

"I have good news and bad news," Sophia said to Clara that afternoon, as soon as they were out of earshot of the groom, who rode behind them in Hyde Park. Both in their riding habits, crops in hand, they sat high in their sidesaddles, maintaining a leisurely pace along the bridle path.

"Did James know anything?" Clara asked.

"Yes, if he was talking about the same Seger. The good news is, he's a peer. His name is Seger Wolfe, and he's the Marquess of Rawdon."

"Truly. A marquess, you say. Mother would swoon."

"Yes, she would, but I must inform you that James wasn't particularly pleased to learn that you were at a Cakras Ball. He warned me to be more careful in the future, and he suggested that you be especially mindful if you ever meet the marquess again."

"He has a reputation, then?" Clara asked as her horse's hooves tapped lightly over the soft ground. "Is that the bad news? Did he lie to me about not being married?"

"That, I do not know, but it would be easy to find out now that we know who he is. All I know is what James told me—that the marquess was involved in a divorce scandal. He had to testify in court about his affair with a married woman, and for that reason, he is not invited into polite society."

Clara absorbed this news with disappointment, though she shouldn't be surprised. She knew the marquess seduced married women regularly at the Cakras Balls. That sort of behavior was bound to ruin a man's reputation eventually.

"Will society not let him back in?" Clara asked. "Or is it his choice to refuse invitations?"

"I wish I knew."

Clara gazed up at the sky. "I wonder if he learned a lesson from that scandal. Perhaps he's more cautious these days. He must be, given the way he tossed me out the door when he discovered I was unmarried—a hot potato to him apparently."

"You are not a potato, Clara, and you're still hoping for the best where he's concerned, aren't you?"

"I can't help it. He's still the most interesting man

I've met since my arrival in England. I want to understand why he is what he is, and I can't seem to shake that desire."

Sophia regarded her sister. "What about the Duke of Guysborough? I only mention him because Mrs. Gunther asked about him this morning. She wanted to know if we encountered him last night."

Clara laughed. "How would we even know? Everyone was wearing a mask."

"Indeed. But do you remember meeting the duke last week?"

"The tall fellow with the dark mustache? Yes, I do."

"And what did you think of him? He would be an excellent catch, given his rank. His title is not quite as old as James's, but he's favored by the queen. She admired his wife for her charity work. The duchess passed away just over a year ago."

"A widower." Clara ducked below some low-hanging branches. "I hadn't considered marrying someone who had been married before. I suppose it is an option."

"Did you find him attractive?"

Clara shrugged. "Not as attractive as the marquess, though he would probably be a more sensible choice."

"Yes," Sophia agreed. "And I do want you to be sensible, Clara. I was supportive about going to the Cakras Ball, but when I think about what could have occurred if we were discovered.... I don't wish to take that kind of risk again."

"I'm sorry I put you in that position." Clara sighed. "But I begged you to take me there, so don't blame yourself."

They rode in silence for a few minutes, enjoying the cool breeze.

"I just wish," Sophia said, "that there was a way for you to see the marquess again without risking another appearance at a Cakras Ball."

"If only he came out into society."

Sophia considered it for a moment. "Well, there's always the obvious. I could host a party and send him an invitation. He knows I'm your sister. If he's interested in seeing you again, he'll come."

"He told me he despises the Marriage Mart."

"That may be so, but if my eyes were telling me anything last night, it was that he was as taken with you as you were with him. You might be the very thing to bring him out of his shell. Perhaps deep down, he wants to be accepted again and we can help him. The worst thing that could happen is he would simply not attend—in which case we would at least know that he is determined to remain alone."

"Or that he is not attracted to me."

Sophia urged her horse into a gallop. "Impossible."

Clara began to gallop as well.

"Shall I arrange an assembly then?" Sophia called out to Clara as she came up beside her.

Clara experienced a delightful thrill of anticipation. "Most definitely."

Seger sat down for supper in his dining room with his stepmother, Quintina, at one end of the table and his cousin by marriage, Gillian, to his left. Lobster puffs with hollandaise sauce were served, followed by tarragon chicken with artichokes, at which time

Quintina set down her glass of wine and broke the customary silence.

"I received an invitation today, from the Duke and Duchess of Wentworth."

Seger paused, his fork in midair. "You don't say."

"Are you surprised by this?"

He did not look up from his plate, for there was very little he ever chose to reveal to his stepmother. "Should I be? I wouldn't know, since I haven't been following your social calendar."

Quintina bristled. "Surely you know that I do not receive invitations from dukes or duchesses, but we won't go into the reasons why." She gave a cursory glance at Gillian, as if she didn't want to soil the girl's virgin ears with talk of Seger's personal exploits.

Instead, she'd cast the blame without actually saying it, which was her way. She blamed Seger for the family's social descent, all because of what had occurred three years ago with Lord and Lady Edmunston.

Though if one were analytical, one could go back much further than three years and find another source for blame. The true origin of Seger's current manner of existence—the reason why he preferred to remain an island.

"The odd thing about it," Quintina said, "is that the invitation was addressed to you and me both. *Now* tell me that you're not surprised." She raised a dark, arched eyebrow.

Seger wiped his mouth with his napkin and sat back. "All right, you win. I am surprised."

This was, in fact, an understatement. He hadn't been invited into those upper echelons for years. The duchess couldn't be playing matchmaker for her sister, could she? He wasn't exactly a respectable catch, although he did hold a title, and that was the singular purpose behind most of the American heiresses' shopping excursions to London. Perhaps she or the duchess didn't care about his reputation. Or didn't know about it.

Not that any of it mattered. He was not interested in being bought for cash. He was one of the few English aristocrats who had enough cash of his own to buy three lifetimes of freedom.

"So, what do you make of it?" he asked.

"I would call it a gift," Quintina replied. "Despite the unpleasant fact that the duchess is American, it's a chance for us to be accepted in the right circles again, which is an opportunity this family desperately needs. An opportunity Gillian needs." She smiled warmly at her niece. "I promised my sister on her deathbed that I would do everything I could to see her daughter married well. This is Gillian's first Season and I must seize this opportunity."

Seger glanced at Gillian, who kept her eyes lowered and said nothing. She was a quiet little bird at the table most nights. Barely noticeable sometimes. *Shy,* Seger thought. Though not completely unattractive in a youthful sort of way.

"You will go, I presume?" he asked Quintina as he leaned forward and reached for his wine.

"Naturally. But may I request that you decline?"

He raised his eyebrows. "The first decent invitation I've received in years, and you want me to decline? What was all that talk about this family finally getting back into the right circles?"

To be honest, he didn't care a whit about that, nor was he interested in a stuffy Mayfair assembly where most of the old matrons would likely hiss at him anyway. He would, however, like to see the lovely masked creature who'd kept him up most nights for the past two weeks. He still hadn't gotten over her departing words—that she'd been unable to stop thinking about him.

To say he was flattered was an understatement. He hadn't expected her to say such a thing. He had expected some roundabout answer, perhaps an aloof claim that she was simply looking for adventure, because that's what most women said to him when flirtations began. They knew by instinct that that was what would lure him into their bedrooms.

He remembered suddenly that Miss Wilson had initially reminded him of Daphne, and he felt a twinge of discomfort.

Quintina spoke up and interrupted his thoughts. "I am of the opinion that your presence at the assembly would evoke whispers, and I want to do what is best for Gillian."

He glanced at his cousin again. She smiled sheepishly.

"What would you have me do, Gillian?" he asked.

Seeming surprised that he had spoken to her directly, she went suddenly pale. "I...I would have you do whatever you please."

She certainly was a nervous little thing.

Quintina cleared her throat. "There is a more critical reason why you should not attend, Seger."

"And why is that?"

"Because I suspect the motive behind our invitation concerns the duchess's younger sister—that garish girl we read about in the paper. The duchess is holding this assembly to gather all the unmarried peers into one room, so that they may be sized up like merchandise. Surely, you would prefer to avoid such a vulgar affair."

Seger slowly blinked. "Ah. You don't want me to meet the American. Afraid I'll become infatuated with someone inappropriate?"

Her voice was cool and subdued. "It's not as if you haven't made that mistake before."

Like a venomous snake, tension curled around the table. Seger made a fist on his lap. "You are correct, Quintina, and there were disastrous consequences."

His stepmother's cheeks flushed with fury. "Seger, for eight years you have refused to take a respectable wife and produce an heir. Don't you think you have punished this family enough for those consequences that no one could have predicted?"

Seger tossed his napkin onto his empty plate and stood. "I believe I am finished. If you will excuse me." He bowed politely to Gillian, left the dining room, and went upstairs to reply to the Wentworths' invitation. He would let the duchess know that he would be most pleased to accept.

Chapter 6

Dear Adele,
That splendid gentleman I told you about? I
hope to see him again tonight....
Clara

B Y NIGHTFALL, THE ANTICIPATION OF being in the
same room with the marquess had reached a
fevered pitch. Would he even come? Clara wondered
as she moved about the crowded drawing room. He
had accepted Sophia's invitation to the assembly, but
it was getting late and he had not yet arrived. Perhaps
he had reconsidered, changed his mind. It wasn't every
day, after all, that a man re-entered a society that had
rejected and expelled him.

A gentleman stepped up to the door. The majordomo
announced, "His Grace, the Duke of Guysborough."

James and Sophia greeted him, then invited Clara
to join them. The duke bowed elegantly. He was one
of the peers under consideration as a potential husband, at least by Sophia and Mrs. Gunther, and this
made Clara pay attention.

He was, she supposed, a handsome man. With dark
hair and mustache, he possessed a certain impressive
maturity. There was something about him, however,
that made her feel ill at ease, as if she would always

have to sit up straight while in his presence.

As soon as he moved on to mingle about the room, Clara glanced at Mrs. Gunther who was sitting forward in a chair, watching Clara's every move. She sat back, however, after the duke turned away.

"It's getting late," Clara whispered to Sophia when there was a free moment. "Do you think he changed his mind?"

"I don't know. I hope not."

At that moment, an older woman approached the door with a younger lady at her side. The woman was of medium height and proud looking. The girl appeared shy and nervous.

The majordomo announced: "Lady Rawdon and Miss Gillian Flint."

Clara's stomach went *whoosh*. It was Seger's stepmother.

Sophia greeted her warmly. "Lady Rawdon, welcome."

"Your Grace. May I present my niece from Wales, Gillian Flint." She gestured toward the girl behind her, who curtsied.

Sophia smiled. "It's a pleasure to meet you." She turned toward Clara. "This is my sister, Clara Wilson."

They exchanged light pleasantries, but when Lady Rawdon moved on, she scrutinized Clara's extravagant gown from top to bottom and gave her a cool glare. The younger Miss Flint admired Clara's jewels enviously then followed with her head down.

Pulse pounding, wondering if the marquess would arrive next, Clara watched the top of the stairs, but a group of ladies ascended. No wild-looking, wavy-haired gentlemen in sight.

Another half hour went by and the frequency of arrivals began to diminish. Clara's feet were getting sore. *He's not coming,* she thought. *He changed his mind.*

The disappointment was difficult to keep at bay, though she did her best not to show it. She glanced at Lady Rawdon across the room, speaking with a group of older women. At that moment, Sophia nudged her. Hard.

Knocked slightly off balance, Clara stepped to the side, then turned to the door just as the majordomo announced, "The Marquess of Rawdon."

The world seemed to stop turning. All Clara heard was the noisy, thunderous rush of her blood in her ears.

He was here. At last.

Her gaze went first to his eyes, for she'd never seen them without the mask. They were deep green, large and expressive. She had known before that he was handsome, but this was mind-altering. He was everything she had imagined, and more, with the divine presence of a Greek god. Her body pulsed with sizzling, nervous excitement, and her stomach whirled with butterflies.

It wasn't until a few seconds later, as the marquess was shaking James's hand and saying something that made James laugh, that Clara noticed he had cut his hair. Though it was by no means short, it was not wild about his shoulders any longer.

Had he trimmed it because of this single assembly? Had he gone out and changed himself just for her? Or would he have done it for any other invitation?

Either way, the sight of it made her feel joyful inside. He had come out of hiding.

Clara watched him greet Sophia. "Duchess, it is an honor."

"The honor is mine," Sophia replied, turning casually toward Clara. "May I present my sister, Clara Wilson of New York. This is Clara's first Season in London, Lord Rawdon."

He moved to stand before her. He was so tall, grand and sophisticated that she almost forgot to breathe. "At last," he said, bowing his head to her.

A shiver of desire tingled across her flesh. "Welcome to Wentworth House, my lord."

Locked in his smoldering gaze, Clara melted at the grandeur of his face—the masculine line of his jaw, the discerning intelligence in his eyes. Neither of them spoke, until the moment was broken by Sophia, who cleared her throat. Clara felt wrenched out of a trance.

The marquess smiled again, more broadly this time, as if he recognized that she was enamored. Not that he hadn't seemed enamored himself, but perhaps that was just his way. Perhaps he was enamored with all women.

The divorce scandal of three years ago flitted across her mind. She reminded herself to be wary.

The marquess's gaze swept across the crowded drawing room, but before he ventured inside, he faced her one more time. "I would enjoy hearing about America this evening, Miss Wilson, if you would be inclined to describe your home to me."

"I will seek you out," she replied.

"I look forward to it."

He entered the room, and Clara faced the door again to greet two more guests, while struggling to wipe the silly grin off her face and quiet her trembling heart.

There were very few people whom he could talk to, Seger realized as he moved about the room and felt more than a few disapproving gazes follow him to the buffet table. He had not attended a proper assembly in three years, and consequently did not move in these circles. His acquaintances were of a different breed now—not so strict and straight-laced, less judgmental of others—and his entertainments were less correct, by Society's standards. Apparently, most of these people knew that.

Did they think he wanted to be accepted again? He hoped not, for he had never wished to reconcile with them. They had forsaken him, as was their prerogative, and he had accepted that. He was here for quite another reason this evening. To satisfy a lusty curiosity. Quench it if he could, for he was not interested in marriage for profit.

Yet he could not deny that he was interested in *something*.

He noticed his stepmother and Gillian in the far corner but was not inclined to join them. Instead, he reached for a glass of champagne as a footman passed by and downed it in a single gulp.

Setting the empty glass down on a table, he slowly made his way around the perimeter of the room, feeling very much like an outsider. The only pleasant distraction was Miss Wilson still at the door, teeming with charm as she greeted the last few guests. She had smelled like strawberries again.

Her sister, the duchess, was also charming. She had welcomed him without a hint of contempt.

The duke had been cordial as well. Seger wondered if His Grace knew about his wife and sister-in-law attending a Cakras Ball. From what Seger knew about the duke, he was not the sort of man one kept secrets from, nor was he the sort who would remain in the dark for long about any and all events involving members of his household. Regardless, if His Grace had known about his wife's little adventure, he certainly hadn't revealed it. Still, he was a man Seger should not underestimate.

Seger did manage to meet a few gentlemen he knew from his current social circle, gentlemen who had the rare ability through certain connections to cross over from one sphere to the other. They were surprised to see him at the duke's assembly and made no secret of it as they waved him into their conversation.

There, he was introduced to a few respectable ladies and gentlemen, and the first crack in the barrier of his expulsion became visible to both himself and others in the room. He wasn't sure how he felt about that. He had not come there to chisel his way back in.

A short time later, he was still intensely aware of Miss Wilson's presence on the opposite side of the room, her gaze locked on his from yards away, her eyes smiling with mischievous anticipation. He turned away from a group of laughing gentlemen to walk toward her.

They met in the center of the room but did not settle there. Seger led her toward the wall.

"You wanted to hear about America," she said cheerfully.

"That, and whatever else you wish to tell me about. I'll listen to bible recitations if that would please you."

Her whole face beamed. She gazed over her shoulder at the other guests and spoke softly. "I wasn't sure if you would come."

"I wasn't sure myself, but I'm glad I did. May I mention that the wig you wore the other night does not do you justice?"

She sighed. "Still full of flattery, I see. I thought you might be more reserved in a more...*normal* situation."

"You call this normal?" He glanced around. "I'd forgotten how completely *abnormal* these things could be. No offense to the hosts intended."

"I'm sure none would be taken. My sister is American, as you know, and I assure you, all of this was a culture shock to her in the beginning."

"And what about you? You're American as well. What do you make of our English ways?"

She paused. "I don't know yet. I'm still trying very hard to fit in. I wish I knew how to act blasé."

"I'm glad you don't."

Clara smiled at the compliment. "May I just say that you have given me hope, my lord, that not everyone is as reserved as they pretend to be."

He pushed away from the wall. "No, I suppose I am not as reserved as most of the people here tonight, and I can certainly feel the chill. Perhaps we should take a turn about the room. I forgot that lingering in private corners with unmarried ladies is frowned upon."

He offered his arm to Miss Wilson and she laughed. "You certainly *have* been out of circulation if you'd forgotten something as fundamental as that."

"I have indeed."

They walked through the crowd, nodding politely to people as they passed.

"I heard about your court scandal three years ago," she said quietly, when they were out of earshot of other guests.

Seger felt his eyebrows lift. "My word. Don't you know how to talk about the weather with gentlemen you've only just met?"

She touched his arm with the closed fan that hung on a string from her wrist. "Yes, but you and I have met before and I'd like to think that we've moved beyond small talk. Pretending to be prim and proper would feel hypocritical. Besides, I've already discussed the weather at least fifty times tonight, and your scarlet past is much more interesting."

A smile touched his lips. "I suppose my scarlet past is the subject matter of most conversations here tonight. Were you shocked to hear about it?"

"I was, but I'm over it now. You see, I didn't learn of it tonight. I learned of it from my sister a week ago, after she asked her husband about you."

Seger glanced at the duke across the room. "And he knew everything? I'm surprised he invited me into his home." He gazed down at Miss Wilson with a devious smile. "He doesn't know what happened between us that first night under the stairs, does he? Perhaps that was his motivation to bring me here—to either squash me like an insect or force me to propose."

She laughed again. "No, my lord. My brother-in-law is a very open-minded man. He was on the fringe of good society himself at one time. He believes there is more to a person than what first appears on the surface. He believes in second chances. That is why he invited you."

"Do you believe that, too?"

"Of course. People are not all good or all bad. They are more complicated than that, but we seem to have strayed off topic. I was hoping you would tell me about what happened three years ago and why you felt you could not re-enter society."

He shook his head in disbelief. It felt odd to discuss such scandalous topics in a setting like this, but Miss Wilson, he supposed, was not like other debutantes. She was not like any other woman he'd ever met, to be honest.

Nevertheless, she seemed genuinely eager to hear about it, and far be it for him to disappoint a lady.

"It's not that I felt I couldn't re-enter," he said. "I simply did not wish to. It was my choice, and I believe my lack of penitence exasperated certain self-righteous people who would have liked to see me beg."

"So, it was your pride that kept you out? You would not apologize?"

"Partly. But mostly, the scandal was more of a final straw. I had been displeased with society for a long time before that. As I told you before, I never wished to be a part of the Marriage Mart." He was surprised he was telling her all this. It was not why he had come there. He had intended to enjoy a lighter, more friv-olous encounter.

"You don't *ever* intend to look for a wife?" she asked.

He felt his shoulders stiffen. "Not among society in this manner, when everything is a mad scramble for position. I admit I am jaded. When it comes to mar-riage, I will take my chances with fate."

She seemed to accept that.

"But don't you wish to hear about the actual scan-dal, my dear, or at least my side of it?" He wanted to steer her away from the deeper, more ancient issues regarding his lifestyle choices.

She looked him directly in the eyes. "Yes, I would like to hear your side."

They moved to a vacant sofa in the corner and sat down. "First, tell me what you heard, and I will tell you if it's truth or fiction."

Keeping her voice low, she explained what she knew—that he had been called as a witness in a divorce case in court, to prove a lady's adultery.

Seger leaned back. "All true."

Miss Wilson's voice lost its confident coquetry. She suddenly sounded like an innocent child. "So, you *were* the lady's lover?"

He did not flinch. "I was."

She nodded and lowered her gaze to her gloved hands in her lap. She became very quiet.

Seger swayed closer to her. "You were very liberal a few minutes ago. Now you're different. Are you horrified?"

She shook her head. "I'm not horrified. I knew it had to be true. Consider where I met you."

He leaned back again. "Ah, yes, in a den of wicked-ness. So, there you have it. My character unveiled. Be warned, I am depraved."

"I was warned already. Many times, in fact, by you and by my sister and by my own self."

His voice became a husky whisper. "If you know I am a scoundrel, why, then, are you sitting with me?"

She seemed to consider the question for a long moment, then she finally looked up. "If our acquain-tance were of the more conventional sort, I would tell you that I am sitting with you because I believe no man is ever completely irredeemable. But since we are being liberal and honest and admitting to all sorts of depravities, I will confess that I am sitting with you for the plain and simple reason that I find you very attractive."

Seger smiled. This heiress was delicious. His pred-atory instincts began to hum, and he leaned toward her, close enough that he could smell the fresh, clean scent of her skin. "Then I believe we have something in common."

She inched away from him and glanced around self-consciously because he was most definitely push-ing the limits of propriety. "And I believe, sir, that you should sit back. We are not at one of your Cakras Balls."

Taking a deep breath to subdue the intense desires welling up inside of him, Seger forced himself to rise. He held out his hand. "You are absolutely right, and what a shame it is. Hungry?"

She laughed and gave him her hand. "Ravenous."

Together, they went to the buffet table. Seger picked

a few grapes from a large bunch and offered them to Miss Wilson in his open palm. Eyes never leaving his, she took one and popped it into her mouth.

He watched her moist, pink lips as she ate the grape, and felt a stirring of arousal. What he wouldn't give for the honest liberties of a Cakras Ball now.

Miss Wilson glanced over her shoulder and spoke softly to him. "My lord, despite the fact that I've witnessed your debauched underworld, I will have you know that I am a respectable young lady. You shouldn't be looking at me like that."

"In my defense, you shouldn't be licking your lips like that."

She grinned, then became more serious. "I'm not looking for trouble."

God, how he wanted to touch her. "Are you trying to tell me something?"

"Yes."

"That you have no intention of taking any more risks?"

Just then, an older woman approached. Seger recognized her from the first night he had met Miss Wilson. She was the chaperone.

"Good evening, my dear," the woman said. "You have found the grapes, I see."

Miss Wilson seemed to tense at the woman's question. Seger cursed to himself. No wonder he'd not missed the Marriage Mart. The frustrations in situations like this were unbearable.

"My lord," Miss Wilson said, "may I present Mrs. Eva Gunther? Mrs. Gunther, the Marquess of Rawdon."

They greeted each other. It was clear to Seger that the older woman recognized him as well, though naturally she did not acknowledge it.

She stayed to make conversation for a few minutes, then gestured toward the other side of the room. "I believe there are some ladies who would like to make your acquaintance, Clara. Would you be so kind as to excuse us, Lord Rawdon?"

Seger recognized the obvious intent to pry her out of his company. He was not surprised. Politely, he inclined his head.

"Perhaps we can continue our conversation later?" Miss Wilson said as Mrs. Gunther practically dragged her away.

"I certainly hope so." He bowed and retreated.

The marchioness watched her stepson turn away from Miss Wilson. "They *have* met before," she whispered to Gillian. "I am sure of it. Did you see the way she traipsed across the room to talk to him? It was the crudest thing I've ever witnessed in my life. Heaven help us all if she's picked him out of the crowd." Quintina glanced toward the fireplace, where a group of gentlemen were standing in a circle. "Why isn't she hounding after the Duke of Guysborough, for pity's sake? He's the best catch in the room."

"For the same reason as myself, I believe, Auntie," Gillian replied. "He's not the one she wants."

The marchioness clenched her jaw and sighed. "I hate to admit it, Gillian, but you could learn a few things from the American girls, despite their brazenness. In fact, I believe that brazenness is precisely what has all our men tripping over themselves to talk to them." She squinted her eyes in disgust. "It's because those girls are smiling and laughing all the time, telling stupid, unbelievable stories. I *despise* Americans."

Gillian regarded her aunt with surprise.

"They don't know their place," Quintina continued. "They are overconfident. They think that they can buy their way in with money their fathers earn. *Working,* I might add. You have no idea how it broke my heart to see my family home go to a vulgar American laborer, who earned his fortune panning for gold. Panning! I hate that word. I've never so much as touched a pan in my life. Nevertheless, Americans remind me of leeches. They're here to latch on. They don't realize the greatness of England."

"You forget Yorktown, Auntie."

"Oh, *hmph.* Do you have any stories to tell, Gillian? Have you never done anything wild or different? I heard, for example, that the duchess, before she came to London, went on a buffalo hunt once. She said she knew how to throw a tomahawk. What is a tomahawk, by the way, do you have any idea?"

Gillian shook her head.

"No, I didn't think you'd know. It's just as well. It's probably an American sport of some kind."

They sat down on a settee. "You're going to have to try harder to *say* something," the marchioness said to her niece. "And keep your head up. You never look at him when he talks to you."

"I can't help it, Auntie. I become nervous."

She patted Gillian's hand. "I understand, dear, but you must endeavor to get over that. You must try harder to put a sparkle in your eye. It looks as if Seger is finally ready to move forward with his life. The fact that he came here this evening was astonishing, to say the least, so you must be first to take advantage of this opportunity. Watch the American girls and see what they do. Perhaps I'll have a few new gowns made for you, like the ones they are wearing. Would that help, do you think?"

"I believe it would, Auntie. Miss Wilson's dress is very pretty."

"Well, well, well," Quintina replied, patting her niece's hand again. "It's the least I can do. You have no mother to see to your future, and if she were alive—my dear, dear sister—she would want you to be happy, to have everything you desire. You're a good girl, Gillian. You deserve a husband you can be proud of, and I would like to see our family's bloodline continue in such a prestigious vein. I wasn't able to give the marquess any children, but you could be the one to provide the next heir. We shall not give up hope, darling. Now do as I say. Watch the American and see how she handles herself."

As an afterthought, Quintina added, "She looks a little bit like Daphne, don't you think? It's rather disconcerting."

Gillian turned her gaze toward Clara Wilson, the famous heiress, the sister of the Duchess of Wentworth. The girl was surrounded by a crowd of doting gentlemen, all of them laughing at her stories, enchanted by her smile, just as Seger had been only moments ago.

A tiny muscle twitched at Gillian's jaw, and she

squeezed her reticule so tightly that she broke the looking glass inside it.

Chapter 7

Dear Adele,

Sometimes I feel so out of place here. I am not like the other English ladies. I try to be reserved, but at heart I know that I am not. What I really want is to be an open book with those I care about, and I want to find a husband who is that way, too. I'm tired of talking about the weather. I want a soul mate, someone who will not be superficial.

The marquess, interestingly enough, is not afraid to break the customary rules of conduct. He's quite different from the rest, but I fear that Mrs. Gunther does not approve of him....

Clara

"Is it time to continue our conversation, yet?" Lord Rawdon whispered in Clara's ear.

He had come up behind her unexpectedly, startling her with the heat of his breath upon the side of her neck. Her entire body erupted in gooseflesh.

Champagne glass in hand, she turned. "I'm willing if you are."

He smiled and offered his arm. They walked into the music room where a German pianist was scheduled to begin shortly. "Shall we take our seats?"

"Yes." Clara allowed him to lead her to the front

row. They were the first guests to sit down. The pianist's assistant was arranging sheet music; a liveried footman stood near the open doors.

"You've been very popular this evening," Lord Rawdon said. "Why is it that Mrs. Gunther hasn't dragged you away from any of the other gentlemen? She doesn't disapprove of me, does she?" His last comment dripped with sarcasm.

Clara gave him an apologetic look. "She is on a mission for my mother, I'm afraid. She wants to be sure I am married off to the highest-ranking peer possible, and the most respectable."

"Ah, the respectable part... That is where I fall short."

Clara tried to explain. "She's a very proper lady. She comes from old money. Mother was thrilled when Mrs. Gunther agreed to accompany me to London. She knew Mrs. Gunther would have the highest standards conceivable, and that I needed someone with a very strong hand to lead me in the right direction."

His eyebrows rose. "And she took you to a Cakras Ball?"

Clara gave him a quick, heated glance, then returned her cool gaze to the front of the room. "That was a mistake, and I do *not* thank you for reminding me of it."

He grinned and sat forward. "Well now. This is becoming interesting. Your mother felt you needed a strong hand. I detect something naughty in your past." He watched her for a moment. "Why didn't your mother accompany you herself?"

"Because she is with my younger sister, Adele, who

is having her own first Season in New York."

"You didn't wish to debut in London together?"

Clara felt her spine bristle at the direction of their conversation. Unlike most of the other Englishmen she had met, the marquess had no qualms about asking indiscreet questions.

They were heading into dangerous territory.

"No," she tried to explain. "We did not wish to debut together." She glanced up at him, uneasily.

"I see," he replied.

"I wanted her to have her own special time," Clara explained. "Without her older sister around. Things didn't go that well for me the year before last. Hence Mrs. Gunther's strong hand."

Clara didn't know why she was telling him all this. It pointed back at her mistakes. She supposed she felt that he, of all people would understand.

Maybe that's why she was so attracted to him. He didn't make her feel inadequate. He lived by his own rules and did not judge her or anyone else by society's strictures.

Most people—if they knew the whole story—would call her fast or unprincipled, which she was not. Yes, there was a thrill-seeker lurking in her heart, but she was not fast. She believed in love and marriage and fidelity and she wanted a decent man for a husband.

That was her struggle, she supposed. Her definition of decent wasn't quite as black and white as the rest of the world's.

"How could a New York Season possibly not go well for you?" the marquess asked. "You are the loveliest creature I've seen since...well, since forever."

She warmed at the compliment, but still wanted to be cautious where her heart was concerned. She stared straight ahead at the piano.

"What, no answer?" He urged her to look at him. "Don't tell me you botched it up. Made a few social blunders?" He sat back and laughed. "Is that why you're here? Because you used the wrong fork once and can't show your face in New York?"

"Stop teasing me," she said, slapping his arm with her fan. "I can certainly show my face. I just wished for different surroundings and fresh conversation, that's all."

He gave her an exaggerated nod as if he didn't believe her. "You must realize that now you *have* to tell me what happened, and spare nothing, I need all the shocking details."

She glared at him, astounded. "Sir, you are impossibly rude. And there are no shocking details."

"There must be. You're blushing. There are red blotches on your neck, right there."

He pointed just below her earlobe.

She slapped his hand again. "You are very wicked."

He chuckled and leaned back again. "Yes, I suppose I am, but you still haven't told me how you stumbled and landed on your face during your New York debut."

"I did not land on my face." She said nothing for a moment. "All right, fine. A man proposed to me—a very unsuitable man my parents did not approve of."

"That's hardly your fault."

"But some would argue that I encouraged him, and maybe I did. My sister had just married a duke and I was feeling pressured to follow in her footsteps and marry well. I didn't like it."

"So, you rebelled."

Clara felt suddenly agitated. Not at the marquess, but at the subject matter of this conversation. Why were they talking about this? She had wanted to bury it.

Yet she also wanted to be an open book.

The marquess raised his hands in mock surrender. "Please, I'm on your side. I fully support a good rebellion from time to time. Lord knows the world has witnessed a number of my minor social revolts. You didn't marry him, I take it."

"Of course not." She chose not to reveal how close she had actually come to marrying Gordon. How her father had arrived just in time, as they prepared to board a ship ready to set sail for Europe, with plans to tie the knot in the middle of the Atlantic.

Thank God for her father.

"The story has a happy ending, then," Lord Rawdon said. "And you had an adventure. Well done."

The marquess was certainly relaxed about scandals and social blunders, which was probably a good thing. She doubted she would ever tell any of the other London gentlemen what she had just shared with the marquess. She couldn't imagine how the Duke of Guysborough would respond.

"So, if your younger sister doesn't succeed in America this Season," he asked, "will she come to London next year as well?"

"Probably."

He glanced in the other direction. "The newspapers

were right. It is becoming a stampede."

Clara threw him a cantankerous look.

He chuckled. "What? That's not why you're here? To bounce back from your close brush with social pauperism and, as you said, marry well?"

She shook her head at his insolent manner. "I am here to find a decent and respectable man to share my life with. It doesn't matter to me if he has a title or not." She shifted on the chair, raised her chin high, then turned to look at him when she sensed his amusement. "You don't believe me!"

Still smiling, he shook his head. "To be honest, no. You seem ambitious. Like the sort of woman who wants the very best after narrowly avoiding disaster once before."

"What I consider to be the 'best' might surprise you. Perhaps it has nothing to do with a mere accident of birth."

She heard the sarcasm in her tone and knew she was the one being insolent now, but she couldn't help it. He was always teasing her and trying to provoke her. She suspected he enjoyed watching her fight back. It amused him. Perhaps it amused her, too.

"I don't think anything about you could possibly surprise me," he said.

Clara lowered her voice and regarded him intimately. "It often feels like you are trying to steer me toward trouble. You say the most improper things. Or maybe it's the way you say them."

Other guests, two by two, began to trickle into the room. Clara sat up straighter in her chair, resolving not to get pulled into the tempting heat of this man's flame just yet. She had to be more careful. She was still not entirely sure she could trust the marquess to be "decent," therefore she could not allow her passions to take her to what might be a dangerous, ruinous destination.

"I would prefer if we changed the subject now," she said.

Lord Rawdon stretched his legs out in front of him and began to look bored. "A decent and respectable man, you say. I guess that counts me out."

He was unbelievable. "And you are no doubt relieved."

"Intensely."

The room filled up and they had to refrain from speaking so candidly with each other. It was time to stop, anyway. Clara recognized the marquess's body language and the tone in his voice and knew that he was both pulling back and pushing her away. Their conversation had become too serious, and he wanted only to flirt.

She felt a stab of disappointment.

From everything he'd said tonight, it was obvious that he sought only brief, frivolous affairs, not deep soulful ones. He was not the sort of man who was suited to a marriage based on fidelity—like that of Clara's sister, Sophia, and her husband James. They were devoted to each other in every way. They knew each other's hearts as well as they knew their own, and they had no desire to stray.

Feeling discouraged, Clara watched the pianist take a seat on the bench. He placed his fingers on the ivory keys.

Clara realized miserably that her desires created a paradox. She craved excitement. In her heart she wanted to burst out of the box of polite behavior, yet she wanted to be respectable. She wanted a man who believed in piety and the institution of marriage. She wanted a morally upright man, but not a dull one, which was likely a difficult combination.

Gordon had been wild, but he had not possessed any honor. She had learned a sturdy lesson with him. Because of that, she was determined now. Just as the marquess had said, she was ambitious toward that end and would not settle for less than what she wanted.

She felt another wave of disappointment course through her. She did not believe the Marquess of Rawdon could be what she wanted. Like Gordon, he was far too wild. He did not seem interested in what was socially proper. He did not seem inclined toward true intimacies of the heart, only pleasures of the flesh. He continually pulled back when she tried to move away from flirting. He had said he was relieved he was not the kind of man she would want for a husband.

But oh, he was so beautiful, and so far, he was the only man in London who made her heart go pitter-pat.

Well, at least now she knew. The fantasy of him was indeed just that—a fantasy. He could only be a lover in the physical sense. She had to keep her head on straight about that.

What a shame, she thought. What a sad, frustrating shame.

The very next day, a letter arrived for Clara. Not

recognizing the penmanship, she took it upstairs to her room, flopped down on her belly and broke the seal.

My Dear Miss Wilson, it began...

Her heart began to pound.

> *You must forgive me this indulgence, but I could not resist the inclination to write to you and tell you how thoroughly I enjoyed our discourse last evening at your sister's assembly. I had considered calling on the duchess today, but decided against it, as I felt it was too much progress for a man like me, in too short a time. I cannot, I'm afraid, delve into a complete recovery from my wicked ways and evolve overnight into a proper gentleman who pays calls to respectable young ladies, sipping tea in brightly lit drawing rooms.*
>
> *Instead, I choose to write you a letter, where I would be free to say the things I would have wanted to say, had I been in your delightful, delectable company this afternoon.*
>
> *Why am I writing this? you must be wondering. I am wondering that myself. I have no idea. As I mentioned last night, I am not presently seeking a wife and I usually confine myself to less perilous associations. Perhaps it is the French wine I am sipping. No, it is not. It is you. You enchant me.*

Clara's heart flipped over inside her chest. She rolled over and sat up, then walked to the window to continue reading.

I have no wish to spoil your chances of meeting the decent and respectable man you desire, yet I find I cannot sit idly back and accept that I will never see you again, or—forgive me for my plain manner of speaking—kiss you again. I could not stop looking at your lips last night. I wanted to find another dark staircase.

But I digress. As you see, I am too frank for the society you accept as your own. If I were like other gentlemen, I would say goodbye to you now and wish you the best. But I have not behaved as a gentleman for many years, and I find myself plotting other ways to kiss you again and satisfy my passions without causing too much damage in the process. Do you understand my meaning? Do you have any ideas?

Sincerely,

S.

Clara could hardly breathe. Was he serious? Surely not! He must be teasing her again. This was scandalous! She could not reply to something like this. What if someone found out?

She read the letter again. Heaven help her, her blood was rushing so fast, she felt faint.

This was madness. She could not take part in a wild and wicked affair. She'd brushed up against scandal once before and did not wish to do so again. She had come to England to meet respectable gentlemen and avoid that sort of thing. How had she managed to stumble across the worst, wildest rogue in London?

And she'd allowed him to kiss her!

She paced back and forth across the room, telling herself that she would not, under any circumstances, reply to this letter. That would be social suicide. She must break all contact with him, for it was clear he was exactly the kind of man she should avoid. The kind of man she had initially feared he was—a rake and a libertine. The kind of man who was very dangerous to her, for over the past week, she had discovered that she was not as strong as she thought she was. Where the gorgeous, tempting marquess was concerned, she was actually quite weak.

Clara squeezed her eyes shut and breathed deeply. She must concentrate on meeting the *right* sort. The kind of man she had hoped to meet when she'd steamed across the Atlantic dreaming of a proper future. She wanted a man who would be faithful to her. A man who would have the integrity not to stray outside of his marriage, because that's what it took to be faithful. Honor and integrity. Everyone felt passion and temptation. Those with honor did not act upon it. The marquess seemed to act on every base impulse he felt.

Clara read the letter again. It was shocking. She lifted her chin and folded the paper and stuffed it deep into the back of one of her drawers.

No, that wasn't a good place. Her maid might find it. She pulled it out and stuffed it under her mattress, then made a firm decision to thrust the Marquess of Rawdon out of her mind once and for all. For good. For eternity. She would not think of him again. No. She would forget him. He was not the man for her.

There. She went to her door and ventured out into the corridor to join Sophia for tea.

He was forgotten.

The next day she read the letter again. It had taken every ounce of self-control she possessed not to pull it out in the middle of the night and read it. Somehow, she had resisted that urge and congratulated herself in the morning.

It was almost noon now, however. She had not been able to get through even half the day.

I could not stop looking at your lips last night. I wanted to find another dark staircase.

Her toes curled inside her shoes. Something tingled in her nether regions. She should not have read it. It had been a foolish thing to do. She was weak, to have been seduced from clear across the city by ink and pen. Weak, weak, weak. He was an expert at love-making to be sure.

She should have known better. She should have burned his wicked words right after she'd read them. She should not be infecting her brain with them now.

She read the letter again.

What a scoundrel he was. *Any ideas?* he had asked. As if she would entertain such thoughts.

Heaven help her, she had quite a few.

But she would certainly *not* tell him what they were.

That night, by candlelight, Clara dipped her pen in the ink jar and paused above her stationery. How to begin, how to begin... It was necessary to inform the marquess that she was not interested in anything untoward, and that she would prefer it if he refrained from any insinuations in the future.

She looked at his handwriting again and felt a warm fluttering in her belly. This was his personal penmanship. The ink on this paper had come from his very own desk. His big, masculine hands had touched this paper not long ago. Perhaps he had blown gently on the ink to dry it.

Her belly quivered as she imagined all of that.

Clara shut her eyes and shook her head, forcing herself not to think about him sitting at his desk writing to her, or doing anything else for that matter. She had to focus on the task at hand.

If only she knew what to say. There was a part of her that did not want to end this. It was exciting and invigorating and flattering. He was a grand and beautiful man and he found her attractive. All her sexual instincts were telling her to encourage him and see where this might lead, but her head was telling her to be careful and prudent and not be foolish. She wanted so very badly to be virtuous.

Oh, dear. She was having a barrel of a time listening to the right voice.

Sighing deeply, hoping she was not doing anything *too* terribly risky, she lowered her pen to the page. Then it came to her. She smiled and began to write.

> *My lord. You are very naughty.*
> *Sincerely,*
> *C.*

The next morning, another letter bearing the marquess's seal was brought by a footman to Clara's boudoir, who picked it up off the silver salver and calmly thanked the young man. She set the letter on the corner of her desk and feigned disinterest until the footman left the room and closed the door behind him, upon which time she could not help herself. She snatched up the letter, rose to her feet and tore at the seal.

> *Miss Wilson,*
> *I laughed out loud when I read your note. You are enchanting. Again, I implore you. Any ideas?*
> *S.*

Clara covered her mouth with her hand. She'd never felt like this before. What was it about this particular gentleman that brought out such overpowering impulses in her? She had not felt this way with Gordon. It had been naïveté and pressure from her parents that drove her to make mistakes with him, not this kind of blatant, hungry desire. She should not be communicating with this man in such a wicked fashion.

Clara stuffed the letter under her mattress with the last one and returned to her more respectable correspondence. That was impossible, however, with her mind where it was—frolicking in the house of sin, entertaining all sorts of lewd, indecent thoughts about a gorgeous, golden-haired marquess.

Ten minutes later, she realized she was still resting her chin on her hand, staring blankly at the wall. She felt inebriated.

Shaking her head at herself, Clara realized she could not possibly resist replying to his letter, depraved as it was. She pulled a blank sheet of stationery out of her desk drawer.

For a moment she sat there, tapping the clean end of her pen against her lips, wondering if it was possible for the marquess to ever be faithful to one woman. Perhaps he had simply not met the right lady yet. All boys grew up to become men eventually, didn't they? Wasn't it possible he could have arrived at that cross-roads? She was his first debutante, after all, or so he claimed. Perhaps he was ready to change. Perhaps she could teach him about real love. Was she foolish to hold on to that hope? Probably.

Nevertheless, she dipped her pen in the inkwell and began to write, while forcing herself to be serious and scrupulous.

> *Lord Rawdon,*
> *You must realize that this manner of correspon-*
> *dence is utterly inappropriate. I do not wish to*
> *continue this, as I have explained that I am not*
> *interested in any kind of immoral affair. If you*
> *wish to see me, please do so in a proper, respectable*
> *place, at which time I would be happy to converse*
> *with you.*
> *C.*

She congratulated herself on her most inspiring self-restraint.

Another reply arrived that very afternoon.

*But I don't wish to see you in a proper, respect-
able place. I wish to be quite alone with you, Miss
Wilson, so that no one will witness my hand sliding up your dress.*
    S.

Clara gasped in shock. Of all the cheeky nerve!
The audacity! What kind of wanton woman did he
think she was? She would not be lured into sin simply because he suggested it in a note, no matter how
clammy her palms were at the moment, or how loopy
she felt at the thought.

Congratulating herself again for her impressive iron
will in the face of such astounding provocation, she
picked up her pen to reply:

*My lord, your suggestions are appalling. Is it
your intention to ruin me?*
    C.

Clara received the marquess's reply the next morning. She had to admit, she was exceedingly curious
about how he would respond to her blunt accusation.
She tore open the letter and began to read:

*My Dear Miss Wilson,
    I apologize if I gave the impression that I wanted
to ruin you. I have no desire for such an outcome.
You have my word that I will do everything in my
power to prevent it. I am discreet and I know how
to give pleasure without destruction. You may trust*

me completely in that regard.
    S.

Clara could not believe the marquess's reply. He was still trying to seduce her after she had made it clear, in no uncertain terms, that she wished to remain respectable. Had he no shame?

The time had come to put an end to this. For real this time. She could not see him again.

She was about to write another reply and communicate her decision when a knock sounded at her door. A maid said, "Miss Wilson, the duchess requests your presence in the drawing room."

Clara called out, "Is it important?"

"There is a gentleman caller, miss."

A swarm of butterflies exploded in Clara's belly. She rose and went to the door. "Do you know who it is?" Clara pulled the door open, but the maid was gone. Standing motionless, holding the doorknob, Clara wondered if the marquess had come to call upon her properly. Was he willing to make this concession, or was it another man wishing to pay his respects?

Clara hurried to the mirror to look over her appearance. She pinched her cheeks and smoothed her hands over her upswept hair. Perhaps it was the marquess. Perhaps it wasn't. She would know soon enough.

With a hand on her belly to quell her nervous stomach, Clara made her way into the corridor and walked slowly toward the drawing room. She entered and saw her sister sitting near the fireplace pouring tea, laughing at something, then she turned her eyes toward the other occupant in the room.

Her entire being swirled with a dizzying current of desire. It was indeed the marquess. And he was smiling wickedly at her.

Somehow, she managed to enter the room on steady feet.

She had not told Sophia about the letters. She wasn't sure why. She usually told Sophia everything—she'd told her every word the marquess had said to her at the assembly—but this was different. Perhaps she was afraid Sophia would begin to disapprove of him, and whether it was wise or unwise, Clara did not wish to be told that she should not respond. She wanted to make up her own mind about that.

Sophia stood. "Clara. How lovely that you are here. See who has come to pay us a call today. You remember the Marquess of Rawdon? He attended our assembly the other night."

It was all so proper. Sophia was a brilliant hostess. "Of course I remember you," Clara replied. "Good day, my lord. How good of you to call."

"It is entirely my pleasure, Miss Wilson."

Not knowing what to expect, Clara took a seat next to Sophia, who poured her a cup of tea. The conversation then turned toward the usual topics—the current events in *The Times,* the most recent debates in the House of Commons, and of course, the most agreeable topic that could always be depended upon for propriety—the weather.

At the end of the obligatory fifteen minutes, the marquess reached for his hat and walking stick. "I must thank you, duchess, for a delicious cup of tea. It was second to none."

His behavior was impeccable. He moved toward the door. One would think he had been a respectable member of society forever.

He bowed toward Clara. "Miss Wilson." Then he turned and left the drawing room.

As soon as the front doors opened and closed downstairs, Sophia rushed to Clara and took hold of both her hands. "He came to call."

Clara didn't know what she felt. She was in shock. She was confused. What exactly did he want—a torrid affair or a proper courtship? Perhaps he had changed his mind after he'd sent the last letter. Perhaps he was giving in to the idea of reforming himself.

"I wonder if we should call on his stepmother," Sophia said. "Lady Rawdon seemed to enjoy herself here the other night. I believe she was pleased to receive the invitation. From what I've heard, she has not been received in most houses, not since the marquess was involved in that beastly court case."

Clara sat down again. She picked up her teacup and took a sip but set it down again when she realized it was cold. Sophia sat beside her. "He came for you, Clara. You're the one he wanted to see."

"But he has a reputation, and I am quite certain that Mrs. Gunther disapproves of him."

"It's your future. You are the one who must choose, and it's obvious that you fancy him."

"But how do I choose when I still know so little about the marquess, except that he is not respectable? The Duke of Guysborough on the other hand is very well regarded, but he does not interest me, not the way the marquess does. Perhaps it's just a foolish desire to possess something that cannot be possessed—like the wind or the sun." She gazed imploringly into her sister's eyes. "I feel like I'm losing my mind. My head is telling me that he is all wrong, but I can't stop thinking about him."

Sophia rested her hand on Clara's. "Sometimes the heart does not make sense. It only knows what it feels. I still believe that the marquess should not be ruled out as a possible match for you. He came here today, which suggests that he is at least willing to make an effort to act respectably. Perhaps he does want to change. Perhaps he was only waiting to be invited back into good society, and now that he has been, he will be able to court proper, unmarried young ladies like yourself and look to a brighter future. Perhaps that just wasn't an option for him before."

Clara narrowed her eyes at her sister. "First of all, I do not want him courting proper, unmarried young ladies like myself. I only want him to court *me*. But do you think there's hope for him? That I should give him a chance?"

"He came here today. He made a promising effort. Yes, I do think you should give him a chance."

But you haven't read his letters.

Oh, who was Clara trying to fool? She knew very well that she could no more forget him than she could forget to breathe. Perhaps she simply had to leap in headfirst and take a risk. If it all blew up in her face and he broke her heart, well, she would simply have to live with that. At least that way, she would never have to ask herself, *what if?*

She only hoped he was as discreet as he claimed to

be in his last letter, and that he would not lead her down a winding path to ruin.

Chapter 8

Dear Clara,
The marquess sounds like a very dangerous
man....
Adele

SEGER WALKED OUT OF WENTWORTH House and wondered if he had taken leave of his senses. What was it about Clara Wilson that brought him to such heights of desire? It was entirely out of his realm of experience. It bordered on obsession.

He climbed into his coach and tapped his walking stick against the roof to signal the driver, then he tried to ground himself. He labored to remember the sorts of relationships he was accustomed to. He was not like other men. He was not seeking a socially acceptable wife. He enjoyed his life exactly the way it was.

Why then, had he just taken the first step toward a proper courtship with a respectable young lady, after swearing to both himself and the lady in question, through a number of audacious letters, that he was only interested in a brief, secret affair? The usual stuff where he was concerned. He had made it clear in no uncertain terms that that was what he wanted, but at the last second, after he sent the letter, he panicked—yes, panicked—and feared he had gone too far, come on too strong. Consequently, he made a complete about-face and bloody well contradicted himself. He had called upon her. Properly.

He remembered suddenly that he had dreamed about her the night before. Seger felt a disturbing jolt of confusion, as if two conflicting musical notes were chiming in his head at the same time. He winced at the discord.

He wasn't even sure what he wanted at this point. It had been a number of years since he'd desired a woman who was innocent. (Presuming the heiress was in fact untouched, which he did presume, rightly or wrongly).

Daphne had been innocent. He had loved her unreservedly without any thought to whether or not it was wise. That led to disaster.

He was, however, no longer a boy. He was a man, and he was the Marquess of Rawdon. His father was no longer alive to dictate Seger's future. If Seger wished to marry someone completely unsuitable—such as a bold American heiress—no one could stand in his way.

Seger chided himself. He did not wish to *marry* Miss Wilson. He certainly didn't need her money. He only wanted her in the physical sense. He wanted to hear her sigh with contentment after he'd brought her to the most ferocious climax she'd ever experienced in her life—all the better if it was her first. What he wouldn't give to show her that kind of pleasure for the first time.

Which was, he supposed, the primary problem. One couldn't enjoy an innocent without repercussions. Without responsibility and commitment and permanence. Without the young woman's expectations of love and devotion.

He had been living too long outside the lines. He'd forgotten how to play by the rules. After Daphne died, he'd lived the life he'd wanted to live, without caring what other people thought about him or wanted from him. Women especially. He had removed that particular instinct from his repertoire and chose to offer a different sort of pleasure altogether. He was renowned for it, and the women with whom he associated rarely expected anything outside of that infamous reputation. They knew the rules, knew what he could give them, and most of them accepted it quite happily without making the mistake of asking for more.

Because he always made it very clear he would not give them more.

Wouldn't or couldn't?

He took a small breath. He wasn't sure. It seemed like he had always been isolated. Emotionally removed from everyone—from society, his family, his acquaintances. He'd never had any brothers or sisters.

Was his lifestyle really by choice, or was he incapable of intimacy?

No, he could not be incapable of it. He had loved once, very deeply.

But only once. Eight years ago, when he had been devoted to Daphne.

Was it possible for a man to permanently banish from his heart the capacity for true emotional connections with other people?

Seger exhaled and shook his head. How many times

over the past few weeks had he questioned his lifestyle and remembered Daphne? He hadn't thought of her in years, but lately, their relationship had been coming back to him in little flashes of memory.

Perhaps it was the way Miss Wilson made him feel. She, like Daphne, possessed innocence, and consequently whatever existed between them was fresh, not sordid as most of his relationships had been since Daphne left this world.

Suddenly, he felt dissatisfied with everything about his life. He remembered the things he had wanted when he was twenty, and how eager he had been to become someone's husband. He had wanted Daphne to be his partner for life, to share his joys and pains. He'd wanted a home filled with children.

He sat in silence, staring unseeing out the window at the passing traffic, barely hearing the clatter of the coach or the noise from the street. He had not wanted anything like that since then. He had given the idea of marriage a very wide berth.

Seger tipped his head back against the seat. Daphne disappeared from his mind.

Instead he thought of Miss Wilson sitting in the duchess's drawing room across from him only moments ago, sipping her tea. What a vision she had been, beautiful and charming and glowing with smiles. Intelligent as well, discussing light politics and other things. She was a remarkable woman, and she inflamed his senses like no other. She possessed some kind of magic. A power that he feared could bring him to his knees.

Strange, how he feared it and wanted it at the same

time.

Then he thought of Clara reading the last letter he had sent. He imagined how she had comprehended his promise not to ruin her. *I know how to give pleasure without destruction.* What was her expression when she'd read such licentious words? Surely no gentleman had ever written anything like that to her before.

He felt a sudden urge to apologize—a strange and extraordinary impulse for Seger, who had written similar things to other women in the past and never thought twice about it. It was a jarring reaction now. He wished he could take the letter back. He wished he could start over where she was concerned and handle everything differently. More politely.

Those thoughts brought a frown to his face.

Wearing a low cut, royal blue velvet gown and feathers in her hair, Clara walked into the large opera box with James, Sophia, and Mrs. Gunther. Before she sat down, she glanced at the brightly lit theater below. People were filing into rows, taking their seats. A hum of conversation filled the auditorium while the orchestra warmed up with a dissonant array of violins, flutes and trumpets, all practicing scales.

Many seats below were still empty. Clara gazed across to the other side where the more luxurious boxes were filling up. She found herself staring at every fair-haired man who caught her eye, searching for one in particular.

"It's quite a magnificent theater," Mrs. Gunther said as she sat down and withdrew her mother-of-pearl opera glasses from her beaded reticule. She held them up to her eyes to examine the elaborate set on the stage.

Clara sat down as well, while Sophia and James remained standing at the back near the open curtain, conversing with someone.

It had been a full week since Clara had seen or heard from Lord Rawdon, and she was desperate to know why. She had not responded to his last letter, taking a chance that his unexpected afternoon call had been his way of retreating from the scandalous nature of their acquaintance and beginning a proper courtship. She had watched for him at every social event since, hoping he would continue his re-emergence into society, but she was disappointed at every turn.

She began to wonder if she had made a mistake in not replying to his letter. Perhaps he had taken her silence as a rebuff.

It seemed all she ever did where he was concerned was analyze the situation and wonder endlessly what he was thinking or how her actions had been received. If only they could be honest with each other and communicate freely and candidly.

She supposed that was what he'd been trying to do when he wrote those scandalous letters. He'd wanted to escape the pretensions of the Marriage Mart, which he openly admitted to despising.

Just then, someone touched Clara's shoulder. She turned to discover that the tall Duke of Guysborough had entered the box.

"Good evening, Miss Wilson." He moved to the empty chair beside her and sat down. "It's been an exceptional week for entertainment, has it not?"

She had encountered the duke at most of the assemblies and balls she'd attended the past few days and had danced with him more than once. "It certainly has been," she replied. "How is your mother?"

They talked about the dowager's health, then discussed the opera they were about to see. Mrs. Gunther listened politely to all that was said and smiled and nodded with approval. Then the duke gave his farewell and stood up to converse with James for a few more minutes before leaving the box.

"What a charming gentleman," Mrs. Gunther said, leaning in close.

Almost too charming, Clara thought. Too perfect. Could she live up to that sort of ideal on a daily basis?

"I believe he fancies you," Mrs. Gunther added.

Sensing that the performance was about to begin, Clara reached into her purse for her opera glasses. "It's difficult to say. He's very friendly to everyone."

"Yes, but especially to you. I've been keeping count of his dancing partners and you hold the highest honor for most waltzes each night."

Clara raised her opera glasses and looked more closely at the stage decorations. "I didn't realize you were keeping count of anything."

"Only because he's such an excellent prospect. Has he spoken to you about his children?"

"A few times, yes."

"He has only one son, you know. The boy is eight I believe."

Clara continued to use the opera glasses to discreetly search the boxes on the other side of the theater.

"I would suspect," Mrs. Gunther continued, "that

he would like to have more sons to secure his line. One can't take chances with a dukedom."

Clara perused each box and peered at the audience below.

"You're not listening to me," Mrs. Gunther said, sitting forward and looking over the rail. "I ask you, what down there could possibly be more interesting than the Duke of Guysborough?"

"I'm just looking at the fashions, Mrs. Gunther. There are some lovely gowns this evening."

Mrs. Gunther continued to peruse the audience below. "Poppycock. You're looking for that disreputable marquess. Is he here?"

Clara sat back and stared at Mrs. Gunther. "No, I do not believe he is."

"Good." She sat back, too, and lowered her voice. "He is not the sort you should mix with, Clara. I realize he is a peer, but his reputation overshadows that fact. There is your own reputation to think of. I must insist that in the future, you give him the cut direct."

"Cut him? I couldn't do anything like that."

"You must, in order to deliver a clear message. You cannot afford to sully yourself. You mustn't do anything to discourage more respectable men—like the duke—from considering you as a bride. You must convey perfection."

"I'm hardly perfect, Mrs. Gunther. No one is."

"But some people are more perfect than others, and despite his elevated rank, the marquess is very low down on that scale. The gossip about him, may I say, is detestable."

Clara was beginning to feel ill. "Gossip can sometimes be exaggerated."

"Do not defend him, dear girl. Even if it is exaggerated, appearances are as important, if not more important, than the truth."

Clara knew she shouldn't argue with Eva Gunther, a grand New York matriarch, but she couldn't help herself. Her hands had closed into tight fists. "How can you say that? What if he is, in actuality, a good man, merely misunderstood?"

Not that she believed that herself. She had no idea. Well, she had some idea. Judging by the letters he had sent, he was every bit as notorious as the gossips claimed.

"It wouldn't matter."

The lights dimmed and James and Sophia took their seats. The curtain at the back of the box lowered as if by magic.

Clara sat stiffly in her seat, contemplating everything Mrs. Gunther had said. She felt a great pressure squeezing around her heart at that moment—an obligation to ignore what she wanted and do what was expected of her.

Another part of her, in angry response, wanted to see the marquess again for the single purpose of rebellion. Of proving that he was not all bad, and also to prove that she had a mind and will of her own and she would not relinquish her personal happiness for the mere sake of appearances.

Clara chided herself. She had felt this way once before, and there had been terrible consequences.

The opera began. Clara sat agitated for a while, then she tried to calm down and use the time to come to terms with what Mrs. Gunther had said. The woman could not be faulted for acting in a way that she believed was in Clara's best interest. The woman came from a very old family, after all. She had traditional values that were not easy to renounce.

Clara sighed.

Who was she fooling? She knew she could never act rebelliously for the mere sake of rebelling. She had learned to be smarter than that. Well, most of the time.

She raised her glasses and glanced at the box across the way and saw the Duke of Guysborough sitting alone, watching the opera. His wife had probably occupied the seat beside him when she was alive. How sad that she had died so young and left her husband and children behind. Clara felt a strong wave of sympathy for the man.

Perhaps she *was* being foolhardy, dreaming about a wild, dishonorable marquess when a decent, genteel man with proven high moral and family values was within her reach, expressing his interest in her. Treating her with the utmost gentlemanly respect.

Clara lowered her opera glasses and sighed heavily, then promised herself she would keep an open mind.

Three days later, the Duke of Guysborough called upon Clara. He walked into the drawing room, sat down on a sofa, and proposed.

Sitting opposite him, in a chintz upholstered chair, Clara stared at him blankly.

"I would be a good husband to you, Miss Wilson," he said. "I am highly regarded by the queen herself.

My estate is comprised of some of the most prestigious lands in England, and my children are obedient.
You would almost never see them."

Never see them? That was supposed to be a good
thing?

"You would become a duchess, like your sister," he
added with a proud nod.

Clara tried to think straight. It was the offer of a
lifetime. Hundreds of young women on both sides of
the Atlantic would give anything to be in her shoes at
this moment. Why then, could she not feel her toes?

Clara tried to smile. "You flatter me, Your Grace. I
had not expected such a wonderful speech from you
today."

Just before he'd proposed, he had told her that she
was lovely—a rare jewel. Purity and perfection.

But she was not perfect. She was far from it. Would
he still want her if he knew the passions that dwelled
in her heart? Passions of the mind as well as the flesh?
She suspected that any wife of his would have to hide
or completely smother that side of herself.

"May I deliver good news to my family this evening?" he asked.

Clara's skin prickled all over. It was too much too
soon. How could she possibly accept? At the same
time, she did not want to pass up this opportunity—
which was indeed a great boon—and later live to
regret it.

"Your Grace, you must give me some time to think
about it. I am honored by your proposal, truly I am,
but as I'm sure you can understand, I must consult my
family on the matter."

He smiled. "Of course you must. It is an important decision. I'm sure they will guide you in the right direction. Shall I return tomorrow?"

"That would be very good of you."

He made a bow and took his leave.

Clara sat in her chair, unable to move. The walls seemed to be closing in all around her. The Duke of Guysborough had just proposed marriage, and before twenty-four hours were out, she must make the biggest decision of her life and choose her destiny.

She stood up and went to the window to watch the duke step into his carriage and drive away. He was a handsome, distinguished man, admired by the Queen of England. Mrs. Gunther approved of him. Clara's parents would undoubtedly also approve. The duke had been married once before and had from all accounts been a good husband.

He was, as some would say, a sure thing. As far as appearances went, he was exactly what she wanted. Or at least what her head told her she wanted. Her heart told her something else, however. There was something about him that didn't ring true. He was simply too perfect.

The carriage disappeared at the end of the street, and Clara turned away from the window.

Sophia entered. "Did he propose?"

Feeling almost numb inside, Clara nodded.

"What did you say?"

"I told him I would give him an answer tomorrow."

"I see." Looking worried, Sophia regarded Clara. "Are you still thinking about the marquess? Because I don't think he's the sort of man who would offer a proposal marriage quite so quickly." She moved fully into the room and stood before Clara, who felt suddenly nauseous.

Sophia continued. "What do you want, Clara?"

"I don't know. Or rather, I do know, or at least I thought I did. I want to marry a man who will be a good husband. A man I can respect. Everyone is telling me that the duke is that man, yet my heart is not quite so certain. He said something about his children today. He suggested that I would never have to see them—as if that would make me more likely to accept his offer. What does that say about his love for them, and his devotion to his family?"

Sophia nodded with understanding.

"Besides," Clara added, "I am still attracted to the marquess."

Sophia led Clara to the sofa and sat down. "I remember what it felt like when I was falling in love with James. If I had been pressured to marry someone else, I don't know what I would have done. I don't envy you."

"If only I could see the marquess again."

"But would it make a difference?" Sophia asked. "I believe the marquess would require a fair bit of wooing, so to speak, to be enticed into marriage, and unfortunately you don't have time to do that. It's a shame the duke had not waited a little longer and given you a chance to get to know him better."

"You know me too well, Sophia." Clara gazed down at her hands on her lap. "What am I going to do?"

Sophia shrugged. "Only you know the answer to

that question. It's your future."

After a long pause, Clara looked into her sister's eyes. "I must see him again."

Sophia considered that for a moment. "I suppose you could send him a note and tell him that you've received an offer. That might give him a little nudge."

"But I don't want to pressure him into proposing to me. I just want to see him and talk to him. Find out for sure if there is any hope."

"But would you be prepared to refuse a decent man's offer on the off chance that a notorious rake might reform?"

Clara stared out the window again. "I'm not sure. That's what I need to find out."

Clara sat alone in her room that evening and read all the letters again. After some careful deliberation, she knew that the time for playful flirtations must come to an end. She could not simply wait and hope that the marquess would appear at a society ball. She had to take the bull by the horns.

She dipped her pen in the ink and scrolled a quick note.

> *Dear Lord Rawdon,*
> *I must see you. Can we arrange a time?*
> *C.*

Clara sealed the letter and gave it to a footman with instructions to deliver it immediately. He returned an hour later with a reply.

Miss Wilson,
The urgency of your letter intrigues me. My
carriage will be outside of Wentworth House this
evening at two a.m.
   S.

Two a.m.! Clara could barely believe her eyes. Did he think she would be able to convince her chaperone, Mrs. Gunther, to escort her out to a gentleman's carriage at that hour of the night?

Obviously not.

Which was precisely the point. He expected her to sneak out alone.

Clara squeezed her forehead in her hand. Could she do such a thing? Perhaps this was fate attempting to provide the evidence she required to prove that the marquess was not the man for her.

Or perhaps it was the opposite. This was fate delivering the *real* marquess to her on a silver platter. Alone without pretensions. Without restrictions. There was no time, after all, to get to know the real man through superficial encounters in crowded drawing rooms.

He'd told her she could trust him to do everything in his power to protect her from ruin, and oddly enough, she did trust him in that regard. Every instinct she possessed—and she was operating wholly on instinct where the marquess was concerned—told her that he would not ravish her if he had the chance. He had on two other occasions proven that to be true when he'd instructed her to leave the Cakras Balls and not return.

Her belly swarmed with apprehension. Could she

sneak out of the house undetected and not get caught? By Jove, she was going to try.

Chapter 9

Dear Adele,
Have you met anyone interesting in New York?
I hope there are some new faces, because sometimes
I fear that I will be a complete failure here and end
up back there before I have a chance to blink.
Love,
Clara

WEARING A DARK GOWN, NO jewels and sensible shoes, Clara tiptoed down the stairs, then down another flight to exit the quiet house through the servants' back entrance. She left the door unlocked and moved quickly through the foggy night along the side of the house to the front—where indeed, a carriage was waiting in the shadows across the street, a considerable distance away from the nearest street lamp.

She approached slowly, her heart pounding like a mallet in her chest. This was an adventure, to be sure, but presently the excitement was translating into a dreadful, nauseating knot in her stomach, for she did not know what to expect. She had never been out alone at night before, nor had she ever agreed to such a scandalous, secret rendezvous with a rake. In his carriage. Just the two of them.

She neared the shiny black vehicle and circled

around the back of it. The door opened onto the sidewalk and light from inside the carriage spilled onto the ground. The marquess stepped out into the chilly mist. He wore formal attire—a black jacket, white waistcoat and white necktie. No hat or gloves.

"I knew you would come." He stepped forward and kissed her gloved hand. "Your carriage awaits."

Clara glanced over her shoulder. The large coach blocked the view from the house, so Clara could at least relax about being seen.

He assisted her inside, then climbed in and closed the door.

A small lamp gave the lush, leather interior a dim, dreamlike glow while crimson velvet curtains covered the windows. Clara tried to breathe normally as she sat down and arranged her skirts.

"Where are we going?" she asked.

"Nowhere. We'll remain here. Unless you *want* to go somewhere."

She shook her head. "No, here is fine. Then I can leave when I wish."

You're thinking out loud, Clara.

"Precisely my thought as well." With all his attention focused on her, he rested an arm along the back of the seat behind her.

She stared at his face. He was so handsome in the lamplight, it hurt just to look at him.

"So, tell me," he said with a friendly, open expression, "what was the emergency?"

Clara tried to think clearly. She did not wish to tell him that she brought him here to inform him that someone had proposed to her. She was certain he would not be attracted to such desperation—a single woman carrying a torch for him, begging to see him immediately and sneaking out in the middle of the night to do so. He'd bolt like a fox. He would think she was entertaining foolish, romantic hopes that he, too, would propose, when in actuality, Clara was doing everything possible to shun those hopes.

"It wasn't an emergency," she said, "I just suddenly realized that I did not respond to your last letter, and I haven't seen you for an entire week."

The marquess was quiet for a moment, then he began to stroke her arm with the tip of his finger. "You know, I thought I might have shocked you with that last letter. Did I?"

She cleared her throat. "No. Well, perhaps a little."

He continued to stroke her forearm, causing gooseflesh to erupt in every corner of her body.

"You can take off your glove if you like," he said.

"Why would I want to do that?"

He merely shrugged.

She gazed at him for a moment that felt electrified, then swallowed hard and took both gloves off. She set them on the seat beside her.

It was strange that on all their previous encounters—except the first perhaps—she had felt confident around him and had become bold and flirtatious. Tonight, she was nothing of the sort. She was nervous and frazzled and shaky. He had all the power.

As if he could read her mind, he said, "You mustn't worry. There's no need to be nervous."

She swallowed uneasily. "I can't help it. It's very late and we are very much alone and... I shouldn't be out here with you. I have no idea what to expect. Will we talk? Or are you going to kiss me?"

Amused by the question, he chuckled. "What would *you* like to do?"

"Talk," she instantly replied. "At least, to begin with."

His expression warmed and he leaned back. "For the record, I prefer to talk first, as well. What would you like to discuss?"

Clara considered it. "Well, here in your carriage at two a.m., I doubt that polite rules apply, so can we get around talking about the weather?"

"Absolutely."

"Then I would like to ask some questions I've been told are too forward for polite society. Tell me about your family and your home and your childhood. I would also like to know something about your past romantic affairs."

His head drew back with surprise, but he still looked amused. "I'll tell you anything as long as you promise to oblige me the same way."

"I'd be happy to."

He casually pushed a lock of hair away from her forehead. "Where shall I begin?"

"How about with school?"

"All right, then." He told her about attending Charterhouse and she learned that he'd been an exceptional student, academically.

"Were you well-behaved as well?"

"I was a model student, usually a favorite of my professors and prefects. I was one of the few lucky ones who never once received a caning."

Clara grinned. "An achievement to be sure, but I doubt it was luck if you were well-behaved. Did you attend university?"

"Yes, I went to Cambridge, then I went abroad for a few years to Paris and India." He told her about his travels, the things he had seen and done.

Clara listened to everything with keen ears, fascinated by all of it, soon forgetting that she was there on a mission to gather information and decide whether or not he was redeemable.

They chatted about their favorite pastimes, unusual tastes, embarrassing moments. The marquess had a surprising interest in botany. Clara enjoyed sketching people's faces. The marquess once posed for an inexperienced artist in Paris who was attempting to paint Zeus. It turned out very badly. Clara had once drawn a picture that made the model look like a pomegranate.

He could be very amusing, she discovered as she laughed at his tales. He seemed to greatly enjoy many little things in life, like the sound of a dog snoring, or a warm hat on a cold day.

Before Clara knew it, an hour had passed, and she realized she had not uncovered half of what she'd wanted to learn about this man. There suddenly seemed to be much more to learn than she had initially imagined.

"Do you have any brothers or sisters?" she asked.

"No. My mother had a difficult time bringing me into the world and the doctor told her not to have any more children. Seven years went by and she made the mistake of forgetting his advice. She and the baby died before she made it to the birthing bed."

"I'm so sorry. Do you remember much about her?"

His expression softened. "She was a quiet, unassuming woman, and very kind. When my father remarried, he chose a more outspoken woman—my stepmother—but they were unfortunately unable to have children, which I believe partly explains the marchioness's deep affection for her niece."

"Miss Flint? The young woman who attended my sister's assembly?"

"Yes. Her own mother died a few years ago. She was Quintina's twin."

"Ah, it's no wonder she is close to her."

They sat in silence for a few minutes, then Clara answered the marquess's questions about her upbringing and education in America. She described her early childhood in Wisconsin, what it was like living in a one-room cabin in the woods before her father moved them to the city and slowly but surely earned his fortune on Wall Street. She told him about learning to speak French in Paris with her sisters, and she described her etiquette training in finishing school.

Then she decided it was time to broach a new subject. "What about your affairs?" she asked directly, knowing she had to become more efficient in this conversational quest before it was time to go back inside. "That woman from the divorce case. Did you love her?"

He sat forward slightly. "Now we're getting somewhere. No, I did not love her, but neither was the sentiment returned."

"How long were you involved with her?"

"Only a few months. She was a regular patron of the Cakras Balls. I was not the only man she carried on with but was I the only witness in court that day." He looked away for a few seconds. "She was a kind-hearted woman. Quite witty on occasions."

"Where is she now?" Clara asked.

"She went to Ireland. Her husband is still here, though he hides away in the country most of the time."

Clara settled back onto the deeply buttoned uphol-stery. "Have you never been serious with anyone?"

"Ah. The questions are becoming more interesting, aren't they." He gazed up at the roof of the coach. "Yes, I was serious once."

Clara sat forward. "How serious?"

"As serious as a young man can get. I was in love and wanted to be married."

Clara nearly lost her breath.

"You're surprised," he said.

"Well, yes." But it was more than that. A thousand questions were darting around inside her brain. "Why didn't you marry her?"

"Because I was young and according to my father and stepmother, not aware of the 'importance' of my marriage. I was heir to a very old title, and I had the unfortunate luck of falling in love with a merchant's daughter. Not even a very prosperous merchant, at that."

Still digesting her shock, Clara probed further. "How old were you?"

"Sixteen. I knew within a week that she was the one for me, and I was hers, secretly, for four years before I proposed. When my father learned of it, he was livid. The marriage was of course forbidden, and she was sent away, rather unexpectedly."

"By whom?"

"My father."

Clara was brimming with curiosity. "Where did she go?"

"He sent her to America, but the ship sank, halfway across the Atlantic."

A lump formed in Clara's throat. "I'm sorry to hear that."

He looked the other way toward the small red velvet curtain that covered the window. "It was a long time ago."

"Have you not cared for anyone since then?"

He turned to look at her again. "I've cared for many."

Clara's heart began to race as he leaned closer and his gaze settled on her lips. He was so close that his nose was almost touching hers. The proximity roused her desires.

"Are you going to kiss me now?" she asked, breathlessly.

"Only if you want me to." He remained where he was, waiting for her to give him some direction. Anticipation sizzled in the air around them.

"I'm not sure what I want," she replied. "This feels dangerous."

"Sitting in a carriage alone with a notorious libertine at three o'clock in the morning, asking all sorts of intimate questions, seems dangerous as well. Yet here we are."

"Yes, here we are." His nearness was overwhelming. The flow of blood through Clara's veins throbbed in her ears.

She moistened her lips and the marquess smiled.

He was still smiling a few seconds later when he kissed her, his lips reaching hers almost experimentally. Clara closed her eyes and gave in to the mad rush of desire, welcoming his touch after so many days remembering what it had felt like that glorious first night under the stairs. Now, here it was again—the passion, the eroticism, the sweet, pounding ache of lust being fulfilled.

He cupped her face in his hands and grinned roguishly. "Still delicious."

"That was nice," she said, trembling all over, a blush warming her cheeks. She wished she could be more in control and know what she was doing, but she had no idea. This was unlike any experience of her life.

"You even taste like strawberries," he said. "I'm afraid I'm going to have to kiss you again. There's simply no getting around it."

"Please do." But before he had a chance to follow through, she lunged forward and pressed her open mouth to his.

The kiss was deep and fierce and utterly intoxicating. A sweet shiver ran through Clara's body as she clutched at his shoulders, realizing she had been starving for this, far more than she realized.

The marquess eased her down upon the seat, never breaking the intimacy of the kiss. His hands roamed leisurely over her hips, then he rose to move her leg to one side and adjust her skirts so that he could settle himself between her thighs.

This was risky, she knew—to let him lie on top of her like this—but she did not wish to stop. She wanted to feel the weight of him, tight upon her body. She had not known that lust could have such an overpowering effect on all her senses and reasoning.

Laying hot, open-mouthed kisses on her neck, the marquess whispered, "You must tell me how far you wish to take things, so that there are no surprises or disappointments later on."

"I don't know," she said breathlessly. "I've never done this before."

He drew back slightly. "Not even when you ran away to elope?"

She shook her head. "No. My father arrived before anything could happen."

"Then I say 'Bravo' to your father." The marquess kissed her cheeks and nose. "You're very charming." He kissed her on the lips again, then eased her mind with a tender smile. "And you needn't worry. I've given you my word. There will be no destruction tonight. But are you sure you want to continue? It might leave you hungry for more."

"I'm sure, because I can't imagine saying no to anything right now."

He considered that for a moment, while gazing down at her face in the dim light. "Then we might as well get comfortable." One by one, he unfastened the covered buttons on her bodice and kissed lower… down the length of her neck and across her collarbone.

When her bodice finally fell open, he thrust his hips

against hers and slid his hand up over her corset to her bare neckline. Clara's pulse quickened at the softness of his caress. He smiled seductively as he kissed the swell of her cleavage, unhooking the corset clasps over her breasts.

Sucking in a breath, Clara marveled at the quivering in her belly. This was all so deliciously wicked. If anyone caught them! Oddly enough, the danger only served to pour fuel on her already flaming desires.

The corset came loose, and she reveled in the physical freedom. Seger tugged at the ribbons to loosen it and pull it down. He took one of her breasts into his mouth and every tingling fiber of Clara's being cried out with shock and delight at the incomprehensible pleasure of such intimacies.

Together, they moved on the seat, thrusting, kissing and laughing softly, touching each other intimately.

"You are delightful," he said with a rakish grin.

He closed his hand around hers and proceeded to teach her how to touch him. As soon as she caught on, he closed his eyes and returned his mouth to her breast. Clara tilted her head back on the seat, surprised when a tiny moan escaped her throat.

"Lord Rawdon," she whispered, feeling strange.

"Call me Seger." Then he reached down and lifted her skirts until they were bunched around her waist. He slid a hand over her thigh, then into the heated confines of her drawers. "I'll be gentle," he said.

Clara clutched at his shoulders. "Seger..." While he kissed her on the mouth, he stroked with his fingers, causing her insides to quiver with an unfamiliar need. Soon, her body began to tremble and quake, then an extraordinary sensation licked over her like hot, advancing flames, followed by an intense shudder of release. It was divine, perfect ecstasy.

Afterward, she relaxed and Seger sat back, draping her legs over his lap.

"Good heavens," she sighed, utterly depleted of strength. "Am I dying?"

"No, you just glimpsed heaven, that's all."

She shook her head in disbelief. "I've never glimpsed heaven like that before." She tossed a limp arm over her forehead. "Did you glimpse it as well?"

He chuckled. "Not tonight."

"Have you ever?"

He chuckled again. "Yes, and your innocence is delightful."

"But I'm not so innocent anymore, am I?" she asked, and then frowned. She leaned up on both elbows. "I'm not ruined, am I?"

Seger caressed her cheek. "No. You're still a virgin."

Sensing his affectionate amusement, she reclined on the seat again. It was obvious that he found her entertaining and intriguing, and she couldn't deny the satisfaction that came from that knowledge.

"But was it enjoyable for you?" she asked. "If you didn't feel what I felt…. Is it better with other women?"

"No, not better," he replied, shaking his head.

"But different."

"I suppose."

She thought about that. "Then this wasn't quite as gratifying for you as it was for me."

He touched a thumb to her lips. "It was gratifying

enough. I made you a promise."

"But you gave me pleasure. Can't I do the same for you?"

He raked a hand through his hair. "That's a very tempting offer, but we mustn't overdo it. My self-restraint does have its limits."

Still feeling tremendously amorous, Clara sat up. "What if I *want* to overdo it? I promise, I'll be a very enthusiastic pupil."

"Trust me, I believe you."

"Besides, I'm not ready to go back inside yet," she continued to argue. "The servants won't be up for at least another hour."

She slid across the seat, took Seger's face in her hands and kissed him fiercely. "Show me what to do. I don't want to leave yet."

He responded instantly, lifting her onto his lap, kissing her with unleashed abandon. Feeling aroused all over again, Clara straddled him. Her drawers were still on the floor, so she could feel the rigid length of him easily through the barrier of his trousers.

"What can I do to help you glimpse heaven, without losing what's left of my virtue?" She blew gently in his ear.

He kissed her neck. "I'm warning you, you should quit now, while I'm still in control of my impulses."

Heart racing, she untied his cravat and let her fingers slide into his shirt, across his smooth bare chest where she felt his heart beating.

"What I wouldn't give to be inside you right now," he whispered huskily, thrusting his hips, lifting her up.

She watched his face in the lamplight, and he watched hers. It all seemed so natural, intimate, and tender. How she loved being with him and feeling this way. How could she dream of doing this with any other man?

Clara rested her forehead against his. Their pace quickened until his grip on her hips grew tighter and firmer. He pulled her close and kissed her and she threw her arms around his neck and held him close.

After a while, he groaned in frustration. "You'll be the death of me."

"I wouldn't want that."

His eyes softened. "Promise me you won't feel guilty about this in the morning."

"I'm not sure how I'll feel. But I hate that I can hear the birds chirping and the sun will be up soon. I'll have to leave, or I'll be seen. Mrs. Gunther would tan my hide."

"Mine as well," he replied.

She chuckled and nuzzled his face. "This was all so new to me. I never imagined…."

"It might surprise you to know, but it was new to me as well. We should do it again."

"Yes, definitely."

"How can we arrange it?"

"I don't know," she replied. "I'll have to think about that."

As she began to button her bodice, she suspected she would be thinking of nothing else until she was back in Seger's arms again, by any means possible.

Chapter 10

Dear Clara,

No, there are no new faces in New York, so you had best make a success of it in London. You haven't given up on the handsome marquess, I hope? Have you become better acquainted with him yet? I am anxiously awaiting more news.

Adele

CLARA WOKE TO THE SOUND of a knock at her door. She grumbled, rolled over in her large, soft bed and opened her eyes.

The curtains were drawn and the sun was shining outside. What time was it? She squinted at the clock. Almost noon.

The knock rapped again.

"I'm still sleeping!" she called out, rolling to her side and curling up with a smile, gathering the covers into a ball and hugging them with her whole body.

"Are you all right, Clara?" It was Sophia. "You're not ill, are you?"

No, I'm not ill. I've never felt so good in my life.

Clara sat up. "I'm fine. Come in."

Her sister peered inside. "You missed breakfast and you're about to miss lunch, too, if you don't get your lazy bones out of bed."

Clara waved her in. "I need to talk to you."

Sophia shut the door behind her and moved fully into the room where Clara was sitting up in bed, smirking, feeling as if she might burst.

"What's going on? You look like you know a secret." Sophia sat down.

"I do, but if I tell you, you have to promise you won't be angry, nor will you breathe a word to anyone. Not even James."

"You know I don't like keeping secrets from James."

Clara hated asking her sister to lie, but she couldn't let anyone else find out what she had done. More importantly, she didn't want her brother-in-law—who had always been supportive of her despite her past mistakes—to think badly of her. She couldn't imagine anything worse than disappointing someone she respected so much.

"I don't want James to know because I don't want to fall short of his generous regard. Besides, there would be havoc if he knew."

"Havoc? What's going on, Clara?"

Clara stared at her sister for a few seconds, hoping she wouldn't be too shocked by what she was about to hear. "I...I did something rather impulsive last night."

Sophia covered her face with a hand. "Oh, no."

"Don't worry, no one knows. I was careful."

"What did you do?"

"I snuck out to meet Lord Rawdon."

Sophia's cheeks went pale. "You did what? How?"

"I sent him a note saying that I wished to see him, and in his reply, he told me his carriage would be out front at two a.m. I knew I had to take advantage of the opportunity, since the duke is expecting an answer today, so I was very quiet and went out a servant's door. The marquess was outside, just as he said he would be. We didn't go anywhere. We just sat in his coach and talked."

"You talked," Sophia said skeptically. "That's all?"

"Well, no, but I'll explain the rest in a minute. The point is that I've made up my mind about the Duke of Guysborough. I can't marry him." Clara continued to explain. "And after I talked to the marquess, I realized that we were right about him, Sophia. There is hope. His unconventional behavior makes perfect sense."

"Why?"

"First of all, he was an exemplary child and model student, very well-behaved with excellent academic performance. It was only later in life that he began to live recklessly, and there is an explanation for it. You see, he fell in love with someone but was forbidden to marry her because his father considered her to be beneath him socially."

"Interesting," Sophia replied. "But I'm still waiting for the reason why you think there is hope."

"Yes, I'm getting to that. The young woman was sent away to America by Lord Rawdon's father, but she died when her ship sank halfway across the Atlantic. It's tragic, I know. It was after that that the marquess retreated from society because he blamed its severe, restrictive rules for his heartache. The point is, he loved once before, Sophia, deeply and faithfully. He wanted to marry the girl, and the loss of her cut him so deeply, he has not yet gotten over it."

"And you think this makes him more attainable?"

"Yes," Clara replied. "If a man is capable of loving a woman once with that much devotion, he is capable of it again. He needs to be rescued and I can help him. I am sure of it. It's in his nature to love."

Sophia stood up and paced the room. "This is very dangerous, Clara. No woman should ever believe that she can change a man. When you marry, you must marry the man for who and what he is, not what you hope he will become."

"You rescued James."

"But I didn't know that's what I was doing when I agreed to marry him. I believed he was perfect as he was. It was only later that I realized there was more beneath the surface than I knew. You, on the other hand, know that the marquess is not the kind of man you ever intended to marry. You should not forget that."

Clara tossed the covers aside and stood up. She went to her dressing table to sit down and begin combing her hair. "There is an attraction between us. We could have talked all night long."

"He's a very skilled lover," Sophia argued. "That's what he does. He seduces women, makes them feel desirable."

Clara bristled at the words. "No, there was something special between us."

"I'm sure all women feel that way after a night in his arms. He's very handsome and charming. Tell me you did not do anything foolish. You didn't give yourself to him, did you?"

When Clara turned and faced Sophia, she recognized the anxiety in her eyes. "You needn't be concerned. I am still a virgin."

Sophia let out a breath of relief and collapsed into a chair. She rested a hand on her chest.

"Which is another reason why I believe he is honorable beneath the infamous notoriety," Clara added. "He's had three opportunities to take advantage of me, and all three times he has resisted and done everything in his power to protect my virtue. I trusted him completely last night. There was not a single fear in my mind that he would ravish me against my will or do anything to harm me. The fact that he could act with honor in that way leads me to believe that if he makes any kind of vow or promise, he will be faithful to that vow."

"You think he could be a reliable husband?"

"Yes, I do."

"We're talking about a lifetime, Clara, not one night with a virgin. Maybe he didn't ravish you because he knew that if he did, he'd have to marry you, and the idea of commitment and fidelity outweighed his temporary desires."

Clara pulled the brush roughly through her hair. "There was nothing temporary about what happened last night."

"But you are not experienced with this sort of thing! Some men can make love to a woman and forget her the very next instant. Their dalliances are merely conquests. What did happen, exactly?"

Clara shook her head. "I wanted to tell you before, but now I don't. You'll only disapprove."

Sophia approached Clara and rested her hands on her shoulders. "I only worry that you're going to get hurt. That you're romanticizing what happened."

"You were supportive before. You were encouraging me to find out all I could about him. Why have you changed your mind?"

"I haven't changed my mind. I just feel that you must tread carefully where the marquess is concerned. Guard your heart as well as your virtue until you can be sure he is worthy of you. Be vigilant and act with caution. That's all I'm saying."

Clara knew deep down that her sister was right. Clara's head was in the clouds this morning.

But how could it not be? She had glimpsed heaven the night before.

"All right, fine" she said to her sister. "I promise to be careful. But I must refuse the duke."

Sophia nodded. "Mrs. Gunther won't be happy. You probably shouldn't tell her beforehand. She'll spend the whole day trying to talk you out of it."

"Good point. I'll tell her after the fact, then she'll have no choice but to accept it." Clara sighed heavily. "Well, now that we've got all that out of the way, do you want to hear what happened in the carriage *after* the marquess and I talked?"

Sophia smiled and sat down next to Clara. "Of course. And spare nothing. I want every delicious detail."

Later that day, the Duke of Guysborough was announced and entered the drawing room. After a short time, Mrs. Gunther mentioned that she needed to speak to her maid about something, and left Clara alone with him.

As soon as her chaperone was gone, the duke stood up and moved closer to the fireplace. "You've had a chance to consider my proposal?" he asked, looking down at Clara where she sat on the sofa. He appeared confident. She supposed it was natural, considering his status. Clara was not looking forward to rejecting him.

"I have, Your Grace, and I am very flattered."

He smiled and moved closer to sit down next to her. A cold knot tightened in Clara's belly. She hated this.

"I am honored by your offer," she continued, "but...I'm afraid I must decline."

The duke's head drew back in surprise. "I beg your pardon?"

"I'm so sorry."

"Is there a reason? There must be a reason."

"I do apologize. This is most difficult. I...I am simply not in love with you."

His eyebrows drew together in a frown. "Not in love with me?" He rolled his shoulders as if he were struggling to keep his anger in check. "Perhaps I should have taken more time for a courtship. I've heard that you American girls have certain expectations in that regard."

"First of all, I am not a girl," Clara replied. "I am a woman. But yes, your proposal did come rather quickly."

"Because I was certain that if I did not make an offer, someone else would. The competition for you is intense, Miss Wilson. You are the talk of the town, so to speak."

Clara was no fool. She knew she was popular because she was a wealthy heiress and it was a well-known fact that her father would furnish her husband-to-be with a very generous marriage settlement. Her own sister, Sophia, had made James one of the richest men in England. Sophia's dowry, if one included the railroad stock, had been the largest in English history. Clara's would most certainly match that.

"Thank you for the compliment, Your Grace," she said.

But he was not satisfied. "May I indulge in some hope that you might reconsider if I give you more time?"

She didn't know what to say. She hated rejecting the duke, and there was of course a chance that Lord Rawdon would break her heart in the coming weeks. The possibility that she might be burning her bridges loomed over her.

"I really don't know, Your Grace. I don't wish to give you any false hopes."

He stared into her eyes for a moment, and his darkened. "Is there someone else?"

Clara swallowed nervously. "I cannot say."

"Cannot say?" His voice revealed agitation, and an uncomfortable tension moved through Clara's neck and shoulders. "You're making a foolish mistake, Miss Wilson. You know that, don't you?"

The duke's harsh tone cleared her of any regret about rejecting him. She was now certain that she had done the right thing.

When she did not reply, he grabbed hold of her

hand and pressed it against his cold lips. He began to drop hard kisses up her arm. "Maybe this is what a woman like you wants."

All the hairs on the back of her neck stood up in disgust. Heart racing, she quickly wrenched her arm out of his grasp.

The duke's petulant gaze shot to her face. Recognizing her revulsion, he sat up straighter. "I was right. Your interests do lie elsewhere. But I will have you know that I am still willing to marry you, and I would treat you with the respect that you deserve. You would not find that to be the case with the Marquess of Rawdon."

Clara stared at him, dumbfounded. What did the duke know? No one had seen her leave the house the night before. The marquess had come to call on her properly once, but surely that wasn't enough to suggest....

"I beg your pardon, Your Grace?"

"It is your choice, Miss Wilson. You can be a duchess, or you can be a slut."

Clara sucked in a breath. She had never been spoken to in such a manner. She certainly had not expected this from the duke, who had always appeared to be the epitome of proper, gentlemanly behavior.

Fury began to rage inside her and she stood. "Please leave."

She made a move to walk around the sofa and open the drawing room door for him, but he seized her arm.

"I will leave," he said, "when you have realized your folly. You've attended two Cakras Balls and you have become besotted with a notorious rake. I saw the two of you together here in this very room at your sister's assembly. Others did as well. I assure you, there were whispers. You do not emit purity, Miss Wilson. There is something unchaste about you, and you have associated yourself with the marquess—a known degenerate. I am willing to overlook that fact because the damage is still reparable at this point. I can offer you a respectable escape."

"A respectable escape?" Clara jerked her arm from his grasp. "I asked you to leave."

"I don't believe you want me to do that."

"Why ever not?"

"Because I have the power to destroy you, Miss Wilson. To put it in plainer terms, if you do not accept my offer, I most certainly will."

"He said *what?*" Sophia asked, her voice brimming with indignation as she rose to her feet.

Clara sat numbly on the sofa, still in shock. "He told me that it was my choice. I could be a duchess or a slut. Needless to say, I didn't tell Mrs. Gunther any of that. She is very curious about what happened."

Sophia walked to the mantel. "I'm so angry I could spit. The Duke of Guysborough of all people. I always took him for a gentleman."

"So did I. I was stunned."

"As you had every right to be! He behaved deplorably!"

"Yes." Clara gazed around the room. "But I, too, behaved foolishly, and I must accept some responsibility for this unpleasant state of affairs. If I had not lost my head with the marquess, none of this would be happening." She stood up and paced the room. "If you must bar your door to me, Sophia, I will understand. Perhaps I should leave now and go back to America before this situation spins out of control. I don't want you and James to be sullied by it."

"Don't say such things. We would never bar our door to you."

"James might wish to, and he would have every right. He might want to protect Liam and John."

"James will not wish it. You are a member of this family, and as far as he is concerned, you are under his protection." Sophia crossed to the sofa and sat down. "Besides, this is as much my fault as it is yours. I should never have taken you back to that Cakras Ball. I've been a terrible chaperone."

"No. If you hadn't taken me, I would have found some other way to see the marquess again, and things could have been much worse. Or maybe I would have accepted the duke's proposal and paid for such naïveté later."

For a long time, neither of them said anything. The mantel clock ticked and Clara felt a heavy weight upon her shoulders—the uncomfortable, cumbersome weight of her precarious future.

"Sometimes," she said softly, gazing up at the flowers on the mantel, "when I think about the marquess, I feel possessed. I don't know if it is love or something darker...something purely hedonistic. But I can't suppress my desire to give myself to him in the physical sense. Completely."

She turned her eyes to her sister, expecting shock

and condemnation. Instead, she saw compassion.

"I understand how you feel," Sophia said. "I remember...with James." Sophia stood again and took both Clara's hands in hers. "Do not be distressed. You are a normal, healthy young woman with very human desires, and I agree with you on one point—that the marquess acted honorably, having spared your virtue when clearly you could have been easily persuaded. Compared to Guysborough, he is a gentleman through and through."

"I agree."

"It appears," Sophia continued, "that the marquess and the duke are very different from how they are perceived. Things are not always as they seem, are they? I've always believed there was more to a person than what is visible on the surface. That's why I despise the gossip mill."

Clara sighed. "I'm afraid I might be dragged through the gossip mill very soon, if the duke doesn't get what he wants—which is undoubtedly a mammoth settlement from Father."

Pursing her lips, Sophia turned away from Clara. "It is nothing short of blackmail. I will not stand for it. James will not stand for it. We must tell him. He will know what to do."

A wave of apprehension moved through Clara. It was colored with shame and remorse. She hated causing problems for the two people she respected most in the world, and she did not want her sister's husband to think poorly of her. "Please don't tell him about how I snuck out in the dead of night. Everything else, but not that."

Gazing uncertainly at Clara, Sophia spoke softly. "Don't worry, it will not change how he feels about you. James is a man of the world. Besides that, he *must* know, because we cannot allow him to take steps without knowing all the facts."

Clara sat back down. "He won't go to the marquess, will he? I would die if he did."

"I'll ask him not to. Either way, it will not be his first priority. The marquess will not be the one to face the heat of his wrath today."

In the end, Clara told James everything that had occurred between her and the marquess over the past few weeks. She even confessed to the letters and the scandalous rendezvous in the carriage, though she spared him the more intimate details.

Standing by the window in his study, James gave her a responsible speech about the importance of propriety, then made her promise never to do anything like that again. Clara agreed without hesitation.

James glanced out the window briefly before turning his attention back to Clara, who sat in a small chair.

"You're certain that the duke knows nothing about the rendezvous in the coach?" he asked.

Clara nodded. "He would have used it against me if he knew. He only mentioned the Cakras Balls and the way the marquess and I behaved at the assembly."

James nodded. "The duke should have known better than to reveal his knowledge of a Cakras Ball and use it to threaten *anyone's* reputation. He'll pay for that mistake, I assure you. You have nothing to worry about, Clara."

She gazed up at her brother-in-law. "You're sure?"

"I'm positive."

"But what about Mrs. Gunther? She has no idea why I refused the duke and she is pressing me to explain."

"I will speak to her," James replied, "and tell her that you simply did not favor the man."

All Clara's fears drained away in that instant but were quickly replaced by another cause for concern. "You won't intimidate the marquess, will you? As I told you before, he has behaved honorably toward me. Well, with the exception of certain things he said in the letters...and inviting me out in the middle of the night, but even then, he did not take advantage when he could have. Will you think of that, James?" *When you are face-to-face with him, as I'm sure you will be later today.*

Her brother-in-law stepped away from the window and came around the desk. "I will indeed endeavor to think of it. Now, do not spend another moment troubling yourself with this disturbance. Guysborough *will* back down, and you can be certain that he will behave in the future. Go to the nursery now and try to smile, Clara. I believe Sophia is waiting for you to play peek-a-boo with Liam."

She rose from her chair and allowed James to escort her out of his study.

Sickening dread poured through her, however, when she stood at the top of the stairs a few minutes later, watching her brother-in-law slip into his long, black greatcoat and place his top hat on his head, and inform the butler that he was going out to take care of a thing or two.

Chapter 11

Adele,
I have fallen hopelessly in love with Lord Raw-
don, and everything is in a terrible, terrible mess...
Clara

S EATED AT THE DESK IN his study, Seger glanced up
from the newspaper when his butler entered and
informed him that the Duke of Wentworth wished to
see him.

Seger laid his newspaper aside and let out a sigh.
"Send him in, Cartwright."

As soon as the butler disappeared, Seger stood up,
went to the sideboard, and poured himself a brandy.
"Here we go."

A moment later, the duke entered the room. Hands
at his sides, he said simply, "Rawdon."

Seger poured another glass of brandy and approached
the duke with it. He held it out, and without a word,
the duke removed his gloves and accepted it.

Seger noticed the duke's right knuckle was blood-
ied. "Were you practicing on a tree outside in the
garden?"

Wentworth glanced absently at his hand, then took
a deep swig of the amber liquid. "It wasn't practice."

For a moment, the two men regarded each other warily, then Seger gestured toward the chairs in front of the fireplace. The duke sat down and waited for Seger to sit before he spoke. "Shall we dispense with small talk, then?" the duke asked.

"By all means."

Wentworth nodded. "You're no fool, Rawdon. I'm sure you know the motive behind my call."

Seger swirled the brandy around in his glass and took a sip. "I can hazard a guess. You want me to stay away from your sister-in-law."

Wentworth's shrewd eyes narrowed with scrutiny, as if he were attempting to determine what to make of Seger. "To be frank with you, I'm not certain. I'd like clarification from you first."

"Concerning what, in particular?"

"I will come straight to the point. Clara informs me that she is still in possession of her virtue. Is that true? I will have the truth, Rawdon."

Seger considered the material facts. Images of his encounter with Clara in the privacy of his coach the night before flashed like fireworks in his mind. He remembered sliding his hand into her drawers. He remembered what she tasted like and sounded like when he'd brought her to a climax. Then he recalled Clara sitting on his lap, straddling him.

If anyone had peered in at them, it would have appeared they were making love.

When one looked at it that way, he had certainly helped himself to her so-called virtues the night before, but for all practical purposes, he'd left her with the most important thing—her maidenhead.

He'd ensured she would still have choices.

"It's true," he replied, then downed the rest of his brandy in one gulp. "She is still a virgin. You have my word on that. Most of the time, we just talked." That, too, was the truth.

The duke continued to scrutinize him.

"Do you believe me?"

At last, Wentworth nodded. "Yes, unless some evidence in the future points to the contrary, in which case you would regret our conversation today."

Seger understood. The duke would not be lied to.

"So, I take it," Seger said, "that you are not here to muscle a marriage proposal out of me?"

"Not today."

"But you want me to keep away from her."

Because that's what male relations of Seger's paramours *always* wanted.

For a long time, Wentworth appeared as if he were considering the question. Then he set down his glass. "Clara is my wife's sister. She is a kindhearted, intelligent young woman and her happiness is my primary concern. From what I can discern, she has an affection for you, and I will not be the one to tell her that her affections are misguided. I do not know one way or another if they are. I will, however, watch carefully over the coming weeks to ensure that she is not treated in a cavalier fashion. You will see her only in respectable situations, and you will not continue to encourage her if there is no future in it. If you do, there will be consequences. Do you understand?"

"Perfectly."

"I must also inform you," the duke added, "that

you are very close to the center of another scandal, a scandal I attempted to avert just over an hour ago."

Seger glanced down at Wentworth's bloody hand and felt the muscles of his forearm tighten as he clenched his own hand into a fist. "What scandal? It doesn't involve Clara, does it?"

"Your concern for my sister-in-law does you credit. Yes, it involves her. The two of you were seen together at two separate Cakras Balls, and a certain gentleman who covets Clara's marriage settlement has threatened to reveal it. Under other circumstances I would have words for you in that regard, but from what I understand, Clara's attendance at the ball was accidental, at least the first time, and you steered her away and suggested that she leave. You did the same the second time, when it was *not* accidental."

Was Seger receiving a commendation? he wondered, staring at Wentworth's dark expression. Why was he telling him all this?

"You said just now that you attempted to avert the scandal," Seger mentioned. "Were you successful?"

"I made an impression," the duke replied, "but it wouldn't hurt for you to make an impression as well. I believe we should present a united front."

Seger tried to keep his anger in check. "Who, may I ask, is the gentleman in question?"

"Guysborough."

"The duke? Bloody hypocrite. He, of all people, should know the rules of the Cakras Society. He'd tried something like this once before, didn't he?"

"Yes, two years ago he was suspended for speaking about a particular lady who had rejected his attentions at one of the balls, but I think in this case, Clara's value financially was worth the risk of being suspended again."

"Society won't take kindly to a second misdemeanor. A suspension would be the least of his punishments."

"I reminded him of that," Wentworth said. "Perhaps you should, too. Tell him that we spoke."

"Will that do the trick?

"Who's to say for sure? All I know is that I don't trust him." Wentworth stood. "Thank you for the brandy, Rawdon."

Seger stood as well. "I'll show you out."

They went to the door where the butler was waiting with the duke's coat and hat. Wentworth was halfway down the steps outside, almost to his coach, when Seger called out to him. "Wentworth!" The duke stopped and turned.

"I appreciated the invitation your wife sent—for my family to attend your assembly."

A bluebird flew by, then swooped down and perched on the stone wall by the gate.

"It was our pleasure to welcome you, Rawdon." Wentworth touched the brim of his top hat and continued toward his coach.

Seger stood for a moment or two, watching the vehicle drive off.

The meeting had not gone the way he had expected.

Finally, he closed the door and returned to his study. All he could think about was Clara and the fact that a scandal had come dangerously close to her shores, no thanks to him. He loathed the idea that he had brought her even the smallest measure of grief or anxiety. She had trusted him with her reputation, and he had let her down.

Seger sank onto the chair at his desk and stroked his chin. He gazed at the empty grate in the fireplace and let his mind wander where it would. He recalled the taste of Clara's open mouth when he'd kissed her the night before. The memory of her irresistible sighs when he'd been busy with his hand beneath her skirts brought on an inconvenient surge of arousal that accompanied the heated recollections. Along with that came a wave of regret for what she had suffered today.

With resolve, Seger decided that he would take care of the scandal. He would see Guysborough, and ascertain what exactly had transpired, then he would ensure the man behaved himself in the future and never so much as looked at Clara again. Then Seger would call on Clara to assure her that all was well.

But who was he trying to fool?

He didn't want to call on her to ease her mind about a scandal. He simply wanted to be in the same room with her. To touch her if possible.

With some apprehension, he rose from his chair and summoned his butler to have him ready the coach, for he had an important personal matter to attend to.

Just when Clara thought the day could not possibly provide another surprise, an under butler entered the nursery. Clara was holding John, singing a lullaby.

"You have a visitor," he said. "The Marquess of Rawdon."

Clara shot a glance at Sophia, who froze.

"Tell him I'll be right down," Clara replied, and the young man took his leave.

"What's he doing here?" Sophia asked, picking Liam up off the floor and laying him down in his crib. "James hasn't even returned yet. We haven't had a chance to find out what happened."

"You don't think James coerced Lord Rawdon into proposing, do you? Because I will not agree to a forced wedding."

"I don't know." Sophia took John out of Clara's arms. "Just go, Clara. Don't keep him waiting. Offer him tea. I'll give you a few minutes before I follow."

"Thank you. You are the best sister."

Clara tidied her hair on the way to the drawing room. Nervous twitters gathered in her belly at the mere thought of seeing Seger again. She stopped and paused outside the drawing room doors, fighting butterflies, then entered.

The marquess stood at the window, hands clasped behind his back as he looked out. The sunlight shone on his face, illuminating the square cut of his jaw, his full lips and straight nose. All Clara's senses came alive. Such power he could wield over her, merely by standing there, doing nothing.

He turned and faced her, and they stared at each other for several sizzling seconds. Excitement swirled in Clara's belly.

"What are you doing here?" she asked, moving forward at last.

It was not the sort of question she would pose to a regular caller, but to say anything else to this man— whose hand she had allowed up under her skirts the night before—would be putting on airs, to say the least. They were beyond the usual protocol.

He spoke matter-of-factly. "Your brother-in-law paid me a visit today."

Clara's stomach careened. What happened between the two men? She couldn't imagine.

"I was afraid he might do that," she said apologetically.

Clara moved fully into the room but kept the sofa between herself and the marquess. She was afraid that if she were within arms' reach of him, she would not be able to resist touching him.

"What did he say?" she asked.

"He came to warn me not to take any more risks where you are concerned, as any responsible brother-in-law would do. From now on, I may only see you in respectable settings."

"That's all?"

The marquess sauntered seductively around the sofa. She knew he wasn't trying to be seductive. He simply couldn't help it.

Feeling suddenly breathless, Clara backed up a step.

Seger stood before her, barely a foot away. "He also informed me that a possible scandal involving both you and me had come to his attention after you received a certain gentleman caller earlier today."

Clara's muscles tensed at the mere mention of what had occurred between her and the Duke of Guysborough. She was still shaken by it. "Did he tell you where things stood? Was he able to clear things up?"

Seger's eyebrows drew together with surprise. "You don't know?"

"No, James hasn't come home yet." Wondering what had happened, she began to feel ill. Perhaps the scandal had already exploded, and she would have no choice but to return to New York on the next ship.

The expression on Seger's face softened. "You needn't worry. It's been addressed."

"By whom? By James, or you?"

"Both of us. If Guysborough knows what's good for him, he'll never speak your name again unless it is to compliment your kindness or your grand sense of morality."

Clara held her hand over a lump of dread in her belly. "Are you sure?"

"Absolutely."

In that instant, Clara noticed a drop of blood on his collar. "Oh, I see."

Seger saw what she was staring at and glanced down at the blood, too. He tried to rub at it. "I do beg your pardon. I didn't notice this." Then he glanced up at her face and his expression softened with understanding. "I'm not generally the violent sort, Clara, but the duke pulled a pistol on me and I had to disarm him."

"A pistol!"

"Don't worry, it went out the window."

"Are you all right?" The image of Seger staring into the barrel of a gun sent her emotions into a rapid spin.

"I'm fine."

"What about the duke? He's not...." She couldn't finish.

"He's fine, too, though his ego is probably bruised. This blood.... It's from a bloody nose, that's all."

She decided she did not wish to know any more

details concerning his or James's "conversation" with the duke. The bloody nose was more than enough information.

Seger looked her up and down. *"You* are all right, I hope?"

She nodded.

"Good." He reached out a hand, his eyes warm with an open invitation. "Come and sit with me."

What could she do but follow? She was charmed. Clara placed her hand in his, and they sat on the sofa, facing each other.

"I am sorry for what happened with Guysborough," he said, "and I accept all responsibility. I should not have come to your sister's assembly. People know what I am, and they are not accepting of me. I should have remained outside your circle."

"No. You have honor, Seger. Surely you know that. It was Guysborough who behaved dishonorably."

With a swift glance toward the door to ensure they were alone, Seger raised her hand to his lips and kissed her open palm. Clara tried to maintain her composure, but it was impossible. Seger stirred every passion-filled longing that existed inside of her.

"I will continue to blame myself for what happened," he whispered. "I only wish I could make it up to you somehow."

He laid soft, open-mouthed kisses on her wrist and she sucked in a breath of arousal. No wonder every woman in London wanted him. His ability to please was addictive. Having experienced his lovemaking skills in the coach, it was now impossible for Clara to forget how he made her feel. How quickly he had become an obsession.

Slowly, he kissed his way to the inside of her elbow and Clara's heart thundered in her ears. She trembled at the sheer, unbridled roar of her desires from the sensation of his tongue on the inside of her arm.

"I'm very sorry for what happened," he said.

Her voice was breathless. "You're quite forgiven, my lord."

Just then, Sophia entered and cleared her throat.

Seger reacted calmly, with the unruffled demeanor of a man who had been caught like this a hundred times before. He sat back, then stood. "Duchess. What a pleasure."

Before Sophia had a chance to reply, Mrs. Gunther appeared. Clara—still in a dazed stupor—said a silent thank you that Sophia had arrived first.

The two ladies entered the room and moved around the sofa to sit across from them in two facing chairs. Sophia's face was pale. Mrs. Gunther's chin was high in the air as she glared hotly at Seger. No one said anything for a few seconds until a parlor maid arrived with a tray of tea and scones.

"May I pour for you, my lord?" Sophia offered with a smile, trying to ease the tension. It would not be eased, however. Not with Mrs. Gunther's nostrils flaring on the other side of the room.

All Clara could do was sit quietly and try to quell her racing heart and force the hot, stinging blush from her cheeks. Her body was still heated with an insatiable need for more love play with the marquess. Her mind was besieged.

She glanced warily at her sister. How long had she

been standing there?

Without batting an eye, Sophia led the conversation into lighter matters. She inquired about the health of Seger's stepmother and asked polite questions about his home in the country. Mrs. Gunther was grimly silent.

Ten awkward minutes later, Seger set down his cup and addressed Sophia. "I wonder if you would be so kind, Duchess, as to permit me a moment alone with your sister?"

Clara gazed at him in shock. His meaning could not have been more clear. Gentlemen did not request private conversations with unmarried ladies in drawing rooms unless they intended to discuss something personally significant.

Something momentous.

Something that involved questions that were asked on one knee.

Had James forced him to do this?

Heart racing, Clara had to remind herself to breathe. The marquess did not meet her gaze.

All Seger's attention was focused on the duchess as he waited for her reply because he wanted everyone out of there.

"Of course," she said at last, looking uncharacteristically flustered. "Mrs. Gunther, won't you join me in the library for a few minutes?"

The woman refused to move. Her cold gaze darted from the duchess to Seger, then back at the duchess again as if she were struggling for a way to prevent what was about to happen.

But Seger wasn't even sure he knew what that was. He was at the mercy of his desires, his unquenchable lust for this alluring young woman who had shattered his ability to stave off emotion. When he was with her, he lost all sense of reason and strength of will, and he was astonished by his malleability. He could not be blasé with her, for this entire experience was fresh and new. He had not known it was possible to want a woman this badly.

"Mrs. Gunther," the duchess repeated more forcefully, rising to her feet. Seger rose also.

The woman gathered her aplomb and finally stood, sending a seething glare in Seger's direction as she passed by on the way to the door.

He wondered suddenly what he was going to say next. He gazed down at Clara and saw in her eyes a hopeful but cautious expectation.

So, there it was. The first step toward the life he had been avoiding for eight years, the life that went beyond superficiality where a woman was concerned. He realized suddenly that a partial reason for his avoidance of it was to punish his stepmother and his late father for what had happened with Daphne. Even though the old marquess was long cold in his grave, Seger had wanted to deprive him of the next heir.

Now, for the first time, that meant nothing to Seger. All he knew was what he wanted, and that he could not bear the thought of anyone else proposing to Clara Wilson. He wanted her for himself. In his bed. Forever.

The thought shocked him. He had never meant for Clara—or any woman for that matter—to become so important to him.

As soon as the duchess and chaperone were gone, Seger sat down again and turned to face Clara. He should end this now...say goodbye, but his mental faculties could not gain a foothold over his lust and need. He wanted Clara. He wanted access to her rare inner beauty, and there was no fighting it. All he could do now was try to say the right things without becoming a man he did not wish to become. A man at the mercy of his emotions.

Consequently, he searched for bearings, and fell back into the habits that had become the foundation of his existence. He summoned his surface charm and forced a lid on anything deeper.

Clara's thoughts were screaming inside her head. What were his intentions? Was she being presumptuous, imagining that he meant to propose?

"I don't wish to cause any more scandals," he said.

"Then maybe we shouldn't be alone right now."

"But we must be, if I am to say what I wish to say."

She had to struggle to keep her voice steady when every nerve in her body was buzzing like an electric current. "And what is that, my lord?"

Looking relaxed and confident, he smiled. "That I desire you. That I want you."

Despite her anxiousness, she somehow managed to return an equally confident smile. "You didn't need to come all the way over here to tell me that. I already knew it. You made it more than clear to me last night."

His brow lifted with amused admiration. "Marry

me."

Clara's body seemed to stop functioning. Everything within her went still.

"Marry you? Just like that? No romantic proposal? No attempt to win me over with a few choice compliments?"

"You said yourself that you already know how I feel about you, and you don't seem like the sort of woman who needs to dance around a point before coming straight to it. There is scandal on our heels, and it is certain to catch up with us again if we continue in the direction we are going. I desire you, Clara, and since I am now confined to seeing you only in respectable situations, I will have to make everything respectable, because I do intend to see you. Quite often, in fact. Every night in my bed, if you take my meaning."

Clara stood and walked to the window. Her heart was racing, her thoughts swimming. She had not expected a marriage proposal from Seger, at least not this soon. She thought she'd have to employ some clever persuasion tactics to encourage him to reform, and she'd expected that to take some time.

Then again, she hadn't expected James to learn all about their secret encounters either and visit the marquess. Nor had she expected the Duke of Guysborough to try and blackmail her into marrying him.

She faced Seger. "What is the real reason you want to marry me?"

"The real reason?" He stood also and moved to stand before her at the window. "Because as I said, we are heading for a scandal, and I desire you too much to give you up."

"What do you mean, heading for a scandal? Do you mean the duke's threat, or something else? Some ambiguous future scandal?"

"Both. I can't promise that I'd be able to restrain myself if we were alone again." He considered that statement, then added with a captivating smile, "Actually, I can promise you that I would *not* be able to. Next time, you would not walk away a virgin."

Clara felt dazed by his suggestion. "My brother-in-law didn't put you up to this, did he?" she asked. "He didn't give *you* a bloody nose, I hope."

"No, he did not. In fact, he has no idea I am here, let alone proposing to you. Even if he knew, I'm not entirely sure he would approve."

Breathing deeply as she gathered the facts—and her composure—Clara searched for understanding. She needed to know what this was about and how the marquess truly felt about being married to her for the rest of his life.

"I don't want a forced marriage," she said. "I want my husband to be sure that he wants me."

"There are no worries there. I am sure."

She narrowed her eyes at him.

"I can see you want more from me," he said. "You want me to pour my heart out to you."

Clara saw the reluctance in his eyes and knew that he had already said more and done more than he ever intended to say or do with any woman.

A sudden thought of all the other women shook her confidence, and she reminded herself what kind of man he was. She told herself it was dangerous to hope for too much.

Seger moved to the mantel. "I am not a poet, Clara, nor am I inclined to lie to you. On top of the reasons I already gave you, I've always known that I must marry eventually. I require an heir, and I would enjoy having children with you. Making them, especially."

Even when he was giving her the cold, hard truth, he was delivering more flattery than she'd ever known in her life. He looked at her like he wanted to devour her, and it made her feel weak in the knees. She felt as if he could pull a yes from her lips with a mere smile.

"So, it is duty," she managed to say.

"Only partly."

"And desire."

"Definitely that. I can't resist you."

She took some pleasure from the compliment, for he was in his own way telling her that she was special. She had done something no other woman had been able to do. She had gotten a proposal out of him.

"What about the marriage settlement that is sure to be offered?" she asked. "Have you been seeking that all along? Did you somehow manipulate all of this to cause a scandal and force my hand?"

"Good heavens, no. I have enough money of my own. I don't dabble in politics, so I dabble in other things. The American stock market for one. I am probably as rich as your father."

Clara's eyebrows lifted. "I had no idea."

"Not many people do."

She moved away from him to pace around the room. "So, you're not one of the infamous impoverished English lords? That will certainly surprise the New York newspapermen," she said with bite. "They don't seem to believe that any Englishman would marry an American for anything other than money."

"We will break the mold, then."

Clara stared at him for a moment, considering all of it. "What about love?" she finally asked, knowing she was pushing the limits. "Since we're being honest with each other...."

If he were unnerved by her question, he didn't show it. He seemed more amused than anything by her "negotiations."

"I wondered if you would bring that up." He gazed out the window for a moment, then looked directly into her eyes as he spoke. "I won't lie to you, Clara. You're an intelligent woman, and you must realize that we barely know each other."

"I do."

"As I told you last night, I've only loved one woman in my life, and it ended catastrophically. I admit I am jaded, but that doesn't mean our marriage cannot be a success."

He was being honest and sensible, admitting that he did not truly love her, and she couldn't deny that she respected him for that. If he'd told her he loved her, she probably wouldn't have believed him and would have felt as if she were being tricked or patronized.

But still, in her deepest heart of hearts, this was not what she wished they were saying to each other right now. She didn't want to hear about other women from his past or have him mention the only woman he had ever loved. The mere thought of her cut Clara to the quick. She had dreamed of so much more where Seger was concerned. *She* wanted to be the only woman in his heart and mind, forever and ever.

"Are you suggesting that you would grow to love me?" she asked.

A reasonable question that she hated asking. It hurt. It made her feel rejected and humiliated.

"Possibly."

Possibly. Not definitely. The response sank like a cold, hard stone into her belly.

Would the mere possibility of love be enough? Could she take such a risk with a man like him? What if he only grew bored with her?

Seger must have recognized the doubts in her eyes, for he strode toward her and spoke with conviction. "I would treat you well, Clara. You would become a marchioness and live here in England near your sister. It would be a life of privilege and grandeur. In addition to that, I desire you and you desire me. Can't that be enough, at least for now?" He gazed at her for a few intense seconds. "Imagine the pleasure."

Oh yes, she could definitely imagine that.

He lowered his lips to hers and kissed her, and she wrapped her arms around his neck, reveling in the passion that had taken up permanent residence in her heart.

Holding her face in his hands, he looked into her eyes. "I want to marry you because I desire you. I want you in my bed, and I want no other man to ever touch you but me. Yes, I need a wife and an heir, but this is not about anything as dull as duty, nor is it about money. Believe me. I want you, Clara. Passionately."

It was about passion, but not love. Could she live

with that? She had wanted love.

But wait, no, she had not. She had wanted a decent man who would be a good husband and father. A man who would be faithful to her.

Seger's heart was decent. She was certain of that—as certain as she could be where any man was concerned. He had always kept her best interests in mind, doing what he could to protect her when she'd ventured outside the safe circle of her proper world. He'd even tried to push her back in. Except for the previous night in his coach, when he had lured her out, but that was because he desired her. Passionately, as he put it.

Perhaps it would not take much to turn that passion into love.

But was she certain he could be reformed and become a faithful husband? Or was that simply what she wished? Everything to do with him had been a fantasy from the start. She couldn't be sure where the fantasy ended and reality began.

He was very passionate. That much she knew. He enjoyed physical pleasure with women. Would she be enough for him? Would she be able to keep him satisfied for the rest of their lives?

He kissed her again and she melted in his arms. "Say yes, Clara."

Senses blazing, she returned the kiss with abandon. Then, before she realized what she was saying, she blurted out, "Would you be faithful to me?"

This, she realized, was the final question that would determine her future.

He pulled back to look at her. For a long moment

he considered her question while her stomach turned over with a sickening fear that his answer would be no. Or that he would say yes, and she would know he was lying.

"That's a difficult question. I don't have a crystal ball."

She wasn't satisfied. "Answer the question, Seger."

His shoulders rose and fell with a deep sigh that held a note of surrender. "I would try to be."

Clara knew it was as honest an answer as she would ever get from *any* man. He was right about the crystal ball. No matter who she married, there could never be any guarantees. Marriage, by nature, was a leap of faith for everyone.

He kissed her again and she gave herself over to the passion, for that was the one thing she knew they shared, the one thing she trusted. Then she let that passion carry her to a decision.

Clara smiled up at him and said, "I believe, my lord, that you have secured yourself a wife."

Chapter 12

Dear Clara,
You said in your last letter that everything was
a terrible mess. I hope things have improved. Just
remember, don't do anything hasty. Be careful in
your decisions. Be sure to listen to the advice of
Sophia and James. They have your best interests at
heart....
Adele

CLARA, SOPHIA, JAMES, AND MRS. Gunther gathered in the drawing room after Seger left. The tea was now cold, but the parlor maid had not been allowed in to take the tray away.

"Sophia," Mrs. Gunther said, as if Clara were not in the room, "you must realize the mistake your sister is making. The Duke of Guysborough proposed first. He is the wiser choice. He outranks the marquess, not to mention the fact that he is respected by society, where the marquess is not even invited into it."

James strode to the mantel. "May I remind you of the old adage, not to judge a book by its cover?"

"How else can one judge it," she asked, "when appearances are everything?"

"Not to me," Clara said.

"Or me," Sophia added, gazing up at her husband, who smiled down at her.

"You have lost your senses, all of you," Mrs. Gunther said. "Your Grace, you must do something. The ladies are smitten simply because the marquess is a handsome man. They must be made to understand."

Hands behind his back, James moved to stand behind his wife's chair. He rested a hand on her shoulder. "I believe, madam, the only one here who must be made to understand anything is you."

"I beg your pardon?"

"I mean no offense, Mrs. Gunther, but you are not in full possession of the facts, and it is time someone enlightened you. The duke acted in a most ungentle-manly manner and he threatened to destroy Clara's reputation if she did not accept his proposal. There. Now may we dispense with the arguments?"

Mrs. Gunther stared blankly at Clara and Sophia. "Is this true?"

"Yes," Sophia replied. "He knew about Clara attending the wrong ball that first night. He threat-ened to use it against her."

"But did he actually threaten it," Mrs. Gunther asked, "or merely suggest that she would be better off avoiding the possibility that such a thing might get out?"

"It was a clear threat," Clara said firmly.

Mrs. Gunther's voice took on a desperate tone. "But he is the Duke of Guysborough. You should not have crossed him by refusing him, Clara."

Everyone, including James, gaped at Mrs. Gunther. "Are you saying I should have accepted his proposal, regardless of his behavior?"

"*His* behavior? *He* is not the one with a scandalous past, Clara."

Her meaning was the same. Make a mistake and pay the price. For the rest of your life.

James held up a hand. "I believe this discussion is over. Clara has made up her mind."

"But Your Grace, the duke is.... Well, he's a duke."

"Meaning what, exactly?"

She shifted in her chair. "Meaning Clara would be a duchess. Imagine, two American duchesses, and sisters! It is too good an opportunity to—"

James narrowed his gaze at her. "You would have Clara marry a man who threatened to publicly destroy her?"

"No one would ever have to know about that."

"But I would know!" Clara practically shouted. "I wish to be happy, Mrs. Gunther, and I would not be happy with the Duke of Guysborough."

The older woman's cheeks flushed with smug condescension. "Why not? Because he is not as handsome as the marquess? Mark my words, Clara, a handsome face will not keep you happy when your husband is cavorting with other women right under your nose."

Clara bristled.

James held up a hand again to hush everyone. He turned toward Mrs. Gunther. "I believe, madam, that your duty to my sister-in-law has been fulfilled."

Though she spoke to James, Mrs. Gunther turned her admonishing gaze toward Clara. "She is making a grave mistake, Your Grace."

"I do thank you for your attendance to her," he

added, "but perhaps it is time you returned to America."

Mrs. Gunther rose from her chair and smoothed her hands over her skirt. "If you will excuse me, I am suddenly in need of a rest. I will be in my boudoir." She walked out with her nose pushed high in the air.

Clara sat in silence staring after her chaperone and felt a great weight lift from her shoulders.

After Seger broke the news of his engagement to his stepmother, he retired to his study and realized that the expression on her face had been the same as it had been eight years ago when he'd told her he intended to marry a merchant's penniless daughter.

Only Clara wasn't penniless. She was, however, American and not "one of them."

After Quintina realized that she would not be able to change Seger's mind, she made a point of mentioning that at least with an American bride, their vulgar in-laws would remain on the other side of the Atlantic and would not be dropping by for tea.

Seger sat down at his desk and realized with some chagrin that he was experiencing a slightly perverse pleasure from her exasperation.

A knock sounded at his door just then. "Come in."

Quintina entered. She strode all the way in and stopped before him with her hands clasped in front of her as if she were nervous.

"Yes, Quintina, what is it?"

She hesitated a moment. "I believe, Seger, that I...I would like to invite your fiancée as well as the Duke and Duchess of Wentworth to dine with us one evening next week."

Seger leaned back in his chair and stared. "Pardon me?"

"You heard me the first time. You're just making me repeat it to punish me further."

"None of this is intended to punish you," he replied. "I want to marry Clara Wilson because she delights me. It's as simple as that."

She nodded quickly, almost as if she needed to hush him, as if she did not wish to hear any more explanations of that nature. "Either way, if we are going to be related, we must come to know these people."

He supposed it didn't hurt that Clara's sister was a duchess. American or not, a duchess was a duchess. That was likely what was behind this.

Well, he'd take it. "Magnificent. Send the invitation first thing in the morning."

"Very well." She turned to leave but stopped at the door. "And Seger. Congratulations."

He gazed with surprise at his stepmother, feeling uneasy at her remark, for he knew it was taking every bit of willpower she possessed just to speak the words.

"Thank you," he replied, then returned to his correspondence.

Quintina walked out of her stepson's study and closed the door behind her. She met Gillian in the hall and stopped abruptly. The girl's eyes were red and puffy. She was clutching a handkerchief.

Quintina felt her heart throb painfully in her chest.

"Well?" Gillian asked in a shaky voice.

Quintina put her arm around her distraught niece

and led her toward her boudoir. "Don't worry, my dear. Dry your eyes. I will handle this. I have an English acquaintance—a woman currently abroad in America. She will be a useful connection in New York. Everything will work out just fine. You'll see. Now let us go and fix your hair. From now on, you must always look your best. Come, we will talk about what you will need to do next."

Clara entered Rawdon House with James and Sophia, and handed her cloak over to the butler. She looked up at the crystal chandelier over her head in the entryway, and the numerous, large family portraits that lined the wall up the wide, carpeted staircase. It was difficult to believe this was going to be her home one day, when she became Seger's wife.

Never in her life had she imagined such a future for herself, certainly not when she was a child living in Wisconsin, where stories of princes and dukes and duchesses with coronets on their heads were just fairy tales.

Then, after what had occurred two years ago just after Sophia had married James, Clara believed her future was doomed forever. She never expected to marry a man she adored. She'd expected to have very little choice in the matter and consider herself lucky if anyone was willing to take her on. Or she had expected not to marry at all.

But two years had passed, and that particular time in her life seemed like a distant memory. She could barely even picture Gordon's face in her mind. Thank goodness she had been able to move on.

Clara walked with Sophia and James upstairs to the drawing room. She continued to gaze at the portraits on the second floor. Everyone was very grand. Her belly quivered suddenly at the daunting notion of becoming part of a family such as this.

She followed the butler toward the double doors of the drawing room and tried not to feel intimidated. Instead, she focused on the simple fact that in the very near future, she would share a bed with Seger and it would all be perfectly respectable.

That was the best part in all this. She would not need to worry about being ruined. In fact, it would be her duty to let him "ruin" her. She could hardly wait.

The butler showed them into the drawing room where Lady Rawdon stood by the window, and her niece, who Clara remembered from the assembly, sat by the fireplace. She stood, however, when they all walked in.

"Your Grace," Lady Rawdon said, turning toward James with a warm smile. She approached and greeted each of them, then invited them to sit down.

The woman's gracious manner and her amiable welcome caused a whole slew of Clara's apprehensions to fall away. She found herself smiling in return as she shook hands with Gillian, realizing that this shy young woman was her future cousin by marriage.

Just then, Seger appeared in the doorway. Clara's heart tumbled over itself at the mere sight of him looking so handsome in the light from a wall sconce next to him. He wore a formal black jacket and white waistcoat. His face was pure perfection—all fine lines and classical elegance. But beyond his physical beauty, he possessed a free and open disposition that was such a large part of his extraordinary charisma. In this era of restraint and sexual repression, he was quite the opposite. He exuded an offer of pleasure and laughter.

That, perhaps, was what made people uncomfortable around him. He drew attention. He was extreme in his pursuit of gratification, and he made women think lustful thoughts. Perhaps they worried that it showed. Perhaps they felt their cheeks flushing with desires for this, that, and everything, and they feared the whole world would know it.

Seger's gaze fell upon her, and he smiled. "Clara."

All her senses came alive at the husky sound of his voice and the fierce intensity in his eyes as he entered and approached her, kissed her hand, then greeted James and Sophia. He was so suave and irresistible that he took her breath away.

Oh, she hoped Mrs. Gunther had been wrong about him. Clara prayed she was not making a serious mistake, agreeing to marry a man who would have the power to break her heart into a million pieces, because she adored him so much and he was not so ardent in his affections.

He had told her he would *try* to be faithful. *Try*.

How hard would he try?

A footman entered the room and brought a tray of champagne around. Clara gratefully accepted a glass.

They all stood and talked about wedding plans and about Clara's family: when they would be able to travel to London, where Clara planned to purchase her wedding gown, and other topics related to the upcoming nuptials.

"Had they set a date yet?" someone asked. "Why not next spring?" Lady Rawdon suggested. "Sooner," Seger had replied, with a seductive, knowing glance in Clara's direction.

She felt as if she were watching the conversation from a great distance away.

A short while later, Seger lured Clara to a quiet corner of the room and watched the others, as if to make sure no one was watching.

"You look lovely tonight." He ran a finger along her forearm and up to the top of her long glove. "But you always look beautiful."

"Thank you. I'm nervous, Seger."

"Why? We are engaged now. All is right and proper."

She glanced uneasily at the others, who were laughing about something. "Yes, but it all happened so fast. Aren't you worried? You don't have cold feet?"

He smiled. "If anything, I want to move the wedding date forward. That's how badly I want you. I'd like to move straight to the honeymoon."

He touched her briefly behind the ear, kissed her on the mouth, and sent a wave of gooseflesh down the length of her body. It was all done so quickly, so discreetly, that it left her trembling with desire for something more.

How skilled he was at seduction. He could reduce her to a blob of besotted pudding with a single touch.

She wondered suddenly if he would ever do something like that to another woman in another drawing room one day. Was that how easy it would be?

No, Clara, she quickly chided herself. She had to stop thinking these things. He had told her he would try to be faithful. He had told her he wanted her more than he'd wanted any other woman in a very long time. She would be content with that and enter into this marriage with favorable expectations.

Clara swept all that jealous nonsense away. "I admit, I am looking forward to our honeymoon, too."

"Then let us marry in September."

"Your stepmother suggested the spring."

"Yes, but she's not thinking about what I am thinking about."

Suppressing a chuckle, Clara replied, "I'm afraid to ask."

"Good, because I don't think there are words for it." They walked leisurely around the room, aware of the others talking and laughing.

"October, then?" Seger asked.

Clara raised an eyebrow. "A wedding should not be rushed. There are things to plan, like flowers and music and food."

"It can all be planned in a day if one is focused."

"My gown must be designed and made. That can't be done in a day."

"It can be done in a week for the right price."

"A week! You'd have me wear something plain or unoriginal?"

"I'd have you wear nothing at all if we could do it in private. Honestly, all that wedding business is just for show. I've never cared about what other people think and I would marry you tomorrow in the back garden with only the necessary number of witnesses if you would agree to it."

She sipped her champagne and spoke with a teasing tone. "Are you afraid I'll change my mind?"

He pressed a hand to his chest as if he had been shot. "Good God. I hadn't thought of that. Now that you mention it, I suppose I must consider the possibility. How will I ever keep your interest through the winter, which is so dashedly long and cold?"

"I think the question of the hour is how I will keep *your* interest," she replied.

He stopped walking and leaned in closer. "That will be easy. Just smile like that, wear more dresses like that, and every once in a while, send me a lewd letter."

Clara laughed out loud. The others quieted and glanced at them, then resumed their conversations. Seger and Clara chuckled privately with each other.

"I would give anything to be alone with you right now," he said softly. "I fear this proper behavior where you are concerned will be the death of me."

"I wouldn't want that."

His gaze smoldered. "Then marry me in September."

"You are very persistent."

"When I want something, yes. September?"

"But it is now June. That gives us a little over two months."

"That's two months too long. Let's tell everyone tonight. The wedding will be in September. I can make arrangements for our honeymoon immediately. Would you like to go to Italy? Or perhaps America? You choose, as long as it's in September."

She shook her head at him in disbelief. "Do you never give up?"

"Not when it comes to what I want. Will you agree?"

His tenacity was amusing and flattering and left her feeling warm and excited inside. Unable to resist his enticing, pleading expression, she set her empty glass down on a table and grinned wickedly. "Yes."

"Superb. Now that leaves us two whole months to figure out a way to avoid another scandal."

"What do you mean?" she asked, concern suddenly clouding her thoughts.

"You don't expect me to survive that long without kissing you, do you? Did I mention you might be the death of me?"

Clara laughed again and tapped his chest with the tip of her closed fan. "What are we going to do about that?"

He touched her arm where it was bare, just above the top of her glove and below her short, lacy sleeve. She felt instantly aroused and glanced at the others to make sure they weren't watching.

Seger whispered in her ear. "I still know how to give pleasure without destruction, and I believe you know how to enjoy it. All we require is a location."

She gazed up at him in disbelief. "You're not trying to lure me out to your coach in the middle of the night again, are you?"

"Actually, I had somewhere else in mind. Somewhere much more comfortable, but a good deal riskier. How about tomorrow night?"

Could she even pretend not to be interested in hearing his shocking and appalling plan? Not a chance.

Her mouth curled up in a smirk as she flicked open her fan and waved it in front of her face. "All right. I'll bite. What, pray tell, are the scandalous particulars?"

Seger woke the next morning feeling famished. His future wife was turning out to be a bold and adventurous woman, unlike any of the proper young debutantes he'd met in the past.

He was not sorry, he decided as he sat down in the breakfast room and picked up his newspaper. He needed a woman like her as a wife, someone who would enjoy a little spice in their marriage. Or presently, in their engagement. He could never have married a tame and spiritless young woman. He needed excitement, and Clara, innocent as she was, was proving to him again and again that she suited him absolutely. She had agreed to his shocking proposition—even *he* thought it was shocking—and he would see her tonight. In private.

Maybe with a few well-timed trysts like these, he would survive until September after all. Though it would be a challenge not to deflower her completely. Could he survive that? He had already plucked a good number of petals.

He looked up from the paper when Gillian walked into the breakfast room. "Good morning," he said.

Under her arm, she carried a large, heavy package wrapped in brown paper, and set it down on a chair at the table. She served herself breakfast from the sideboard and took a seat. "It was a nice dinner last night," she said. "Did you enjoy yourself?"

He glanced up from his paper again. His cousin did not usually initiate conversations at breakfast. She was painfully shy, and this attempt to converse surprised him.

Seger casually folded his paper and set it aside. "I did enjoy myself. And you?"

Rarely did Gillian meet his gaze when she spoke to him—or anyone else for that matter—but this morning she made the effort. A few times, at any rate.

It was a shame that she was not more confident, Seger thought. She was not an unattractive young woman, if only she would smile and speak up more often.

"It was delightful," she replied. "I must say, I like Clara very much. She's lovely."

"I'm pleased to hear it."

The conversation stalled for a moment while Gillian ate her breakfast. Seger considered picking up the paper again but did not wish to be rude. He sipped his coffee instead and stared out the window.

"September is a wonderful time for a wedding," Gillian said, surprising him again by resuming the conversation. "Will Clara's family come from America? I understand she has another sister."

"Yes, her name is Adele and she's eighteen. I'm sure she will look forward to meeting you, Gillian. She is out this year for her first Season, just like you."

"I wonder what it would be like to have a Season in New York," Gillian replied. "America sounds like an exciting place. I would like to visit it sometime."

"Perhaps you will."

She smiled at him, though he saw very little joy

in her eyes. He had never seen Gillian sparkle the way Clara did, and he'd known her since she was an infant, when she came with her mother from Scotland to attend Quintina's marriage to Seger's father. Seger had been seven at the time.

Seger also recalled the day they buried Gillian's mother, two years ago. Gillian had wept silently through the entire service. Seger had sat in a pew across from her and watched her wipe her cheeks incessantly under the black netting of her hat, but she never uttered a sound.

She, like him, was an only child—except that she had been extremely close to her mother. Quintina had explained the uncommon bond between them when she received the telegram about her sister's death. Seger had marveled at the bond, realizing he was not able to understand what it could have been like growing up in a house where one did not feel completely alone. Seger had grieved deeply for the young woman's loss.

She must feel very alone now, he thought with more than a little sympathy, though Quintina did her best to be a mother figure.

Gillian finished her breakfast and set down her fork. She reached for the package beside her. "I have something for you, Seger. It's an engagement gift." She stood and brought the gift around the table and handed it to him.

He gazed up at her warmly. "What an unexpected surprise. Thank you, Gillian."

She sat down in Quintina's usual spot while Seger used his breakfast knife to cut the string and open the package.

"The latest edition of *The Popular Atlas*," he said with delight. "What a perfect gift, Gillian. How did you know I enjoy maps?"

"I've noticed that you read a lot of travel books, and the atlas you have is very old. This one is new and has more detail."

He leafed through it. "I dare say it does. This is magnificent. Thank you again." He smiled at her, reached across the table and patted her hand. "I will treasure it always."

Her eyes lit up at the compliment and he was pleased to at last see some evidence of a spark.

Chapter 13

Dear Clara,

Mother is determined to have me follow in your footsteps next year. She has hired an English-woman as my new governess. Mrs. Wadsworth is helping me to learn all about aristocratic etiquette. Just today I learned that if I was ever to break a vase or a glass in a noblewoman's home, I should not offer to pay for it. That would be very bad form. Keep that in mind if you are ever so clumsy, dear sister...

Love,
Adele

SHORTLY BEFORE THREE O'CLOCK IN the morning, Clara tiptoed downstairs to open the door she and Seger had decided upon—the same one she had used to sneak out on the night she met him in his coach.

Tonight, however, she would not go outside. He would come to her. For one hour, while everyone slept, he would share her bed.

It was risky and imprudent she knew, but she was overwhelmingly desperate to be alone with him again. And they were engaged. It wasn't as if she was doing this with a stranger. Seger was going to marry

her. Besides that, it was never too soon to start building upon the foundation that she hoped would grow
into something more. That was perhaps her primary
objective, why she couldn't help but be accommo-
dating to his needs, which at the moment were solely
physical.

Consequently, she had given him detailed instructions on how to make his way through the house in
the dark, and how to find her room. She told him
she would leave her door ajar and light a candle. She
explained which floorboards creaked, and which
doors were routinely left open. Thankfully there
were no dogs in Wentworth House to raise a ruckus,
so Seger could be sure of reaching her room without
incident.

Clara sat on her bed on top of the covers, her
nightgown unbuttoned at the collar, her hair freshly
combed, feeling as if she were waiting for a train to
crash through her door and plow across her bed. Her
heart was pounding, her senses humming as she listened for the slightest sound from outside her room.
The nervous excitement coursing through her veins
was enough to make her giddy.

The clock chimed three times in the entryway
downstairs, then a few more minutes ticked by. Anxious about Seger's safe and undetected arrival, Clara
slipped off her bed and padded to the door to peer out
into the hall.

He wouldn't forget, would he? she wondered uneasily. Maybe he did this sort of thing all the time—snuck
into ladies' bedrooms in the middle of the night—and
it was easy to disregard. He might have fallen asleep.

He might be at a party somewhere and lost track of time.

But then suddenly, without warning, there he was. He appeared like a phantom out of the darkness, backed her into the room, and closed and locked the door quietly behind him. "Let's hope your maid is a sound sleeper," he said in a low, husky voice as he took her face in his hands and kissed her passionately.

The next thing she knew, Clara was being eased down upon the bed. Seger removed his jacket and waistcoat and lay down beside her, leaning over her while running his forefinger down her cheek and neck, causing her to shiver all over with thrilling anticipation.

"I thought you'd never get here," she said.

"Well, I'm here now. Can I convince you to let me stay for two hours, not one?" he whispered with an appealing boyish grin.

"I suspect that in a few minutes, you'll be able to convince me to do just about anything, so give me your word, while I still have control of my senses. One hour, then you must go. Promise."

He nodded and unfastened another button at the collar of her nightgown, gazing flirtatiously into her eyes the whole time. "I'm always making promises where you are concerned. But yes, I promise."

His mouth covered hers and she drank in the exquisite taste of him as he gathered her nightgown in his fist and slowly tugged it upwards.

For a while they kissed and pressed their bodies together on the bed, thrusting and heaving as he used his hands to stroke and pleasure her everywhere. Before long, Clara's nightgown became too great of a hindrance, so she sat up and pulled it off over her head. Suddenly she was naked in the candlelight, without shyness, allowing Seger to gaze openly at her body. Sitting up on her heels, she realized she never knew couples did this sort of thing together. She'd imagined that everything would take place in pitch darkness, under the covers, with the lovers' eyes closed.

"You are so lovely," Seger whispered. Then he eased her onto the soft mattress again and swept his tongue over the rigid peaks of her breasts. Clara wriggled with rapture and had to fight not to let out an impassioned sigh that might wake others in the household. Soon, she was breathless with desire and twisted lasciviously as his mouth covered hers and he kissed her deeply.

It was enough to drive her mad into the beyond. She tore at his neckcloth, then sat up again to pull his shirt off so that she could rub her hands up and down his beautiful muscled chest.

A moment later he was on top of her, kissing, stroking her thighs with his warm hands and flicking his tongue over her swollen nipples. He still wore his trousers, and she suspected it would take a great deal of convincing to get him to take them off. But oh, how her body yearned for more, though more of what she had no idea. There was still so much she had yet to experience.

This was some kind of seventh heaven of rapture, she thought as she squeezed her eyes shut and arched her back and tossed her head to the side on the pillow.

She kissed him deeply, tasting the flavor of her own feminine arousal and losing control of all her senses.

"Please, take these off," she pleaded, tugging at his trousers. "I want to do everything with you. I want you to make love to me."

Seger felt his defenses slip beneath the erotic force of her plea and the pounding ache in his loins. He could not seem to locate the discipline that had always been his unwavering armor. It was that very discipline that had protected him from ambitious debutantes or lonely wives of philandering husbands. He had managed to live a gratifying eight years without ever causing an unwanted pregnancy out of wedlock.

Yet here tonight, he was suddenly willing to risk it all. Consequences meant nothing. He wanted Clara with an overpowering need, but she was his future wife. Could he not relax just this once? Could they not begin their journey now? Why wait for the marriage papers? That was just a formality. Even if he got her with child, they could simply claim that the baby had come early. It happened all the time, didn't it?

He was making excuses. He would say anything to justify making love to her now, with unfettered abandon.

Clara, delightful sexual creature that she was, began to tug at his trousers. He grabbed hold of her hand in an effort to stop her, knowing it was his last vestige of restraint.

"What are you doing, darling? That's dangerous territory."

"I don't care," she said. "I want you. We're engaged. Why not? I've heard it's painful the first time. Why not get that over with now, so that I can enjoy our wedding night without any fears or anxieties?" She kissed his neck and chest and sent him spinning into a world of savage yearning. "I can feel it. Please, Seger...."

She was thrusting her hips against him while she begged. It was too much. He was losing the fight. Then she reached into his trousers and took a firm, determined hold of his desire.

"Please," she whispered again in his ear, more urgently.

The bed seemed to shift beneath him, and that was that.

He reached down in a fumbling panic that was completely outside his natural smooth approach and ripped his pants off like a randy schoolboy.

How much time did they have? A quarter of an hour? Let it be more than that.

A second later he was nude, pressing himself into the soft moist heat between her thighs.

"Are you certain?" he asked one last time, praying she wouldn't change her mind now.

"Yes."

No hesitation there.

She nibbled on his earlobe, leading him into a swirling eddy of pleasure until he was long gone, past the point of no return.

His whole being trembled with need as the head of his desire came to a quiet pause at the entrance to her sweet, welcoming haven. Slowly he edged himself inside as wave upon wave of pleasure enveloped him. He kissed her deeply and she wrapped her legs around his hips, and she pulled him into her, her fingernails digging into the firm flesh of his back.

Her body arched into his. He shifted, hesitated for a moment, then thrust slowly forward, as gently as possible, into the tight hollow between her thighs. It wasn't long before he felt the rupture of her delicate womanhood.

Clara whimpered in his ear and the awareness of the physical pain he had caused her brought him to a halt. "I'm sorry for that," he whispered as he kissed her neck.

She clung to his shoulders and squeezed him tightly. "Don't be. I wanted it."

Pushing himself up on one elbow, the other arm stretched across her, he gazed down at her face in the flickering candlelight. She was the most beautiful woman he'd ever seen. The vision of her beneath him with her hair splayed out on the pillow was so astounding, so humbling, it made his chest ache.

She took his face in her hands and stroked his cheek, then closed her eyes and inhaled deeply.

Feeling a passionate jolt, and awakening from what felt like a dream, Seger paused for a moment to think, realizing this was only the second time in his life that he had taken a woman's virginity. It had been twelve years since the first time, and he had not thought about it in ages. Tonight, he felt almost like a virgin himself.

Lowering his mouth to hers, careful not to hurt her, Seger pushed more deeply into her soft, heated depths. Together they moved in harmony, seeking a satisfaction they had both been craving since the first night they'd met and kissed under the stairs.

She was his now. Forever. She would be his wife and share his bed each night. He wanted it to begin now. He didn't want to wait two months, but this was how the world worked, he supposed.

Suddenly a pounding wave of pleasure crashed over him and he quickened inside his future wife, feeling a blinding rush of gratification. She dug her fingernails into his back and pushed her hips upward, squeezing around him.

Just then, somewhere in the house, a clock chimed four times. He collapsed upon Clara, utterly spent.

Clara tried to lift her head off the pillow, but it fell back. "Stay where you are," she whispered. "You're not going anywhere."

"But I made you a promise," he replied, ribbing her on, without withdrawing from the splendors of her womanhood.

"This is the one and only time I will let you break a promise to me."

He chuckled at that.

"Unless we are in this same situation again," she added, "in which case I hope you will do whatever I ask." Her voice trailed off. *"I had no idea it could feel like this."*

He kissed her cheeks and nose and felt a great groundswell of affection.

She'd just said *she* had no idea it could feel like this, when in fact it was he who was bewildered. He had just made love to a virgin—a virgin he'd already proposed to—and he felt wholly content. All seemed right with the world, except for the fact that he would soon have to slip out of her bed and make a hasty departure.

His gaze roamed over her face, then he rolled off her.

He was accustomed to this routine—rolling off a lady, then reaching for his trousers and making himself scarce—but tonight it felt wrong and frustrating and the reaction was completely foreign to him. He felt like he was already home, and he should not have to leave.

Clara snuggled into him and rested her cheek on his chest. "I wish you didn't have to go."

"Me too."

"When will we be able to do this again? I'm not sure I can wait until September."

He was quite certain that he couldn't. "Then let's get married sooner."

She rose up on an elbow. "Really? How soon are you thinking?"

"Tomorrow would be nice."

She chuckled softly. "Tomorrow would be nice indeed, but my mother won't arrive until next week."

"I look forward to meeting her," he magnanimously replied. "What about next week, then, by special license?"

Clara's eyebrows lifted. "All of my family needs to be here."

"They could all get here within a week, couldn't they?"

She stared at him for a moment, considering it. "Your stepmother is making plans for September."

"Plans can be changed. There is no reason to wait.

In fact, it's dangerous to wait because I am sure I won't be able to stay away from you, and we can only rely on luck for so long. We'll get caught eventually, and on top of that, we'd go insane. I would at any rate."

"I would, too."

He held her cheek in his hand. "Then marry me sooner than September. Put me out of my misery."

"There would be talk."

"You know I don't care about that sort of thing."

Clara sat up and grinned at him. "Why are you so persistent all the time? I can never say no to you."

He brought a finger to his lips to remind her to speak softly. "Shh. And I don't want you to say no. I want you to say yes."

"I already said yes. To everything so far. We have to draw the line somewhere."

Seger frowned. "Why draw a line? Why deny ourselves? Why not simply have what we want?"

She stared at him in the candlelight, then her face changed. Her voice lost its playful tone. "You're used to that, aren't you?"

"What do you mean?"

"Taking what you want without considering the practicalities or social restrictions. Must everything be about pleasure and immediate self-gratification? Is that all you want?"

"Clara," he whispered as he sat up. "Don't."

She continued whispering angrily, as if he hadn't spoken. "Can you not abide by society's rules just this once and suffer through the usual betrothal?" She reached for her nightgown and pulled it on over her head, then climbed off the bed and walked to the window where she stood with her back to him.

Seger raked a hand through his hair. "Something tells me there is more to that question than the obvious."

It almost seemed as if she wanted to make him wait—in order to use their engagement as a test of his ability to resist temptations.

She merely shrugged.

He climbed off the bed and went to her. He stood behind her, feeling the soft fabric of her gown against his nude front. He tried to ignore the urge to take her into his arms, carry her back to the bed and plunge into her again, to go back to the way they were feeling only a few moments ago.

"I don't deserve this," he whispered. "I've never taken what I wanted from you when I had every opportunity. Even tonight I would have resisted if *you* had not been so persistent."

The fact that he was even discussing this was astonishing. Any of his previous lovers would be shocked to see him defending himself like this. It was a tremendous concession, and he wished she knew that.

She dropped her face into her hands. "Maybe you should go."

"Go? Why?" He tried to keep the shock and anger out of his voice because he was afraid that if he didn't, someone might hear them. He had to keep this argument to a whisper. "What's this really about?"

She said nothing for a few seconds, then turned to face him. Her eyes were filling with tears. "I'm nervous about marrying you."

He tried not to let her confession vex him, but it

did. It damn well did. He had come forward leaps and bounds to reach this point with her. He had proposed to her, for pity's sake!

She bowed her head. "You can't blame me for being unsure. I am a prime target for fortune hunters, and you have made it very clear that you don't truly love me. How can I be sure you will be a good husband?"

He backed away from her. "I am no fortune hunter. You know that."

She merely stared at him.

"This is about my being faithful to you," he said.

God, women were so bloody complicated. Normally, he would walk away when his bed partner began to talk like this, or even hint at talking like this, but with Clara, he couldn't. He was in for the long haul and there was no turning back now. Not after what they'd done tonight.

She let out a heavy breath. "If you can't endure two months, how can I be sure you'll be able to endure any reasonable length of time in a marriage? Sometimes there are temptations, and I'm afraid you are not even going to try to resist them. What about when I am enormous with child and unable to perform my wifely duty? What if I become ill? I won't be attractive to you then. Will you go back to your usual entertainments?"

He turned away from her and picked up his trousers. "Maybe I *should* go."

She watched him pull them on. The volume of her voice rose a fraction. "Wait, Seger."

"The servants will be up soon."

He donned his shirt, then sat down on a chair to

pull on his boots in a hurry. He wanted to get out of there. He felt her hovering over him. Women never did that to him. They knew better than to push. They knew that if he was going to return another day, they would have to let him go without a fight.

He felt impatient with Clara, for he was not accustomed to rules or controls. For eight years he had lived freely. He had steered away from responsibility and commitment.

He didn't like feeling impatient with her. She was different from the others. He didn't want to feel this way with her, but he supposed that old habits were not so easy to change. *This bloody boot!*

Clara followed him around the bed. "I didn't mean to make you angry. It's just that a lot has happened these past few days, and we just.... We just...."

Her voice shook and Seger looked up.

She was distraught. He'd just taken her virginity and all her choices were gone. She probably felt vulnerable and confused, and—what was wrong with him?—she was most certainly sore down there. Bloody hell, he was an idiot. He knew nothing. In eight years, he had never let himself feel responsible for a woman's happiness. He'd avoided women who pushed toward intimacy and commitment. Now suddenly here he was, up to his ears in commitment and obligation and probably tears, too, if this continued in the direction it seemed to be going.

He was completely out of his realm of experience. He was fine with seductions and physical attachments—more than fine—but he didn't know the first thing about emotional intimacy and how to handle a

woman who was upset. But now he was to be someone's husband and he had no choice but to stay. He
couldn't don his boyish charm and tease his way out
the room like he normally did.

He suddenly felt as if he had bitten off more than he
could chew.

Then he saw Clara's nightgown quiver and knew
she was fighting a full-blown sob.

He couldn't let her cry. Someone would hear. He
felt a shameless, shallow need to stop her from crying,
only to keep the silence, and an even more shallow
need to get out of there as soon as she collected herself.

Something else took over, however. Perhaps it was
compassion or affection for Clara. Perhaps it was
merely the need to fix the situation. He had no idea.

Before he knew what he was doing, he had crossed
the room and was gathering her into his arms. All that
mattered to him was her comfort and happiness. Her
needs became more important than his own.

His voice was gentle and soothing. "Why did you
insist we make love if you weren't sure?"

She shook her head and whispered, "I couldn't
think about anything except that I wanted you. Now
it's settling in, and I think I've just realized the gravity
of what we've done, and I'm scared. I feel very alone."

Alone. She felt alone? His heart began to pound.

"But I can't do anything about it," she continued,
wiping under her nose, "because I can't turn back the
clock."

He rubbed her shoulders and stroked her hair. "And
the fact that you can no longer change your mind

about marrying me has spooked you."

She nodded.

It bloody well spooked him, too, but he knew better than to say it.

"There is nothing to fear, Clara. We'll be married soon. If we hadn't done this tonight, we would have done it eventually—on our honeymoon at least, which is only two months away. A mere sliver in time. Do not feel that you are alone."

But how would he ever prevent her from feeling that way? He was here. He'd just made love to her, and she felt alone. Even though he was holding her in his arms.

Clara nodded, and he relaxed somewhat, knowing he had eased her mind a fraction, at least. Still, the urge to leave lingered, and he wasn't sure how much of it was a result of the servants' impending appearance, or the subject matter of this conversation.

Either way, he had to go, and she knew it. At least he had a good reason to slip out. Quickly, he pulled on his waistcoat and jacket while she watched him in silence. "I really do have to go before people are up and about."

"I know." She crossed toward him, looking vulnerable and uncertain. Even her voice had changed. It did not hold her usual confidence. "I'm sorry, Seger. Now I feel foolish for the things I said. I wish you didn't have to leave."

He gathered her into his arms again. "No need to feel foolish. You did something you hadn't planned to do tonight. It's only natural."

Natural that she would regret what they'd done.

Something tightened in his chest, but he tried to ignore it because he didn't understand it. He'd never felt any self-doubt after making love to a woman. He'd always walked away secure in the knowledge that he had pleased his partner and the session had been a success.

He should walk away now. He wanted to, but he couldn't seem to do it. He couldn't leave her like this. "Let's do it sooner."

Her eyes were wide with innocence as she blinked up at him. "Do what?"

"Get married, like I said before. I know that's what started this argument, but you don't need to make me wait to test me against temptation. Let me marry you and prove that I am completely devoted. If I were not, I would be putting it off. I want you and no one else. That is what lies at the heart of this. It's why I want to skip the elaborate wedding and keep it simple. We could do it the week after next."

What the bloody hell was he doing? The more uncertain he became, the faster and deeper he dug the hole.

"Seger, you don't have to say that to make me feel better."

"I'm not trying to make you feel better." But he was, and he knew it. "I just don't want to wait, it's as simple as that. Besides, you might be carrying my child."

Worry flooded her eyes.

It was wretched of him to resort to that, but he forged ahead. "Let's make the leap. You will have my total commitment and I promise, after the wedding day, all these doubts and fears will disappear." What he really meant was that if he put a ring on her finger and signed the papers, she wouldn't feel guilty about making love to him, and they wouldn't need to have this difficult conversation again.

"You will be my wife," he added, "and we will become a respectable married couple. Who could ever have imagined it?"

That at least got a smile out of her. "I think I'd like to be respectable."

Seger chuckled. *"You* would? I'm about to enter a whole new world."

The tension lifted and she rested her forehead on his chest. "What about the honeymoon? You've made arrangements for September."

"We'll simply wait and go then. This way, you'll have time to settle in to your new home."

She laughed at the absurdity of such a rushed affair. "Go, before someone catches you sneaking out of here."

"Not without an answer." She was still resting her forehead on his chest and he wished he could see her face. "An answer, darling. The week after next?"

She gazed up at him in the candlelight, then at last she replied, "All right, but only because I want to share a bed with you again."

Her answer pleased him greatly. What could he say? He was a man, and bed was the one place he felt confident in knowing his way around.

He turned to leave, but Clara stopped him with a question. "Seger? Was I your first virgin?"

He halted, closed his eyes, and wished she had not

asked him that. "What does it matter?" He did not see the point in the question.

"But was I?"

He slowly turned, faced her, and paused. "No."

"Have there been many?"

"No. Only one."

She blinked a few times. "Daphne?"

"Yes."

Hearing a thump in one of the upstairs bedrooms, Seger knew it was time for him to vamoose. He hesitated a moment, however, for he could see the distress in Clara's eyes and wished he could stay to make it disappear. He wanted her to know that Daphne was in the past. She was forgotten. There was no need for Clara to feel as if *she* were not the most important woman in the world to him.

Another thump sounded over their heads.

He had to go.

He kissed Clara on the mouth, then backed out of the room. He noted however, that he left without his usual indulgent, flirtatious smile.

When the news of her stepson's sudden haste to marry the American heiress reached Quintina's ears the next day, she gazed helplessly across the breakfast table at Gillian. Time seemed to stand still for a few seconds.

An *American*. Quintina could have spit on her toast.

All was quiet, until Gillian burst into tears and ran out.

Quintina sat in her chair, staring blankly at the wall. She felt numb. Sick. Disgusted. How could this have happened? Marriage terrified Seger. He had never been willing to face the permanence or the commitment. Nor had he been willing to let go of the past, in particular the daughter of an insipid, working-class merchant.

At least *she* had been English.

Quintina had foolishly believed that she had all the time in the world to make Gillian the next Lady Rawdon. She had thought her niece was the only young woman with even the slightest chance with Seger because she was the only one Seger spent any time with on a regular basis—the only unmarried girl who didn't apply any pressure, the sort of pressure that always made him rebel into extreme bachelorhood.

Quintina had also believed that she could put an end to his engagement and send Gillian in to take over where the heiress had left off, after having lit the stove, so to speak.

A sudden heated rage rose up inside Quintina. Gillian had been waiting forever. She'd wanted Seger since she was a girl!

Quintina rose from her chair, picked up a vase full of flowers from the sideboard, and smashed it on the floor.

The American. In two weeks. It couldn't be true.

She took a number of deep breaths to calm herself, then left the breakfast room and informed the housekeeper that she required a carriage right away. She had to send an urgent telegram to America. She could not let this marriage take place.

Chapter 14

Dear Clara,
He must truly love you if he is willing to give up
his way of life for you. If you want to be happy,
you must believe that in your heart.
Love,
Adele

BEATRICE WILSON OF NEW YORK stepped out of
the grand ducal coach and onto the pavement.
Wearing a flounced traveling gown that made her look
even shorter and plumper than she was naturally, she
gazed up at Wentworth House from beneath a wide
brimmed, purple plumed hat.

This was the home of a duke. Her daughter's home.
A wave of satisfaction washed over her.

Her maid stepped out behind her just as Beatrice's
two daughters came running out the front door to
greet her.

"Mother," Sophia said. "You're here at last."

They hugged and laughed, then Clara and Sophia
stepped back to give their mother room to breathe.

"You both look beautiful," Beatrice said. "Congratulations, Clara. I can't wait to meet this marvelous
young man you have captured, and Sophia, I must see

my grandchildren."

"Of course. Come inside."

A footman took care of the trunks, while the house-keeper greeted Beatrice's maid and showed her to her room in the servants' quarters.

A short while later, Beatrice was in the nursery picking up her newest grandson, John, second in line to the dukedom. "What a beautiful boy you are," she cooed, letting him clasp her finger. "Sophia, what an accomplishment. Two sons in two years. The dowager must be pleased."

"She is, Mother. I never thought I would say it, but we've become very close."

Clara gathered Liam into her arms.

"And you...." Beatrice said, turning to Clara. "You are about to marry a marquess. My two girls. What legends you have become back home. Sophia tells me your marquess is devastatingly handsome. No doubt your children will be the envy of all the mothers in England."

Clara smiled, wondering if the future heir to the title was already planted in her womb. "He is handsome, Mother. And charming and wonderful. I'm very happy."

"I'm glad. You deserve it. The world has come around right, has it not?"

"Yes, Mother," Clara replied, knowing her mother was referring to that dreadful time two years ago, when it felt like any hope for respectability had been lost forever.

"How is Adele?" she asked, wanting to change the subject.

"Adele is having a wonderful time going to parties and balls, but she has not written off the possibility of a London Season of her own. She might wish to come next year and explore the spoils London has to offer—spoils which seem to be quite impressive, judging by what you two have accomplished."

She winked at Clara and swayed from side to side to rock the baby. "I've hired an English governess for Adele," she continued, "and the woman is spectacular. She knows all about the aristocracy and tells me she has connections here as well. Though of course, what better recommendation can a young woman have than to be the sister of a duchess and a marchioness?" Beatrice's eyes glimmered with pride. "I am so proud of both of you."

"You will be even more proud," Sophia said, "when you meet the marquess and his family at the Wilkshire Ball. May I be the first to tell you that the date of the wedding has been moved up since yesterday? They're going to be married next week, Mother. They are that much in love."

Beatrice's mouth fell open. "You don't say. Then it is true."

"What's true, Mother?" Clara asked.

"That it's a love match. The newspapers in America are churning the story out like butter."

Clara laughed out loud. "But where would they hear such a thing?"

"Heaven knows. The only thing that matters is that you are an American heroine." She affectionately wiggled Clara's nose. "I can't wait to meet this man of yours."

Sophia approached and put her arm around Clara. "You will approve of Lord Rawdon, Mother. I am sure of it."

"A marquess? You needn't wonder if I will approve. Handsome or not, I will adore him."

Beatrice Wilson did, of course, adore him. Clara watched her mother meet Seger in the ballroom with a look of pure wonder—a look that had more to do with how handsome he was than the simple fact that he was an English lord.

After their engagement was announced publically, everyone seemed to suddenly share her mother's opinion. It had been many years since Seger frequented society ballrooms, and Clara guessed that most of these people were finally admitting to their fascination with him, for he was like no other man in London. He had always been a novelty, and now the powerful Duke of Wentworth had welcomed the fallen marquess into his family, and people were at last free to admire him. He was accepted.

Clara stood off to the side alone, watching Seger dance with his cousin, Miss Flint, and watching his stepmother beam with happiness. The woman appeared pleased to see her son moving about in good society again. Clara was proud to have played a part in that.

Just then, an attractive woman wearing a dark crimson gown, with rubies sewn into the skirt, approached her. She was Lady Cleveland and she was exceptionally beautiful.

"You mustn't stare," Lady Cleveland said. "Everyone else is doing a fine job of that, and you shall have him all to yourself soon enough."

Clara turned to face her, and the woman raised a coquettish, arched eyebrow.

"You must tell me how you did it, Miss Wilson."

Clara tried not to squeeze her champagne glass too tightly. "And you are referring to...?"

"How you snared him. He doesn't need your foreign money, so however did you manage to turn a man who has such a great predisposition toward bachelorhood into the marrying kind?"

Clara could barely swallow as she gazed at the woman beside her, whose eyes raked over Clara with a sneer. "I didn't snare him."

The woman smirked. "Well, whatever you did, I could kill you for it. I only hope you will allow him some freedom eventually and won't become one of those jealous wives."

Clara had to fight to breathe over the fury welling up inside her. "If you would make your meaning clear, Lady Cleveland."

The woman kept her gaze on the dancers as she sipped her champagne. "I thought I already had."

The dance ended and Seger escorted Miss Flint to Quintina, then immediately made his way across the floor to where Clara stood with Lady Cleveland.

"My lady," he said, bowing over her hand and placing a kiss on her gloved knuckles. "It is a pleasure, indeed."

"The pleasure is all mine, my lord," she replied in a low voice that held a dozen-and-one hidden meanings. It was more than clear that these two had a history together and Lady Cleveland wanted it known. "I believe congratulations are in order."

"Yes, I see you've met my fiancée."

The woman gave Clara a haughty look down the length of her nose. "I have indeed. She is very sweet, Seger. Not your usual type."

The intimate manner in which she spoke his given name made all the tiny hairs on the back of Clara's neck stand up. She would have liked to empty her champagne glass over the top of the woman's head, but resisted the urge, tempting as it was.

Seger merely watched the dancers. "It's been awhile, Lady Cleveland," he said.

"Indeed, it has. Where have you been hiding, Seger? Besides the usual haunts."

"I haven't been hiding at all," he replied.

"Then why haven't I seen you?"

He paused. "Because I've been occupied lately. But I expect you'll see more of me, now that I am 'out.'"

Lady Cleveland threw back her head and laughed. "And a magnificent debut it was, Seger." She gave his arm a little squeeze as she moved around him to take her leave. "I hope I will see you later," she said quietly in his ear. "These things can be so frightfully dull. I may be in need of some entertainment after supper."

Clara watched her fiancé's eyes follow the other woman across the room, then he picked up a glass of champagne from a passing footman and turned his attention back to her. "Clara, I feel your ire like a cold North wind."

"Can you blame me?"

He glanced back at Lady Cleveland. "Don't worry

about her. She's just bored, that's all, and she enjoys a little competition."

"She said she hoped I wouldn't be a jealous wife, and that I wasn't your type."

"She didn't mean anything by it. In fact, I would take it as a compliment." He sipped his champagne.

Clara watched the woman on the opposite side of the room. "She didn't intend it to be a compliment. Not if she considers herself to be your type."

"She doesn't. She's just a friend."

"A friend? I hardly think so."

Seger downed the rest of his champagne. "So, you *are* going to be a jealous wife. That might be a problem, Clara. How will I ever live up to my scandalous reputation after next week?"

Her eyes widened in horror until she realized that Seger was joking. He was gazing down at her with a teasing smile.

"Why don't we dance?" he said, setting his champagne glass on a tray. "Are you free for the next one?"

"I am."

She followed him onto the floor and worked hard to bury her insecurities. She wanted to be close to Seger and making accusations like these would not foster a sense of confidence between them.

She shook her head at herself. "I apologize. I didn't like how she was flirting with you, that's all. It was her fault not yours."

He drew her into his arms to begin a waltz. "Let's not talk anymore about Lady Cleveland. Let's talk about you. Your mother is delightful," he said. "She is everything I imagined she would be. Cheerful, high-spirited and thoroughly American."

Clara tried to push Lady Cleveland from her mind. "My mother adores you. It was obvious the second she laid eyes on you."

"But does she know you refused a duke before you accepted my proposal?"

Clara chuckled at the reminder. "I told her everything on the day she arrived. Don't worry, she is not like Mrs. Gunther. My mother covets British titles, certainly, but to her, one is as good as any other. Precedence is merely incidental."

They moved to the center of the ballroom, and Seger held Clara with confidence as he led her through the dance.

"When will your father and sister arrive?" he asked. "You'll be pleased to see them, no doubt."

Despite the pleasant subject matter of their conversation, Clara began to feel a distance between them that had not existed before. She knew it stemmed from what happened the other night, when she'd made demands on him. Her displeasure over Lady Cleveland didn't help matters.

But perhaps this change was a good thing, she tried to tell herself. Perhaps they were moving beyond the surface flirtations and she was getting to know the real man beneath it all. Perhaps it was time to be serious.

"They'll be here for the wedding," she replied, "but with not an hour to spare. My father is a very busy man. He works hard."

"I don't doubt it. To have built such a fortune from nothing, he must be ambitious."

Was she being foolish, or did this feel like polite small talk between strangers?

"Speaking of fortunes," Clara said carefully, "I read, in one of the New York newspapers Mother brought, that you turned down what my father offered as a marriage settlement. It was the biggest headline on the society page."

Seger gazed into her eyes. "We live in strange times indeed if you learn of those details in the newspaper. How in the world did something like that get out?"

Clara shrugged as she let him lead her through another turn. "What I want to know is why you turned it down. The newspaper called it a love match and we both know that's not true."

His brow furrowed at her comment and the tone with which it was delivered. "I beg to differ. Why so cynical, Clara?"

"I don't mean to be. It's just that I came here expecting my engagement to be a financial transaction, and you've insisted that's not why you want me. Maybe I'm just finding it hard to believe, that it could be so perfect. I'd hate to think that you only wanted me in your bed, and now that you've had me, you might regret proposing so impulsively."

She stopped on the dance floor.

Seger stopped, too, and he looked tired all of a sudden. His shoulders rose and fell with a sigh. He glanced around the room. "That is not the case."

"But *why* did you turn down the settlement?"

He took his time answering. "Because I didn't want there to be any speculation that I married you for your money. I didn't want you to have to worry about that."

"Why would you think I would worry? And I thought you didn't care what other people thought."

He was quiet for a few seconds. "Come, we're missing the dance." He gathered her into his arms again and moved across the floor.

"I still don't understand," she said, knowing she should let it go. She was pushing him to talk when he didn't seem in the mood. This—after she'd just told herself to let go of her insecurities. "It's just not the way these transatlantic marriages are usually done," she said with resignation.

Seger spun her around. "You underestimate your charms, darling. And don't worry, your father didn't get off entirely scot-free, and you won't have to decrease your spending. He insisted on providing you with a monthly allowance for his own peace of mind, and I agreed. You will, like your sister, have your own bank account and your own money, so you will have the freedom to spend what you like without having to ask your husband for a handout."

Clara absorbed his meaning and gazed up at him with consternation. "No, no, that's not why I'm asking you about the settlement. I don't want you to think that I'm worried about my financial situation. Truly, I don't care about the money. It's you I want."

He raised a flirtatious eyebrow at her and smiled. "I'm glad. And at least we agree on one thing—that the wedding night can't come soon enough."

His seductive gaze traveled over her face and caused an intense flare of heat inside her. It was the first time he had flirted with her all evening and she was surprised by how relieved she was to bob back to the surface—back to the superficiality. She was relieved that he was behaving more like his old self, the charmer that enjoyed flirting with her.

The following week passed quickly for Seger, with decisions to make about the honeymoon and ten-dozen details about the ceremony to work out. He was glad. Glad to be busy, glad to be one day closer to the finale. He would be even happier when it was over, when all this commotion would settle down.

He woke on his wedding day, however, to the unfortunate sound of thunder booming just over the house. Rain beat noisily against his window and poured down the panes, almost as if someone were standing on the roof, dumping buckets of water.

He tossed the covers aside and sat up on the edge of the bed. Sleepily, he walked to the window. The fog was so thick, he could not even see the street. Lightning flashed, then thunder boomed again.

A fine day for a wedding.

He washed and ate breakfast in silence in his room. Calmly, he read the newspaper. An hour later, he decided it was time to dress. He was about to summon his valet when a knock sounded at his door and a footman entered carrying a silver salver with a letter upon it. A telegram, Seger discovered as he picked it up.

It was from an anonymous person in New York.

YOU SHOULD HAVE TAKEN THE SETTLE-MENT STOP YOUR BRIDE IS A LIAR STOP

YOU'RE NOT THE FIRST STOP ASK HER
ABOUT THE EMBEZZLEMENT STOP

He read it again. "What the bloody hell?"

Seger turned it over, looking for a clue about who would send such a thing, but there was nothing to reveal who had written it.

Perhaps it was a scandalmonger who had read about their marriage in the newspapers and wished to create havoc.

He flipped it over again. *You're not the first.*

Of course he was the first. He knew he was. He had made love to Clara a week ago and she had been a virgin. There was no doubt about that.

But then, what the hell was the person referring to, and what embezzlement?

Seger rose from his chair and walked to the window. Looking out at the storm, he made a fist and tapped it a few times against the dark oak frame. They were to be married that day. In three hours to be exact.

He felt an urgent need to know the facts behind this note before he said "I do."

A half hour later, he was stepping out of his coach in front of Wentworth House and dashing through the cold, hard rain to the door. He noticed the look of concern on the butler's face when he informed him that he wished to speak to Miss Wilson but paid it no heed. He followed the butler upstairs to the drawing room, where he had to wait a significant number of minutes before Clara appeared.

Finally, she walked in wearing a simple green morning dress. Her hair was elegantly adorned with pearls and white flowers and combs that sparkled.

He saw the apprehensive expression on her face, watched her wring her hands together in front of her, and regretted coming there unexpectedly and in a panic. He was surely causing her great distress. She probably feared he was about to call everything off.

"You look lovely," he said, crossing the room to take her hands in his, kissing them and hopefully easing her mind.

She spoke with uncertainty. "Thank you. Why are you here?"

He tried to convey warmth with his voice and expression, for he did not wish to cause her any further anxiety. Surely a woman's wedding day was filled with enough anxiety as it was, without the groom barging into the bride's house two hours before the ceremony to ask accusing questions. He would try not to let it sound that way, at least until he knew the particulars.

"I received a telegram this morning from someone in America, but it was anonymous. I wanted to ask you about it. The sender mentioned an embezzlement. He suggested you were not being entirely honest with me."

Clara felt her heart go *thump* inside her chest. All she could do was stare bewildered at her fiancé and wonder how and why this telegram had come to him today at the worst possible time.

She had told Seger about Gordon proposing to her, but she had not told him everything. She had not explained all the details and complexities. Now she wished she had.

Looking back on it, however, there had never been an opportunity to bring it up. After Seger proposed, she thought she could tell him later, when it would hardly matter.

It hardly mattered now, she tried to tell herself. The embezzlement had nothing to do with her. She had known nothing about it. She was merely an innocent bystander.

She would tell Seger that.

Clara sat down on the sofa. "You remember the man I told you about? The man who proposed to me two years ago?"

Seger remained standing. His expression was calm. "Yes."

Clara's heart began to pound faster. "Well, the reason I didn't marry him was because…he was arrested for theft and embezzlement."

Seger stood motionless, staring down at her. She gazed into his eyes. He didn't seem angry. He didn't seem anything.

"It's a rather strange story, actually," she said with a smile, trying to keep things light.

She hoped he would be understanding about this. He, of all people in the world, should be. He—the king of scarlet pasts….

"Tell me."

She nodded and complied. "His name was Gordon Tucker, and when he proposed, my father refused to let me marry him. I told Gordon I would marry him anyway, despite my parents' wishes, but he knew he could never afford to take me away, so he stole from his employer. I assure you, I knew nothing about that.

All I knew was that he had somehow managed to pay for our passage to Europe. He told me he was in possession of enough savings to tide us over until he could find work when we got there. We were going to get married on board the ship. I suppose he thought that once we were married, Father would have no choice but to provide us with an allowance."

Seger's eyebrows drew together, and for the first time, she saw mild anger in his face. "Did you love this man? You must have felt very passionate if you were willing to run off with him."

She bowed her head and paused a moment before answering. She had been enamored with Gordon, certainly. He was handsome and he knew how to charm her, how to manipulate her, but she had never been in love with him. Not in the deeper sense. "No," she answered at last.

"How can I be sure you are telling me the truth? The telegram warned me that you could be...."

Clara looked up. "That I could be what?"

He paused a moment before speaking candidly. "It said you were a liar."

A lump rose up in Clara's throat. "No, that's not true. Please, Seger. You need to believe me when I tell you that I was terrified getting on the ship with him, and I wept with relief when my father came to take me home. When I said yes to Gordon's proposal, I only wanted to escape the pressure."

"The pressure to marry well," Seger said, needing clarification.

"Yes."

He took a moment to consider this, while she sat

helplessly, not knowing what to say, wishing she knew what was going on inside his head. Was he furious with her? Did he hate her?

Or was he hurt?

"So, you didn't love him," Seger said, beginning to pace. "Did you desire him? He didn't take your virginity, but did you ever let him touch you?"

The question unnerved her. It was clear that for Seger, desire was paramount.

"Yes, I did."

He stared at her for a moment, then turned toward the window. "Where is this man now?"

"He went to prison for the embezzlement."

Seger faced her again. "Prison? Good God. There was a trial? Were you involved in the scandal?"

"No, my father took care of that. I was removed from the situation."

Seger's broad shoulders rose and fell. He looked fatigued. "So, there was much more to this than what you told me at your sister's assembly. This is very serious, Clara. You should not have kept it from me."

She saw the disappointment in his eyes and wished more than anything that she had told him about it sooner. She hadn't set out to keep a secret from him, but she'd considered it to be a stain on her character and she had feared that no one would ever want her if they knew. She had therefore pushed it from her mind. Perhaps it had been her way of pretending—at least to herself—that it hadn't happened, because she regretted it terribly.

"I couldn't tell you at first," she said. "I barely knew you. It's not something I would ever talk about with a stranger. Then, when things started to progress between us, I simply forgot about it when we were together."

"Forgot about it." His tone suggested he didn't believe her. Then he faced the window again. "Have you told me everything?"

"Yes."

"Are you sure? There is nothing else I should know about? Because whoever sent this telegram knows about what happened, and if you are guilty in any way...."

"I am not guilty."

"You're telling the truth?"

"Yes!"

Clara wondered again if he was hurt. If he was, he certainly wasn't showing it. He was focusing on the facts, not his feelings. She should not be surprised.

"Who do you think would have sent this?" he asked. "And why?"

"I don't know."

"Perhaps it was your jilted lover."

"Perhaps." She hated to hear him use the word *lover* to describe another man.

Seger paced about the room, considering everything. "Do you realize that in my position, I would be perfectly justified to call off our wedding?"

His coarse words cut painfully into her heart. She nodded.

"But we have already made love," he continued, "and you were, as it turned out, a virgin." He paced the room, thinking for a long time.

Clara waited nervously for him to make a decision.

What would it be? He had been hurt once before by a woman. Perhaps he felt defeated again. Powerless. Perhaps he was disappointed in Clara and would not be able to forgive her. Or maybe this turn of events had spooked him and reminded him of why he had spent the past eight years avoiding marriage.

This was torture.

At last, he stopped pacing. "I believe we are tied to each other," he said.

Clara closed her eyes. Of course, that was how he would see this—as if she had roped and bound him and he could no longer get away. He would not speak of hurt feelings or disappointments. He would speak only of the necessity of duty and obligation.

"It was not my intention to trap you," she said. "And you're free to go if you want to. I won't hold you to your proposal." It was her pride talking because the last thing she wanted was to lose him.

He did not respond to that. He merely went on as if she had not spoken. "I am hardly in the position to call the kettle black, so we will be married as planned. And I hope that this matter will not arise again after today, and that whoever sent this telegram will let it die. If not, and there is a scandal, then I will deal with it."

"I don't wish to be a problem you have to deal with," she said.

"Scandal is rarely a problem for me. I've learned that one can be perfectly happy outside of society. Sometimes I wonder why I ever wanted to get back in. Oh, yes. Because of desire."

And now because of obligation. Clara's mood sank.

He came around the sofa and stared down at her with cool, detached eyes. "We must simply put this behind us, Clara. You are a beautiful woman and I still desire you."

Was that all? A basic physical attraction? Had this conversation spoiled their chances for anything deeper?

She felt as if she had taken one step forward with Seger—they were getting married after all—but two steps back as far as true intimacy was concerned.

Finally, a small fragment of affection found its way back into his eyes, and he kissed her hand. "I will see you in a few hours?"

"Yes."

"Good."

With that, and nothing more, he walked out, leaving Clara feeling as if she knew him less now than she had the first time she'd met him.

Chapter 15

"*I* CANNOT BELIEVE HE IS GOING through with it," Quintina said to Gillian in the carriage on the way to the church. "What in the world did she say to him to prevent him from calling it off?"

Gillian gazed listlessly out the rain-soaked window. "Maybe she lied."

"We can only hope. If she did, there might be a chance for an annulment. He could claim fraudulent misrepresentation or something of that nature."

Gillian turned to her. "How do you know about that sort of thing, Auntie?"

Quintina's eyes bored into Gillian's. "I've been reading up on it, my dear, trying to find ways to shift things in our favor. The last time this happened, Henry—God rest his soul—had used an iron fist to stop Seger's marriage, but I don't have that option. Seger is the marquess now and he has an iron will of his own. We must be more conniving and move him to end it himself. Believe me, if there is any way to terminate this, I will find it. I am not one to give up hope."

"But he is going to marry her today, Auntie. After that, there won't be any hope."

Quintina gazed at her niece, saw the pained look in her eye, and remembered the day Susan had died. A sickness had spread through her body, and for weeks leading up to the end, it caused her excruciating pain that made her writhe on the bed. Quintina had found it difficult to stay with her, for it was too horrific to watch. Grotesque, really. She had not been there when Susan died, though Susan, her twin, had asked for her repeatedly.

Quintina still felt guilty about that.

At least Gillian had been there at her mother's side the entire time, waiting, praying, and hoping. She had been dutiful to the end.

There was such a desolate finality in death, Quintina thought as she watched her niece stare out the window at the passing traffic. No wonder the girl found it difficult to imagine happiness now.

Quintina squeezed Gillian's hand. "Do not despair. This is happening very quickly, and a man who marries in haste often finds himself nursing regrets later on. Fortunately for us, Seger is not the type to worry about divorce scandals. I believe he would be the first to leap on an opportunity for freedom if he is not happy." She leaned back and pulled on her gloves. "We must hope there won't be any children right away. That would only complicate things."

"What are you saying, Auntie?"

"I'm saying that even if he does marry the American today, it doesn't mean he will remain married to her. I know, it sounds scandalous to even suggest that there should be a divorce in our family, but I cannot bear to see you hurt. You have been hurt enough, with your dear mother departing this world and your father nothing but a cruel brute, God rest his putrid

soul. Your mother was my twin, and you are as precious to me as my own daughter. You deserve to get
what you want, Gillian, and you have wanted Seger
all your life."

"I've more than wanted him, Auntie. I've loved
him." The carriage swayed back and forth and rumbled over the bumpy cobblestones. Gillian smiled at
Quintina. "Do you remember when I was twelve,
and I fell in the courtyard at Rawdon Manor and cut
my knee?"

Quintina nodded, her heart squeezing with sympathy as she recalled that cloudy afternoon.

"I remember how badly it hurt and that I couldn't
get up, and I wanted to cry, but I couldn't because
I was afraid Father would find out. He always got
so angry when I cried. Then Seger appeared out of
nowhere and scooped me up in his arms and carried
me inside. I buried my face in his coat collar, and he
said, 'Don't worry, Gillian, I've got you. You'll be
fine,' and I burst into tears. Nothing ever felt so good
as to cry that day. My knee was throbbing, and all I
could think about was how wonderful Seger was, saying to me, 'There, there now,' and rubbing his cheek
against the top of my head."

"Then he returned to check on you that afternoon,"
Quintina added, encouraging Gillian to continue.

"Yes, and that's when I fell in love. No one knows
what he's really like, Auntie. Not like I do. I know
the real Seger. Society has always judged him wrongly
and most unfairly."

Quintina remembered that day very well. That's
when the seed had been planted, and it had grown

into something far too substantial to be ripped from its roots now. Especially by an American.

Straightening her shoulders, Quintina spoke with fresh resolve. "This wedding is impulsive for both of them. There is room to maneuver and to manipulate the situation. We will all be living together in the same house very soon, and I for one will not simply hand the reins over to a vulgar, opportunistic foreigner. She has no heart invested in this marriage, while you have half of your lifetime invested in loving Seger, deeply and truly. It is not fair, and we will do what is necessary to find a way around this obstacle. You will have him. It won't be difficult. With all that we know about that woman and her past, we *will* find a way to put an end to this."

He should not be troubled, Seger told himself, as he spoke his marriage vows in front of the reverend and the small number of guests. Clara simply had a blemish in her past, which was nothing compared to the complete discoloration of his own tainted history. He should think of it as further proof that they were a good match. She was a kindred spirit, so to speak. She was by nature impulsive and somewhat rebellious toward social restrictions, even though, since her near brush with scandal, she had tried to walk the straight and narrow.

He had witnessed that wild impulsiveness in bed when she had pleaded with him to make love to her. He had given in and reveled in her passion.

So, what was the problem now? he wondered, resisting the urge to rub the tense muscles at the back of his neck. Why did he not feel elated on this day when he was securing a beautiful, spirited woman as his bedmate, and he was removing the cloud of duty that had hung over his head his entire life—the duty to marry and produce an heir and continue his line.

He should be relieved. He should feel that a great weight had lifted, but he did not. He felt only apprehension.

Perhaps it was because he was entering into a permanent relationship with a complicated woman, and he would have to deal not only with the problems of life, but with her resulting emotions.

He'd dealt with a problem that morning, and it had not been a pleasant discussion. He hadn't enjoyed asking her those questions. He'd tried to be impartial, and had wanted the same from her in return, for he had only once let himself near a woman's emotions, and in doing so, he had fallen in love. Then he had been devastated beyond words when it came to an end.

No, he said to himself as he slipped the ring on his bride's slender finger. He should not feel apprehension or any other convoluted emotion. This was all very simple. Clara had made a mistake once, and almost married a swindler. She did not care for the man, and it was ancient history. He knew about it now, and he would very quickly forget that.

In fact, he should try to see this as a good thing. Clara's secret had put some distance between them. They did not really know each other, and this morning that truth had been brightly illuminated.

Yes, he should be able to relax somewhat. There

was a small measure of space now.

So. All he had to think about was the very pleasant task of providing his line with the future Marquess of Rawdon. He would devote himself entirely to his wife's pleasure, hour upon hour, until she was completely satisfied and sighing in his arms.

Not such a terrible fate after all.

Clara waited in her room that night for her husband to come to her.

Her husband. It hardly seemed real. One day, she was adoring him from afar, not even knowing his name. Now she was married to him—to her mysterious dream lover.

Just then, the doorknob turned, and her husband entered the room. Her breath caught in her chest at the awesome sight of him. He wore a black silk robe and approached the bed like a panther—all confidence and suave seduction. If there was any resentment in his mind left over from that morning, he certainly didn't show it. He looked completely at ease and full of anticipation.

"You were right," he said, climbing onto the bed. "It was a good idea to consummate our marriage in advance of the wedding. Tonight, there will only be pleasure."

Pleasure. It was always the priority.

She gazed at him with a sense of bewilderment. This was her wedding night, but she didn't know how to feel. She couldn't be frightened, because they'd already made love, and there was nothing to fear as far as her body was concerned. She should be looking forward to the pleasure he promised to give her.

But there was a small part of her that worried that he did not trust her, and that they would never be able to move past this wrinkle in their relationship because of what he'd learned about Gordon that day.

Seger rolled onto his side, rested his cheek on his hand and gazed at her with rakish eyes. She couldn't help but smile because her new husband was clearly in the mood for fun, and it wasn't much of a stretch to find her own yearnings for such delights. This was the basis of their marriage, after all. At least up until now.

"I thought it went well today," Seger said. "The food was superb."

"Delicious. I especially liked the cream cakes."

"Ah, you like desserts. I knew it," he said wickedly.

"Knew what?"

He ran his finger along her jawline and down the front of her neck. "Some women enjoy appetizers, while some prefer the main course. But you...I had you pegged for a dessert woman."

"We women fall into such simple categories," she replied.

Seger laughed. "But is it true? You look forward to the dessert, even when you've already eaten enough and are completely sated."

"Yes, it's true," she said with laughter. Then her voice became sultry. "And what do *you* like, Seger?"

He sat up and helped her remove her nightgown. "Everything. I do enjoy the appetizer, but when the main course arrives, I think it's the best—the most substantial part of the meal."

He gazed at her naked form in the flickering lamplight. Clara laid her head back on the pillow, enjoying the way he admired her with such voracity.

"Tonight, I would like to be your appetizer, main course and dessert," she said. "Consider it my wedding gift to you." She tossed her arms up behind her head and crossed one leg over the other.

Seger devoured her with his eyes, then he removed his robe and tossed it onto the floor.

Clara loved that she could have this effect on him in bed. This part of their marriage, at least, was perfect. If only that perfection could spill over onto everything else.

Naked, her husband rolled on top of her and pressed his mouth to hers.

"Perhaps we could forego the appetizers this time around," Clara suggested breathlessly. "After a week away from you, I'm afraid I am craving the main course."

He laughed and gathered her close. "You are a dream."

A moment later, smoothly and skillfully, he entered her. Clara sucked in a breath, elated by how he filled her. Bliss shot straight to her core. Seger moaned and withdrew. He rose up on his arms above her, drove forward again, and struck that part of her where pleasure seemed to begin and end, all at once.

Losing herself in the feverish ache that reduced her to something sweltering and unfamiliar, Clara sighed as Seger made love to her in the flickering light. Before long, she felt her senses reach a peak and clutched at Seger's broad shoulders. Clara drove her hips upward to meet each of his firm, deep thrusts.

Afterward, her body relaxed, and she didn't care about anything outside of that moment. All her doubts and insecurities disappeared, replaced by a physical satisfaction that somehow went beyond the physical—so much so it was confounding.

She opened her eyes and looked up at her husband. He was still inside her, moving with the hypnotic cadence of a poem. His eyes held hers, and for a brief instant, she felt as if she were floating.

Seger then let his own passions take him where they would, and he groaned with the ultimate fulfillment. Clara hoped he was putting a child in her womb. She wanted a baby with him. She wanted to do and share everything with him.

Slick with sweat, he collapsed on top of her and held her for a few minutes, then rolled off her and smiled.

"I have only one question," Clara said.

He turned his head on the pillow to look at her.

"I don't want to be presumptuous, but when is dessert being served?"

He laughed out loud and rolled to face her. "As soon as my cake rises, darling."

She laughed as well and nibbled on his earlobe. "How long will that take?"

"Not long."

She slid her hand down his muscled chest. "The main course was delicious, but you're right—even when I'm satisfied, I'm still hungry for a little more. Strange, isn't it?" She leaned up on one elbow and laid a trail of kisses down his abdomen. "Do you mind if I turn up the heat in your oven?"

Seger lifted his head to look at her. "Kitchen skills

too?" He weaved his fingers through her hair, then closed his eyes and relaxed back down on the pillow. "I had no idea I married a woman with so many hidden talents."

"I don't mean to brag," she replied, "but I'm a very fast learner." And down she went.

Clara woke the next morning to bright sunlight streaming in through the windows. Seger's arm was stretched across the bed, just below her pillow in the crook of her neck. She was still naked.

This was bliss.

She inched a little closer, admiring Seger's beautiful face as he slept. She touched her nose gently to his, wanting to kiss him but not wanting to wake him, for they had slept very little the night before. Chivalrous to the end, he had given everything to her pleasure, delivering ecstasy again and again, and for that, he deserved another hour of slumber.

Gazing at his face as he slept, looking at his peaceful countenance and the divine structure of his cheeks and nose, she felt drunk with fascination. She remembered the exquisite feel of his hands on her body in the darkness, and the way she had opened herself to him. He was a man of infinite skill when it came to a woman's desires. His energy was limitless, his desire to satisfy never ending. She had been exhausted when dawn came. Then he'd finally let her sleep, knowing with certainty that she was fulfilled. Her hunger for what he offered had been satiated, her thirst quenched, and afterward, she had slept better than any other night of her life.

Suddenly, a knock sounded at the door. Seger awakened sleepily, gazing around as if he didn't know where he was. As soon as he saw Clara's face, he rolled toward her, took her into his arms, and tried to go back to sleep.

"Seger, the door," she whispered.

The knock sounded again, and he lifted his head. "Who is pounding at my door the morning after my wedding night? It had better be important."

Sluggishly, he rose from the bed, pulled on his robe and went to see who was knocking. He opened the door a crack and Clara recognized the butler's voice.

"I'm sorry to disturb you, my lord, but there is a gentleman caller here to see you. He says it's urgent."

"Urgent? Who is it?"

"His name is John Hibbert, my lord."

Seger stepped back and began to close the door. "I don't know anyone by that name. Tell him to come back later."

The butler persisted. "He says it concerns Miss Flint, and it is a *very* urgent matter."

Seger held the door half open. "Gillian? Has something happened? Tell him I'll be right down."

"What's going on?" Clara asked, tossing the covers aside and slipping out of the bed. She reached for her wrap and pulled it on.

Seger pulled on his trousers. "I have no idea, but I must find out right away."

"Yes, of course you must." With no shortage of concern, Clara watched him leave.

Chapter 16

SEGER ENTERED THE DRAWING ROOM where the gentleman was waiting. He wore a shabby-looking suit and held a bowler hat in his hands and straightened uncomfortably when he locked eyes with Seger.

"Sir, you have disturbed me at a most inopportune time. I hope this is important."

The man spoke shakily. "It is, my lord. Gillian Flint...is she a relative of yours?"

"A relative by marriage, yes. She is my stepmother's niece. What of her?"

The man turned his hat over in his hands. "I regret to inform you that Miss Flint fell from her horse in front of my house this morning. She was unconscious and a good civilian brought her to my door. My wife is with her now. The young lady mentioned your name."

Seger tensed. "Is she all right?"

"Shaken up, to be sure, but I reckon she'll survive."

"Have you summoned a doctor?"

"No, my lord, I came straight here."

Seger nodded. "Thank you for bringing this news to me, sir. Wait here, if you please."

Seger left the drawing room and requested that his coach be brought around to the front door posthaste. He returned to the room just as Clara appeared in a simple morning dress with her hair in a loose knot.

"Gillian has been hurt," he told her.

"What happened?"

"She fell from her horse. I must go and fetch her right away. Will you tell Quintina to send word to my physician to meet me at this gentleman's home?"

Seger questioned the man, who related the address to Clara.

A short while later, Seger was stepping into the coach with John Hibbert, but paused when he heard Clara call his name from the front door.

"Wait!" Without so much as a shawl or gloves or hat, she bounded down the steps and practically leaped into the coach. "I'm coming with you."

Seger helped her inside and shut the door behind her.

Clara sat by the sofa where Gillian rested in the Hibberts' front parlor and listened to the physician speak to Seger at the door.

"She'll be fine," the doctor said. "No signs of bruising or any broken bones. I believe she is simply distressed, as any lady would be. You might want to take a look at that horse, however. Miss Flint said he bucked suddenly without any cause whatsoever."

Seger shook the man's hand. "I will, Dr. Lindeman. Thank you." A few minutes later, Seger entered the parlor. "You gave us quite a fright, my dear girl," he said to Gillian.

She squeezed Clara's hand. "I'm so sorry. I didn't mean to cause this much trouble. I was riding too fast, I suppose."

Sensing the girl's embarrassment, Clara pushed a lock of hair away from her forehead.

"Why would you do such a thing?" Seger asked. "And why did you go out alone without your groom? It's not like you to be so careless."

She shrugged. "I know it was foolish...I...I simply couldn't help myself. I felt reckless this morning." Gillian leaned up on both elbows. Her gaze flitted back and forth from Seger to Clara. "I didn't mean to disturb you, the morning after your wedding."

An uncomfortable silence ensued, and Clara tried quickly to dispel it. "Nonsense. Don't be silly. We're just glad you're all right."

Gillian smiled up at her. "Yes, me too."

Mrs. Hibbert entered the room. "Would anyone like a cup of tea?"

"No, thank you, Mrs. Hibbert," Clara replied. "You've been very kind."

The woman bowed slightly and left the room again.

"All this reminds me of the time I fell at Rawdon Manor," Gillian said. "I was only twelve. Do you remember, Seger?"

He smiled kindly at Gillian. "Of course. I remember how you cried."

Clara gazed down at Gillian's face and saw a warm radiance in her eyes.

"What happened?" she asked.

Seger reminisced. "Gillian was running, that's all I saw. I don't know where she was running to, only that she fell. You went down very hard. Your nose scraped the rocks."

She touched it. "I still have a small scar."

"Barely noticeable," he replied.

Gillian tried to sit up. "But you came to my rescue."

"I merely carried you into the house."

Clara watched the exchange and realized that Gillian was like a sister to Seger. She hoped Gillian would become like a sister to her, too.

Seger glanced toward the front hall. "Perhaps it's time to leave the Hibberts to their day," he said. "Will you be able to walk, Gillian?"

"I believe so."

"I won't have to carry you this time?" he said merrily.

Eyes flashing with delight, she giggled and shook her head. "No, Seger."

"Good. I'll summon the carriage, then. Are you ready, my dear?" he said to Clara.

She nodded and took his hand as he helped her to her feet.

Gillian chose her newest, most fetching gown when she dressed for dinner that evening. Quintina had convinced her that the color amber brought out the best in her complexion, especially in candlelight, and went well with her sand-colored hair. Quintina also chose a pearl-and-diamond choker from her own collection to go with the gown and lent it to Gillian.

Gillian watched herself in the mirror as her maid hooked the choker at the back of her neck. She wished she had been more daring with her appearance before now, when it was probably too late.

She supposed if things didn't work out with Seger, at least she would have learned a thing or two from

Clara about how to attract a man. She'd never experienced admiration from a man before—at least not a man worthy of her notice.

Gillian touched the pearls at her neck. Yes, if things didn't work out here, she would put this new knowledge to good use and do even better than Seger. A duke, perhaps? That would be very satisfying. She would outrank Clara at social functions. Her blood quickened at the thought. Perhaps one day, she would have an opportunity to give her the cut direct.

Just then, a knock sounded at her door and Quintina walked in. She waved the maid away and moved to stand behind Gillian, who looked at her aunt in the mirror's reflection. "Well?"

Quintina rested her hands upon Gillian's shoulders. "You look stunning, my dear. He will be very surprised. We should have been dressing you like this all along."

"I thought the very same thing a moment ago, Auntie. Why didn't we?"

Quintina released a sigh. "I thought he would prefer someone demure for a wife. Someone like...well, you know."

"Yes."

Someone like Daphne. A merchant's daughter who dressed like...like a merchant's daughter.

Gillian bristled just thinking of her. Daphne hadn't even been all that pretty. Seger's affection for her had never made any sense to Gillian. She thought the girl was no better than a dairy maid. Surely, Seger would have realized that eventually. Even if Daphne had not gotten on that ship to America, he probably wouldn't have married her in the end. He would have come to his senses.

Quintina fiddled with Gillian's hairstyle in the back, folding locks into place. "It went well this morning, don't you think? We got them out of bed at any rate."

"Yes, and the Hibberts were very helpful."

"Did you feel badly about lying to them?" Quintina asked.

"Gracious, no. They think they did a good deed, and Seger thanked Mr. Hibbert, who is probably bragging about it at the local pub as we speak."

Quintina nodded. "Well, let us go."

Gillian gathered up her gloves and stood.

They crossed the room toward the door, but Quintina paused before opening it. She turned around to face Gillian. "Remember, look directly into his eyes when you speak to him, darling. You must make him see you in a new light. Meanwhile, I will handle Clara. I know exactly what to do. She won't last long."

Quintina glanced down at Gillian's low neckline, then lifted her gaze and smiled. "I believe you have larger breasts than she does."

"Auntie!"

"It's true, my dear. That gown is perfect. Now come along."

That evening after dinner, Seger retired to his study to attend to some business matters, while Clara played the piano for Quintina and Gillian in the drawing room. Gillian sat under a lamp, embroidering a small pillow. Quintina read a book.

When Clara finished her piece, Gillian set down her needlework and applauded. "You play beautifully, Clara. It is such a joy to have you here."

"It's a joy to be here," she replied. "You've both made me feel very welcome."

"I'm so glad. We are going to be wonderful friends, I know it. We must stay up late and enjoy each other's company like this every night. We'll be closer than sisters."

Clara stood and moved to sit on the sofa beside Gillian. "But you're forgetting the parties. The Season is far from over. There were a number of invitations today."

Gillian sighed and looked down at her stitching. "Yes, I suppose we must go out. I certainly must, if I am ever to find a husband."

"You will find one in no time, Gillian. You look radiant tonight. Wear a dress of that color to a ball and you'll be danced off your feet."

Gillian continued to look down at her embroidery. "I don't think I should like that—to be danced off my feet. Some might call me dull, but I prefer to stay at home in the evenings. I've always preferred it. Everything that makes me happy is in this house."

Clara inclined her head questioningly. "Have you been living here long? I thought you were just visiting, that you normally live with your uncle."

On the far side of the room, Quintina looked up from her book and listened.

"Yes," Gillian replied, "and Auntie has been very kind, always letting me stay as long as I like. My uncle doesn't mind. He knows that even when my parents were alive, this was like a second home to me. I was close to Seger, you see." Gillian lifted her needle high over her head. "We've always been friends," she continued. "I was only a baby when Seger's father married Auntie. Seger was eleven, and he used to play with me and teach me things. We've been through a lot together. When my mother died, he was such a comfort to me, and before that, when he was suffering with a broken heart over Daphne...." Gillian paused and glanced up from her embroidery. "Forgive me. Perhaps you don't know about Daphne. I have no manners sometimes. I can be so clumsy."

Gillian resumed her needlework.

"Please, do not concern yourself," Clara said. "I know all about Daphne. Seger told me everything. It's a very sad story, isn't it?"

Clara wasn't sure why she felt such a strong compulsion to inform Gillian that she knew about Seger's first engagement, and why she felt suddenly competitive. It made no sense at all. Gillian was Seger's cousin, not Lady Cleveland.

But Gillian had known Seger her entire life. She knew so much more about him than Clara did.

You'll catch up, Clara told herself. Soon, you'll know him better than anyone.

"You are the most beautiful creature here," Seger said as he escorted Clara onto the terrace at Weldon House.

The breeze was warm on Clara's cheeks, the champagne sweet on her lips. Seger had not stopped looking at her all evening, and she felt beautiful in her red silk, form-flattering Worth gown, with embroidered pearls on the bodice, and a flowing, flounced train. At her neck she wore a large diamond pendant that flashed and sparkled. Seger's gaze had dropped many times to her cleavage, though she doubted he was admiring the diamond.

Clara gazed up at him flirtatiously over the rim of her champagne glass as she sipped. "You are a shameless flatterer."

She couldn't wait to go home and be alone with him.

He gave her a look that offered promises for later. "Shameless is my middle name. And I can flatter you all night long, if you wish it."

Just then, a woman approached Seger from behind and spoke close in his ear. "You must flatter me, too. I haven't heard your delicious talk in a dog's age. I'm sure your lady-friend won't mind sharing."

Clara drew back in surprise. "Sharing?"

Seger turned to face the woman but she suddenly seemed more interested in talking to Clara. Her breath smelled of whisky and she nearly lost her balance as she whispered in Clara's ear, "Your bed or mine, darling? We can take turns, back and forth, five minutes each. What do you say, Seger?"

Horrified, Clara gazed up at her husband. He stared blankly at the woman. Clara wasn't even sure if he recognized her.

But then he spoke her name. "Mrs. Thomas, allow me to introduce my wife, Lady Rawdon." He gestured toward Clara.

The woman blinked a few times. "I beg your pardon, my lord. Did you say your *wife*?"

"Yes."

"Dear me." Her cheeks colored. "I didn't know. No one said anything." She backed up a step and laid a gloved hand on her chest. "I'm mortified. I've been in Paris, you see, and I only just returned yesterday and...."

Seger turned to Clara. "Darling, this is Mrs. Abigail Thomas."

The woman held out her hand. "How do you do?"

"Very well, thank you," Clara replied, shaking her hand. The woman fiddled absently with a lock of hair around her ear as the three stood in awkward silence, then Mrs. Thomas commented on the weather. Finally, she made a move to leave. "It was very nice to see you, Lord Rawdon, and a pleasure to meet you, Lady Rawdon." She turned and left.

Seger watched her go. "I apologize for that."

Clara tried to keep her voice steady. "It wasn't your fault."

"I hope that sort of thing doesn't happen again," Seger added.

I'm surprised she hadn't heard about our marriage."

"We married quickly. And she was in Paris. The news will make its way around soon enough."

He downed the rest of his champagne and smiled at her understanding, then escorted her back inside. Clara forced herself to forget about the incident and did not mention it again, but she did feel a tension between herself and her husband for the rest of the evening.

The following morning, Clara sat in the breakfast room sipping tea and reading the newspaper.

Gillian entered, served herself breakfast from the sideboard, and sat down. "Did you have a good time at the assembly last night?" Gillian asked.

Gillian had arrived later in the evening with Quintina, and Clara had seen her talking to a number of handsome young men. "Yes, I did, and it looked like you were having a good time as well. Who was that man with the red hair? He always seemed to be smiling when he spoke to you."

"That was Stanley Scott. His father is a baron from the north, so dear Stanley is only a mister. He seems young, don't you think?"

"I don't know. I thought he looked very nice."

Gillian rolled her eyes. "Nice, and limp in the head."

Clara didn't know what to say to that. She picked up her tea and took another sip.

"I noticed that you barely left Seger's side," Gillian mentioned a few minutes later. "Don't you trust him?"

The question caught Clara off guard, and she set down her teacup. "Of course I trust him. We simply enjoy each other's company, and there were a some people he wanted to introduce me to."

"Like Mrs. Thomas?" Gillian replied. "I saw her talking to you. Well done, Clara."

Clara felt her insides begin to churn. "I don't know what you're referring to."

"I saw you shake her hand. You were very composed. One would never know."

"Never know what?"

"That you must have been seething inside. I would have been, too, in your position."

Clara closed the newspaper and sat back. "I was not seething."

Gillian gave her a look. "Please. You don't have to lie to me. I know how it is with Seger and all the women who want him. But you were very good last night. You're just the kind of wife he needs."

Clara tried not to choke on her tea. "Gillian—"

"I'm not sure I could do what you do," she continued, "especially being an American. I've heard you people have different expectations about marriage, that a man who strays is frowned upon." She returned to her breakfast.

"Gillian, I don't like what you are insinuating."

Gillian stopped chewing and stared at her. "Oh, my goodness. It *does* bother you, doesn't it. I'm so sorry. I can be so tactless sometimes."

Clara swallowed over the agitation rising up within her. "Nothing bothers me, because there is nothing going on. Seger was very apologetic about Mrs. Thomas's behavior."

"Of course he was. Pretend I didn't say anything." Gillian watched Clara pick up her newspaper but did not take the hint. "I just don't want you to get hurt, that's all. I see how you look at him."

Clara set down her paper again. "I'm not going to get hurt."

"I just know how I would feel if *I* were his wife. He is such a handsome man. It would be difficult not to be possessive."

Clara felt like she was going to blow a gasket.

"Permit me to offer you some advice," Gillian said. "You must try to remember that you are an English-woman now, and English wives look the other way when their husbands take lovers. If he were *my* husband, that's what I would do. I wouldn't think twice about it and I'd be the perfect wife for him because he's worth it. Not only is he a marquess, but he is handsome and charming as well."

By this time, Clara's blood was boiling in her head. "You're telling me it wouldn't bother you if he was unfaithful?"

Gillian sipped her tea and tossed her head. "No. I'd be happy that he chose me as his wife above all the rest—especially when no one thought he would *ever* marry, because of Daphne. He loved her very deeply. If only you could have seen them together…. I thought they were made for each other. They were kindred spirits, the best of friends. Some say that kind of love comes along only once in a lifetime."

Everything—from the tabletop to Gillian's mouth moving clownishly as she chewed—turned Clara's vision red. She had not expected this from Gillian, who had been very sweet up until this moment. Why in the world was she saying these cruel, hurtful things, and reminding Clara that she was not the great love of Seger's life?

Then it dawned on Clara, like a gaslight exploding brightly inside her head.

Gillian was in love with Seger.

Chapter 17

THAT NIGHT, WHILE WAITING FOR Seger to come to her, Clara couldn't stop thinking about what Gillian had said to her that morning. She tried to tell herself that she was jumping to conclusions about the young woman's feelings, but it did no good. She couldn't get over how Gillian had suggested that she would be the perfect wife for Seger because she would turn a blind eye to his philandering.

Clara wasn't angry with Seger. The rational part of her brain knew that he had done nothing wrong, at least not that she knew of. She was angry with Gillian for saying those things, and she was angry with Mrs. Thomas and Lady Cleveland for reminding her that her husband was coveted by other women, and that he would face temptation every day for the rest of his life.

Women would offer themselves to him. Desperate, lonely women who knew how skillful he was in the bedroom. Beautiful women, who wanted nothing more than a few casual hours with an expert lover—a man who knew by instinct exactly what they wanted.

A chill cooled Clara's skin at the thought of all the women her husband had made love to, but she was sensible and knew better than to dwell on that. It was in the past.

Later, after Seger had entered her bedroom and made love to her, he rolled onto his back and sighed. "I like being a married man."

Clara tried to smile. "More than being a bachelor?"

He turned his head on the pillow and looked at her. "With you as my wife, definitely."

She considered that for a moment. "But what if I were sick for a month? What would become of our marriage if there was no sex? Would you wish for a different wife then?"

He rolled to face her and rested his cheek on his hand. "I told you before that I desire no one but you."

Desire, yes, but love? Will you ever love me like you loved Daphne?

"You've asked me that question before," he said, "and I've answered you, yet here you are asking again. Is it because of what happened at the assembly last night?"

Clara realized how foolish she was sounding. He was right. She had asked this question before and he kept giving her the same answer. She had to try to accept it.

"I'm sorry, I'm asking silly questions. I think it's because of the conversation I had with Gillian this morning. She said some things...."

He frowned. "What did you talk about?"

Clara hesitated, not sure if she should tell him, but then she decided it was worth discussing. Perhaps it would bring them closer together on an emotional level, which was what she wanted after all.

"Gillian told me that she saw what happened with Mrs. Thomas, and she congratulated me for not making a fuss. She said that if *she* were your wife, she would give you the freedom you needed."

His eyebrows drew together. "I cannot believe you had this conversation."

"Neither can I. All day long I've been thinking about it, and I've come to the conclusion that Gillian might be.... Is it possible that she might be in love with you, Seger? Have you ever suspected it?"

Seger sat up and gaped down at her. "That's ridiculous."

Clara sat up, too, hugging the covers to her chest. "Is it?"

"Of course. She has never so much as glanced at me in that way. She thinks of me as a brother. I cannot even imagine such a thing."

"But if you could have heard her talking this morning. Haven't you noticed how she's been dressing lately? How she's been changing the way she looks?"

"No, I have not. I think you are letting your imagination get the best of you, and you always seem to think the worst of *me.*"

"No, I am not accusing you of anything, Seger. I believe it is all on Gillian's side, and maybe she doesn't even know it herself."

"Know what? That she wishes she were my wife? Good God, if *she* doesn't know it, it hardly seems possible that *you* could."

"I just sensed it."

He got out of bed and pulled on his robe. "This is absurd, Clara. I understood your reservations about marrying me in the beginning, and I understand if you are upset about Mrs. Thomas's solicitation last night, but this, Clara—this is getting out of hand."

Her temper began to rise. "You think I am having delusions?"

He sighed with resignation. "I think you are worried about your decision to marry me because of what happened last night, and it has caused you to be irrational."

Irrational?

"Gillian is just a girl," he continued, "a shy, quiet girl. She's not like Mrs. Thomas, so do not think what you are thinking. To tell you the truth, I'm getting tired of your lack of confidence in me. I told you I would be a faithful husband, yet you keep bringing up this sort of thing. I'm tired of discussing it." He crossed to the door.

"Where are you going?" Clara asked, her anger rising. Seger had not understood any of what she was saying. He didn't believe her, he couldn't bring himself to doubt Gillian's sweetness, and he thought she was irrational.

Even if she was completely wrong, he could have at least been sympathetic and tried to ease her mind about it. Instead, he had called her feelings absurd. He had defended Gillian. He was walking out. He did not want to delve into her emotions. He wanted only light conversation and sex.

"I am going to get a drink and read for a while," he replied. "Suddenly I don't feel much like sleeping."

Nor do I, Clara thought miserably, flopping onto the bed after the door swung shut behind him.

Clara couldn't sleep. She needed to talk to someone,

but she couldn't go to Gillian, nor could she go to her stepmother, who adored her niece and would probably react exactly as Seger had.

Clara wished she could talk to her sister, but Sophia had gone to Bath with James to spend a few weeks with his mother and his sister, Lily, who had wished to escape the pressures of the London Season this year. Sophia had explained to Clara that Lily had gotten into some trouble a few years ago, shortly after James and Sophia had wed. Lily had run off with a Frenchman. The whole thing had been covered over, but Lily, unfortunately, had not yet gotten over it. She was uneasy around men and didn't trust her own judgment.

She and Clara would probably have a lot to talk about.

After a moment's deliberation, Clara decided to write a letter to Sophia. If nothing else, it would help her to express how she was feeling. She went to her desk, pulled out a clean sheet of stationery, and dipped her pen in the inkwell.

> *Dear Sophia,*
>
> *It is the middle of the night and I cannot sleep, for I am distraught. This morning, Gillian said things about Seger that made me uncomfortable, and I can only assume she said them to hurt me, for she is secretly in love with him.*
>
> *I know it sounds absurd, and perhaps I should have waited until I had something more substantial to base my beliefs upon than my womanly instincts before I mentioned it to Seger. But I wanted so*

*desperately for us to be close. I wanted to share my
feelings with him. I told him my suspicions, but
it did not go well. He did not believe a word of it.
He called me irrational, for he cannot believe that
Gillian would ever see him as anything other than
a brother figure.*

   *Now I feel worse than ever about my marriage. I
feel as if I expected too much too soon, and I have
pushed Seger away. He was angry with me, and
he left our bed, and I fear that if he loses interest in
me (you know what kind of interest I mean) that
there will be nothing to keep him from leaving me,
for there is really so little depth of feeling between
us to begin with.*

   *I miss you, dear sister, and I will look forward to
seeing you when you return.*

   Love, Clara

"Look what I found?" Quintina said to Gillian the
next morning, entering her niece's boudoir and wav-
ing a letter in her hand. "It was sitting by the front
door waiting to go out with the rest of the family's
correspondence, so I decided to take a peek."

Gillian was sitting at her dressing table, trying different hairstyles. "What is it, Auntie?"

Quintina handed it to her niece. "It's a letter Clara
wrote to her sister last night. I almost feel like cele-
brating."

Gillian stared at it uncertainly. "Aunt Quintina, it
is unconscionable to read someone else's mail. How
could we be so devious?"

"You can't pretend to believe that Clara wasn't

devious when she did whatever she did to get Seger to propose. I can only imagine what tactics she employed."

Gillian considered that for a moment, then slowly opened the letter and read it. "Oh, sweet mother of God! She told him what I said! I could brain her!"

"Now, now, it's not such a bad thing," Quintina replied. "She says Seger didn't believe it and he called her irrational. *Irrational,* Gillian. He would have absolutely no patience at all for an irrational wife. I believe we've found our strategy."

Still reeling with rage at the image of Clara telling Seger about their conversation that morning, Gillian glared impatiently at her aunt. "Which is what?"

"You must continue to say things that make her mad with jealousy. Hint at things—even things about Daphne—but never be clear. When you are with Seger, behave as you always have. Even ignore him a little more than usual, so he will think that Clara is imagining everything. If we can drive her to tears, that will be even better, because you know how he hates that sort of behavior. He'll think she's unbalanced. Then, I will top it all off with my trump card."

"What's your trump card, Auntie?"

Quintina smiled. "Would you really like to know?"

A glimmer of malice lighted Gillian's eyes. "Of course."

Quintina sat down on the bed. "As it happens, there is a gentleman traveling here now from America. His name is Gordon Tucker, and he has agreed to do something for me."

Clara spent the afternoon riding with Gillian through Hyde Park. She had not wanted to go, but she hadn't wanted Seger to learn that she'd refused, so she accepted Gillian's invitation, donned her black riding habit and top hat, and pasted on a smile.

The sky was overcast and the air cool, and as Clara galloped over the grass, she was surprised to be enjoying herself. Perhaps it was because Gillian was so quiet. She spoke very little, never mentioning their conversation the morning before. She merely rode ahead of Clara, who gladly brought up the rear. She had no desire to race with the girl.

They were on their way home, however, when Gillian slowed her pace and waited for Clara to ride up beside her. Their horses nickered and flicked their ears.

"What a glorious day for a ride," Gillian said. "We should do this every afternoon."

"It is lovely indeed."

"I enjoy our friendship very much, Clara. I am so happy Seger married you."

The statement surprised Clara, who instantly doubted her feelings from the day before. Perhaps she had jumped to conclusions, and Seger had been perfectly justified to react the way he had.

"I enjoy it, too, Gillian," she replied, patting her horse's neck.

They trotted side by side. "Did you know," Gillian said, "that my father had once wanted me to marry Seger?"

Clara's mood took a sudden dive. "Is that so?" She did not want to be having this conversation!

"Yes," Gillian said brightly. "I refused, of course. I told my father that Seger was only a friend to me, that I could never imagine him as my husband, and then after the scandal with Daphne, and Seger's withdrawal from society.... Well, Father changed his tune after that. He wouldn't hear of it. He wanted someone respectable for me. Of course, I never believed that Seger was not respectable. I knew he had more honor than any other man in London, and he was merely pining away over Daphne, whom he had loved very deeply. But Father could never see that. He didn't know Seger as I did." She gave Clara a sidelong glance. "But you must know him intimately as well, because you're his wife. He must share everything with you. He probably tells you he loves you every time you're together." She looked up at the sky. "You are a very lucky woman, Clara."

Clara didn't feel so lucky at the moment. She felt like she was losing her mind. Nothing Gillian said hinted at anything untoward between her and Seger. Gillian had said that Seger had been a friend to her, and that her feelings went no deeper than that. Yet there was something in her tone. Something that goaded Clara—and seemingly on purpose. Gillian's voice was condescending, and she seemed intent to have Clara recognize it.

And she kept bringing up Daphne.

"I'm so happy we're like sisters now," Gillian said, "and that we can tell each other everything. It must be wonderful to be married. I envy you. Tell me about it, Clara. How many times a day does Seger tell you he loves you? Do you ever get tired of hearing it?"

Clara swallowed over the urge to tell Gillian to go ride her horse straight into the Thames. She reminded herself, however, that Gillian was a member of Seger's family, and she could not be so rude. And for all she knew, maybe she *was* imagining things. She could be feeling vulnerable because of all the other women in Seger's life—whether they were former lovers propositioning him at balls, hateful cousins, or the ghosts from his past.

Clara wasn't sure of anything anymore.

"Forgive me, Gillian," Clara said, "but I would prefer to keep certain things private. I'm sure you understand."

Gillian shifted her riding crop from one hand to the other. "I'm sorry, Clara. I'm the one who should be asking for forgiveness. I sounded like a busybody just now. I loathe people like that. Don't you?"

Clara merely nodded, and they rode out of the park toward home.

That night, when Seger came to her bed, she smiled flirtatiously and removed her nightgown, and pushed every thought of Gillian and Daphne, and all those other women, from her mind. She would not again make the mistake of spoiling the only intimacy that existed between herself and her husband. She would enjoy the pleasures of the marriage bed and be the adventurous woman Seger had fallen in love with.

"Has he ever shown you a picture of Daphne?" Gillian asked Clara over breakfast the next morning. "He had a miniature of her at one time. He must still have it somewhere. I can't imagine he would ever discard it."

Clara spoke with a pretense of indifference, though she was tempted to throw her toast in Gillian's face. "No, I can't imagine he would either."

"Well, she was very beautiful, and the reason I ask is because you are beautiful, too. To be honest, you resemble Daphne. We've all noticed. Auntie mentioned it the first time she saw you. The housekeeper mentioned it, too."

Clara struggled not to reveal her surprise. She tried to sound unruffled and merely curious. "In what way do I resemble her?"

"You have the same color hair, and your mouth is the same." She pointed at her own mouth. "It's the lips. Seger has an appreciation for lips, doesn't he? Have you noticed that about him?"

Clara could barely believe Gillian's audacity. But under no circumstances would she take the bait. Instead, she smiled playfully. "Yes, I suppose he does have an appreciation for lips. I can certainly attest to that."

She was pleased that her voice hinted at all sorts of wicked innuendo. It knocked Gillian off kilter. The poor girl's cheeks flushed bright red.

Clara returned to sipping her tea.

Gillian was quiet for a moment, then she made another attempt to knock Clara off balance. "Do you know about the gravestone?"

Clara saw the competitive glint in Gillian's eyes, and realized that things were spiraling out of control. There was nothing subtle about Gillian's desire to attack Clara. Her intentions were not up for debate.

Gillian was charging ahead at a full gallop, sword drawn, and she didn't care if Clara knew it. The space between them was now an open battlefield.

"What gravestone?" Clara asked dryly.

Gillian raised an eyebrow in a spiteful manner. Was she not even going to try to be subtle?

"Daphne's gravestone. He had one erected, you know."

Clara had to admit defeat on this point. She sipped her tea and set the cup down in its saucer. "I didn't know that."

"No, I wouldn't think he would mention it. He had it erected in their private meeting place at his country estate, and planted daffodils all around it. Daffodils were her favorite. He told me about that once, when he was lonesome for her."

Clara took a calming breath and leaned forward in her chair. "Gillian, your comments about my husband are beginning to give me a headache."

Gillian's chin rose up a notch. "I don't know why that would be the case."

"Are you sure?"

"No." There was such challenge in the cursed woman's eyes!

Clara squeezed her fists with fury. "In the future, let us try to talk of other things. You have other interests, don't you? Music? Books?"

Gillian smiled sardonically. "I understand, Clara. I understand completely."

Clara had just finished brushing her hair before bed, when Seger entered her bedchamber carrying a bottle of red wine and two glasses.

"I thought you might be thirsty," he said, his voice low and seductive, his eyes warm.

Having never shared a bedroom with a man other than Seger, Clara wondered if all husbands were as gracious and charming as he.

Not likely, she decided, feeling quietly aroused. "You always know what I'm in the mood for."

With great appreciation, Clara took in the breadth of his shoulders and the sheer perfection of his body as he moved across the room. He was flawless beyond contemplation. He looked like the statue of David, if one could imagine David wearing a black silk robe. She, for one, preferred to imagine her husband quite *without* the robe.

And yet, her marriage was not all red wine and roses. For one thing, her monthly had begun and she wasn't sure how to handle that. What did husbands and wives do when the wife was indisposed?

Additionally, neither of them had mentioned their argument about Gillian. It was as if it had never occurred. They'd made love the night before, but Clara had felt distanced from Seger and didn't know how to breach that distance without starting another argument.

She rose from her chair and forced herself to smile, all the while feeling like she barely knew her husband. Nor he her. They were like two casual acquaintances, making light conversation, laughing about trivial things, and making love. Though he picked up on each and every desire she had sexually, and satisfied her beyond any expectation, he didn't want to hear about her anxieties or emotional insecurities. He just wanted her to smile and be beautiful and amusing.

She was thankful that it was easy to smile and be beautiful when he was making love to her, for that was how he made her feel.

As she watched him pour the wine, however, she realized uneasily that the persona she was forced to keep up when he was *not* making love to her was beginning to try her patience.

There were moments when she wanted to shout at Seger or throw a vase at him to stir up some real emotion between them. But she feared that if she did that, he would think she was irrational again, and she did not wish him to see her that way. It was important to her that she hold on to his respect.

He handed her a glass. "Try this, darling. It's the best we have in the house."

She sipped the wine and felt the most pleasant sensation of heat pouring through her body, relaxing her mind. "It's delicious."

"Not nearly as delicious as you." He held up his own glass. "To your beauty."

Clara watched him in the dim lamplight and marveled at his beauty—the square line of his jaw, his strong, masculine hands. Sometimes he seemed to have no awareness of the strength of his appeal. Other times, he knew exactly how to use his charm.

Distracted as she was by her husband's charisma, she still could not get the image of Daphne's gravestone out of her mind. Seger had erected it on his country estate, and the memorial to his first love would always be there, even after Clara had taken up residence.

She wondered if he still went to visit it.

Shaking her head at herself, she endeavored to sweep those thoughts from her mind. She did not want to spoil their evening together. Instead, she sat down on the bed and asked him about his day, resolving to make this a pleasant, memorable night.

As she watched him saunter toward her, sleek and irresistible, she knew it wouldn't be difficult.

Seger gazed down at his wife and wondered how it was possible that any woman could be so exquisite in every way—from her earthly beauty down to her angelic, bright charm. Her smile was everything to him. Sometimes it was sweet and adorable, other times confident and poised, and still other times, it was sexually charged and drove him around the bend with need. She was the perfect combination of innocence and sophistication.

He had put aside their conversation of a few nights ago, and she seemed to have forgotten it, too. She had not mentioned Gillian again, and he was glad. He did not want to be reminded of the fact that Clara did not completely trust him when he had done everything in his power to earn and deserve her trust. Nor did he want to talk about Gillian when he was with Clara. Gillian was the last person on his mind.

He set down his glass and climbed onto the bed, then took Clara into his arms. With the exception of a few small impediments, marriage was bloody spectacular so far.

Though he couldn't imagine it being this good with anyone else—which was why he had never been the least bit inclined to take this route with any other woman.

Well, he had with one woman, but that had been a very different time.

He eased Clara onto the soft pillows and began to unbutton the top of her gown, but she stopped him. "Seger...."

Stalled briefly—a tad surprised—he drew back. "Yes?"

"I'm not sure we can do this tonight."

He blinked a few times. "What do you mean?"

"I mean...." She slipped out of the bed and folded her arms, as if she were shivering in the cold. "My monthly arrived today."

A small breath sailed out of his lungs, and he felt slightly out of his element. It wasn't often he'd had to deal with this problem. Most women he knew simply avoided "social" situations when they weren't fully able to consummate them.

"I see." Then it occurred to him that this meant Clara was not with child. "Are you disappointed?"

"Disappointed that we can't make love tonight?" she asked, in a sweet, innocent voice that melted his heart.

"First of all," he said, sitting up, "we can make love if you wish to, but that's not what I mean. Are you disappointed that we didn't conceive a child?"

Her face softened. "A little, I suppose. I do want to give you a son."

He rose from the bed, approached her and took her into his arms. "Don't be disappointed, darling. It often takes some time, I've heard. Look on the bright side, we will have to try doubly hard in the weeks to come. I don't think I'll mind that very much. Will you?"

Clara smiled. "No, I won't. But what will it mean for tonight?" She touched his lips with her thumb. "Will you go back to your room?"

"Do you want me to?"

"No." Her voice became breathy like a whisper. "There is still your pleasure to consider."

He smiled and felt his arousal grow. "What exactly are you suggesting?"

His delightful wife didn't answer the question. She simply went down on her knees and untied the belt of his robe. Her eyes were dark and mischievous as she looked up at him.

He cupped her head in his large hand. "I didn't want to presume...."

"Presume anything you like. There's no point wasting a good bottle of wine." Then she smiled again and lit his body on fire.

Seger lay on the bed, stroking Clara's soft cheek and kissing her in the darkness, realizing that he was not the least bit disappointed to be lying in bed with a woman, having agreed to refrain from making love to her.

He hadn't felt such tenderness in a long time. Eight years to be exact. He'd forgotten what it felt like.

Then he remembered the look on Clara's face earlier when she told him she was not with child. She was clearly disappointed, but he had taken away that disappointment with a compassionate smile and a few choice words.

Maybe there was hope for him, after all. Maybe—as he and Clara grew closer—she would begin to trust him, and he would not feel so inept when it came to her more complicated emotions. He certainly felt close to her now, and not just in the physical sense.

He closed his eyes, pulled her into his arms, and fell asleep.

Chapter 18

Dear Clara,

Last night, I made the mistake of asking the hostess at a dinner party to pass me the gravy, and a dreadful silence fell upon the table. No one spoke to me for the rest of the evening. Mrs. Wadsworth, my lovely English governess, has since informed me that one should never ask the hostess for anything. Ask the servants. But you probably knew that already....

Adele

SEEING HER SISTER ENTER THE London ballroom, Clara excused herself from the other ladies. "Sophia, you're back. How was Bath? Were you able to convince James' sister to come home?"

"Bath was wonderful, and Lily seemed in good spirits. I tried to have her finish out the Season here, but she wouldn't have it. She has not yet regained her confidence."

"It might take some time." Clara understood because she had been there.

They strolled around the room together, smiling and nodding at the other guests, then Sophia looped her arm through Clara's. "I received your letter."

"I was wondering if you had. I regret writing it now."

"Why?"

"Because everything seems so much better. I haven't mentioned my feelings about Gillian to Seger since that first night we argued, and we've been very happy the past few weeks."

Sophia stopped and faced Clara. "But you seemed so upset when you wrote the letter. Has Gillian said anything else like that since then?"

"A few things, yes, but I've learned to ignore it and do my best not to let it bother me. I believe she is unhappy and spiteful, but I wouldn't say that to anyone but you. I can't insult or scorn Seger's relations. His stepmother would hate me, and I don't want that. I want to be accepted by his family."

They began walking again. "But if she is saying things intentionally to hurt you, you should tell your husband."

"I can't right now. When I imagine myself repeating the things she says, it truly does sound like nothing. She's never said anything outwardly damaging. It's merely her tone and the look in her eye that insinuate things. Seger would think I was being 'irrational' again. In his opinion, Gillian is a harmless, shy girl who wouldn't know a nasty thought if it bit her on the nose. Besides, I think it bothers him that I don't trust him."

Sophia spoke softly. "But do you think he would take her side over yours? He should realize by now that you are not irrational. Certainly, there must be some deeper affection between you. Is there?"

Clara swallowed uneasily. "I don't know."

Sophia led her to an alcove where they could sit down and speak in private. "Has he told you he loves you?"

Clara lowered her gaze. "No, and I have no idea if he is even moving in that direction. He treats me with kindness and consideration, but...."

"Does he sleep all night with you?"

"Yes, every night."

"Well, that's something."

"I suppose. He is very tender and loving and he flatters me, but I believe that is his natural way when he makes love to women. It's why they all want him so badly."

Sophia shook her head. "You mustn't think about other women, Clara. His bachelor days are over, and you are his only bed partner. Unless.... You don't suspect that he is—"

"No, no. We are together every night and there has never been any evidence of...well, another woman's perfume or anything like that."

Sophia leaned back and looked the other way. "I can't believe we are even discussing such things. There is no need of it, really."

"No, you're right," Clara replied. "Truly, I have banished such concerns over the past few weeks. Well, for the most part. He really has been wonderful, Sophia."

"I'm glad. And if Gillian continues to strike out at you, it will all come around. Seger's an intelligent man, and he will see the truth for what it is."

Clara sighed gratefully. "I don't know what I would

do without you."

Sophia clasped her hand. "You would get along just fine."

After meeting with his solicitor to discuss a small financial matter, Seger walked through Piccadilly and found himself dreaming about his wife.

He'd never imagined marriage would turn out to be so immensely pleasurable. He'd certainly had his doubts.

Well…. He still had his doubts. There was the issue of Clara not trusting him, which continued to trouble him, but he hoped that would soon take care of itself. He was doing his best to work through it.

Other than that, Clara was beautiful, amusing, enchanting. He was surprised to discover how much he enjoyed simply talking to her. They often stayed up late, conversing about their days as well as books and art and society. He adored her impressions of life and people. Her original, insightful opinions always fascinated him. Perhaps it was because she was American and had been brought up with different values. He appreciated how she made him look at life.

He also realized that he was beginning to feel less awkward in relating to her on a personal level. It was as if something inside him had awakened. He didn't know what to say about it, though…or if he should say anything at all. Things were so easy between them, maybe there was no need. Clara seemed happier in their marriage. Perhaps she could sense what was growing between them and would learn to trust him over time.

If only he could go back and repeat that unfortunate argument they'd had about Gillian. He would handle it differently. He would be less defensive. He certainly wouldn't walk out on her. Perhaps tonight he would apologize for the way he had handled that conversation and ask Clara if she still felt uncomfortable around his cousin.

He passed a dress shop and stopped to look at a ball gown in the window. It would look stunning on Clara. She would outshine every woman in London. In the world, for that matter, with her dazzling smile and winsome laughter. The color of the dress was magnificent. He moved on and decided he would tell her about the dress that night. She might want to have a look at it herself.

Good heavens, he thought with a smile, tapping his walking stick along the ground. He must be deeply besotted if he was going to talk to his wife about a dress. Imagine that.

He became aware of his stomach growling, so he turned into a small cafe. After being seated at the back, he ordered the lamb and requested a newspaper.

Not five minutes later, he heard someone speak his name and looked up.

"Quintina. Gillian." He set down the paper and stood. "What are you two doing here?"

As he rose to greet his stepmother, he realized that their relationship had not been quite so strained lately. He had not thought about his anger toward her concerning Daphne, which had been the leading wedge between them for years. He wondered if Clara's companionship was affecting him in imperceptible ways that were influencing other areas of his life.

"I was just about to ask you the same thing," Quintina said. "We've been shopping and thought we would stop for a bite to eat."

Seger gestured toward the empty chairs at his table. "Please join me."

The ladies ordered their meals and told Seger about their purchases—hair ribbons and combs for Gillian, a hat for Quintina. Just before the food arrived, however, Quintina pressed a hand to her head.

"My word, I have developed the most painful headache."

Gillian touched her hand. "Can I get you anything, Auntie?"

"No, no, thank you, dear." She touched her head again. "Ooh. It is quite severe." Glancing around the cafe, she said, "I believe I will skip lunch. Would you mind, Seger, if I leave you to bring Gillian home? I wouldn't want to spoil her afternoon."

"Certainly."

"That's not necessary, Auntie," Gillian said. "I'll go with you."

At that moment, the food arrived. "Don't be silly, my dear girl. Enjoy your lunch."

Seger walked Quintina to the door, then returned to his table. He spent a pleasant hour with Gillian, though as usual, he had to work hard to keep the conversation going.

Clara dressed for dinner and walked to the drawing room. She did not expect to see Seger, for he had told her he would be dining at his club with an old

friend from Charterhouse who now lived in India—
but who was in London for a fortnight.

Clara entered the drawing room. Gillian stood in
front of the window, looking out. She turned and
smiled brightly when Clara entered the room.

"My, don't you look lovely this evening," Gillian
said.

Clara wondered how it was possible that Gillian
could be so hateful at times and so sweet at others.
Sitting down on the sofa, she wished she had brought
a book with her so she wouldn't feel obligated to talk,
but she had not thought of it, so here she was.

Gillian sat down next to her. "Did Seger tell you?"

The look in the young woman's eyes made Clara's
stomach careen with dread. "About what?"

"About the dress? We had lunch together in Piccadilly today, and he told me how much he liked it. I
believe he was thinking of it for you."

"You believe?"

And my husband met you for lunch?

They're cousins, she told herself. Cousins sometimes ate together.

Gillian stared at her blankly. "Yes, I think that's
what he meant when he mentioned it, though I suppose one can never be sure."

Clara decided not to respond to that. In fact, she
was not going to say one single word. She would not
help Gillian spin any tales.

The tense silence caused Gillian to rise to her feet.
She wandered to the mantel and fiddled with knick-
knacks as if she were bored. "It was a very nice lunch,
except for when we talked about Lady Cleveland. I

hope I didn't sound too angry."

The normal response would have been "Angry about what?" but Clara didn't let herself ask the question, because that's exactly what Gillian wanted her to do.

Nevertheless, the girl chattered on. "I really do despise that woman. I suppose you must feel the same way. I wish there was some way we could ruin her, you and I together, but I don't think Seger would like that very much, would he?"

Still, Clara said nothing, but her teeth were grinding together.

Gillian continued. "I know I once said that if I were Seger's wife, I would look the other way, but now I'm not so sure. I do see your plight. When I bumped into Lady Cleveland today in one of the shops, my blood literally boiled, because I knew Seger had just left her house. He said he'd gone to see his solicitor, and maybe he did, briefly, but I knew the truth." She gazed down at Clara. "I suppose it's our lot in life to suffer through that sort of thing, isn't it?"

That was it.

Clara could not endure one more minute of this petty harassment. She stood up. "I've had enough of this, Gillian."

Gillian put on an innocent air. "Clara, what's wrong? I don't like your tone."

Clara almost laughed out loud at the nonsense spurting from this woman's mouth. "Nor do I like yours. And I doubt Seger would think too much of it either, if he could hear you now. Your purpose is obvious. You're like a bad actress in a bad play, and if

I weren't so appalled by your duplicitous behavior, I might find it amusing."

The color drained from Gillian's cheeks. "How dare you. I am a member of Seger's family."

"And I am his wife," Clara firmly said. "The mother of his future children, heirs to his title. Mistress of this house."

Gillian narrowed her eyes and approached Clara. "You think *I'm* being obvious, but do you know what is *really* obvious? How much you hate me, but that is not surprising, is it?"

"What are you insinuating?"

"I'm insinuating nothing. In fact, I hope I am being very frank. You can't stomach the fact that I am close to Seger and you are not. I know that you are not, because I know him so well. He shares his deepest feelings with me, and he tells me that you are little more than a stranger to him. So, do not blame *me* for what is missing in your marriage, and do not go complaining to him about me either, because he will see right through you. If Seger is distant and that upsets you, it is not my fault. I have done nothing wrong. I assure you I am still only a close friend to him. Nothing has happened, at least not yet, but you hate me anyway, don't you? Even though I've done nothing to deserve it." She turned away from Clara and walked to the window. "If you're going to hate someone, hate Lady Cleveland."

Clara stood motionless. Words failed to come. She couldn't think of how to respond to Gillian's outburst. She was in complete and utter shock.

Just then, Quintina entered the room and kissed

Clara on the cheek. "Good evening my dear. What a beautiful day it was." She sat down on the sofa. "I believe Seger is having dinner at his club tonight, isn't he?"

Gillian raised an eyebrow at Clara, as if to suggest he was not at his club. Her expression was triumphant.

When Clara did not respond, Quintina glanced at Gillian in the corner and said with a jolly tone, "Well, you both look famished. Are you ready to eat?"

They nodded and moved into the dining room. It was the worst meal Clara had eaten since she'd set foot on English soil.

Clara was removing her earrings, feeling angry and nauseous, when a knock sounded at her bedchamber door. Hoping it would be Seger—yet not at all sure what she would say to him if it was—she went to answer it.

Her mother-in-law stood in the corridor. "Quintina."

"Hello, my dear," the woman said with a sympathetic tone. "May I please come in?"

"Of course." Clara stepped aside.

Quintina moved to the center of the room. "You were quiet at dinner. Is everything all right?"

Clara thought carefully about how she should answer that question. She could hardly confide in Quintina and tell her that she'd had a huge fight with her niece, especially knowing how much the woman loved and doted on her twin sister's only child.

Nor could Clara tell her that she was worried, rationally or not, that her husband was in another woman's bed at that very moment.

"I was just tired, that's all."

Quintina nodded but seemed unconvinced. She let her gaze sweep the room. "You have so many lovely things." She picked up a framed photograph on Clara's desk. "Is this you and your sisters?"

"Yes. It was taken when I was twelve."

"Indeed. You were all so lovely, even then." She set the picture down and met Clara's eyes again. "Please tell me what has upset you. Is it the conversation you had with Gillian this evening?"

Clara stared in silence at her mother-in-law.

"I sensed the two of you had argued, and when I asked Gillian about it, she told me you discussed Lady Cleveland. Poor Gillian. She's very concerned about you and feels terrible for even mentioning that horrid woman's name in this house. I'm afraid she'll never forgive herself."

Quintina stepped forward and hugged Clara. The warm gesture was unexpected, and Clara had to work hard to keep her guard up.

"It was kind of you to come and check on me," Clara said.

The woman drew back and touched Clara on the nose. "I couldn't help it. You seemed so miserable."

"Truly, I'm fine."

"You're sure?"

"Yes."

Quintina was reluctant to let go of Clara. "You mustn't worry about Lady Cleveland. The woman just appeals to Seger's rebellious side. It won't last. They never do. The important thing to remember is that he married *you*. You're the one he chose. I would offer to talk to him about it, but I don't think it would do any good. He would only deny the affair, as any married man would."

For the second time that evening, Clara was at a loss for words. She couldn't imagine what Gillian had said to Quintina. All she could do was stare at the woman before her, while the reminder of Lady Cleveland burned hotly inside her heart.

After a few seconds, Quintina moved to the door. "Promise you will come and talk to me if you ever feel unhappy or unsure about anything. I would like us to be close, Clara. I never had a daughter of my own."

She walked out, leaving Clara to ponder everything that had occurred that day, and finally decide to talk to her husband about it as soon as he arrived home.

Clara would be calm and rational in her quest for the truth, and under no circumstances would she give in to the urge to throw a vase.

Seger walked into Clara's bedchamber shortly before midnight. His breath smelled of whisky and cigars.

"Did you have a nice time tonight?" Clara asked in a pleasant voice, though she was reeling with doubts and anxieties about Gillian and Lady Cleveland. Even that wretched dress Gillian had mentioned.

Seger tugged at his neckcloth and began to unbutton his shirt. "I did. Lord Cobequid is looking well. He intends to return to India in a few weeks."

Seger told her about their dinner and billiards game. Then he related some of Lord Cobequid's tales of the

British colony abroad and slipped into bed beside her.

"How was your evening?"

"Interesting. Strange," she replied. "I'm not sure where to begin."

"How about at the beginning?" He sat back and waited patiently for her to elaborate.

"All right. I spoke to Gillian tonight," she finally explained, not caring if the subject exploded in her face and drove her husband from the room like it did the last time. At this point, she would welcome a fight if it meant honesty and candor between them, no matter how disagreeable it was for Seger.

To her surprise, he sat forward and took her hand. "I've been meaning to speak to you about Gillian."

Clara felt her brow furrow.

"I wanted to apologize," he said, "for the way I reacted the last time we spoke about her. It was wrong of me. I should have been a better listener."

Clara sat up. "Seger, I..."

She what, exactly? She hadn't expected him to offer an apology, and she didn't have a clue what she wanted to say in response. She was relieved, of course, but something inside her was suspicious about why he was offering an apology on this, of all nights. He'd had lunch with Gillian that day. Had he suspected, like Clara, that Gillian had feelings for him? Was he ready to take Clara's side and tell her she'd been right all along?

Or was he trying to appease her because he was hiding something else—a rendezvous with Lady Cleveland perhaps?—and he wanted to keep her happy and prevent her from asking pointed questions?

He pushed a lock of hair behind her ear. "I have come to realize that I haven't always been easy to talk to."

"Well...."

"I apologize for that as well. Our marriage came to fruition very quickly, and I will admit now that I was apprehensive during our engagement, but I've since learned that the reality of marriage is not nearly as frightening as the idea of it. The decision was the hardest part, and now that it's done, I find married life far more pleasant than I ever could have imagined."

Clara regarded him warily.

"I believe," he said, "that we've been getting to know each other better. Do you agree?"

She gazed up at him with parted lips. "I suppose."

Where was this coming from? She wished she could accept it as a simple move toward a deeper intimacy between them, but knowing his previous lifestyle, his reckless desire for women—and considering everything that had occurred that day—how could she help but have doubts?

"You don't feel that you have given up a great deal?" she asked. "Your whole way of life?"

Assuming that he had actually given it up.

Seger inched closer and kissed her lightly on the mouth. "What I gave up cannot compare to what I have gained."

He kissed her again, more deeply this time, and despite her desire to hash things out with her husband, Clara couldn't help but revel in the warmth of his kiss. All that mattered when he touched her was that he continued to touch her, with his masterful hands and his irresistible talent to please. All she wanted was his body.

Clara feared suddenly that deep down, she *wanted* to be appeased. She wanted him to make her forget all their troubles. She wasn't proud of that, but there it was.

How thoroughly English she had become.

If only she could believe him. If only Gillian had not been planting seeds of doubt in her mind.

In that moment, the thought of Gillian woke her from her passions and evoked an urgent need to clear the air. Clara could not continue to guess and brood about matters when she did not know the facts. That way lay madness.

Perhaps she was not so English after all.

"I heard you had lunch with Gillian today," she said.

Seger gazed at her questioningly. "Yes, but it was a chance meeting."

She recognized how intent he was to assure her of that. How she hated this.

She reminded herself that Gillian was not to be trusted. The woman was determined to make her feel unstable, and Clara would not, under any circumstances, let that happen. She had to keep an open mind and not rush to blame Seger. She must not look at the vase on the mantel.

"Seger, I must be truthful with you. I'm going to tell you what Gillian said to me today, and you can form your own opinions about it. I just need to relate it to you, for my own peace of mind."

He sat up, too, and began to look concerned. "What did she say?"

"She said things about Lady Cleveland. She made references and suggested that you were still involved with her. That you were with her today. Were you?"

His eyes darkened. "No, I was not."

Clara inhaled deeply. One down, one more to go.

"Gillian also said that you confessed all your deepest feelings to her, and you thought I was little more than a stranger to you."

"I beg your pardon?" Seger replied. "She said those exact words? You are not paraphrasing?"

Clara's heart was clamoring, her stomach churning with dread. What if he thought she was hysterical and imagining things? What if he took Gillian's side? What if he truly was still involved with Lady Cleveland and lying about it?

"That is exactly what she said," Clara replied. "Almost verbatim. Truly, I do not want to cause trouble, but Gillian has said some terrible things to me, and I don't think I can bear it another minute. She has tried to make me doubt you, and I must admit, I am a vulnerable target in that regard."

He gazed at her for a moment. "Do you doubt me?"

As difficult as this was, the most important thing was to nurture what intimacy existed between herself and her husband, and to close the emotional distance between them. She needed Seger to understand her heart, and she needed to understand his. There had to be truth between them.

"I will be honest with you," she said. "I am not sure."

There. The truth was out in the open. And the vase was still standing on the mantel.

Seger pulled her into his arms. "Clara, my darling, you mustn't believe a single word Gillian has said. I have not seen Lady Cleveland since the night you met her at that wretched ball. Gillian had no reason to say those things. I don't know why she would even think it."

Clara fought the tears that were threatening to fill her eyes. "I don't know either, except what I suspected weeks ago—that she has feelings for you, and she hates me because I am your wife. Even if it were true—that you were having an affair with Lady Cleveland—why would Gillian want to tell me and hurt me by doing so?"

He held her close and kissed her cheeks and then her mouth. "It is not true. Clara, have you been miserable because of this?"

"I've tried not to let her get the best of me, but I admit, I do not completely trust you."

Seger held her in front of him so that he could see her face. His eyes were dark and growing darker with every second. "I don't know what to do to change that. I want your trust, and I damn well deserve it, for I've done nothing wrong." He pulled her into his arms again. "I swear on my life, I am not seeing Lady Cleveland. I care for you in ways I never thought possible. I didn't think I was capable of this."

Because of Daphne, she thought.

Clara almost sobbed. "I want to make things better between us. I want to believe you."

He kissed her again, then slipped out of bed and reached for his trousers.

"Where are you going?" Clara asked.

"To speak to my cousin. She will apologize to you, and if she refuses, she will be packing her belongings this very night."

Clara realized the ramifications of such an action, and climbed out of bed, too. "You mustn't do that. Quintina would be devastated. She would hate me."

"She would not be justified in that hatred."

"Perhaps not, but it wouldn't matter in the end. Emotions don't always make sense, especially when they concern a loved one. Quintina adores her niece, and I don't want to be responsible for a rift between them. Quintina might resent me."

"What would that matter?"

Clara paused a moment. "Earlier tonight, after she learned what Gillian had said to me about Lady Cleveland, she came to my room and was very kind to me. I believe that her intentions were good. She said she never had a daughter of her own, and I feel there might be a chance for affection between us. I don't want to spoil that. Please, all that matters is that you and I are clear with each other. If I am confident in your faithfulness, Gillian cannot hurt me."

But was she truly confident? She wanted to be. She wanted to believe that he was sincere in everything he'd said tonight—that he was no longer seeing Lady Cleveland, that his grief over Daphne was fading away, and that he was finally ready to love Clara.

Seger hesitated, then walked around the bed. "Are you sure?"

"Yes. I don't want a confrontation over me to divide this family. I'll be able to handle Gillian from now on. Now that you know what she is trying to do, she has no power. I will tell her that you know, you can even say so yourself, and I wouldn't be surprised if she leaves quietly on her own."

He shook his head, as if in disbelief, then urged Clara down onto the bed and covered her body with his own. Soon, she was writhing with pleasure, feeling the onerous weight of the day lifting. Her body grew warm, and she buried her fingers in her husband's thick hair.

"I wish we could go on our honeymoon now," she whispered. "If only we could be alone together."

She wanted to forge a deeper bond.

Seger kissed her tenderly on the mouth. "I would like that, too, but I have an interview with a business speculator at the end of the week that cannot be rescheduled. I have many questions I want to ask him, and he is only in town on the twenty-third."

"Could we go somewhere closer and be back in time?" Clara asked. "What about your country estate? I haven't seen it yet, Seger, and I am desperate to see your home. Our home."

He stopped what he was doing and looked down at her. "Why not just stay here? We could spend the days together."

Clara sighed. "There are so many distractions. I want to be alone with you. Just the two of us. I want to stay in bed all day and not worry about my mother-in-law knowing what we are doing, or my sister dropping by to visit. I want to go for long walks across country meadows with you and listen to the birds. I want to make love in the woods."

A slow, lazy smile touched his lips. "You know that

I am always at your service. Anywhere and anytime."

She ran her fingers through his hair, and replied playfully, "I've come to discover that. Please say you'll take me, Seger. I want to see our home."

Seger rolled to the side to lean on an elbow. "You should know, Clara, that I don't consider Rawdon Hall to be my home."

Surprised, she gazed at him blankly. "But it's where you were born and raised, isn't it?"

"Yes, but I haven't been there in a very long time."

She felt a heaviness settle in her chest. "Why ever not?"

"I've always traveled abroad during the winters, and when I return to England I come here to the London House. I deal with estate matters from a distance."

"But why?" she asked again, fearing she already knew the answer.

He shrugged. "The place does not hold happy memories for me."

Clara stared at her husband in bleak silence and sat up. "Because of Daphne?" *There it was...out in the open at last.*

For a long moment, Seger said nothing. Then he sat up as well and touched her cheek. "You look wounded, Clara."

"No, I'm not." But her voice was trembling.

"I promise you, my feelings for Daphne are ancient history. She might have been my reason to leave eight years ago, and the reason why I haven't returned, but that's merely because I became a creature of habit. I assure you, she is forgotten. You're all that matters to me now. Come, lie down. Seger inched toward the pillows. "There has been too much talk of other women tonight, and I don't want to think of anyone but you."

Clara forced herself to lie back and snuggle close to her husband.

"And you're right, my darling," he added. "We are newly married. We need to spend some time alone together. I will send word to Rawdon Hall first thing in the morning and tell them to expect us the day after. It's time we embarked upon our new life."

Clara rested her cheek on his warm shoulder, smiled when he kissed her forehead, and wished she could feel better about the new life she had begun.

Gillian stood at the window in her bedchamber and did not even try to fight the tears that were pouring from her eyes like two cascading waterfalls. Her cheeks were drenched. Her nose was running, and she couldn't stop sniffling.

She pressed her hand to the cool pane of glass and watched Seger's coach disappear down the road. She cursed that vile American cow. Clara had lured him away with sex. How could Gillian compete with that?

But when had she ever been able to compete with anyone where Seger was concerned? Gillian had been fooling herself to think that Seger could ever fall in love with her. She had no idea how to charm a man. How to be coquettish. Everything Gillian had told Clara about her father wanting her to marry Seger had been a lie. He would never even have considered such a thing. He'd always called Gillian an embarrassment.

Gillian should not have let Quintina manipulate her. She should have given up on those dreams the day of the wedding. Quintina had been wrong to suggest that things could change. She had given Gillian false hopes.

Quintina entered the room, saw her niece sobbing by the window, and immediately embraced her. "There, there darling. Go ahead and cry, get it all out. That's better. All will work out, you'll see."

But Gillian did not see. She pushed her aunt away and wiped the tears from her eyes. "No! I have tried and tried, but she will not be broken! I can't do it anymore. She is not behaving the way you said she would. You said she would be driven to tears, but I am the one who is crying."

"Get a hold of yourself, dear. The war is not over."

"This is not a war, Auntie. It is a marriage, and I am an outsider. I do not belong here. I should go home to my uncle's house and forget about Seger. I should prepare for a Season of my own next year and find someone else."

Quintina moved forward again and took hold of Gillian by the shoulders. "You are upset because they just left, but they will be back, and we still have one more scheme to execute. Do not give up now. I want Susan, God rest her soul, to know that I made your dreams come true, and to be frank with you, dear, I cannot bear to think that my future grandchildren will be half American. Wait until we at least exhaust all possibilities."

"I'm beginning to think this is more for you than me!" Gillian replied. "You hate the fact that your parents lost their home to an American, and you can't bear for it to happen again. But Clara is mistress of this house now, Auntie, and there is not one single thing we can do about it."

"But there is!" Quintina replied desperately.

"No. I can't do this anymore. It's humiliating! I hate being in this house when he goes to her bed every night!"

"Gillian, calm yourself. Sit down and listen to me. Something significant is about to happen. I have been communicating with that man I told you about—the one from America. He has incriminating information about Clara and his very presence will knock her clear off her glowing pedestal. I have asked him to come to London, and I assure you, it's going to be sordid. He is on his way here as we speak."

Gillian sat down and tried to stop crying as she listened in foggy comprehension to what her aunt told her would happen next.

Chapter 19

Dear Adele,

I love Seger and I want to make him happy, but there are still so many barriers between us. While I believe I have overcome the problem with Gillian, I am still not at ease. I must continue to live with the knowledge that what happened to the woman he loved eight years ago has left a deep hole in his heart. She is the sole reason that his heart has been so inaccessible, and while I knew that from the beginning, I believed my love would fill that hole. I have just learned, however, that he has not returned to his home in the country since she died. We are traveling there today, and I do not know what to expect....

Clara

$\mathcal{A}$S THE CARRIAGE APPROACHED RAWDON Hall and drove around the circular fountain in front of the house, Seger realized with unease that an emotional awakening did not come without some discomfort, for he could not seem to escape thoughts of Daphne.

He had always been able to avoid reminiscing—he had spent eight years teaching himself how to bury his feelings—but at present, he could not push her from his mind. She was so much a part of his youth and his memories of this house, which was why he had never returned. Until now.

He gazed out the carriage window at the south garden. All at once, a host of vivid images came hurling, spinning back at him. He recalled the excitement and anticipation of running through that garden, sneaking away in the evenings before dinner, to meet her secretly down at the lake. He remembered how his feet would carry him across the lawns and through the woods, how his heart would race at the thought of seeing her. For four years she had been his best friend, his confidante. She was—and would always be—his first love.

A knot of tension formed in his gut as the carriage rolled to a stop. He remembered the last time he had been there, when he'd driven away devastated and shattered—emotionally bruised and beaten down into a state of complete and utter grief over Daphne's death. He had not looked back. He couldn't. He'd been so full of rage toward his father for sending Daphne away. For being the cause of her death.

Why had she gotten on that ship? he had wondered so desperately afterward. Why hadn't she come to him? If she had, they could have run away together.

The question had haunted him for years. He had wondered what he'd done wrong. In the end, he finally accepted that she'd chosen to leave, thinking it was for his own good. She'd always worried about his parents' disapproval. She had not wanted to be the reason his father would disinherit him, as he had threatened to do.

The carriage stopped in front of the house, and Clara squeezed Seger's hand. He smiled at her, pleased at least that she was here to distract him from those memories and remind him that life was not the same as it was. Now he was married to an extraordinary woman he desired beyond any imagining. He had come around full circle. He was home, and he was about to start a new life.

He helped Clara out of the carriage and escorted her into the front hall where the servants were standing in two straight lines, eager to greet the new marchioness. Seger recognized almost no one. He supposed many of the former servants must have moved on and been replaced over the years. Even the butler was strange to him.

A short while later they were shown to their rooms, and Clara seemed genuinely pleased with her boudoir and the house in general.

"It's lovely," she said. "I'll be very happy here, Seger. We will live here, won't we? You won't continue to manage things from London?"

Seger kissed her hand. "If you wish to live here, then we will make it our home."

He was surprised to hear himself speak those words so quickly, without really thinking it through. He had expected more of a resistance from his deeper self—from the place where the memories lived.

But he supposed he had faced those memories just now and had not suffered so much after all. Yes, he had remembered things—things he had not permitted himself to revisit before now, because they were too painful. But they were only memories. Scattered and dim. Small, individual fragments of the four years he had spent with Daphne. Sad memories of a difficult and turbulent time, yes, but there were pleasant memories, too, and for the first time since he couldn't remember when, he had faced them. He had remembered how he had felt when he was sixteen.

Perhaps he could let himself remember other things as well. Face all of it at last and put it behind him.

Clara spent an hour in her room with her maid, unpacking her things and freshening up after the journey from London. Then she met Seger in the drawing room at the agreed upon time.

He took her on a tour of the house, which she enjoyed immensely for it was a wonderful house, full of antiquities and art as well as all the modern conveniences. Then they ventured outdoors to the stables where a groom was waiting for them, with two horses saddled.

She and Seger went riding over the green hills and through the trees along a narrow river. Seger told her about the childhood games he used to play with two boys who were sons of a nearby squire. He showed her the squire's house from a distance and wondered if the family still lived there.

"Would you like to call on them?" Clara asked, but Seger said no, reminding her that this was their time to be alone together.

"Another day," he said, and Clara felt a rush of happiness.

Later, they arrived at a lake, and decided to give the

horses a rest. Seger dismounted and tethered his gelding, then helped Clara down, too.

"Shall we walk?" he suggested.

A short time later, they sat down on the grass in the shade of some towering oaks. Seger leaned back on his elbows and crossed his ankles. He stared at the calm lake.

There was not even the hint of a breeze. Clara breathed in the clean, damp scent of the water and listened to the birds chirping. The trees were still.

"It's so peaceful here. I believe I could come every day and just sit here and do nothing but daydream." She gazed up at the leafy branches over her head, blocking her view of the sky.

Seger said nothing. He was very quiet.

She watched him for a moment or two and wished she knew what he was thinking about, then it occurred to her that he might be thinking about Daphne. Remembering....

Clara felt a tightening sensation in her stomach and cleared her throat. Maybe she should suggest that they leave now and go back to the house. They could go to her bedchamber. They hadn't made love yet. Perhaps they could steal some time before dinner.

Then she reminded herself that she had come to Rawdon Hall with her husband get to know him better. To forge a deeper connection between them—a connection that continued outside of the bedroom.

"Does all this remind you of Daphne?" Clara gently asked him.

He met her gaze and he looked surprised at first, then his face softened. "Yes."

Clara tried not to feel hurt that he was thinking about another woman now, in this beautiful, idyllic place, when she was thinking of no one but him.

Wanting him to feel that she was offering comfort—and *not* wanting him to know that she was fighting a pang of jealousy—she reached out and touched his shoulder.

"Did you come here with her often?" Clara asked.

"All the time. We used to swim over there." He pointed.

Clara didn't know what to say next. He seemed melancholy and was particularly quiet.

Finally, Seger turned to her. "It was a long time ago, Clara. Don't think that I still want her. I want *you*."

Clara took in a breath as he leaned toward her and cupped her head in his hand, pulled her close for a kiss. She moaned blissfully at the feel of his mouth on hers and his tongue parting her lips and venturing inside. The kiss was full of reassurance—intentional reassurance, she believed. It was unlike any other kiss they'd shared.

Perhaps they did know each other in certain ways, she thought. Her husband wanted to soothe her. He did not want her to feel like she was second choice.

Gently, he laid her onto the soft grass and came down upon her, tilting his head this way and that as he kissed her. With roving hands, he reached lower and raised her skirts. The sensation of his fingers feathering over her thighs roused her senses and caused a flurry of butterflies deep inside her belly.

Oh, how she needed to be the object of his desire at that moment. She wrapped her legs around him and

held him close as he kissed her neck, his hot breath
tickling her skin and filling her with need.

"Let's make new memories," she whispered in his
ear. "I love it here, Seger."

Her husband recognized the passion in her voice.
Sensitive lover that he was, always willing to answer
to a lady's longings, he called up his extraordinary
charms.

Clara felt beautiful, as if she were the most important person in the world to him. He had such a talent
in that regard. All he had to do was smile suggestively,
and she opened to him like a spring flower.

Glancing down with teasing eyes, he unbuttoned
the top of her bodice and kissed along her collarbone.

"Tell me what you'd like this afternoon." His voice
was husky, provocative.

"Why don't you surprise me?"

Her body relaxed and surrendered as Seger unfastened his breeches. A moment later, he was easing
himself into her, slowly with grace and control, never
taking his eyes off hers.

They watched each other in the twilight as they
made love at the water's edge. It was peaceful by the
lake. Clara had never known such contentment, such
deep, soul-blazing love.

After a time, his pace quickened, and he closed his
eyes. He pushed into her firmly and held himself deep
inside—so deep it felt as if he was filling her completely.

A moment later, passions spent, Seger collapsed on
top of her. "I think I just gave you everything I had."

"But I hope there will be something left for later,"

she replied playfully.

He propped himself up on both elbows and gave her the rakish grin that always melted her heart. "I'll see to it. A hearty dinner should fill me up again."

He glanced at her hair and picked a few crisp, dead leaves out of it. "I've made a mess of you."

Clara laughed.

He fixed his eyes on hers and rolled onto his back beside her, tossing his arms up under his head. "I'm glad you suggested this makeshift honeymoon. It's been a delight so far."

Clara rested her cheek on her hand and rolled to face him. "Thank you for bringing me here. I know it wasn't easy."

She saw in his eyes that he knew exactly what she was referring to. "No, Clara. It has not been that difficult."

"But you were thinking of her for quite some time, and you were very quiet a little while ago. You looked sad."

"Only because I haven't thought of her in a long time, and that was my own choice. Being back here makes it impossible to ignore the memories, that's all. And I suppose I've finally accepted that it's time to say goodbye." He hesitated before adding, "I want you to know that if she miraculously returned from the dead and knocked on my door this very night, I would still choose you."

For Clara, those words were music to her ears. She dropped her gaze to the matted grass, but there was still one more thing that had been weighing heavily on her mind.

"Do I remind you of her?" she asked. "Is that why you married me?"

Seger leaned closer. "Of course not." He cradled her chin in his hand. "Clara, look at me. I admit that when I first saw you, I noticed a slight resemblance. Perhaps it's what made me approach you, but since then I have not seen it. You're different in every way. I don't see her when I look at you. I only see you."

Clara accepted his explanation and reminded herself that even though this conversation about Daphne was painful in a way, it was a good thing. He was being open with her, and that was what she had wanted.

"I understand if you need to think of her," Clara said. "It's been a long time since you've been here."

He touched her cheek, then leaned back on his elbows. "You've been very understanding. Most women would have slapped my face and stormed off by now."

She tried to smile. "It means a great deal to me that you are honest with me, Seger, and if at anytime, you want to talk about her, I'll listen. I want you to share your feelings with me."

He considered that for a few seconds, then kissed her. "Thank you, but I believe I will refrain from talking any more about my tragic youth. Let's put it behind us, shall we?"

He was right. It would hurt if he talked about Daphne constantly and told her private things about their relationship, because as much as Clara tried to be understanding, her heart was aching on the inside. She was only human after all.

Seger fastened his breeches while Clara arranged

her skirts, then he rose and helped her to her feet. He pulled the leaves out of her hair.

As they mounted their horses, she thought about Seger coming there with Daphne, and how often he must have pulled leaves out of *her* hair. Clara imagined Seger making love to Daphne, telling her that he loved her, as he must have done hundreds of times.

He does not love me, at least not yet. Not like he loved her.

The thought came unbidden, made her stomach clench, but she forced herself to banish it.

Chapter 20

Dear Clara,
It sounds like he romanticizes his first love, and now you must compete with the ghost of a perfect woman. I hope he will eventually see how fortunate he is to have you, for I know how deeply you love him. Every man should be so lucky...
Adele

CLARA WAS THE ONE HE wanted. Seger knew it with absolute firmness of mind when he climbed into bed with her that night.

Yes, he had thought of Daphne a number of times since he and Clara had arrived at Rawdon Hall, but the memories were distant. They were vague and seemed almost childish, for he had been a mere adolescent when he'd first met Daphne. He was only sixteen. He had fallen madly, hopelessly in love, but he was no longer that innocent, optimistic young boy. He had changed a great deal in the years since. He had lived a completely altered existence.

He wondered how he would feel about Daphne if he met her now, for the first time. He would probably not even notice her in a crowd of other women. He was far too experienced, or perhaps jaded was a better word.

"I enjoyed myself today," Clara said sweetly as she inched down under the covers. "I love this house, Seger, and I love the countryside. I will look forward to returning here after the Season has ended."

"As will I," he replied with some surprise. He rolled on top of her, pressed his lips to her delicate mouth, and smiled. "Because this bed—with you in it—is like a little corner of heaven on earth."

His "experience" had moved him to choose Clara out of an endless sea of eager, predatory females. Now, Clara was there with him, in the flesh. She was no ghost. Her patience and understanding—knowing that he was thinking of another woman from his past—only served to shore up his respect for her. She had understood the complexities of the situation—that he couldn't help but think of Daphne after returning to Rawdon Hall for the first time since her death—yet Clara had been sympathetic and tolerant.

How could he not love her for that?

Seger kissed her with an unruly passion and helped her pull her nightdress over her head.

Seger did not mention Daphne again during the rest of their stay at Rawdon Hall, but Clara took note of the times he was quiet and melancholy and suspected that he was thinking of her.

Nevertheless, she enjoyed their private time together and felt that by being understanding and patient, she had gained Seger's respect. They had, in fact, forged a closer bond.

Now, back in London and riding alone in the coach

on her way home from a brief shopping excursion, Clara reflected on her marriage and began to believe that a deeper love between herself and her husband was indeed possible. Likely even, if they continued in the direction they were going. They had come forward a great distance since their wedding day. Seger had opened up to her completely at Rawdon Hall. He had held her tenderly in the night, and he had appreciated her understanding.

Clara sighed heavily as a wave of relief and contentment moved through her. She felt optimistic about her marriage now, for the very first time.

The coach stopped at an intersection, and without warning, her door opened, and a man stepped inside.

"Sir!" she shouted. "This is not a hackney cab! Get out please!"

Before she had a chance to call to her driver, the coach lurched forward, and the man settled himself on the seat beside her.

She gazed at the familiar face, and it was as if all the air had been sucked out of her lungs. All she could do was murmur his name.

"Gordon."

"Yes." He stared at her for a few seconds. "Upon my word, Clara, you are more beautiful today than you were the last time I saw you. How is that even possible?" He placed his hand on his chest, as if he were trying to still his beating heart.

Panic surged into her veins and Clara had to fight to think clearly. "What are you doing here? I thought you were in prison."

"I was released three months ago."

"But you promised you would never contact me again. What do you want?"

He lounged back in the seat and rested both hands on his walking stick. "Straight to the point, as usual. It's what I always admired most about you, Clara. You always knew exactly what you wanted. Well, almost always." He smiled—a sinister, knowing smile—and leaned toward her, as if he wanted to sniff her.

Clara slid away from him. "I am married now, Gordon. I don't wish to see you. I must insist that get out of my coach immediately. Driver!"

But the driver didn't seem to hear her.

"Yes, I know all about your triumphant marriage," Gordon said. "It was splashed all over the New York papers."

Clara tried to keep her breathing slow and steady. "You still haven't told me why you're here."

"Why do you think I'm here?"

"I don't know. All I know is that I want you to leave." How could she ever have been so young and foolish as to allow this man into her life?

He shook his head at her. "You must know I've never stopped loving you."

Clara frowned. "That's the most ridiculous thing I've ever heard. You never loved me. You wanted my father's money, and you got it when we parted—a great deal of it—so you had better leave now before he finds out about this, and takes steps to see you back in prison for blackmail."

"I don't wish to blackmail you," Gordon replied. "I only wanted to see you."

"Why?"

"Because I've been thinking of you every night since we parted...every wretched night I was in prison. Surely you remember what we had together. How exciting it was."

She slid away from him again, disgusted by his mendacity. "I remember nothing! You manipulated me and lied to me." When he did not respond to those accusations, she narrowed her eyes at him. "Did you send that telegram to my husband on our wedding day?"

He considered the question for a moment. "No, that wasn't me."

"But obviously you know about it. Who did you tell? Who sent it?"

"To be honest, I don't know, and I don't care. I'm here only to see you again for my own personal reasons, and to remind you of the love we shared."

"It wasn't love, and the only thing I am reminded of is filth. Get out of my carriage, Gordon, and do not ever contact me again."

"But I don't want to get out."

He moved closer until she was pinned up against the side of the coach. He moved his face in slow circles in front of hers, so close she could almost feel his mouth touching hers. She turned her face away in disgust.

"I want to be with you again," he said. "We belong together. Surely your husband of all people will be open to his wife taking a lover. Based on what I've heard about him, he would probably encourage it."

Clara tried to squirm out of his grasp. "I don't know what you've heard, but it isn't true. Our marriage isn't like that."

He continued to paw at her, kissing the side of her head. "You're dreaming if you think he isn't taking lovers of his own. If nothing else, why not get revenge?"

"Let go of me!"

Just then, the coach bumped, and Clara glanced out the window. "We are almost at Rawdon House," she said in a panic. "Get out of here, Gordon, or I will call my husband out to remove you himself, and I guarantee he won't be gentle."

Gordon glanced out the window as well. "Damn. I suppose I should hop out now before he finds out about us." He slid away and picked up his hat. "As the English say, *Cheerio*."

He opened the door and leaped onto the street, leaving Clara behind to still her racing heart.

"There is no us!" she shouted after him.

The coach reached Rawdon House and stopped. Clara bolted inside to tell Seger what had happened, for she had vowed on their wedding day that there would be no more secrets, and she intended to keep that promise.

Seger descended the stairs at his club. He had been informed that Quintina was waiting for him outside with an urgent message. She had never come looking for him at his club before.

"What's wrong?" he asked, exiting the building and letting the door fall closed behind him.

Quintina was pacing back and forth on the pavement. "Seger, I apologize for interrupting you, but may we take a walk?"

He stared at her a moment, then met her at the wrought iron gate and offered his arm. "Certainly."

"I have something to tell you," she said, as they strolled down the street, "and I don't know exactly how to say it. It has come as a shock to me, and I hope it will not be unduly painful for you to hear."

"What is it, Quintina?"

She cleared her throat. "I have a friend in New York, and she has informed me that Clara was involved in some sort of embezzlement a few years ago."

Seger glowered down at Quintina. "I already know about that. Clara explained what happened, and she is innocent. But I am curious to know how your friend came by this information, and if this is the person who sent me a telegram on my wedding day. Who is it, may I ask?"

Quintina glanced up at him. "An Englishwoman I knew a number of years ago. She moved to America to become a governess, and when she read about you and Clara in the New York papers, she felt a moral obligation to inform me of Clara's background."

Stopping on the pavement, Seger faced his stepmother squarely. "I would like to know this woman's name, if you please. This is a matter that must be addressed posthaste. I will not have anyone spreading lies about my wife—lies that concern something that is dead and buried in the past."

Quintina sighed. "But Seger...I'm not entirely sure that it *is* dead and buried, which is why I felt it necessary to speak to you immediately. You see, my friend wrote to me about this issue quite some time ago, but I chose not to mention it, because I like Clara very much, and I want your marriage to be a success. But I could not keep it to myself any longer, not after what happened today. Can we stroll again?"

Seger nodded and offered his arm. They walked in silence for a few seconds before Quintina finally spoke. "First of all, I'm not sure that Clara was entirely innocent. My friend informed me that her signature was on certain documents, but that is not what concerns me now. As you said, it's in the past. What concerns me is Clara's association with the man who lured her into this embezzlement in the first place. She was engaged to him, I understand."

"Yes, but Clara severed her relationship with him when she learned about the embezzlement, and he went to prison."

"But he is out now. Here in London, in fact."

Seger stopped again. "In London, you say?"

"Yes, but it's much worse than that. He came to the house looking for Clara, and she went off with him in the coach. Alone. I don't think she realized that I knew who he was. She said he was an old family friend."

Seger glared at his stepmother, then uttered an oath and turned to summon his carriage.

Seger walked into the house, where he found Clara sitting alone in the drawing room, gazing absent-mindedly out the window.

At least she was there, and not somewhere else.

He approached and stood over her where she sat on the sofa. Eyes wide, she gazed up at him.

"What happened today?" he asked directly.

She stared dumbfounded for a moment, then went pale. "Seger...." Her voice betrayed her trepidation. "You know?"

"Yes. But I wish to hear your description of the events."

She continued to gaze up at him with dismay, then rose to her feet, wrapped her arms around his waist and buried her face in his chest.

"I tried to find you when I came home, but you had gone out." Her voice began to quiver. "Oh, Seger, Gordon has come to London."

He would have liked to see her eyes when she spoke, but her cheek was still pressed to his chest. "I am aware. What happened, Clara?"

"He caught me off guard. I was on my way home from Piccadilly, when he opened the door of the coach and got in. There was no warning. He must have been following me."

"He got into the coach with you?"

"Yes. I told him to leave, but he wouldn't."

Seger reached around to pry her arms off him. He stared at her, trying to see the truth.

Just then, Quintina entered.

Seger held up a hand. "Give my wife a chance to explain." He turned his attention back to Clara. "He did not come to the house? You didn't go with him willingly?"

She shook her head.

Quintina stepped forward. "What do you mean, Clara? Of course he was here. Mrs. Carruthers told me who he was, and I watched you leave with him. I watched you from my window upstairs."

A heavy silence descended upon them while Clara and Quintina stared at each other, as if they were each trying to comprehend what the other was saying.

"I didn't leave with him," Clara finally professed. "I don't know what you think you saw, but I did not see Gordon in this house."

Quintina shook her head in disbelief. "You think both the housekeeper and I imagined it?"

"Yes!"

Quintina turned to Seger and gestured toward Clara with a hand. "Perhaps she wishes to spare your feelings, Seger."

Clara's voice took on a more aggressive tone. "I do not wish to spare my husband's feelings. I did not go anywhere willingly with Gordon Tucker. He stepped into my coach uninvited. Seger, you must believe me."

Seger's gaze darted back and forth between his wife and his stepmother. "One of you is not telling the truth." He looked down at his wife, whose face had gone ashen. He felt a stabbing sensation in his heart. It was fear, and it was sickeningly familiar.

He tried to ignore it and focus on the matter at hand—uncovering the facts.

"I swear on my honor," Clara said, "I did not leave this house with that man."

"But what motive would I have to lie?" Quintina asked. "And the housekeeper, too?"

Seger was not about to guess anyone's motives. He had not trusted his stepmother in many years, yet how well did he really know Clara? She had kept the secret about the embezzlement from him until he discovered it on his own on their wedding day. Now Quintina was telling him that Clara was not innocent after all, that her signature had been discovered on certain related documents.

He didn't know what to believe. His gut pitched and rolled.

Clara took a desperate step forward. "Seger, please...."

He held up a hand to silence her, then turned to his stepmother. "Leave us, Quintina. I must speak with my wife privately."

"Seger, I am terribly sorry. Perhaps I shouldn't have said anything."

"I am glad that you did. Now leave us."

Quintina hesitated a moment before she walked out and closed the door behind her.

Chapter 21

Dear Adele,
I pray that all will work out between Seger and
me. I believe that if I lose him now, after we have
come so far, I would never recover from the heart-
break....
Clara

"$\mathcal{I}$T SEEMS TO BE YOUR word against Quintina's," Seger said to his wife.

Meanwhile, the thought of Clara in the presence of her ex-lover—whether she was telling the truth or not—made Seger see red. He tried to push the fury away but couldn't. He wasn't accustomed to such vulnerability where a woman was concerned. It had been years since he'd felt anything like it. Jealousy was not even a word in his vocabulary when it came to his temporary relationships. His hands shook.

"I am telling the truth," Clara said. "I don't know how to convince you, except to ask for your trust."

"My trust? You lied to me once before about this matter. I would be a fool to offer my trust blindly."

"I never lied. I told you about Gordon, I just didn't tell you everything, because we barely knew each other. There was so little time."

"But you could have found the time if you'd wished to."

She sighed heavily, collapsed onto the sofa, and buried her face in her hands. "You're right, I could have. My only excuse is that I was afraid you would change your mind about marrying me, and I wanted you more than anything. If I neglected to tell you, it was only because I was so desperately in love with you."

He almost laughed at the idea. "Love? You just said, Clara, that we barely knew each other."

She looked up at him, her eyes red and puffy, laden with a mixture of anger and bafflement. "Don't you believe in love, Seger? Have you forgotten how you felt when you first met Daphne?"

"I spent four years with Daphne," he replied. "I've known you little more than a month. And Daphne has nothing to do with this."

"But you told me you fell in love with her the first time you saw her. That you decided she was the one for you after a mere week of knowing her. Can't you believe that I might have felt the same way when I met you?"

He did not want to think about how quickly he had leaped into an intimate relationship at the age of sixteen, how quickly he had given away his heart. "I was very young. You and I are not children."

She frowned at him. "You have become jaded and you have not let yourself love me, Seger. I deserve a chance to earn your love. I want to be more to you than just a wife in name."

He suddenly wondered why they were having this conversation, when the issue of her ex-lover still hung in the balance. He paced the room.

"What happened today, Clara?"

She sighed in frustration. "I already told you. Gordon walked into my coach, uninvited. I never met him here in our home. Quintina is lying."

"Why would she lie? She told me today that she wanted our marriage to be a success."

Clara spread her hands wide. "I don't know. Maybe she's lying about that, too."

He remembered the day Quintina had explained that Daphne had gotten on a ship bound for America. Quintina had spoken in sympathetic tones and tried to explain and defend her husband's actions. She had held Seger's hand as she delivered the news, but he had known she harbored triumph on the inside.

Today, he didn't know who to believe.

He watched his wife wipe tears from her eyes. Something inside him throbbed with empathy. He hated to see her cry and he did not want to feel this pain that was cutting him from the inside out. He wanted to crush it, like he'd learned to crush all feelings for other people years ago.

He didn't want to face the possibility that Clara had been dishonest with him, or that she was somehow involved with another man and was lying about it, as Quintina was suggesting.

He didn't want to face the possibility that she had married him for his title, like so many of her fellow countrywomen did these days, because he could not deny that he'd always felt certain there was something more than that between them. He'd always known Clara desired him in a basic, elemental way, and that pleased him. It had been his justification for marrying her. Desire was something he understood and could handle. Now, everything was falling into question.

He wanted to leave this room, to shut himself off.

He also felt the urge to protect what was his.

Seger walked to the door.

"Where are you going?" Clara asked.

He did not look back. "Out."

Seger went to five hotels before he found the one that had Gordon Tucker listed as a registered guest. It was an expensive hotel. Too expensive for an ex-prison convict.

He tapped the ivory handle of his walking stick on the man's door.

A few seconds later, the door opened and Seger found himself standing face to face with his wife's one-time fiancé, a man who had recognized her passion and had taken advantage of it in the worst possible way.

He was a good-looking man, tall with brown hair and blue eyes.

Seger wanted to strangle him.

"Lord Rawdon," Tucker said with a vile grin. "I was expecting you. Eventually."

He opened the door the rest of the way. Seger walked in and glanced around the room. It was familiar. He had been in this hotel—and every other decent one in the city—a number of times, but he didn't want to think about that. He was a husband now, and the sheer, rock-hard density of that role seemed to fill his entire being.

"I presume you have come to ask me to stay away from your wife," Tucker said.

"I am not here to *ask* you anything. I'm here to tell you that she doesn't want to see you, and that you should leave England today."

Tucker pulled a cigarette box out of his breast pocket, removed one and lit it. He took a deep drag and blew the smoke off to one side. "I don't think so."

Seger moved forward. "Clara belongs to *me,* and you will be back in prison by nightfall if you choose to ignore that fact."

"She belongs to you, does she? American women are not little lambs, Rawdon. You should have learned that by now. Clara is a bold and daring woman, and one should not try to put her in a cage."

"My reason for coming here is not to cage my wife. It is to get rid of *you.*"

Tucker raised an eyebrow. He sat down on the bed, leaned back on an elbow and crossed one leg over the other. "If you send me back to America, you will make Clara very unhappy. Is that what you want?"

"She won't be unhappy."

"Yes, she will."

Seger wanted to end this conversation immediately by throwing Tucker out the window, but he smothered the urge because he wanted information.

"I understand that you forced your company upon her today," he said.

"I wouldn't call it that," Tucker replied. "She received me in her drawing room like the proper lady that she is."

Seger cleared his throat. *She received him?*

If that were true, it meant Clara had lied about what had really happened.

But God! Even after hearing Tucker uphold Quintina's claim, Seger still had trouble believing it. He wanted to trust Clara—all his instincts were steering him in that direction—but how could he, when three people were now saying one thing, while she said something completely different?

He loathed being in this position—in a battle, unarmed, ignorant of his enemy. Unaware of the terrain.

He decided to take a risk. "She didn't receive you. You forced your way into her coach."

Tucker rose to his feet. "Is that what she told you? She's a sneaky one. You probably shouldn't have married her. I'll tell you what—I'll take her off your hands and marry her myself, if you'll agree to give her to me. A quiet divorce shouldn't be difficult for a man like you. You're an aristocrat. You must have connections in high places. I reckon she'd be happier with me, anyway. She doesn't have it in her to stay in one place for too long. Besides that, we're drawn to each other."

All at once, Seger felt a rush of blood pounding in his ears. He clenched his jaw, hauled back an arm, and threw a hard punch at Tucker, knocking him flat onto the bed.

"Bloody hell!" Tucker cried, cupping his chin in his hand.

Seger turned to leave. "Be out of here by tonight, sir, or I'll be back in the morning to continue this conversation exactly where we left off."

Gillian heard the hotel door click shut and stepped out of the wardrobe. Heart racing, she smoothed a hand over her skirts and observed Gordon sitting on the edge of the bed, clutching his jaw. He glanced up at her with a feeble expression in his eyes. His lip was bleeding.

"He punched me!"

She crossed over the carpet to stand before him, took a look at his lip, and removed a handkerchief from her reticule. "Here. Use this."

He reluctantly accepted it. "I thought you English were supposed to be polite and reserved."

"Not Seger," she replied. "Well, he's polite when he wants to be, but never reserved."

Gordon shook his head. "I don't know what you see in him. He's a brute if you ask me."

"You were plenty brutish yourself."

He didn't look up at her. He just dabbed at his lip with her handkerchief.

For a long moment, she watched the top of his head. His hair was a shiny brown color. She liked the way it parted in waves.

"I would have thought you'd be used to fighting," she said, "after being in prison."

He tried to give her back the handkerchief, but it was stained with blood.

"Keep it," she said.

He stuffed it into his pocket and stood. He was very tall. He towered over her, and he smelled like cigarette smoke.

"I had a talent for talking my way out of most

fights," he told her.

"I'd wager you did."

The side of his mouth curled up in a careless grin. "Not this one, though. Seemed more like I was talking my way *into* it."

Gillian shrugged. "It's what you agreed to."

"Yes, and I also agreed to a hundred pounds. I said exactly what your aunt told me to say, so where's my reward?"

She paused and looked up at Gordon Tucker.

This man was a criminal. She'd never known a criminal before.

"I have it right here." Gillian reached into her reticule and pulled out a bank note. She held it between two fingers and waited for him to take it, but he didn't right away.

His eyes bored into hers.

She felt an electric current surge through all her nerve endings.

Then he smiled, and slowly drew the note from her fingers.

Clara sat up in bed, waiting anxiously for Seger to come home, but he stayed away for most of the night—which gave her plenty of time to think about what happened that day.

Quintina had lied. She had looked Clara in the eye and spoken a complete fabrication. Clearly, she was carrying out some sort of scheme to disgrace Clara. But why?

The answer was obvious: Gillian wanted Seger, and Quintina wanted her niece to have him.

As soon as Clara realized that, she decided it would be best to remain in her bedchamber and wait for her husband to return, for she had no idea what might occur if she confronted Quintina or Gillian. She did not know how far they would take this.

Finally, after spending the entire evening entertaining every possible scenario about where Seger had gone, Clara heard the coach roll up outside. It was almost midnight. By the time he reached her bedchamber, Clara was wound up tighter than a tall case clock.

He walked in, and despite the fact that she was still uncertain of his feelings, every fragment of her being sighed with relief. At least he was home.

He closed the door behind him and moved to stand at the foot of her bed. "I spoke to Gordon Tucker today."

"Did he tell you what happened? Do you believe me now?"

Her husband circled the bed and stood over her. "He told me you received him in the drawing room."

Clara glared at him with burning eyes. "He's lying, and I won't have it. It's a conspiracy, Seger. If you don't believe me, I will get to the bottom of it myself." She slipped out of bed and reached for her wrap. She'd barely pushed her arms into the sleeves, when Seger laid a hand on her shoulder.

"Where are you going?" he asked.

"To talk to your stepmother. She lied today, and if Gordon told the same lie, that means they are working together. Quintina wants to get rid of me. The only explanation I can see is that she must be doing this for Gillian."

"Wait." Seger turned her around to face him.

"Why should I wait? Despite what you think, I'm not being irrational, and I'm not making this up to hide an affair with my former fiancé. I have never been more serious about—"

Suddenly, her words were smothered by the intensity of her husband's kiss. He crushed her mouth under his, as if he hadn't seen her for a year. A tiny moan escaped her, and her knees turned to jelly. Clara wrapped her arms around his neck, kissed him deeply in return, and could barely remember what she had been saying only seconds ago....

After he finished kissing her quite thoroughly, he drew back and looked into her eyes. Clara felt weak and dazed. She couldn't think straight.

"Do you think I've lost my mind?" she asked.

"No," he replied, "but I spent the entire night thinking that maybe I'd lost mine."

Her anger slowly receded, and she took a deep, calming breath. "Why?"

"Because despite what Quintina and Gordon Tucker profess, I want to take your side in this."

Clara was cautiously hopeful. "Does that mean you believe me? That Gordon stepped into my coach uninvited?"

"My gut is telling me yes, but three people have said one thing while you say another."

She took his face in her hands. "But surely, you must know that I would never do anything to jeopardize our marriage. You know that I love you, even if you aren't ready to love me back."

He looked doubtful.

"Please, Seger. I cannot stay in this house and face adversaries if you do not trust me—or if there is no hope that you will ever love me."

He turned away from her and moved to the opposite side of the bed. "This has been a trying day, Clara. I wanted to kill Tucker because I nearly went mad with jealousy. And I didn't want to feel any of that. I wanted to go back to the way things were before I met you. When life was less complicated."

Clara swallowed over a sudden lump in her throat. "You mustn't believe any of what Gordon said. I tried to get rid of him in the coach, Seger. Honestly." She heard the desperation in her voice. "I told him I never wanted to see him again."

"I want to believe you," Seger replied, "but that's the problem, you see. I can't help worrying that I'm inclined to take your side only because it's what I *want* to believe."

She knew she was grasping at straws. "Quintina and Gillian.... This is all their doing. They want me out of here, Seger. Think about that. It makes sense. If you can't trust your heart, trust that. Ask them."

He nodded, and she almost cried out in relief.

Seger moved around the bed to stand before her. He laid a hand on her cheek and kissed her tenderly. "I will, but not now. It's late, and after what happened today, I want to make love to you. I need to know that you are mine."

She thought about insisting that he go and ask them now, but the weary look in his eyes changed her mind. All that mattered was her husband's confidence in her love for him, so she pulled off her wrap and began to unbutton his waistcoat.

When Clara woke the next morning, Seger was gone.

She took a deep breath, knowing this day would either turn out to be the dissolution of a family or the dissolution of a marriage. There would be a confrontation. Accusations. Someone was going to be ousted and maybe even sent away.

She prayed it would not be her.

Clara rose from bed and rang for her maid. A half hour later, she left her room to go and knock on Seger's door. She wanted to go to the breakfast room on his arm. She wanted to present a united front.

When she reached his room, however, his door was wide open. She saw him standing in front of the window, handsome as ever in his dark morning jacket and waistcoat, so she entered without knocking.

He was holding a letter in his hands.

"Seger...."

He faced her. "A footman just brought this."

His eyes were dark with concern. Clara took the letter and read it.

Dear Lord Rawdon,
I am the one who sent you the telegram on your wedding day. I have information about your wife.
Please meet me at ten o'clock at Hyde Park, under Marble Arch.

"Who sent this?" Clara asked, as panic welled up

inside her.

"It doesn't say."

She swallowed nervously. "Have you talked to Quintina yet?"

"No, and there won't be time. It's almost ten now."

Almost ten! Clara's whole body tensed. "Will you go?"

"Yes. I want clarification."

"What do you mean, clarification? I've told you everything, Seger. There is nothing you don't know, nothing this person can possibly say that you haven't already heard, unless what they say is a lie. Maybe Quintina has orchestrated this."

He studied her face, then nodded. "It is quite possible, but I still have to go. I need to know who sent me that telegram, and why they felt the need to travel all the way here to explain themselves."

"But do you still believe me about Gordon?" she asked.

His shoulders rose and fell with a sigh. "I don't know anything right now, Clara. I want to gather all the information before I form any decision. Surely you can understand that."

She did understand. She always understood, didn't she? But it didn't make any of this easier to bear. "Seger, I want your trust and support. I did nothing wrong."

"But you of all people should know how difficult it is to trust your spouse completely, when there are questions."

Clara shifted uncomfortably. She supposed she deserved that. All she'd done was point her finger at her husband and assign blame, make him feel that he was never giving quite enough, without thinking about how it must have made *him* feel. No wonder he had not been able to hand over his heart to her. He felt she had no confidence in him. He didn't believe that he had her trust.

"Take me with you," she said.

He shook his head. "No."

"Please, Seger. I'll stay in the coach. I need to know who sent this, too, and I deserve a chance to defend myself if need be."

He considered it a moment, then finally agreed. "All right, but I don't want you to show your face. For all I know, this person might be dangerous."

The Rawdon coach clattered over cobblestones at precisely ten a.m., causing a flock of sparrows to flutter noisily from the treetops over Marble Arch.

Clara sat across from Seger in the coach, feeling sick to her stomach, while her husband appeared completely in control. The vehicle came to a slow halt, and Seger reached for his hat.

"You'll be careful?" Clara said, touching his arm.

"Of course." He settled his hat on his head and leaned to open the curtain with one finger. His eyes searched the area, then fixed on something or someone.

"What is it?" Clara asked.

She pushed her own curtain aside as well and peered out.

A woman stood under the arch.

Clara glanced back at Seger. He was still staring at

the woman, then he let the curtain fall closed and sat back. He gazed with a frown at Clara's knees.

"What is it? Do you know who she is?"

All the color had drained from his face. He was as white as a sheet.

"Who is it, Seger? What's the matter?"

Finally, his eyes lifted. They were deathlike. "It's Daphne."

Chapter 22

Dear Clara,
My lovely English governess gave her notice the other day and has now left us for another situation. I am extremely disappointed as I liked her very much. In many ways, she reminded me of you....
Adele

CLARA STARED NUMBLY AT HER husband, who sat unmoving across from her in the coach, his hands clasped together in front of him.

The whole world seemed to shift beneath her. All she could do was stare at him, waiting for a response.

A few seconds passed—seconds that seemed more like hours—then he peered out the window again, as if to ascertain that he had not imagined what he saw.

Clara slid across to the other side to sit next to him. "Are you sure it's her?"

"Yes." He covered his face with his hands. *"My God. She's alive."* He swept his hat off his head and raked his fingers through his hair.

Clara's stomach pitched and rolled. What would this mean for them?

They sat stiffly in the coach until Seger finally met her gaze and stared at her with uncertainty. A vein pulsed at his temple. After a moment, he moved to exit the coach.

She grabbed for his arm. "Seger, wait!"

He paused and looked back, but she didn't know what to say.

He didn't either, apparently.

She let go of him, and he left her behind.

Seger had to force himself to put one foot in front of the other as he walked toward Daphne. *Daphne!* His heart was ramming against his ribcage, and his head was spinning with a dizzying mixture of shock and anger.

How could she be alive? How could she have let him think she was dead all these years?

He stopped a fair distance away, feeling suddenly paralyzed as their eyes met.

Standing in the shade beneath the arch, she looked the same. Older, yes, but still lovely. She no longer looked like a merchant's daughter, however. She wore a deep purple silk gown of the highest fashion, and a matching plumed hat with black netting over her face.

Seger swallowed hard and forced his feet to carry him the rest of the way. When he reached her, he let his eyes roam over her face and saw the years that spanned between them. Tiny wrinkles framed the outside of her eyes. Within them, he saw the experience of a life apart from his. She was not the innocent, buoyant girl she had been when he'd first met her, all smiles and exuberant expressions. She seemed confident. Mature.

He had so many questions.

She took her time studying his face, too.

Slowly the shock of seeing her again abated. Seger took a deep breath and found the will to speak. "I thought you were dead."

She lowered her gaze to the ground. "I know."

Her voice hadn't changed at all. Something deep within him trembled at the sound.

"Why didn't you contact me?" he asked harshly. "Didn't you know how deeply I would suffer?"

She moistened her lips and stared apologetically into his eyes. "I thought it was best. I thought it was the only way to get you to forget about me and move on."

Seger clenched his jaw to try and stifle his anger—anger that stemmed from being lied to for all these years. By Daphne of all people. He needed to understand.

"Explain this to me, please. You were not on the ship that went down? What happened?"

"I was on another ship that left two days later. Your father was afraid that if you knew what ship I had boarded you would trace me to my destination in America."

Seger let that sink in, then his mind groped for other questions. There were so many of them, questions that had haunted him and gnawed at him for eight painful years.

"Why didn't you at least tell me you were leaving, and say goodbye?"

"Because you wouldn't have let me go."

"Damn right I wouldn't have."

She shook her head and met his eyes again. "I

couldn't let you defy your father, Seger. You would have been disinherited. You would have had no family. I didn't want to drag you down."

"*You* would have been my family."

"But we would have been social outcasts. Penniless."

His eyebrows drew together in dismay. "You knew that didn't matter to me. I never cared about society's approval. I ended up a social outcast anyway. By choice."

She nodded.

He realized by her response that from a distance, she had been following his path through life. The knowledge gave him a chill. "You knew that?"

"Yes. It was one of my conditions when I accepted your father's petition to see me leave England. I made Quintina promise to keep me abreast of your news."

Seger tried to stay calm and focus on the questions still burning in his brain, not the fact that his stepmother had been secretly communicating with Daphne all along.

"My father told me you went to him and asked for money in exchange for leaving me."

She shook her head. "No, he came to me with the proposition and the money."

"Which you accepted."

"Yes, and I will not apologize for that. I knew I would have to begin a new life, and believe me, it was a meager consolation."

A meager consolation. Seger's chest constricted. A panicky sensation moved through him, and he found himself breathing hard.

He wanted to hear her tell him that it had been devastating for her, too. He wanted to hear her say that had loved him, because that was the thing that had plagued him all these years and made him wary of trusting women's affections. He'd always believed that his only love, Daphne, had not really loved him so deeply after all. That their years together had been a lie. He had not been able to trust any emotion since then because of that doubt.

His voice shook when he spoke. "Did *you* suffer?"

Her eyes filled with tears, and she took a few seconds before replying. "Yes, Seger, more than you will ever know. I did what I did because of how much I loved you."

He blinked down at her and found himself at a loss for words. He could say nothing, do nothing, but stand there and stare at Daphne. Daphne.

Then something made him look back at the coach. He thought of Clara and how she must be feeling, watching this. She was probably wondering if he was about to leave her and return to the woman who she believed was his one and only true love.

He swallowed hard and faced Daphne again. "Why did you send that telegram on my wedding day? What were you trying to do?"

She nodded as if she had been waiting for that question but seemed reluctant to answer it. She turned and began to pace under the arch.

"For the past eight years, I've known what kind of life you were living, Seger, and a selfish part of me was glad—glad that you had never gotten over me. I liked knowing that I was the great love of your life, and that if things didn't work out for me in America, you would always be there, willing to take me back. Then I read about your marriage in the papers, and suddenly you weren't there for me anymore. Quintina wrote to me and told me that Clara was a terrible match for you, that she was a greedy, title-seeking vixen. I was more than happy to believe it and help her put a stop to the marriage."

Daphne stopped pacing. "But know this, Seger—I wasn't doing it for Quintina. I despised her and I still despise her now for being the cause of our separation. I was doing it for *me,* because learning about your marriage made me want you back. I began to fantasize that when it did end, I would find the courage to return to you. I imagined being held in your arms again."

Daphney paused, gazing intently at him. Seger made no move to take her into his arms now. He wanted only to hear the rest of her explanation.

"So I offered myself to the Wilson family," she continued, lowering her gaze and pacing again, "as a governess for Adele, hoping I would be able to find something to make you reconsider your marriage to Clara. I took things from Adele's room. I went through her letters and diaries, and the scandal with Gordon Tucker was more than I ever could have bargained for. It was like a gift from heaven, I thought. I was sure that would be enough to bring an end to your marriage."

"But it didn't," he said.

"No, it didn't. And then I...I started reading the letters that Clara wrote to Adele, and I realized that she was not what Quintina said she was, and when Clara wrote about Gillian, my heart actually went out to her. I remember Gillian, you see. She was only a young girl then, but she was hateful toward me, too."

Seger nodded. Everything was becoming very clear.

Daphne approached him. "But those letters made me remember how it felt to be with you. I've never stopped loving you, Seger, and I have never married. My only excuse for doing what I did is that I was too young to understand how lucky I was to have the love of a man like you. I thought I would meet someone else one day, but no one ever compared to you. If only I had known that then."

She stood a mere six inches away, her eyes wide and searching. His Daphne. Her face, her lips, they were so achingly familiar. How many nights had he dreamed of kissing those lips again and holding this woman in his arms?

Something wrenched his attention away, however. He looked back at the coach again.

"Seger." Daphne reached up and laid a gloved hand on his cheek to turn his face back to her. "What we had was rare and extraordinary, and if you wanted me back today, I would come. I would marry you if it could be so, but even if it couldn't, I would be yours regardless. There are ways."

A tremor moved down his spine. "You are offering to be my mistress."

"Yes. Some things are more important than the rules of the world we live in. You taught me that, or at least you tried to, eight years ago. It's taken me this long to realize that you were right. I do love you,

Seger."

Seger gently removed her hand from his cheek. He held it in his for a few seconds, then raised it to his lips and kissed it. "I'm sorry, Daphne. I can't be with you."

"Why?" she asked. "Are you afraid I'd leave you again? Because I wouldn't. I'm wiser now, Seger. I know what's important."

He stared into the depths of that statement and felt a great wave of wisdom himself. "As do I."

Daphne slowly pulled her gloved hand from his. "Your marriage to Clara."

"Yes."

She glanced back at the coach and nodded. "Then, I'm too late."

"Yes."

Daphne continued to stare at the coach as if she wanted to see the woman who had, after all these years, reached and redirected Seger's heart, but the curtain was drawn. "She must be very special."

"She is. And she is the reason why you and I must say goodbye to each other."

Daphne shuddered visibly. Then she nodded. "I understand, but first, I...I want to give you something." She reached into her reticule and pulled out a stack of letters tied together with a ribbon. "Take these."

"What are they?"

Was this an outpouring of love? he wondered uncomfortably. Were these letters meant to make him change his mind?

She managed a smile. "You probably think they're

from me, but they're not. They're Clara's letters to Adele. I took them. You should read them."

He accepted the small stack and stared down at his wife's elegant penmanship on the top envelope. "They're not my letters to read."

"Ask her permission first, then, because you need to understand some things about your wife."

His eyes lifted. Trepidation rippled through him. "Such as?"

"Such as how much she loves you."

Seger stared at Daphne, speechless.

She forced a smile that did not seem to come easily. "I knew," she said, "that it would go one of two ways today. You would either take me back, or you would be faithful to your wife. I came prepared for the latter."

He continued to stare at Daphne's troubled face in the morning light. "Why are you doing this?"

"Because when I read those letters, I wept. I realized that she loved you more than I ever did, because I had selfishly allowed you to idealize my memory for eight years, when I should have proven to you that I was not the perfect woman you thought I was. On top of all that, I was ashamed of myself because I was willing to leave you, Seger. For money."

He felt his heart throb with what he realized was an unprecedented sense of freedom. He had thought he was free before, never committing to anyone or anything, but he had not been free. He had been in chains, afraid to love. Afraid to let Clara into his guarded heart.

None of that mattered now. *This*...this new understanding of his misconceptions about the past was opening his heart and mind to the extraordinary gift he had in the present.

Still staring down at the letters, he recalled Clara's patience and understanding when he had not been willing to give her his whole heart. He had never told her he loved her. He hadn't known that he had, but now.... Yes, now he knew.

He had desired her from the first moment he saw her across a crowded ballroom. And every day since, that desire had grown until it matured into love. *Love!* Now that Daphne was here before him, he knew that he loved his wife, and he knew that she had been unwavering in her love for him.

"I don't need to read these," he said. "I already know how she feels." *She has shown me every day. She has persisted, steady in her constancy, while I have shut her out.*

He heard Daphne's voice as if it were coming from a great distance away. "You should know something else, Seger. Quintina paid Gordon Tucker to follow Clara yesterday. I know because I went to see him. He told me that Clara loathed him because he was a threat to what she had with you."

Seger touched Daphne's arm. "Thank you."

She sighed. "I'm sorry for what I did to you, Seger. You've suffered long enough. You deserve happiness. Go and seize it."

He stepped forward and took Daphne into his arms.

Clara peered out the coach window, saw Seger kiss Daphne's hand, and knew she couldn't bear to watch any more of this. Her fists were clenched so tight, she was surely going to draw blood. She needed air.

She opened the door and got out. She walked around to the other side of the coach—the street side, where she wouldn't have to look at them, and where they wouldn't be able to see her—and leaned her head back against the side of the vehicle.

What in God's name was her husband thinking about and feeling right now? Had his love for Daphne come flooding back, and had he already forgotten the fact that he had a wife watching and waiting?

He had a wife.

Little more than a month ago, he had been a free man. He had married Clara very hastily. Was he regretting it now? Had proposing to her suddenly become the worst, most impulsive mistake he'd ever made?

Glancing up at the coachman, who was oblivious to her at the moment, she tried to decide what to do. She had always been understanding when it came to her husband's grieving heart, but this was too much. He was now taking advantage of that understanding, and she couldn't bear the weight of it anymore. She wasn't a saint. She was a woman with passions and fears. Did he ever think of that? No. He was presently kissing another woman's hand right under her nose—a woman he had admitted was the greatest love of his life.

It was just as Mrs. Gunther had said it would be.

Could Clara live like this? Could she survive a marriage that would cause heartache day in and day out? If it wasn't Daphne, it was Gillian or Lady Cleveland or a score of other beautiful huntresses, all of whom wanted a share of her husband, and Clara wasn't sure she could ever learn to trust him enough not to let them bother her.

She couldn't go on like this.

A hackney cab came toward her, and the need to escape this pain and anger displaced all sense of reason. She stepped forward and waved a hand. The cab pulled to a stop in front of her, and she got in. As soon as she closed the door, she looked up at her coachman, who glanced down at her. He lurched forward in his seat, but it was too late for him to do anything. Her cab was driving away.

She was glad. It was time Seger knew that she was not his ever-faithful crutch. It was time he fretted about *her* for a change.

Seger walked back to his coach. He couldn't wait to see Clara and prevail upon her the genuine truth that he wanted no woman in the world but her, and that he now had concrete proof that she was telling the truth about Gordon. He would assure her that he would deal with Gillian and Quintina at once.

When he approached the vehicle, his driver rose to his feet at the reins. "My lord...."

Seger raised a hand. "Not now, Mitchell."

Not giving the driver another thought, Seger opened the door of his coach. His eyes darted from one seat across to the other. Clara was gone.

He stepped back and looked up at Mitchell. "Where is the marchioness?"

The man's face was lined with worry. "Begging

your pardon, my lord. She slipped out of the coach so quietly, I didn't notice until she was driving away. She got into a hack, my lord."

Panic ignited in Seger's veins. He made a fist and pressed it against the side of the coach. "Which way did she go?"

The man pointed. "That way."

Seger ran around the back of the coach to try and see down the street. "How long ago?"

"Just a few minutes."

There were a number of carriages in the street. There was very little possibility of finding hers among them.

Seger bolted around the back and got in. "Take me back to Rawdon House."

He said a prayer that she had simply gone home.

Chapter 23

SEGER PUSHED THROUGH THE DOOR of his London house and did not stop to remove his hat or coat. He dashed up the stairs, taking them two at a time, and went straight to Clara's boudoir.

"Clara!" He knocked once on her door and entered, only to find the room empty. He then went to his own bedchamber and looked there, then headed for the drawing room.

He stopped in the open doorway when he saw Quintina and Gillian both sitting demurely in chairs, embroidery on their laps and a tray of tea and scones on the teacart.

"Seger, you look troubled," Quintina said sweetly. "Whatever is the matter?"

"Did Clara come home?"

She laid her embroidery aside and stood. "No. Why? Gracious, I hope she hasn't gone off with that deplorable Mr. Tucker again. Is that what has you worried? How can we help? Gillian, did Clara mention anything to you? Did she say where she was going this morning?"

Gillian opened her mouth to reply, but Seger moved fully into the room and stopped her with a look. "Don't even bother."

"I beg your pardon?" Gillian said, as if she were

bewildered by his tone.

He stood before his stepmother, glaring down at her coldly. "Clara is not with Gordon Tucker, nor did she ever receive him in this house."

"Seger, how can you take Clara's side, when she has been dishonest and—"

"She has been wronged, Quintina. By both you and Gillian, and I will see the two of you gone from this house by nightfall."

Both women were shocked into silence.

Quintina managed to gather her composure. "Seger, you married Clara impulsively, without a clear understanding of her nature. We now know that she is deceitful, and she has seduced you into believing her. It is not too late. We can get you out of this."

He shook his head. "No, madam. You are the deceitful one. You destroyed me years ago when you came between Daphne and me and informed me that she was dead. You will not do so again."

"*I* did not come between you. It was Daphne's choice to leave, and you cannot blame me for her death."

He took another slow step toward Quintina. His voice became hushed, almost a whisper. "We both know that Daphne is very much alive."

All the sounds in the room—the ticking of the clock, the snapping of the fire in the grate—seemed to recede into nothingness.

Eyes wide, Quintina stared up at Seger. "I know no such thing."

"I've heard enough of your lies." He turned his steely gaze to Gillian. "And I've seen enough cruelty. Clara is my wife, and her happiness is my primary concern."

Quintina made a desperate move to grasp his arm. "You are not thinking clearly, Seger. Jealousy over this Tucker fellow has turned your head."

He moved toward the door. "There has never been more clarity in my mind than there is at this moment." He stopped, however, when Gillian tossed her embroidery onto the floor and shouted at him.

"It wasn't my doing, Seger! Quintina was the one who talked me into everything!"

He recognized the desperation in her voice, saw it in her eyes, but it was too late for that. "You have a mind of your own, Gillian. You could have used it." He faced his stepmother. "I will wire your brother in Wales and inform him that you and Gillian are on your way to his home. I will also ensure that you are settled with an adequate sum to live on, Quintina, since you are by rights my father's widow. All I require in return is that you never set foot in this house again."

With that, he left the room and returned to his coach. "Take me to Wentworth House," he instructed the driver, hoping that he would find his wife there, and that she would agree to hear him out.

Seger stood beneath the portico at Wentworth House, asking the butler if Lady Rawdon was inside. The man did not answer the question. He simply invited Seger in and escorted him to the duke's oak-paneled study to wait.

Wonderful, Seger thought, preparing himself for the certain advent of the so-called "Dangerous Duke's" infamous wrath. *Bloody hell,* he didn't have time for this. He only wanted to talk to Clara.

Finally, the door of the study swung open, and James walked in. He stood tall and grim just inside the door, stared at Seger for a moment, then crossed the room and poured two glasses of brandy.

He handed one to Seger, and said, "This is disturbingly familiar."

Seger accepted the glass, then set it down on the desk without touching it. "Is Clara here?"

James regarded him, then set his own glass down as well. "You made me a promise once, Rawdon, that you would not treat my sister-in-law carelessly."

"Yes."

"It seems you have not kept your word."

Seger clenched his jaw. "No, I have not. I have hurt her, and I know that. But you can rest assured that I have not been unfaithful to her, nor have I ever come close to entertaining the notion."

James considered Seger's defense. "That's not what Clara believes—not after what happened this morning."

"She's here, then?" Seger asked, clutching at the hope that he would be able to make things right.

"Yes."

Seger felt the pressure lift from his chest. "I need to see her."

"But she doesn't want to see *you.*"

"Did she actually say that?" Seger asked. "Or are you just trying to protect her?"

"The answer to both those questions is yes."

Seger swallowed over his frustration and paced

around the room. "That woman I met this morning.... She means nothing to me."

Why was he explaining himself? The only person who needed to hear his explanation was Clara.

"From what I understand," James said, "Clara has endured a certain degree of stress since she married you. She is my wife's sister, and I consider it my duty to make sure that such circumstances do not continue."

Seger's whole body tensed. "Clara is *my* wife, Wentworth, and any duties regarding her happiness are my concern, not yours."

The duke's eyes narrowed. "I'm not sure you are capable of fulfilling that duty. You have not displayed any such tendencies in the past."

"Maybe not," Seger replied irritably, "but we all grow, and some of us even deserve second chances. I thought you embraced that idea."

Tension hung in the air like a thick haze. "I do," James said, "and you were given that second chance. I'm just not sure you deserve a third."

"I did nothing wrong. I had to see that woman. She said she had information regarding Clara, and when I realized who she was, I had to speak to her. You see, she was the woman I—"

"I know who she was."

Seger felt like he was talking to a brick wall. "Then you must understand why I had to speak with her. But it's over now. I'll never see her again. All that matters to me is that Clara...."

His voice broke. He couldn't finish. He wasn't even sure he could remain standing. "*Please,* James," he said, taking an unsteady step forward and pleading desperately, knowing he sounded pathetic. Knowing that his eyes were becoming wet, his voice was breaking. "I *have* to see her."

James stared at him for an agonizing moment, then he went to the door and held it open.

"She is with Sophia in the nursery. Third floor."

Seger regarded his brother-in-law with some surprise, then crossed toward him. "Thank you," he said, pausing before him in the doorway, before dashing up the stairs to find his wife.

Clara sat in the rocking chair by the window, gazing out at the gray sky and the idle leaves on an old English oak, while she rocked Liam to sleep. She leaned her head back, hugged the soft bundle gently to her breast and closed her eyes, but opened them again, slightly startled, when Sophia bent to scoop the babe out of her arms.

"I'll take him now."

"But he was just falling asleep," Clara whispered.

Her sister almost scolded her. "Clara, I'll *take* him."

Realizing something was wrong, she glanced at the door.

There stood her husband, filling the doorway completely with his large, masculine frame.

All her senses trembled, and heart fluttered like the wings of a hummingbird. Even after what had happened that morning, he was still the most beautiful man in the world. He made her weak with desire.

"Seger."

He glanced pleadingly at Sophia, who carried Liam

toward the door.

"I think I'll take Liam to nap in my bed," Sophia said, "while John is out in the pram with the nurse. Perhaps I'll just go and... and...." She gazed awkwardly at Seger and Clara. "I'll just go."

She left them alone in the nursery. Clara rose from the chair, her body tense as she tried to resist her womanly responses to him—the same sexual responses that had given him the power to take advantage of her on so many occasions, and to talk her into believing that he was the man she wanted him to be.

She didn't think he really was. He would always enjoy other women. She had simply been denying it to herself all this time.

Seger slowly walked toward her, as if he wasn't sure if he was welcome, and had to test the waters first.

"Clara," he said softly, "why did you get in that cab?"

She lifted her chin and wondered how it was possible that he could not understand why she had done it. Or perhaps he was just playing innocent. "Because I couldn't watch any longer."

"There was nothing to see." He took a few more cautious steps closer.

She responded by turning her back on him and walking to the other side of the room. "That is a matter of opinion." Every instinct she possessed sensed the intensity of his nearness as he quietly approached.

"No, it is not a matter of opinion," he said. "Listen to me." He turned her to face him. "I had to speak to Daphne to understand what had happened. I was in shock. You must understand that."

"I've understood everything, Seger. I've done nothing but understand, but I can't do it anymore. I can't keep coming up with excuses for my uncertainties about our marriage. I can't continue to be understanding and patient, when I am actually frightened to death on the inside. I don't *trust* you. I realized that this morning. I felt sick watching you go off to talk to her. I was sure you were going to leave me."

"I'm not going to leave you."

She looked into his eyes and saw sincerity. Desperation. But after everything she'd been through, she wasn't sure she could believe it. Maybe this was just his way of appeasing her, so that she would give him the freedom he needed to....

She didn't want to think about the rest.

Clara went to the table beside the crib and began to put Liam's toys back into the toy trunk, one by one.

"She wanted to become my mistress," Seger said.

Clara froze, then forced herself to continue putting the toys away. "That's not surprising. There are a number of women in London who want the same thing."

"But I don't want them. Nor do I want Daphne. I told her that. She is going back to America."

Clara whirled around to face him. "How can I believe you? She's the reason you never married for eight years! She's the reason you haven't been able to love *me!*"

He shook his head at her. "Maybe she was the reason I chose to live as I did, but she has nothing to do with what is between us today."

He moved closer and cupped her face in his hands.

"I'm sorry I have not been able to love you, Clara, but it had nothing to do with Daphne. It was because I had become so accustomed to a certain way of life, it became almost impossible to imagine anything different. I'd begun to believe that I wasn't capable of loving one woman. But from the first moment I saw you, I knew you were different. Everything about you was different, the way you looked, the way you made me feel. All other women were eclipsed by you, and they still are. You have been my friend and my lover, my confidante and my companion. You have made every day feel like heaven, and I think of nothing but you when we are apart. I could no more live without you than I could live without air in my lungs. I would die if I lost you, and that—I believe—is love."

Clara saw the light in her husband's eyes, and slowly blinked. Could she believe him?

"Seger...."

She had no idea what she wanted to say. All she knew was that her husband was kissing her. Holding her in his arms and calming her, soothing her.

He was such a magnificent kisser. Her body throbbed at the exquisite sensation of her breasts pressing up against the firm wall of his chest. Heat issued forth and simmered between them where their bodies touched. The tight, close contact began to melt the ice crystals she had worked so hard to forge around her heart.

He continued to hold her face in his hands as he gazed down into her eyes. Her body ached with desire. "I want no woman but you, Clara. I *love* you, and I will always love you."

She felt herself bending to his will as she always did. How could she not? She was melting in his arms, burning to give herself over to his strong skillful hands, quivering with the need to feel his flesh next to hers.

She labored to subdue such weakness. She had to be strong. She could not give in so easily. This was a turning point in her life. She would set the rules now and demand his fidelity and respect, otherwise give him the power to tramp all over her heart in the years to come.

Her voice was steady as she spoke. "How can I trust that you're telling me the truth? That you're not going to go back to your old ways as soon as this is forgotten? I can't live like that, Seger, and I won't. I would rather spend my life alone than suffer that kind of anguish, and I *will* spend it alone if you cannot be constant."

He stroked her hair tenderly. "Clara, I will be faithful to you until the day I die, and beyond."

"Those are just words, Seger. I need more than that. I need proof."

"Here's your proof!" He placed her open palm on his chest. "I have changed. Every day since I met you, I've moved farther away from the shell of the man that I was. I feel it inside myself. I'm whole again. Surely you can see it, too." He cupped her cheek in his hand. "Can't you see it in my eyes? Hear it in my voice? Feel it in your heart? God, this morning Daphne appeared, *alive,* and offered to be my mistress, and I sent her away. Isn't that proof enough that you are the only woman in the world for me? That my heart beats for you and you alone? *I love you, Clara. You are my entire world.*"

Tears of joy welled up in her eyes as she gazed at her husband and listened to all he said. Really listened. He was right—he had changed, and she could see it in his eyes. Still, she was so afraid to trust her instincts.

But she did love him. That much she knew.

"I love you, too," she said.

He gathered her into his arms and held her tight, kissing her cheeks and neck and finally her mouth.

"Clara, you have given me so much, even when I gave nothing in return. I want to spend the rest of my life showing you how much I love you. I want to have children with you and grow old with you. I want to prove to you that I will be the most faithful husband England has ever known."

A wealth of emotions cascaded over Clara as she stared up at her beautiful husband in the afternoon light that was pouring in the nursery window.

"I sent Quintina and Gillian away," he added. "They will never have another opportunity to cause you pain. No one will if I can help it."

He kissed her again until her lips were burning with need. She clutched at him, feeling as if all her dreams had come true. She did trust him. Deep in her soul, she knew he was the man she'd always believed him to be. Today, she had feared the worst. She had thought she would be heartbroken for the rest of her life, but he had pulled her out of that abyss and shown her what was real.

"Please know in your heart," he said, "that I will never leave you, nor will I ever go back to the empty existence that was my wretched life before you walked into it. You are my whole world, Clara, and I love you with all my heart."

She smiled and gazed into his fathomless green eyes, then wrapped her arms around his neck and cried tears of pure, perfect joy.

Epilogue

Three weeks later

QUINTINA ENTERED THE BLUE GUEST chamber—the room Gillian had taken at her brother's home in Wales. A note lay on the dresser.

> *Dear Auntie,*
> *I'm sorry to disappoint you, but I am leaving. I am going to America to marry Gordon Tucker because I have fallen in love with him. He is a handsome and exciting man, and he tells me I am pretty. I believe I have finally found true happiness.*
>
> *Love,*
> *Gillian*
>
> *P.S. I took the diamond pendent that you lent me, as we were short of funds.*

Quintina read the note twice, then sank onto a chair by the bed. *No, no. No!* Gillian could not have gone off with a prison convict. She could not have been so foolish! She could have married a duke or an earl!

What would Susan think if she were alive today?

She would blame Quintina for not making things right, for not taking better control of her daughter.

Quintina buried her face in her hands and sobbed. She could not accept that her niece—her dead sister's only child—was going to become an American!

Clara raised the covers for Seger to slide into bed beside her, and inched down cozy and warm. "I've been waiting for you for almost ten minutes. What took you so long?"

He smiled that rakish grin that she loved. "I wanted to make sure my robe was on straight and my hair was just right."

"Why?" she asked in a coquettish voice. "It's just me."

"Just you? You are the center of the universe, my love."

"Not for long," she replied.

He gazed questioningly at her. "What do you mean?"

"I mean, there's going to be a new center in our universe very soon. In about eight months to be exact."

His eyes sparked with joy. "Are you sure?"

"Yes. I saw the doctor today."

Seger gazed down at her flat stomach and rested his warm hand upon it. "A baby."

"Yes, Seger. Our first child."

He lowered his lips to hers. "I am the luckiest man on earth. You have made me so."

"Just as you have made me the luckiest woman."

Seger covered her body with his own and kissed her again, more deeply this time with full abandon. His hips thrust forth, gently but firmly, causing a sensuous arousal deep in her feminine core. She pressed her own hips forward and wrapped her legs around him.

"I love you," he whispered in her ear, and laid a trail of soft, open-mouthed kisses down her neck.

"I love you, too. I never knew life could be so wonderful, Seger. Make love to me."

He grinned and nuzzled her nose. "I will fulfill your every desire, my lady. Where would you like me to begin?"

Clara smiled in return. "Wherever you wish. You always seem to know what I want before I know it myself." She lifted her head off the pillow and kissed his open mouth, then relaxed as his lips made their way down her neck to the open collar of her nightgown. Gooseflesh shimmied down her spine. He slid his warm hand inside and Clara sighed with enchantment.

"What did I ever do to deserve you?" he asked, sliding her nightgown up, and cupping her behind in his hand. "You have given me such pleasure."

"More than just pleasure, I hope."

"Much more." He positioned himself above her and paused.

"I want all of you," she said.

His voice was laced with seductive teasing. "You're sure?"

"Yes."

He kissed her on the nose in the flickering candlelight. "Positively sure?"

Her head came off the pillow as her body trembled with need. "Yes!" she cried out, laughing.

Seger smiled. "Then you may have all of me, my love, for the rest of my days and beyond. Thank you for giving me back my life."

Then slowly, very slowly, he pushed into her until she quivered all over with ecstasy.

Author's Note

According to Oscar Wilde, the English gentleman admired the American woman for her "extraordinary vivacity, her electrical quickness of repartee, her inexhaustible store of curious catchwords." If such a woman was also an heiress, all the better.

In the late Victorian period and early in the twentieth century, approximately one hundred American heiresses married British nobles. A fair exchange of titles for money became the business of the day, and millions of American dollars wound up in the hands of impoverished English lords, who certainly couldn't work to replenish their bank accounts. That would have been ungentlemanly.

In that light, marrying for money was nothing new in the British aristocracy. It had been going on for centuries. With modern industrialization in America, however, Wall Street had come into its own. New Money was everywhere, and there was a freshly stocked market for brides who were not only wealthy, but beautiful and spirited as well.

But why were these American fathers willing to send their daughters and their hard-earned fortunes across an ocean to a country they had fought a war against one hundred years before?

As Marion Fowler states in her book, *In a Gilded Cage,* they longed for "the *poetry* of class." They felt the chill from those with "old money" in America, who turned their noses up at a society that had earned its fortune, not inherited it. The "new rich" wanted respectability, refinement, and something more than mere economic standing.

Princess Diana's great grandmother was an American heiress. In 1880, Frances Work of Newport married the Honorable James Burke-Roche, younger brother of an Irish baron. Burke-Roche had traveled to America and spent time in Wyoming, raising cattle, before meeting the woman of his dreams—the beautiful and very wealthy daughter of a Vanderbilt stockbroker. The couple traveled back to England where they had twin sons, one of which was Diana's grandfather.

Winston Churchill is another offspring of a transatlantic marriage. His mother was Jennie Jerome of New York, who in 1874 married Lord Randolph Churchill, second son of the seventh Duke of Marlborough. He proposed to her when she was nineteen, three days after meeting her on board a cruise ship, at a ball held in honor of the Prince and Princess of Wales. In 1895, Randolph died. Jennie married two more times and devoted herself to her son's political career. Jennie had two sisters who also married Englishmen.

I hope you'll look for the other books in my American Heiress trilogy, based on three fictional American sisters: Sophia, Clara and Adele. Sophia's book is *To Marry the Duke* and Adele's story is called *Falling for the Viscount*. Read on for an excerpt from that novel.

After that, you might enjoy the spinoff trilogy about

other members of the Duke of Wentworth's family. That trilogy begins with *Love According to Lily*, the story of the duke's younger sister. A complete booklist follows.

And if you would like to know when an ebook edition from my backlist goes on sale for 99¢ (or is occasionally offered for free), please go to my author profile on Bookbub and click the blue "follow" button. You'll be sent an email whenever there's a flash sale. I am also on Facebook and Twitter where I chat with readers every day.

— *Julianne*

In Love with the Viscount

Could this love nonsense really be worth the trouble?

To Adele Wilson the answer is clear: of course not! She has seen her two sisters dragged through scandal and heartbreak (not to mention every ballroom in London) to find the husbands of their dreams. And that's why she said yes to the first British lord who requested her hand. And why shouldn't she marry him? He is kind, honest, and not sentimental in the least.

Unlike his wilder, more mysterious cousin Damien Renshaw, Viscount Alcester. Ignoring Damien altogether would be easy if he were the sort of man intent on seducing his cousin's betrothed. But he is clearly trying to resist her, and his suddenly proper behavior only makes him more tempting to the usually well-behaved Adele. Indeed, Damien seems to be bringing out another side of Adele, a heady, passionate, exhilarating side. It seems that fate is contriving to teach her — against her best intentions — exactly what this love nonsense is all about …

Excerpt from
In Love with the Viscount
Teaser Excerpt

Prologue

May 1884

*I*NSIDE THE LAVISH INTERIOR OF the *SS Fortune,* steaming smoothly across the deep, dark Atlantic at night, Adele Wilson stood in her first-class stateroom and gazed uncertainly at her reflection in the mirror.

A heavy lump formed in her belly. Why? Everything was as it should be. Her mother was in the adjoining cabin to her left, her sister Clara to her right. Adele had just eaten a delicious supper at the captain's elaborate table and was about to undress for bed and read a most thought-provoking novel before turning down the lamp and going to sleep.

She removed a pearl and diamond drop earring and watched it sparkle in her hand. She closed her fist around it, then looked up at her reflection again.

She felt oddly disconnected from the floor, as if she were in someone else's body. A stranger was staring back at her—an elegant, sophisticated heiress who wore a jewel-trimmed Worth gown from Paris made of the finest silk money could buy, and around her neck, an antique, pearl-and-diamond choker to match the earrings.

She turned away from the mirror and looked around.

Suddenly, even the room seemed wrong. *Wrong.* There was no other word for it. Carved mahogany panels covered the walls, the ceiling was painted gold with extravagant ornamentation around a dazzling crystal chandelier. The sheets on her bed boasted the ship's monogram, and all the fixtures, from the door-knobs to the lamps, right down to the nails in the bulkhead, were polished brass, pompously gleaming.

Sometimes it seemed as if she were living someone else's life. She had not been born into this wealth. She didn't even know how to feel comfortable with it. At the moment, she felt as if she shouldn't touch anything.

Adele sighed. What she wouldn't give to be riding bareback through the woods as she used to do when she was younger, before they'd moved to the city and ventured into high society. Oh, to smell the damp earth and the leaves on the ground, and the green moss around the lake....

She inhaled deeply, longingly, wanting to remember, but smelled only the expensive perfume she wore. Feeling absurdly deprived, she exhaled.

It's nerves, she decided, crossing to her bed and removing the other earring and setting both of them on the night table. Tomorrow she would greet her future husband, Lord Osulton. An English earl. The newspapermen would probably be there to greet the ship and take her picture. No wonder she was ner-vous.

She would get through it, however.

Adele removed the combs from her honey-colored hair and shook out her long, curly locks until they fell loose upon her shoulders. That was better.

The door to the adjoining stateroom opened, and Adele's sister Clara peered inside. Clara had married the handsome Marquess of Rawdon the year before and had left her London home a month ago with her new baby daughter, Anne, to visit her family in New York. "You're still awake?"

Adele faced her sister. "Yes, come in."

Clara, still in her glittering evening gown, her mahogany hair swept into a flattering knot, entered the room and sat down on the chintz sofa. "You barely touched your supper. Are you all right?"

"I'm fine." But Adele knew she couldn't fool Clara who always strove to see beneath the surface of things.

"Are you certain, Adele? You're not having second thoughts, are you? Because it's not too late to change your mind."

"I'm not having second thoughts."

"It would be perfectly normal if you were. You barely know the man. You've met him so few times, usually at dull assemblies with Mother breathing down your neck. You've danced with him only once, which is essentially the only time you've been alone with him. And what was that, three or four minutes?"

Adele sat down next to Clara. "I'm just a little nervous, that's all. But I know in my heart that this is right. I'm sure of it. He's a good man."

"But you haven't had a chance to know for sure if there is any true intimacy between you. Some form of attraction. A spark that leads to a flame. Maybe you should think about enjoying the London Season just once before you marry. Imagine who you might meet. A dashing white knight, perhaps."

Adele shook her head. "I'm not like you, Clara. You and Sophia were the adventurous ones, while I've always been prudent and practical. Isn't that what Mother and Father said every time you and Sophia got into trouble?"

Clara smirked. "I can hear Father now." She put a finger under her nose like a mustache. "Why can't you two girls be more like your younger sister? We can always depend on Adele to behave herself."

Adele smiled and rolled her eyes. "The fact remains, I don't wish to suffer through an entire London Season, being speculated about, forced to wear diamonds every night and flirt in crowded drawing rooms. The thought of it, quite frankly, makes me ill. I'd much rather be in the country—outdoors with the fresh air, which is exactly where my future husband is at this moment."

"You might enjoy the excitement of a Season," Clara said, sounding a little frustrated.

Adele shook her head again. "No, I would not. I am content with my decision to marry Lord Osulton. He is an agreeable gentleman and a very good match for me. From what I understand, he doesn't enjoy the city, either. He prefers his country house."

"But aren't you afraid you might someday wonder what extraordinary adventures you might have missed?"

Adele squeezed her sister's hand. "I don't seek adventure, Clara. In fact, I loathe the idea of it. I prefer a carefully laid out plan, free of the unexpected. Besides that, I believe that sometimes, the best marriages are sensibly arranged. Love comes later, when it has time to grow and become something more substantial, based on admiration and respect rather than a spark and flame. Fire can be unpredictable, and it often burns."

"It can also be wonderful, Adele."

"Can it? Funny, I do recall when it was not so wonderful last year, when you thought your husband was going to leave you. You were miserable. I don't want to be miserable like that. I prefer a sense of calm without any of those difficult emotional ups and downs."

"But Seger did devote himself to me," Clara said, "and we are very happy now. What we have today was worth every minute of misery, no matter how excruciating it was at the time. Some things are worth fighting for, no matter how unpleasant the task. Are you sure you don't wish to postpone the wedding, and suffer through just one Season? You might discover the greatest romance of your life."

Adele sighed and stood up. She crossed to the wardrobe and began to unbutton her bodice.

"You would think," Clara continued, "being bookish, you might have read something about love."

"I've read plenty about love," Adele said with her back to her sister, "and I could never relate to those simpering, lovesick heroines stuck in towers, who stake their happiness on white knights. There are no towers or white knights in real life, Clara. There are only realistic men, and I am quite content to have found a most agreeable one for myself. Besides, it makes me happy to please Mother and Father. You should have seen Mother's face when I told her I had accepted Lord Osulton's proposal. I'd never seen her so proud."

"You cannot live your life to please others, Adele. You must think of yourself and your future. After the wedding, Mother and Father will return to New York, and you will be left in England on your own— no longer a dutiful daughter, but a married woman. You will be responsible for your own happiness and be free to choose what you want to do with your life. You should marry whomever you wish to marry."

"I wish to marry Lord Osulton. *Harold,*" she added, deciding she should probably start referring to him by his given name now that they were betrothed.

Clara smiled lovingly at Adele. "I daresay, you will do as you wish, won't you?"

"As long as it is the right thing to do. I have chosen my path, and I have made a commitment. I will not veer from it."

Clara raised an eyebrow, stood up, and walked to the connecting door to her own stateroom. "I suppose there is no arguing with you. You always were determined to do the right thing, even when Sophia and I tried to convince you to do otherwise. You missed some fun, you know."

Adele tipped her head at her sister. "I also missed many hours standing in the corner."

Clara shrugged. "Adventure has a price."

"And you and Sophia were always willing to pay it."

Adele's maid entered and began preparing the bed.

Clara opened the door. "We'll be docking overnight to pick up some extra passengers, then it won't be long before we reach Liverpool. The captain says we should be disembarking by mid-morning. It sounds to me like you're sure."

"I am."

"Then I am satisfied. I must go and check on little Anne. I'll see you in the morning." She walked out and closed the door behind her.

Adele smiled at her maid and reached for her night-gown.

London's Savoy Theatre
Shortly after four a.m. the same night

It was a well-known fact among certain circles in London that Frances Fairbanks—celebrated actress and hailed by some as one of the most beautiful women alive—enjoyed lying about naked. Especially on the soft, bearskin rug on the floor of her dressing room, when the room smelled of wine and French perfume, and she was gazing at a lover.

Or rather, one lover in particular. Damien Renshaw, Viscount Alcester.

He was by far the most fascinating man she'd ever met—tall and darkly handsome with broad, muscled shoulders and facial features that could have been sculpted by an artist. He was rugged and wild and unpredictable, and what's more, he was the most ingenious, instinctive of lovers. He knew just how to move to give her the most intense intimate experiences she'd ever known.

Yet there was tenderness in his lovemaking.

Frances stretched out like a cat and rolled over onto

her stomach, resting her elbows on the fur. Swinging her bare feet back and forth behind her, she watched Damien sit down on the deeply buttoned settee by the door and pull on a boot.

He glanced up at her briefly with dark eyes that usually promised pleasure and seduction, but at the moment revealed only impatience.

He was in a hurry to leave, Frances realized suddenly with a frown, which was extremely out of character for him. Because Damien Renshaw—the irresistible black lion—never hurried *anything* in the bedroom.

Frances stopped swinging her feet. "You left your shirt on when you made love to me tonight."

She had to work hard to sound confident. It was not something she was accustomed to—working hard at it, that is. She was always absolutely sure of herself where her lovers were concerned. *They* were the ones who did the scrambling.

She swallowed uncomfortably and made a conscious effort to swing her legs again. "You're not angry about the bracelet, are you?"

Pulling on his other boot, Damien didn't look up. "Of course not. As you said, you fell in love with it."

Indeed, she had. So much so, she'd purchased it herself and had the bill sent to Damien.

She sat up on her heels and spoke with pouty lips, hoping to kindle his flirtatious nature. "It was only a small bracelet. I didn't think it would matter in the larger scheme of things."

He rose to his feet, tall and beautiful as a Greek god in the flickering shadows of the candlelight. He searched the shambles of the room for his waistcoat.

He spotted it in a heap on the floor—on top of some purple feathers and Frances's colorful costume from her performance that evening.

He picked up the waistcoat, slipped it on, then reached down to cradle Frances's chin in his hand. He grinned, his eyes sparkling instantly with the allure that reassured Frances that she was still the envy of every hot-blooded woman in London. His voice was husky and sensual when he spoke, but at the same time commanding.

"Next time try to resist the urge. You know my situation."

She did, of course, know. *Everyone* knew. Lord Alcester was in debt up to his ears and had been forced to lease out his London house to a German family and take up residence with his eccentric cousin.

It didn't bother Frances, however. She didn't want Damien for his money. There were others who served that purpose. Damien's talents lay elsewhere.

He dropped his hand to his side and pulled on his overcoat. "My apologies for leaving my shirt on."

"You're not yourself these days, Damien," she said. "I hope it's not me."

"It's not you." He kissed Frances good-bye, leaving her ever so slightly distressed by this unexplained change in him.

It was still dark when Adele woke to the sound of a thump in her cabin. She remembered they were stopping briefly on the coast of England to pick up a few new passengers. She rolled onto her back, wondering how long they would be docked.

She stared up at the ceiling in the darkness and thought about the conversation she'd had earlier with her sister. Clara had suggested that Adele should be reckless for once in her life. This was not a new conversation. They'd had it countless times before as children and young women. Clara and Adele's oldest sister, Sophia, often tried to lure Adele into their mischief.

Adele rested the back of her hand on her forehead and recalled a summer afternoon when they were girls, not long after they'd moved to New York. Clara had gathered them together in the attic of their new house and said, "If we want to grow up, we must have an adventure. And everyone knows that an adventure must always start with running away from home."

Sophia's eyes sparkled, while Adele had been horrified. She had refused, of course, and argued the point of such foolish horseplay, and threatened to tell their parents.

Clara told Adele that if she breathed a word of their plan, they'd string her up by her heels, so Adele promised to keep it secret. Which she did. For about an hour. Then she told her father, who promptly marched out onto Fifth Avenue and brought the girls home and put them to bed with no supper. Adele, conversely, had been given an extra slice of blackberry pie.

Clara and Sophia didn't speak to her for a week after that, but then they forgave her—as they always did—and told her they supposed it was her job to keep them out of trouble because she was the sensible one.

But even now, as women, Clara was still trying to

talk Adele into misbehaving. Adele smiled and supposed it would never change. She'd be an old lady
with a cane and spectacles, and Clara would try to
convince her to dance in the rain. Adele smiled again
and shook her head.

Just then, she heard another thump, almost as if
there were a monster under her bed. Her heart leaped
with panic, but she quenched the sensation because
she'd stopped believing in monsters under beds many
years ago.

Nevertheless, she tossed the covers aside to check.
Her toes had just touched the floor when a man rose
up in front of her. Adele gazed at the dark figure
in terror and tried to cry out, but before she had a
chance, a cloth soaked in a strong-smelling chemical
covered her mouth.

Heart now blazing with terror, she struggled and
tried to scream, but couldn't make her voice work.
Then she felt weak and dizzy, and lost all sensation
in her body before she gave up the fight and remembered nothing more.

Part One

The Adventure

Chapter 1

Somewhere in Northern England

THREE DAYS. IT HAD BEEN three long days, and now it was beginning to rain. A storm was brewing.

Adele rose from the hay-filled tick that served as her bed and walked across the creaky plank floor to the window. All she could see in every direction were endless, rolling hills of grass and rock beneath an angry gray sky, swirling with the oncoming threat of bad weather. Hard raindrops pelted against the glass.

It was barren and lonely, this part of the world, wherever it was. She hadn't seen one person. Not even a lone goat or sheep. There were no trees, and the wind never stopped blowing. It pummeled the stone cottage on top of this sadly forsaken hill, rattled the windowpanes, and whistled eerily down the chimney. The door to the stable knocked and banged constantly. All day long. That—combined with the musty, damp smell of this room—was enough to drive a person to the brink of madness.

Adele made a fist and squeezed it. She had been steered off course into fierce, treacherous waters, and she wanted her calm life back.

If she still had a life to go to…. She wasn't even sure Harold—or any man, for that matter—would want her after this, because she had no idea what her kidnapper had done to her. All she knew was that he had undressed her at some point, because when she woke up, she was wearing someone else's shabby, homespun dress. Beneath it, she wore petticoats and a shift with ivory stockings, but no corset and no shoes. She had no idea what happened to her nightgown, nor did she know why her abductor had undressed her. To be less conspicuous, perhaps, in delivering her to this place of custody? She hoped that was the reason.

Adele breathed deeply in an effort to keep a cool head. She must not panic or lose control. That would do her no good. She had tried everything to escape this room in the past few days. She had pounded on and shaken the door, shouted for help, used all her strength at the window, but her efforts had been futile. All she could do now was wait for something to happen—something she could act upon. Or for someone to find her. Surely her mother was searching, and the police were investigating.

Just then, the front door of the cottage opened downstairs. Heavy footsteps entered the house and pounded across the hard floor. The door slammed shut and Adele's heart quickened with fear. She stood quiet and still, listening.

Voices. It was more than one person, which wasn't the usual routine. There had only ever been one captor here to bring her food and water. What was happening?

Suddenly, a commotion erupted. There was a frenzy

of footsteps. A piece of furniture fell over. Or it was kicked over. Was someone here to rescue her? Harold? But Harold would never face a kidnapper on his own. Or would he?

Her father? If only it could be him! But no, he was at home in America. He wasn't due to arrive in England until the wedding. Perhaps it was a constable. Or a neighbor who had discovered what was happening and had come to her rescue!

Footsteps pounded up the stairs and Adele's breath caught in her throat. Every particle of her being froze with fear and dread. Was someone here to ravish her? Murder her? Her eyes searched for a weapon, but there was nothing. Nothing but a chair. She picked it up. It was heavy, but she would swing it if she had to.

The lock clicked and the door swung open. Two men walked in. One held a pistol to the other's head. The one holding the gun was tall and dark and his eyes smoldered with fury. He wore a heavy, black greatcoat that matched his black hair. Adele feared him instantly.

Was he her captor? She had never seen the man in daylight.

"Your name!" he barked.

"Adele Wilson." It didn't occur to her to ask why he wanted to know. Or to ask anything at all. All she could do was answer the question because he expected an answer.

In that instant, the other criminal—a short, stocky fellow with rotting teeth and thinning hair—whirled around and grabbed the pistol, lunged forward, and took hold of Adele around the waist. He pressed the cold, steel barrel to her temple. She dropped the chair as fear shot through her. She'd never faced a gun before.

"Now the ransom!" The man's high-pitched voice revealed his desperation.

For the first time, Adele looked fixedly at the other man—the dark, wild one—and understood that he was her rescuer.

He held up his hands in a gesture that invited calm, but it wasn't easy for Adele to relax because his dark eyes and windblown black hair gave him the look of the devil, or something worse. Masculine to the core, rough around the edges, he looked as if he'd been traveling for three days straight and hadn't taken the time to shave or bathe or even sleep, because he'd been hell-bent on reaching this house.

Who was he? Where had he come from?

"Harm her and you will die," he said.

His English accent caught her off guard, for he didn't have the look of a polite English gentleman—at least not the type she'd ever met in New York. This man was pure, unleashed aggression.

"Or you can take the ransom and run," he continued. "I recommend the latter."

Adele felt the other man's grip tighten about her waist. She sucked in a breath.

"You won't let me leave," her kidnapper said shakily.

Her rescuer stepped out of the way of the door. "I will let you leave when you let the lady go. But be quick about it because my patience is dwindling fast."

The man pressed the pistol harder against the side

of Adele's head. "I don't believe you will let me go."

Paralyzing fear twisted around her heart. This man was not going to simply walk away. Why should he risk them following?

By the dark calculating look in her rescuer's eyes, Adele sensed he was thinking the very same thing.

In an instant, survival instinct took over. Adele dropped to the floor and sank her teeth into the man's thigh. While he screamed out in pain, her rescuer dashed forward and propelled the man to the wall, where they smacked into it, hard. They wrestled for a few seconds, both grunting as they tried to gain control of the pistol.

It would have been prudent for Adele to run for safety, but some other reflex took over. She darted at the pair of them and leaped onto the shorter man's back. He swung around and threw her to the floor, then aimed the pistol at her heart.

"Damn you!" Her rescuer tackled the man just as he fired. The noise was deafening, the pain shocking. Adele grabbed hold of her thigh and curled forward.

The two men rolled around on the floor until her rescuer swung the handle of the gun and struck his foe on the head. The man's body went still, while thunder rumbled in the distance.

Clutching her throbbing leg, Adele stared numbly at the two of them.

Her rescuer looked up. "You're shot."

"Yes," she rasped.

He crawled across the floor and without so much as a second's hesitation, tossed up her skirt.

Adele leaned back on her hands, trying not to show

her sudden ridiculous sense of modesty in these circumstances. She had been shot. He—whoever he
was—needed to examine the wound.

She looked down at her leg. Her ivory stocking was
stained red on the inside of her thigh. The whole area
burned like nothing she'd ever experienced before. It
was as if someone were branding her with a red-hot
poker.

Her rescuer wrapped his hand around her calf and
moved her legs apart to get a closer look. Adele stiff-
ened. She had to fight the urge to squeeze her legs
back together again.

"I must remove your stocking," he said, "to get a
better look. May I have your permission?"

"Of course."

Her reply came intuitively, but after she'd said
it, she felt her modesty return. She swept the petty
notion aside, for now was not the time to worry about
decorum. She squeezed her eyes shut and focused on
overcoming the pain.

The man's hands were swift as he rolled the stocking down her leg. He barely touched her skin. His
touch was light as silk. He eased the stocking to her
ankle with great care, as if he were handling something very precious. Adele held her breath the entire
time.

"This looks painful," he said.

It was. Her whole leg throbbed, and the pounding
sensation reverberated all the way up to her shoulders.

Adele opened her eyes and watched the man's face.
His dark brows drew together with concern as he
inspected the gash. He slid a hand over her bare thigh

as he touched all around the wound.

"It's just a graze, thank God," he said, sitting back on his heels. "We'll bandage it and you'll live." He stood up and glanced around the room.

Looking up at him, so tall and serious, Adele had to fight the sense of embarrassment and intimidation that made her almost afraid to speak. She had never let a man who was not a doctor touch her so intimately before.

"May I ask who you are? And how you found me?"

He considered her question for a moment. "I apologize, Miss Wilson. I should have identified myself."

Suddenly, he was transformed into a proper gentleman. At least his words were gentlemanly. His appearance was quite another matter altogether. He was unshaven, wild, and rough. His black wool coat looked shabby, dusty, and weathered, as if he'd rolled down a hill in it. There was intensity in everything about him, and it left her breathless and panicky.

Adele was nowhere near ready to relax. Especially when she found herself locked in his dark, gleaming stare.

"I am Damien Renshaw," he explained. "Viscount Alcester. Harold's cousin."

Harold's cousin? Yes...she knew of him. Her sister Sophia had met him in London and described him as the polar opposite of Harold. Lord Alcester had a terrible reputation with women, he was irresponsible with money and his mother had been a scandalous adulteress. He was following in his mother's footsteps, it was said, and led a careless life with a string of mistresses of questionable repute. The current one was a famous and beautiful actress.

"The ship's master at arms informed Harold of your kidnapping," Lord Alcester said, "as there was a ransom note left in your stateroom. Harold informed me of the situation, and it was deemed that I should take care of things."

Deemed? By whom?

"I assured Harold that I would bring you home quickly and quietly," Lord Alcester added. "We will leave here in the morning, after the storm has passed, and travel under assumed names to meet your mother and sister in two days' time, in a village between here and Osulton Manor. It has all been arranged. She will then escort you the rest of the way, as if nothing ever happened."

Adele was in shock. She was to travel alone with this man?

Still fighting the excruciating pain in her thigh, she struggled to collect her thoughts and understand the situation. "No one knows about my kidnapping?"

"Besides the ship's officer, no one except your family and Harold's mother and sister. I suggested he not even tell them, but by the time he contacted me, he had already informed them. They have since been advised to keep quiet."

"To avoid a scandal," Adele said.

"Yes."

She glanced uneasily at her rescuer—a rake of the highest order—then at the unconscious man lying on the floor beside them, who had done God-only-knew-what to her while she was unconscious.

Adele felt sick and dizzy.

Lord Alcester followed her gaze, then crossed the creaky floor to where her kidnapper lay. Kneeling down, he pressed two fingers to the man's neck. The wind from the storm outside moaned like a beast inside the stone chimney and the draft lifted the clinging cobwebs around the hearth.

When at last Lord Alcester spoke, his voice was low and subdued. "He's dead."

Adele swallowed hard as Alcester pinched the bridge of his nose. All the color left his face and he looked as if a severe headache had just taken root inside his skull.

"Are you all right?" she asked.

As soon as he met her gaze, his color returned. "Yes."

He stood up and she found herself trying to read his thoughts but couldn't.

"I'll need to wrap your wound." He was gone before she had a chance to utter a single word.

A moment later he returned with a cloth in a bowl of water and a bottle of whiskey. He shrugged out of his long black coat.

"This house was abandoned long ago. There's nothing downstairs to use for bandages. My shirt will have to suffice."

Adele sat forward to protest—partly because she couldn't fathom the idea of this man walking around shirtless—but the movement caused a stabbing sensation in her leg.

"Sit still," he said. "You'll worsen the bleeding." His voice seemed strained and impatient. Was he annoyed with her?

"I'm sorry," she replied apprehensively. "I wanted to tell you that we could use my petticoat for bandages. It has a bullet hole in it anyway."

He considered that for a moment and nodded.

Adele swallowed. "If you would be so kind as to avert your eyes while I remove it?"

"Do you need assistance?"

Assistance! Her pulse drummed at the suggestion. Based on his reputation, he was probably a master at removing women's underclothes.

Adele was astonished by the sudden depraved direction of her thoughts. It was exhaustion, surely. She'd hardly slept in three days. *Think clearly, Adele. He is merely offering to help in order to spare you pain.*

"I can manage, thank you," she replied.

He left the room but remained just outside the door while she struggled to reach up under her skirts and free the ribbons at her waist. With more than a little discomfort, she slid the garment down over her hips.

"You can come in now." She held the petticoat out to him.

He took it and began to tear it into strips. "If you're in pain, you're welcome to take a few swigs of that whiskey."

She eyed it uneasily. "No, thank you." She wanted to keep her wits about her in the coming hours, for she didn't know what those hours might bring.

While Lord Alcester stood tall above her, ripping and tearing at the petticoat, he glanced around the bare room with assessing eyes. "You spent three days in here?"

"Yes."

He met her gaze. "After I clean and bandage your wound, we'll move you downstairs where you'll be more comfortable."

"I'm perfectly fine here," she replied.

The sound of fabric ripping filled a long, drawn-out silence between them. Adele felt a great need to add conversation to that silence, for she needed to distract herself from her anxiety.

"I don't even know what it looks like downstairs," she said. "I was unconscious when I arrived, and sick when I woke up."

Lord Alcester stopped ripping. "Sick and unconscious?"

"Yes. I was drugged on the ship. He kept me drugged until I woke up here."

"Were you hurt in any way?"

She understood his meaning. He was wondering if she had been violated. She was wondering that herself, with more than a little concern. She knew nothing about such things regarding the female body.

"I'm not certain," she replied. "I didn't feel...." How could she put it? "I felt no pain anywhere. Except for a headache. But I suppose a lady couldn't be sure about a certain kind of pain. Or could she?"

What kind of question was that?

Alcester's expression revealed no hint of awkwardness. He knelt beside her, dipped the cloth into the bowl of water and gently squeezed it out. His eyes lifted to meet hers and he responded with composure.

"It depends," he said softly. "Pardon my candor, Miss Wilson, but did you notice any bleeding when you woke up?"

"No, but couldn't he have...?" *Lord, this was awkward*. "He disposed of my nightgown. Couldn't he have...tidied up afterwards?"

She'd never had a conversation quite like this before.

"I suppose, if he were an exceedingly neat person." Lord Alcester smiled gently at her, and Adele knew he was trying to minimize her concerns.

Continuing to rinse the cloth in the bowl, he said, "My suspicion is that you are probably fine. I believe you would know if something was wrong. But if you wish to be certain, a physician can examine you."

"He'd be able to tell?"

"Yes."

"Would he be able to tell if I was—" She stopped. She couldn't go on.

"If you were what, Miss Wilson?"

"If I was with child?" The idea was unsettling, to say the least, but she had to ask.

"I believe it would be too soon to ascertain the answer to that particular question, but let us deal with one problem at a time, shall we?"

Grateful that Lord Alcester was direct and honest with her about this awkward topic, she considered what she knew about the English aristocratic code. A woman was expected to be a virgin upon marriage to ensure any child born of the union was the true heir to the man's title. Perhaps Harold was worried. Perhaps Lord Alcester was worried, too. He was a member of that family, after all.

"I would like to be examined officially," she said, remembering that she was to become an aristocratic lady herself. It would be her code, too. Best to follow the rules.

Lord Alcester held the cloth above her wound and squeezed water over it. "The Osulton family physician is a very good man," he said. "I would trust him with my life, and you can rest assured that he will be discreet. I hope you are not unduly worried?" Alcester's eyes met hers again. He often seemed to be assessing things.

"I am, but I will do my best to be patient."

He nodded, appearing satisfied, then turned his attention back to the task of treating her wound. The droplets of water tickled her skin. A few times, her leg jerked upward from the intensity of the dribbling sensation—the odd combination of pain and tickling. She wished she could keep her leg still, but it was no use.

"Try to relax," he whispered, glancing up at her again. "Breathe deep and count each breath."

She did as he suggested, keeping her eyes locked on his. All the knots in her muscles began to untie themselves, while she stared at him.

Slowly, the blood washed away, along with the tension in her neck and shoulders. Her breathing slowed.

Lord Alcester bent to look more closely at the gash, then he reached for the bottle of whiskey. "This is going to hurt, but it must be done."

"I understand."

"Squeeze my arm if you have to."

She didn't want to.

He paused to give her time to prepare herself, then poured the alcohol over the wound. He might as well have poured liquid fire on her. Adele clenched her teeth together to keep from crying out.

As soon as he tipped the bottle upright, she leaned forward and squeezed her thigh. "Sweet Mary!" she ground out.

"Apologies." He set the bottle down and reached for the long bandage he'd fashioned from her petticoat. "I'm going to wrap the wound now."

Adele nodded in agreement. He tried to press a smaller bandage to the gash, but she had unconsciously pressed her legs together at the knees. She was clenching her teeth together, too.

He cupped her other knee in his hand and gently pushed her legs apart, again keeping his eyes fixed on hers the entire time. "It's important to do this properly," he said. "Relax if you can."

She struggled to still her racing heart—for no man had ever parted her legs before—and forced herself to surrender to the gentle pressure of his hand.

"Perhaps you could bend your knee slightly?" he politely asked, then he reached for the bandage and wrapped it around her thigh.

His movements were swift and efficient. Before she knew it, he was tying a knot and sitting back. "There. All done. You can breathe now." He lowered her skirt to cover her leg.

She hadn't even realized she was holding her breath until he mentioned it.

He helped her rise but as soon as she attempted to walk, pain flooded through her. She felt suddenly nauseated.

"Let me help you." He wrapped his arm about her waist. "Lean into me. That's it."

She began to limp beside him, and felt the thick, firm muscles of his shoulder and the solid, steady support of his body. He did not waver or lose his balance.

"It will be difficult to walk for a few days," he said.

"But how will we ever get me away from here? For one thing, I don't have shoes. And it will be torture to ride."

"No shoes?" He paused. "Leave that to me. I will ride out at first light and return with a coach and driver for the journey, and I will bring shoes for you."

"What about him?" She gestured toward her kidnapper.

"I will alert the authorities in the morning and have someone come to collect him. Don't worry about a thing. I'll make sure our names are not connected. We'll be long gone by the time they arrive."

They hobbled together into the hall and reached the top of the staircase. Adele stopped and looked down. "This might be a challenge."

"Allow me." He held out his arms.

He meant to carry her? Her heart did a little nervous flip at the thought of it.

Before waiting for her reply, he scooped her into his strong, able arms and descended the narrow steps effortlessly. When he reached the bottom, he carried her to the kitchen, where a faded upholstered chair faced the fireplace. Other than that, the room was unfurnished. There was only a small pile of kindling, some cooking utensils, and provisions to prepare a few meager suppers.

Lord Alcester set her down on the chair. Lightning flashed outside the window. Thunder rumbled almost immediately afterward as darkness began to descend.

"If you will excuse me," he said. "I must take my horse to the stable before the storm is fully upon us."

"Of course." Yet she did not want him to go. She had been trapped alone for three days, helpless and locked in a room. She had just been shot. She was an ocean away from her home, and he was all she had.

Lord Alcester raised his coat collar up around his neck and picked up the hat that lay on the floor. He must have torn it off quickly when he'd first arrived. She remembered the violent commotion that ensued when he'd entered and could only imagine what had occurred.

Settling the hat on his head, he faced her. "The worst is over now."

It was exactly what she had needed to hear. Had he known? He seemed very intuitive.

He opened the door and let in a powerful gust of wind carrying a pattering of cold, hard rain. The gale swept into the cottage and whirled like a tempest, but the room calmed quickly when he slammed the door behind him.

Adele sat alone in the silent kitchen, staring at the door and trying to come to terms with her situation. She couldn't believe that she had been kidnapped and shot. Bookish Adele Wilson, who avoided adventure at all costs....

Her sisters were sure to be shocked when she told them her tale of woe—how she'd been abducted, trapped and finally rescued by a proverbial white knight.

It was embarrassing, actually, to think of him that

way. She had always considered those fairy tales to be silly and unrealistic and would have preferred to read about heroines who rescued themselves.

Either way, Lord Alcester was hardly a white knight. He was more of a dark knight. She remembered how intense and angry he had appeared when he burst into her room. Her knees had turned to jelly.

Then he'd killed a man. *For her.*

A cold shiver moved through her as she replayed that horrific moment when she'd gazed into that dark barrel of death. She had been impossibly lucky. If her kidnapper had fired a fraction of a second sooner....

She was immensely grateful to be alive.

And she owed a tremendous debt to Damien Renshaw—her future cousin. True, his reputation was concerning, and she would never get over the embarrassing fact that he had seen her naked thigh. But he had come to her rescue, galloping across England to what felt like the ends of the earth. He had been her champion, when despite her own efforts, she had been unable to rescue herself.

Adele inhaled deeply, glanced at the door and considered the night ahead, trapped in this isolated cottage with such a man.

All at once, she found herself wishing that the man who had come to her rescue had been Harold instead.

In Love with the Viscount – Available Now

Books by
Julianne MacLean

HISTORICAL ROMANCE

The American Heiress Trilogy:
To Marry the Duke
Falling for the Marquess
In Love with the Viscount

Can This Be Love Trilogy
(American Heiress Spinoff):
Love According to Lily
To Annabelle, With Love
Where Love Begins

Love at Pembroke Palace Series:
In My Wildest Fantasies
The Mistress Diaries
When a Stranger Loves Me
Married By Midnight
A Kiss Before the Wedding–
A Pembroke Palace Short Story
Seduced at Sunset

The Highlander Series:
Captured by the Highlander
Claimed by the Highlander
Seduced by the Highlander
The Rebel – A Highland Short Story
Return of the Highlander
Taken by the Highlander

The Royal Trilogy:
Be My Prince
Princess in Love
The Prince's Bride

Western/Americana Historical Romances
Prairie Bride
Tempting the Marshal
Adam's Promise

Time Travel Romance:
A Time for Love

CONTEMPORARY FICTION
A Curve in the Road
A Fire Sparkling

The Color of Heaven Series:
The Color of Heaven
The Color of Destiny
The Color of Hope
The Color of a Dream
The Color of a Memory
The Color of Love
The Color of the Season
The Color of Time
The Color of Forever
The Color of a Promise
The Color of a Christmas Miracle
The Color of a Silver Lining

ABOUT THE AUTHOR

Julianne MacLean is a *USA Today* bestselling author of more than thirty novels, including the contemporary women's fiction *Color of Heaven Series*. Readers have described her books as "breathtaking," "soulful" and "uplifting." MacLean is a four-time Romance Writers of America RITA® finalist and has won numerous awards, including the *Booksellers' Best Award* and a *Reviewers' Choice Award* from *Romantic Times*. Her novels have sold millions of copies worldwide and have been published in over a dozen languages.

MacLean has a degree in English literature from the University of King's College in Halifax, Nova Scotia, and a degree in business administration from Acadia University in Wolfville, Nova Scotia. She loves to travel and has lived in New Zealand, Canada, and England. MacLean currently resides on the east coast of Canada in a lakeside home with her husband, daughter, and mother. She invites readers to visit her website for more information about her books and writing life, and to subscribe to her mailing list for all the latest news: www.JulianneMacLean.com